THE GODSPILL

THREADWEAVERS, BOOK 2

TODD FAHNESTOCK

PARKER
HAYDEN
MEDIA

Parker Hayden Media
5740 N. Carefree Circle, Ste 120-1
Colorado Springs, CO 80917

Art credits:
Cover design: LB Hayden
Cover Graphic: © Rashed AlAkroka

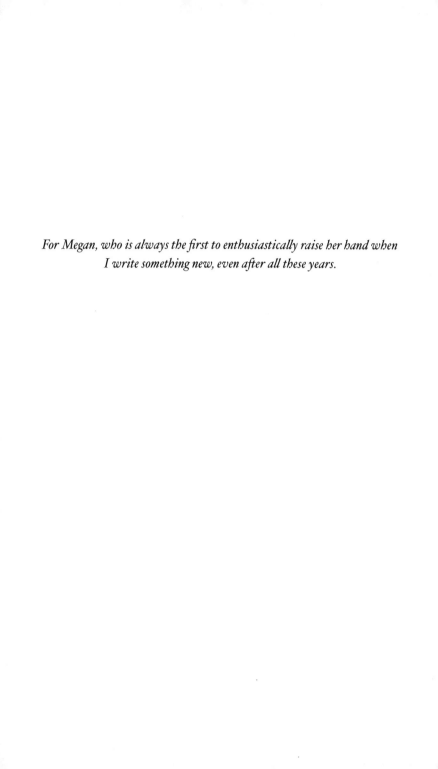

For Megan, who is always the first to enthusiastically raise her hand when I write something new, even after all these years.

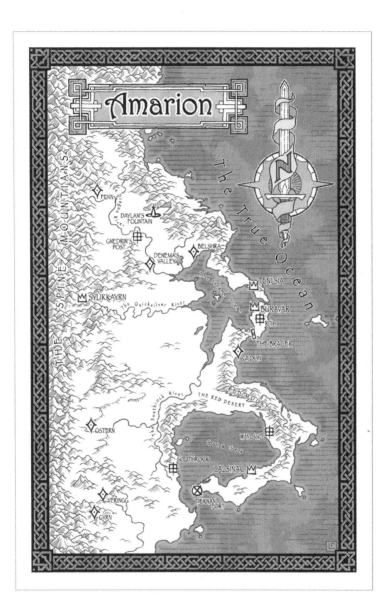

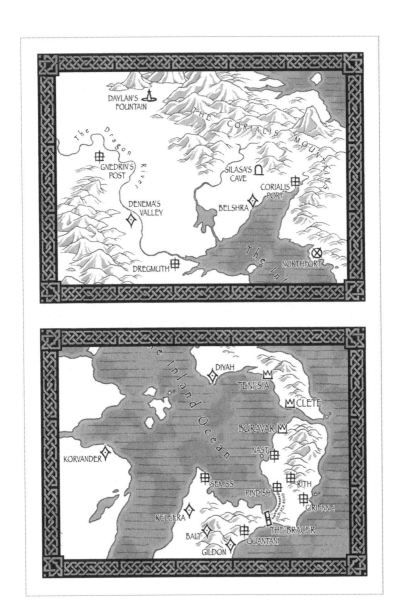

MAILING LIST

If you would like to stay informed about upcoming book releases, giveaways, or enter contests I hold for readers, be sure to subscribe to my mailing list, Todd Fahnestock's Readers Group: https://tinyurl.com/ToddNewsletter

Your email will never be shared and you can unsubscribe at any time.

PRONUNCIATION GUIDE

Main Characters:
Mirolah—MI-rò-lä
Medophae—ME-dò-fä
Mershayn—Mər-SHĀN
Silasa—si-LÄ-sə
Stavark—STA-värk
Zilok Morth—ZĪ-lok Mòrth

Other Characters/Places:
Amarion— ä-MĀ-rē-un
Ari'cyiane— ä-ri-cē-ĀN
Avakketh—ä-VÄ-keth
Belshra—BEL-shrə
Bendeller—ben-DEL-er
Buravar—BYÜ-rä-vär
Calsinac—KAL-zi-nak
Casra—KAZ-rä
Casur—KA-zhər
Cisly—SIS-lē

Clete—KLĒT

Corialis—KȮR-ē-a-lis

Dandere—DAN-dēr

Darva—DÄR-və

Daylan—DĀ-lin

Dederi—DE-de-rē

Denema—de-NĒ-mə

Deni'tri—de-NĒ-trē

Dervon—DƏR-vän

Diyah—DĒ-yä

Elekkena—e-LE-ke-nə

Ethiel—E-thē-el

Fillen—FIL-en

Grendis Sym—GREN-dis SIM

Harleath Markin—HÄR-lēth MÄR-kin

Irgakth—ƏR-gakth

Keleera—kə-LĒR-ə

Lawdon—LÄ-dən

Lo'gan—lȯ-GÄN

Locke—läk

Mi'Gan—mi-GÄN

Natra—NÄ-trə

Oedandus—ȯ-DAN-dus

Orem—Ȯ-rem

Rith—RITH

Saraphazia—se-ruh-FĀ-zhē-ə

Shera—SHE-rə

Tarithalius—ter-i-THAL-ē-us

Teni'sia—te-NĒ-sē-ä

Tiffienne—ti-fē-EN

Tuana—tü-ä-nä

Tyndiria—tin-DĒR-ē-ä

Vaisha—VĪ-shə

Yehnie—YEN-nē
Ynisaan—YI-ni-sän
Vullieth—VƏL-ē-eth
Zetu—ZE-tü

PROLOGUE

BANDS WAITED, watching the other dragons fill the translucent ledges above her. She had a feeling this wasn't going to end well for her. There were nearly a hundred of those ovoid ledges, bordering the enormous natural amphitheater in which she stood, lined with hundreds of dragons. The nearest were right over her head, close enough that Bands could reach up with her long neck and bump them with her nose. The farthest dragons were so small they looked about the size of her knuckle.

In front of her was a half dome over the raised dais where Avakketh would stand when he arrived. Beautiful fountains of water spiraled up from spouts in the ground, rising until they reached each invisible ledge, where they flowed into invisible trenches, allowing the dragon spectators to drink while they watched. Because the ledges could not be seen, the streams of water looked like veins running through some translucent leviathan whose body was comprised of colorful dragons. There were orange dragons. Blue dragons. Silver dragons. Purple dragons. Black dragons. Different dragons of so many shades that no two seemed the same. There were no red dragons, of course. Red was the divine color, Avakketh's color. No dragon had ever been born with red scales.

There were, of course, dragons of multiple colors, like her. She saw Korducalikan, a black dragon with white patterns racing from her nose down her flanks. Her wings looked like forks of lightning. Biridirilaculalan and his family, several purple dragons with light spots, stood halfway down the amphitheater. Bands saw Vidilarrilan, a silver dragon with golden patterns like flames rising up from his claws. He was a childhood friend. She even saw her mother and father, with similar markings to her own. Father rested on his haunches, with his coppery body bearing yellow bands from his chin all the way down his long neck to his chest. Mother had coiled up like a snake, dark green with a light green stripe from her chin to her tail. Her glittering eyes watched Bands, though at first glance, she might have seemed asleep.

Bands glanced over the hundreds of dragons that had gathered, and a familiar feeling of foreboding seeped through her. She had felt this feeling—like a tickle of snowflakes on the inside of her throat and belly—every time she and Medophae went into battle. Returning to Irgakth, land of the dragons, Bands had not expected a warm homecoming. She had expected to be reprimanded. She was an oddity, a deviant; she knew that. Most dragons looked upon humans as ants, barely worthy of attention. Bands, on the other hand, was fascinated with them. She enjoyed watching them, interacting with them. She had fallen in love with them as a whole. And she had fallen in love with a few in specific, a mating kind of love, the kind of bond reserved for two dragons who wished permission to give birth. To most dragons, this was akin to what humans would consider bestiality.

So Bands had expected to face consequences if she wished to re-enter the embrace of her god, like all the rest of her kind. She had hoped at least that Avakketh would reprimand her in private. That was obviously not going to be the case. That Avakketh wanted to see her in the amphitheater with every dragon in the vicinity invited did not bode well at all.

As ever when she felt that cold, tickling feeling in her throat, she felt a sweep of calm come over her. Strangely, it was Medophae's passion that taught her to do this. Whenever she sensed danger, she became icy calm, using those cool prickles and imagining them spreading throughout her body, bringing her a placid state of mind she could use to think, to strategize.

In moments like this, she felt as though her eyes became a separate part of her body, as if they were floating over her head, seeing with a perspective that would allow no fear. She smiled slightly, thinking that her many fellows far down the ledges of the amphitheater looked like a kaleidoscope of butterflies. Dainty, fanciful, purposeless ephemera that flitted on whatever breeze was convenient.

Such a thought would have been a grave insult to any dragon, so Bands kept it carefully to herself, cultivating the mirth that smothered her fear.

She thought instead about what she had seen when she'd come north. Things had changed in Irgakth. There were young dragons she didn't recognize. Dragons lived so long that they rarely asked Avakketh for the gift of creating a new birth. In fact, Bands had met almost every dragon alive before she went south to seek her fortune. But obviously, many had asked for this privilege lately. That meant something. She didn't know what, but it meant something.

Secondly, as she flew north, she noticed many other dragon cities that hadn't been there before. Dragons were not known for change, but they had been industrious over the past centuries, and many of their constructs had been created using threadweaving, which meant Avakketh had been involved. Humans drew their threadweaving power from the GodSpill, the creative god force that had accidentally spilled from the Godgate millennia ago. Dragons drew their threadweaving ability straight from their god, Avakketh. When Bands had left long ago to explore the human lands, Avakketh had cut her off from his power, and she'd had to learn to threadweave like a human, pulling GodSpill straight from the lands, rather than from her god.

At last, the ledges had been filled, and an odd quiet descended on the amphitheater. Bands turned away from the thunder of dragons to the front of the amphitheater, a red granite dais where Avakketh attended on his dragons when there was reason to do so. The smooth, black stone wall behind the dais shimmered, and Avakketh emerged through it like it was a waterfall. The smallest dragons were larger than most human houses. Bands herself was longer than two large houses, tip to tail.

Avakketh was immense, easily five times Bands's size. He could have lay down on the palace at Calsinac and crushed it. He came to the center of the dais, looming over her, surveying the assembled dragons like they might challenge him. Three white dragons came through the shimmering black wall and flanked Avakketh like dogs would flank a hunter. Each of them crouched, serpentine necks arcing up like a question mark, all focused on Bands. She recognized each of them, of course. One was even a childhood friend, Zynderilifakyz.

"Randorus Ak-nin Ackli Forckandor." Avakketh spoke her full name to the crowd without looking at her, and, for a moment, it seemed as if he was demanding that she pop up, raising her wing in the air to be counted.

"My lord," she bowed her head. "Your life is my breath. Your words are my commands. Your eyes, my vision. How may I serve you?" She spoke the ritual words of the dragonhood. Any dragon speaking to Avakketh was required to say these words when first addressed by their god.

His huge, horned head lowered, dark eyes glaring at her. "You mock us," he said.

Her heart dipped. Even though she had known a reprimand was coming, the words hurt. "My lord, it is not my intention—"

"It *is* your intention," he cut her off. "You dare to speak the words of the dragonhood, when in fact you flaunt them with your actions. You claim that my life is your breath, but you have forsaken natural threadweaving for that aberration humans stole from the Godgate. My words have never been your command. Dragons are forbidden to live among humans, yet you prefer their company to the company of your own kind. You claim my eyes are your vision, but you refuse to see the humans for what they really are. You are a liar."

She bowed her head to cover her defiance. Yes, she had disobeyed him. Yes, she had come expecting a rebuke, but her anger flared inside her. Hadn't he already punished her? Avakketh was behind the spell Ethiel had cast; Saraphazia and Tarithalius had deduced that much. No human, even one as powerful as Ethiel, could have imprisoned a god. But Avakketh could have. Avakketh had created that ruby, put it in Ethiel's hands. Avakketh had trapped the brother he hated and punished an errant daughter who had disobeyed him. "I am sorry I have disappointed you, but I return with a completion of the penance you set upon me."

"You return as a traitor."

She looked up. She had seen a dragon reprimanded before. Avakketh should have demanded redress to the rest of dragonkind in the form of service. Sometimes for as much as a hundred years. This wasn't to be a reprimand. This was something else.

She tried to rise above her own thoughts, to consider this dispassionately, but she couldn't. Her anger boiled and, behind it, fear. She had spent four hundred years longing for her beloved, trapped in an abyss with nothing but the constant droning of Tarithalius's bad jokes.

Avakketh watched her, his black eyes hard.

"My lord..." She finally managed to find her tongue. "You...locked me away for four hundred and thirty seven years...."

She glanced at the dragons surrounding her. None seemed the least bit compassionate. She thought of looking at her parents, but she couldn't stand it if she found the same coldness in their eyes, so she avoided that side of the amphitheater. "Yes, I loved a human. Is that crime so horrible that it warranted four hundred years of my life?"

"Was your crime so horrible…" Avakketh echoed the words. "If you understood what you have done…" His eyes flickered with a dark fire. "Loving a human is, in fact, a crime. A spine horse should not mate with a rat. It makes you low, a pitiable thing. But that crime I can overlook, distasteful as it is. What I can't ignore is your threat to dragonkind."

"A threat, my lord? In what way have I threatened—"

"Dragons were meant to think, Randorus, to create, to rule this world my sister Natra and I created. Your kind *earned* their ability to think. Humans, aath trees, whales, equines, all these were given sentience by Natra. They didn't earn it; they don't deserve it. Fine. I was willing to abide Natra's undeserved gift, but when humans first wielded GodSpill, I knew it had gone too far. This was something Natra never intended, and I waited too long to destroy them. They created Daylan's Fountain, an aberration that twisted the natural order of this world, tearing into the fabric of the great tapestry. This is what I call a threat, Randorus. Humans must be destroyed."

Bands's mind raced. If he wanted to destroy humans, why hadn't he done it? And how had she betrayed him? Avakketh said her true crime wasn't loving Medophae, then what was? Bands had been gone for over three hundred years. She couldn't have been a threat to anything, even if she wanted to.

And Avakketh had been waiting. Why? If he wanted humans eliminated, why hadn't he done anything? These past three centuries, humans were at their weakest. They had stopped reading, stopped accumulating knowledge, stopped creating. Tarithalius, the god of humans, was trapped in a gemstone. Even the threadweavers had been slain by Harleath Markin's grand mistake. There was nothing that could possibly stop Avakketh. There was nothing...

It all came together in a rush. Medophae. Avakketh was afraid of Medophae. And then she realized the trap hadn't been to punish her. The ruby Ethiel wielded had been meant to capture Medophae and Tarithalius, the two protectors of humankind, the only two who might be strong enough to fight Avakketh. But Bands had pushed Medophae out of the way. She had taken his place.

Avakketh nodded, as though he could see her piecing it together. "Do you understand now?"

"I saved him," she said.

"You did. You also brought him upon us," Avakketh said. "Your wandering took you to the isle of Dandere, where mortals of the blood of Oedandus could be found. You brought him to Amarion, where he could mix with his god and become what he is."

"But that was good," she protested. "He killed Dervon, who you despised. Dervon's creations killed hundreds of dragons."

"Dervon was a god. Medophae is some stripling human. Did you really think I would condone a human killing one of my own family, no matter how much I hated him?"

Bands couldn't find her breath. Finally, she managed. "Then why wait at all? You're going to have to face him eventually."

"Humans were devolving. If they were to take the path of the senseless equines, so be it. But now, they won't. They have set the GodSpill free again, and I cannot allow human threadweavers to return."

Bands's heart thumped painfully in her chest. She cursed herself for a fool that she had come north. She knew what must be coming next. As her lord and god, he would demand her assistance, her obedience. Bands would submit or he was going to kill her. He'd never let her leave Irgakth without knowing she was on his side.

"It is time for you to atone for your crimes," Avakketh said.

"Please," she said. "They're not what you think. We don't have to kill them. Will you at least let me report what I have learned about humans in my time among them—"

"Your hubris is galling. I know everything I need to know about humans."

"My lord—"

"This is what you will do," Avakketh said. "You will go to Medophae. You will take him on a journey over the True Ocean, back to the isle of Dandere where Oedandus cannot reach him, and then you will kill his mortal form and all the humans who live there, ending Oedandus's line forever. If you succeed in this, then you can return to Irgakth or Amarion, whichever pleases you, and you may live the rest of your days with my blessing once again."

Kill Medophae. Kill all the humans. She looked around at the faces on the ledges. She didn't see any remorse there. Was this what dragonkind had come to?

"Are we completely without compassion for lives other than our own?" she asked, looking farther, turning all the way around, this time looking directly at her parents. And there, she saw what she needed to see. Their scaly faces were tight, eyes narrowed as if readying to fly into an ice storm. They had braced for this moment; they had come to peace with the notion that Avakketh was going to bend their daughter's back— or break it.

They're going to kill me. He knows I can't possibly do that to Medophae. This is his way of passing a death sentence. When I refuse, he'll destroy me.

She had to run, but he would have prepared for that. Even if Avakketh couldn't pull the air from her wings, grounding her, or smash her with air that had suddenly become hard as stone, or just steal the breath from her lungs until she suffocated, even if he couldn't do all these things, there were three white dragons on the dais, hunched and ready to leap on her. She glanced around.

And let's not forget the hundreds of other dragons, many of whom might love the chance to please their lord by slaughtering a traitor.

The irony of it made her heart ache. She had waited four hundred years to be reunited with her beloved. Now she was free, and instead of going to his side, she had chosen to come here. Fool.

She raised her chin. She would face her death with dignity, though. He wouldn't hear her plead.

"You're making a mistake," she said. "The humans aren't your enemies, but you're going to make them your enemies by..." She trailed off. There was a human perched on the edge of the half dome over Avakketh's head, one leg cocked up, one dangling over the hundred foot drop. It was Tarithalius!

Miraculously, none of the other dragons had noticed him up there, simply watching the proceedings, and she forced her gaze back to Avakketh, tried to continue her train of thought. What had she been saying?

"...you'll make them your enemies," she stammered. "By...by attacking them. Why not just..." She flicked a glance upward. Thalius held up a hand like he was waving, five fingers splayed. As she watched, he folded one finger down. Then another. Then another.

Five...four...three...two...one...

Bands leapt into the air with every ounce of strength she possessed. It was a bad idea to rely on Tarithalius. He was capricious. But she had a split second to choose to be part of his plan, whatever it was. And, she had to face it, his was the only plan available.

Her leap took her eye level with Avakketh, and time seemed to slow as their gazes met. His lips pulled back in a snarl, and he gestured even as she spread her wings. He was going to pull the air away from her, or break her wings. She felt the threads around her bend, but then another force took hold of them and bent them back. Her wings didn't break. When she pushed against the air, it pushed back with a ferocious gust.

Bands shot into the sky, whipping past Tarithalius, who winked at her, then vanished.

The three white dragons leapt after, pumping around the half dome, struggling to get airborne. One of them let loose a deadly jet of fire...

...and they dropped like stones. If Bands wasn't so scared, she would have laughed to see the elite three looking like felled pigeons, struggling to untangle their limbs. But gloating could cost Bands her life.

She spun, but a fire jet hit her wing. She yanked it in, wincing. She couldn't afford to lose her advantage. She unfurled it and rode the ferocious gust, leaving the amphitheater behind, which erupted into roars of surprise and anger.

The elites were the fastest flyers among dragonkind. Whatever Tarithalius had done, Avakketh would undo it in a moment, and the chase would begin.

She flew straight and fast toward the crags. It was a lattice-work of crevices and peaks that stretched for miles, and it was her only hope. If she could vanish into the crags before the elites regained the sky, she might lose them.

The crags neared, and she fell toward the first deep crack in the earth like a spear, not daring to look back for fear of losing even a fraction of a second. She dove deep, then began navigating.

She dipped her burned wing and cut the wind as hard as she dared. The wing was injured and, if it split, she was done for. She whipped around the edge of the spire, whispered three words and pulled the necessary threads. The GodSpill was not as strong in Irgakth as it was in Amarion. It made threadweaving more difficult. Her muscles trembled and her joints creaked with the strain, but the threads of the wind shoved her the extra few inches, and she plunged into the ravine without hitting the wall.

Another spire of stone whipped by her. Her claws brushed it, dislodging bits of lava rock that fell into the bottomless crack. She tucked her wings and dove again. Air whistled past her. She unfurled her wings, pulling another hard turn through the meandering trench.

Spying a cave below, she dove one last time. The cave was dark, and she plunged into it at full flight. She whispered, using threadweaving again to stop herself before she slammed into the back wall. She swung around, her tail smashing into a trio of stalagmites, reducing them to jagged rubble.

Just outside the cave, she heard a whoosh of air beneath another set of wings. Damn! The elites were so fast. Another second, and whichever elite had caught her would have leapt on her back.

The white, horned head dipped low, peering into the cave. It was Zynderilifakyz. Zynder was an amazing flyer; of course he had caught her first. But the others would be close behind.

Bands lunged toward the cave's entrance. She only had one chance. She must make it convincing. She whispered words, guiding her focus as she manipulated the threads...

...and vanished.

Zynder blasted the cave with his fiery breath, melting the rough rock until the ceiling dripped onto the floor. Dragons were practically immune to fire, but dragon breath was equipped with a hint of acid. It stripped protections like scales, seeking the tender flesh beneath.

His bright white eyes narrowed to tight slits against the heat, dropping to the lip of the cave.

Zynder entered the melting cavern, checking everywhere. He swiveled his long neck left and right. He even turned and looked behind him into the gloomy expanse of the lava trench.

"You defy the law of our lord," Zynder said in his smooth, strong voice. "Any true dragon would gladly die for him, but not you. You have been so badly infected by the humans that you would rather run."

Bands said nothing; she didn't move.

"What manner of creature are you, Randorus Ak-nin Ackli Forckandor?" Zynder used her full name. His whip-like tongue flicked across the air. "You are not a true dragon. But you are not a human, either. You hide from your betters and pretend to be something so far below your station, our lord must revoke the life that he once gave to you. You sicken us all."

I have learned more than you in my travels, Zynder. Avakketh did not give us life. Natra did. Avakketh does not create.

"Avakketh has shown you more mercy than you deserve." Zynder paused. "I will give you one chance to do the right thing, Randorus. Show yourself. Accept your lord's judgment and pass through the Godgate with honor."

There is no honor in genocide. The honorable path is to fight Avakketh before he wipes out an entire race.

A second of the elites arrived with a powerful flapping of wings. She hovered at the edge of the cave.

"Zynder," the huge white dragon called. "Did you dispatch her?"

He looked up at the new arrival. "No," he rumbled through his teeth. "She has the mean cunning of a rat. She used some spell to transport herself away."

The second dragon rumbled. "Avakketh will be disappointed."

"How did she blunt his spell?" Zynder snapped his teeth in frustration. His scaly lips pulled back to bare his teeth. His white eyes shone malevolently. "How did she do that?"

"She humiliated him. And we have failed our lord."

"If he requires my life as punishment, I will gladly give it," Zynder said.

"As will I."

"She only has one place to go," he continued. "She must return to the human lands, and we will find her there."

The elite showed her teeth.

"I will take my retribution," he said.

He launched himself powerfully into the air. He and the other elite began flying back to the amphitheater.

With the wind whipping past him, he did not notice Bands. Avakketh considered the form of a dragon to be the best form in the world. Stooping to take on the form of another was beneath them all. So Zynder didn't even notice the tiny black dragon beetle Bands had become. She let go of the back of his neck and fell out of sight into the trench, opening her flicking wings and flying south.

She had hoped to spend a hundred years forgetting her beloved. She had hoped to give him time with his lovely human woman, Mirolah.

But she was going to have to break that promise. Medophae had to be protected. The humans had to be warned.

1

MERSHAYN

MERSHAYN PUSHED the rock against the edge of his sword in one long, slow motion. The oil muted the sound a little, but there was still a light ring with each stroke, and it was music to him. After thirty, he hefted the blade, held it out in front of himself and studied it with a critical eye.

"Sharp as my wit," he murmured, putting a thumb against the edge and dragging it lightly. He examined the cut, sucked away the trace of blood. Perfect.

He grabbed the vial of oil and dripped it sparingly on the other edge. He'd only rung the first stroke when a knock sounded at the door.

"Are you in there?" The wood-muffled voice of his half-brother, Collus, came through the door. "Mershayn?"

With a smile, Mershayn grabbed the rag from his bed and wiped away the oil on the blade.

"Come in, Your Majesty," he said.

The door opened, and Collus came in. His copper hair was cut short, high above his ears. The velvet doublet he wore flared out at the top, far beyond where Collus's sloped shoulders actually ended. Mershayn noted with amusement that the fancy doublet looked lopsided.

"Good day, Your Majesty."

"Oh, gods, Mershayn. Is this going to be one of those days? Don't call me that. Not when it's just the two of us."

"Of course, Your Majesty."

Collus let out a long breath and sat down heavily on the edge of the bed. He ran his fingers through his hair, dislodging the crown. He caught it, frowning at it as if he had not expected it to be there, then he tossed it to Mershayn. Mershayn snatched it before it hit the wall.

"Perhaps I'll keep this," Mershayn said, putting on a thoughtful face as he appraised the crown.

"Throw it into the Inland Ocean for all I care." Collus paused then, and put his head in his hands. "I was never meant for this, brother. I liked my life."

Mershayn couldn't argue with that. Watching Collus try to rule was like watching a fish try to fly. "Next time be born a bastard. Nobody expects anything of you," Mershayn said. Collus was Tyndiria's eldest cousin, her closest blood relative. Like it or not, the burden of the crown belonged to Collus by law. The last succession in Teni'sia had almost caused a coup, and the strongest nobles in the kingdom had agreed this time that they would send for, and support, the closest blood relative to their young queen. It should have been Collus and Mershayn's father, but he had passed away three months ago, leaving Collus the lord of a small estate so far to the south that it bordered Clete. Collus wasn't a political mastermind, but even he could see his duty. Teni'sia could descend into civil war if he didn't step in.

"I feel as if there are nothing but sharks in the water all around me," Collus said.

"Behead them all. Start over."

Collus frowned at Mershayn's humor. "Each of them smile and bow and fill me with pleasantries, but I can feel the weight of their intentions, tugging me this way, pulling me that way. And just as I think I am making decisions on my own, I find that I have been manipulated into a corner. To them, I am a puppet brought in to dance to their desires. Galorman Balis wants funds to study the new change in the lands. They're calling it The Wave, and he wants to capture and examine any and all new creatures that have appeared since whatever it is that happened...happened. Bordi'lis wants to kill any such creatures that are found, and confine any of our people who exhibit any unusual talents themselves. Giri'Mar wants me to allow him to bolster the army in case of attack by these same creatures. Captain Lo'gan insists that the army is running quite efficiently, and that it is foolish to build an army upon an unseen threat. Only Grendis Sym seems interested in helping me actually rule the country."

That's because he's a snake that'll tell you anything you want to hear. Mershayn had hated Grendis Sym from the first moment they met. Mershayn liked people who were plain-spoken, and while everyone at the palace seemed to say one thing and mean another, Sym did it so flawlessly that it was barely noticeable. That made him the most dangerous. Publicly, Sym was the most accepting of the fact that Collus's closest advisor was his bastard half-brother. He was all smiles and polite deference. But hadn't his father tried to kill the previous queen and take the throne? Mershayn wasn't a fool. He saw the looks Sym gave him when no one else watched, like Mershayn was a sliver he couldn't figure out how to extract.

"I don't know why you allowed him to become a part of your council at all," Mershayn said. "His father was a traitor. Send him away."

"Lord Sym is the only one who seems to make lucid suggestions about trade, the military, and the damned Wave. He seems to know the way Teni'sia works better than any other. And the others..." He let out a sigh. "They pick and preen and look for every weakness they can find in me. How did Tyndiria do it? She was only sixteen!"

In the last two years, the recently-dead queen had already gained renown in the southern kingdoms of peninsulas for her unanticipated strength. In the south, they'd called her the Bloody Butterfly, after the way she'd dealt with Magal Sym, Grendis Sym's father. She was said to have led a charmed life, surviving a dozen assassination attempts in her first year of rule, but her luck had finally run out. Or perhaps she'd forgotten to pay her top assassin, the notorious Captain Medophae, and he'd ended her life. The man obviously had the skills, and he'd disappeared the day after her funeral. There were also rumors that Queen Tyndiria and Captain Medophae were secret lovers. So he'd also had the access, and what better motivation for murder than the raging emotions of a spurned lover? It all seemed highly suspicious to Mershayn, but nobody in the kingdom seemed willing to even consider that Captain Medophae been the murderer.

"From what I remember," Mershayn said, trying to stay on Collus's topic, "she did not bend under the weight of others' opinions."

"Are you saying that I do?" Collus's eyes flashed.

He spread his hands out, palms up. "What do I know of ruling, Your Majesty? I am nothing more than a fortunate bastard."

"Stop it," Collus growled. "The mouse is an ill-fitting mask for you. Did I ever treat you as anything but a brother?"

"No." Mershayn already regretted what he had said. Some defenses jumped up unbidden. Urg. Mershayn hated politics. There was no way to step rightly. It was all just an opportunity to dredge up all the worst parts of people, to force you to make friends of your enemies, and to doubt those who only wanted to help you. Nothing good ever came of it.

"I didn't deserve that." Collus was sullen.

"I apologize, Your Majesty," Mershayn said. "It was badly done."

"Gods damn it. Stop calling me 'Your Majesty' when we're

alone together. I hate it. You are my brother. I won't have it. That is a royal command, if I must make it so."

Mershayn smiled wryly at the irony. "As you wish, brother."

"Now, be a brother and answer me honestly. Am I a reed that bends to whatever wind blows? Is that what you think?"

Mershayn shrugged. "In the times I have attended your audiences and your councils, I have noticed that, often when an issue arises, you do not seem to know what to do."

"That is because I *don't* know what to do!"

"Can you imagine that your cousin always knew what to do?"

"Tyndiria was an aberration. I don't know how she could have known how to deal with even half of these issues."

"I bet she didn't."

"What?"

"I bet she was clueless, too. How could she not be?"

"Well, that's ridiculous. Everyone raves about her wisdom."

"Perhaps she just acted like she knew."

"And what if she was wrong?"

"Perhaps she wasn't afraid of making mistakes."

"Fair enough. And some mistakes don't matter. But some can cause an open rebellion!"

"If they wanted a war, they would have gone to war and never invited you to take Tyndiria's place. They want to work with you."

"They want to manipulate me."

"Perhaps the trick is listening to them without allowing them to see how much you need them. They called you here to take charge. Take charge! You deliberate and hesitate in front of them. Don't. 'Better to make a mistake with confidence than a brilliant decision with hesitation.'"

"Father said that," Collus murmured. He paused and took a deep breath, glanced at the door with a dread that touched Mershayn's heart. He let out a breath. "Okay. I think I'm ready."

"Good."

Collus stood up. "Will you attend the audiences for today?"

"They are gravely boring."

Collus grimaced. "Yes. But I would like you there. At least for the councils this afternoon."

"If it is important to you, I will be there."

"It is."

"As you wish."

Collus rose and opened the door. Captain Lo'gan and one of the other royal guards stood just beyond, waiting for him. "I shall see you this afternoon, Lord Mershayn," he said, using Mershayn's new title as though that would make him excited about spending his afternoon among pompous windbags and toadies.

"I look forward to it, Your Majesty," he lied.

Collus left and closed the door behind him.

Mershayn let out a long breath. He tossed his sword into the air, snatched it by the hilt, then held it in front of himself. Collus thought too much. Of course, he was a king now. No more gallivanting around the countryside with his bastard brother, poaching rabbits from Sir Gefforak's lands and hatching plans of how one of them would someday climb the keep walls to seduce his beautiful young daughter. The palace life had its amenities, but Mershayn had not felt completely at ease since they arrived. Collus was right. The denizens of the court were snakes. When Mershayn was a child, wrapped in the ignorance that only childhood can allow, he dreamed of being a king someday. That was before he learned the difference between a bastard and a pure born, and that was the end of that dream. The cold reality had stung, but its sting grew less with every week he spent in Teni'sia. He was glad of his spotty heritage now. Better Collus was king than him.

He stood quickly and stepped into a lunge. He thrust the sword forward at the wall by the window. A whisper of dust fell from where the sword point barely touched the stone.

Relaxed. In control. Would that all of life was as easy as swordplay.

2

MIROLAH

AFTER A FEW DAYS' rest, Mirolah and Medophae left Calsinac. In another time, if there weren't so many things that Mirolah had dropped in this last crazy month, she might have liked to explore Calsinac. But her skin itched to get back to Rith, back to Denema's Valley, back to finish all of their unfinished business. So they took a portal to Buravar, bought horses, and came south to Rith.

She stood on the top of the hill, looking at the valley and the city that she had once called home. The sun slowly sank behind distant mountains, a dusky half circle that painted the clouds red. The caravans had pulled into lines outside the city and put up their tents for the night. The workers had shouldered their hoes and gone home. Smoke from the chimneys of dozens of houses rose into the late autumn air.

The smell of cut wheat rose on the breeze that whispered to her in a language she didn't understand. Everything whispered now. The last month of her life belonged to someone else, to some unrealistic hero in a story that could never be real. She had transformed from a scared, simple girl to a woman who could battle the legendary Red Weaver, the undead Zilok Morth, even the god Oedandus, burning inside a hulking Sunrider. Now that it was over, she looked within herself to see if she could find that innocent girl again, but she couldn't.

Last night when they slept alongside the road, she woke up feeling like she was falling. She wasn't that girl from Rith anymore, the one with eight adopted sisters, a job as a scribe, and dreams of a husband and children.

Who was she now?

A humble letter writer from Rith? Medophae's lover? The threadweaver who destroyed the Red Weaver? Or was she that brief goddess, feeling all the power of the GodSpill inside Daylan's Glass, then releasing it all back into Amarion?

The answer should be easy. She should know, shouldn't she?

She closed her eyes and let her senses wander. The voices returned in whispers and garbled sentences. She could feel the valley breathe, gurgling to her. She could feel every living thing within a mile. Squirrels scurried quietly among the leaves of the trees, watching her, talking to her in a tongue she couldn't decipher. Prairie mice scampered through the grass, their intermittent squeaks silent to anyone but her. A fox watched her from the edge of the trees, whispering to her. It was as if they recognized her, and they talked to her as if she should be able to understand them.

Her stomach clenched as she listened, because she knew it had something to do with the GodSpill, with the fact that she had been one with that raging force of creation inside Daylan's Glass for the span of an eye blink. But inside that eye blink was an eternity of time. What had happened to her there? She had thought perhaps these strange aftereffects would fade, but they were only growing.

Everything was filled with GodSpill now; it had transformed the world. The leaves were greener. The mountains seemed taller. Even the air was brighter. Everything shimmered. She remembered her dreams in the rain, of knights riding down the middle of the streets of Rith, resplendent in their armor and their colorful banners, the shine of the sun upon everything, the glow about each and every person because they knew they lived in a land of infinite possibility. That daydream—her daydream—had arrived. Had that always been an effect of the GodSpill in the lands? Had she seen the future when she'd looked at those rainy streets? Or had her imagination infected the GodSpill when she was in Daylan's Glass? Had she *made* this come to pass?

She watched the gorgeous purple sky fade to gray, watched until the mountains lost their definition and became hulking silhouettes in the dark. She felt the air begin to cool.

She had left this place in fear, her life threatened, Lawdon beaten by the magistrate's men, her sister murdered. Back then, this city had been an immense place; it had been her whole world. She had envisioned living the rest of her life on its familiar dirt streets, with the ruins of Historia looming in the background.

Join us....

She spun at the voice, but there was only Medophae, who had just untied the horses. Her heart thumped painfully. The whispers had never been decipherable before.

Who are you?

There was no response. Her stomach burbled, and she wanted to vomit.

Medophae walked up to her, bringing the horses. He was a bonfire in her threadweaver sight, golden flames engulfing him, and the sight of it steadied her. Medophae had a calming effect on people when he wanted to, and she let it wash over her.

When Vaerdaro the Sunrider had taken Oedandus from Medophae, she'd witnessed an evil god come to life in a bonfire of black flame. Medophae had jokingly called the Sunrider "Dark-mane," a counterpoint to the nickname Medophae had been given long ago.

To see that godly flame returned to its rightful color— Medophae's golden color— made her feel safe. It made her feel that all of Amarion was safe.

"Are you all right?" he asked.

By the gods, he was the most beautiful man she had ever seen. Those gray-blue eyes, that towering physique, like he could push over a house. Even the smell of him, healthy sweat with a hint of some spice, intoxicated her. And here he was, smiling at her. He was hers. It gave her a ridiculous thrill, and for a moment, she actually did feel like that girl who had fled Rith so many days ago.

"I'm fine," she said. She had told Medophae about the voices when they were in Gnedrin's Post, but she doubted he remembered. He'd had a lot on his mind. They'd had to run for their lives from Zilok Morth and Vaerdaro.

She didn't bring up the voices now.

"I'm scared of going back," she said, pointedly avoiding her real fear of the enigmatic whispers. "Is that crazy?"

"This magistrate you spoke of sounds at least as formidable as Zilok Morth," he said.

He thought he was so funny. It was adorable.

"I was a girl when I left," she said. "I'd just found my place at Lawdon's and Tiffienne's house, in the community of Rith. I was going to start...well, doing what normal people do." She paused. "Instead, I'm everything they hate. A rotbringer. A threadweaver. A harbinger of death from a frightening past."

"You realize that all the GodSpill just rushed back into the lands. It's going to bring a lot of change, probably has already. You could answer a lot of questions for them. They might welcome that wisdom."

Again, so adorable. How could someone so old cling to such optimism?

"Because the ignorant are always so kind to people who bring change?" she asked dubiously. "No, they're going to take every fear they have and stick it to me. The more I know, the bigger a monster I'll be."

"Well, at least you'll be a cute monster."

"You do realize that you're not that funny, right?"

"Nope." He started back toward the horses. "Come, lovely monster. Let's go find the scary magistrate."

They swung into their saddles, started down the hill, and Mirolah heard the animals whispering in the grass and felt the trees watch them go.

3
———

MIROLAH

MIROLAH REACHED out to knock on the worn wooden door and hesitated. This house had been her home. The only time she'd ever had to knock on this door was when Casra had barred it against her as a joke during a rainstorm. She could hear the voices beyond, distant like everyone was in the kitchen preparing the evening meal.

The girl she had been—who belonged in this house—didn't exist anymore. She had faced dramaths, darklings, and undead threadweavers, and yet she hesitated to step through this door. She had survived the fight with Ethiel, the GodSpill, Zilok, and Vaerdaro. But what worked here? Either she had to lie to Lawdon and Tiffienne, or she had to tell them she was a threadweaver.

Her fist hung in the air.

"They love you, Mirolah," Medophae said softly from behind her. "They loved you before. They're going to love you just the same."

"You can't know that," she said.

"I can and I do."

She turned. "You know you can't just calm me whenever you want to. I'm immune to your glamour now."

"Are you?" He gave a charming smile.

The butterflies in her stomach fluttered away.

She sighed. "You ever do that to me when I'm not expecting it, and I'm going to turn your nose into a potato."

"You're stalling," he said.

"Okay." She let out a breath, turned back around, and knocked.

The muffled noises from the kitchen stopped. She knocked again. Tiffienne's voice rose, the words indistinguishable, but she was probably telling one of the girls to get the door. There was a patter of footsteps, coming closer.

"I *always* have to get the door!" Casra said. Someone from the kitchen retorted.

Casra opened the door, but her head was turned back at whoever had made the comment. She shouted over her shoulder. "No. *Always!*"

Her black hair flung about her shoulders in a lustrous curtain as she turned back around. She looked at Mirolah, and her mouth fell open. She stepped back a pace.

"Gods..." she whispered.

"Hello, Casra," Mirolah said, her eyes filling with unbidden tears. "It's me."

Casra leapt forward and threw her arms around her sister's neck, hugging her tightly. After a long moment, she still wouldn't let go, as if she was afraid Mirolah might disappear. "Oh, Mira, I can't believe it! They told us you were dead."

The voices in the kitchen went silent again, then there was a clamor like a horse stampede. Mirolah's sisters fought to get through the kitchen doorway and flooded into the living room.

Yehnie was first, stumbling over Cisly's feet, her straight yellow hair in disarray. She righted herself, then stopped a few feet from Mirolah and Casra. The rest of her sisters clustered behind Yehnie. Mi'Gan came sprinting down the stairs from the bedrooms and leapt over the bannister. She landed like a cat and ran around the stunned pack.

Shouting with glee, she barreled headlong into Casra and Mirolah and clung to Mirolah's waist.

Cisly and Yehnie moved then, throwing their arms around all of them.

"By Thalius!"

"Mira, I don't believe it!"

When Casra, Cisly, and Yehnie finally moved away, Dederi and Shera enveloped Mirolah in their arms.

"I thought you were dead."

"We cried for days."

Locke, ever the sober and responsible one, was the last of the sisters to step up. She didn't squeal or cry, but the tears on her cheeks spoke louder than words.

"Welcome back, Mira," she said in her husky voice, hugging her. "Thank the gods...."

And finally came Tiffienne. The other girls backed away, and Mirolah's foster mother stood just inside the living room, clutching a wooden spoon with white knuckles.

"Oh, my girl," she said, moving forward. She dropped the spoon, and it clacked on the wooden floor. Her warm, strong arms practically lifted Mirolah off the ground. "Oh, my poor girl. Well..." Her voice broke. She cleared her throat and tried to speak in a steady tone. "You have some explaining to do, to make us worry like this. I want to hear it all. I want to hear it all...." She held Mirolah at arm's-length, clutching her with trembling fingers and inspecting her, then hugged her again, then held her at arm's-length again. Tears wet her cheeks. She wiped one, then the other, then sniffed. "They told us you had tried to escape, and that they had chased you down and killed you." She waved a hand. "But never mind. Never mind." She looked down at Mirolah's youngest sister. "Mi'Gan," she said to the little girl, still attached to Mirolah's waist. "Go and fetch

Lawdon. He'll be in the back. I'm sure he hasn't heard the commotion."

"But Mommy, I want to—"

"Never mind what you want, girl," Tiffienne's stern voice cracked like a whip. "Do as I say and be quick about it."

Mi'Gan sulkily let go, looked up at Mirolah again, then sprinted from the room.

As Tiffienne backed up, Casra, Locke, and Dederi stared past Mirolah, out the doorway, noticing Medophae for the first time. Locke narrowed her eyes and cocked her head. Casra's mouth hung open, again. Dederi walked forward a pace, trying to get a better look, her eyes just as wide as Casra's, though she had managed to keep her mouth shut.

Mirolah came to her senses. "Um, Tiffienne, everyone, this is my..." She suddenly realized that she didn't have an appropriate word for him. Her lover? Her consort? She couldn't say that to Tiffienne. "...Um, my...friend, Medophae," she finished lamely.

"Well, what is he doing standing in the dark?" Tiffienne said. "Come in, Medophae. Please, come in."

He ducked as he entered the doorway. Casra clapped a hand to her open mouth, seeming to suddenly realize it was open. Shera hastily drew her fingers through her hair. Dederi smoothed the waist of her dress.

Mirolah stifled a smile. She remembered what it was like to meet Medophae for the first time.

Even Tiffienne seemed taken aback, but she recovered after a moment, pulling him down into a quick hug. "Any friend of Miro-lah's is family," she said, letting him go then closing the door behind him. "Be welcome here." She pulled a chair out from the dinner table and said, "Dinner is almost finished. You must be starved. Please sit. I'll bring wine."

He nodded graciously. "My thanks. It is kind of you," he said in his light accent, with its over-pronounced T's and lilting flow. He sat in the proffered chair.

"Dinner will be ready in a second." She turned to the girls, shooed them with a wave of both hands. "All of you, back in the kitchen. There's a meal to get on."

"But I want to stay here," Casra protested. Tiffienne stooped to pick up her spoon from the floor. She smacked Casra on the butt with it. "You can gape at our guest when dinner is on the table."

Casra stared at Tiffienne, horrorstruck, then turned bright red. *"Mom,"* she wailed. She glanced at Medophae, embarrassed, then fled to the kitchen. Tiffienne winked at Mirolah.

Seeing the punishment for disobeying Tiffienne's orders, the rest of the girls scurried away like mice.

"So, that's my family," she said.

"They're wonderful," he said. She sat down next to him and kissed him.

Pounding feet hailed Mi'Gan's return. She burst through the kitchen doorway. Her eyes fell on Medophae, and she skidded to a halt. She put her hands on her hips.

"Who're you?" she asked, coming right up to him.

"My name is Medophae."

"You're big." Her mouth pressed into a straight line. The last big man to come through that door had been the magistrate. "Have you come to take Mirolah away? Because if you are, I won't let you."

"Come here, Mi'Gan," Mirolah said. Mi'Gan gave Medophae a wide berth, then squirmed onto Mirolah's lap. "This is my friend Medophae."

Mi'Gan looked back and forth between them. "Do you kiss him?"

"Actually, I do."

"Ick." She wrinkled her nose.

Lawdon arrived then, also through the kitchen doorway. He took his wide hat off and set it on the table just inside the living room. He gave Medophae an appraising glance, then turned to

Mirolah. She patted Mi'Gan, who slid off her lap, and Mirolah rose and hugged Lawdon.

"I missed you so much," she murmured into his ear.

"And I, you." He released her and looked into her eyes. Lawdon was a tall man, but he was still half a head shorter than Medophae.

Medophae stood, and Lawdon reached out to shake his hand. They exchanged introductions, seemingly satisfied with the other's manner.

"Do I have you to thank for saving my daughter?" Lawdon asked.

Medophae shot Mirolah a wry smile. "Actually, no. She saved me."

Lawdon smirked. "Good. That's good." He pointed a gnarled finger at Mirolah. "There's a story here," he said. "Or I'm a Sunrider."

"If you had all evening," Mirolah said. "I could barely cover it."

"As it happens, I do. So you can do your best," he said with finality.

THEIR EXPRESSIONS WERE AS VARIED as the colors of autumn when Mirolah finished the tale of her travels. The dishes lay scattered all about the table, covered with half-eaten rolls and stripped chicken bones. Lawdon sat back in his chair, puffing on his pipe. She felt his emotions flow into her, and he stewed. He had never known Mirolah to be dishonest, yet it was obvious he did not swallow the tale. He kept glancing at Medophae, as though he must be the reason that his foster daughter had become the biggest liar in Amarion.

Mirolah could feel Tiffienne's worry. Her foster mother actually *did* believe Mirolah, and it scared her that there were evils greater than the Sunriders.

Mirolah closed her eyes and forced herself not to "read" her family. She didn't want to invade their privacy, but she couldn't stop all of it.

She could feel that Casra had an instant crush on Medophae. She absently toyed with her fork, stealing furtive glances beneath her eyelashes.

Locke was thoughtful, tense, but not angry like Lawdon.

Cisly was scared, and also furious. She didn't want to be in this room. She was planning to marry soon. A farmer's boy had courted her for half a year. She wanted the world to stay just the way it was. She didn't want to hear that there were darklings and threadweavers and godlike Sunriders. She didn't want her sister to be one responsible for "The Wave," which was what travelers were calling the day the GodSpill returned.

Mi'Gan had fallen asleep in Medophae's lap.

When Mirolah had started, she had asked that all questions wait until the end, as any tangent of the story could take hours to explain. Now that she had finished, she sat back and spread her hands wide.

"And that's it," she said. "We stopped here first because I needed to know that you were okay."

"Us?" Tiffienne said. "Well, that's funny, isn't it?"

"I had to know what the magistrate did to you."

"He knew what was good for him, and he left us alone," Lawdon said. "He wasn't the most popular man when the town heard what he did to you. Been a lot of grumbling from a lot of people since he 'killed' you."

Mirolah smiled. "I don't think I'll feel too badly for him."

Lawdon grunted. He took his pipe from his mouth and pointed the end at Medophae. "So you're Wildmane," he said bluntly, like it was a statement of the ridiculous rather than a question.

"Well, sir," Medophae said. "That's what the poet Thedore Stok once called me. But I never liked it."

"Wildmane isn't real," Lawdon said.

Tiffienne shot her husband an angry glance. "Lawdon, don't be rude."

"I'm supposed to believe that bucket of—"

"Lawdon!" Tiffienne kept him from saying the final word.

"Look," he said, annoyed that Tiffienne was trying to manage him. "I've seen enough swordsmen in my day to know you're probably good with that blade you're wearing. And I'm sure you're good at impressing young women—"

"Lawdon," Mirolah interrupted. "Daddy—"

"Everyone needs to stop interrupting me," Lawdon growled. "If he's a man, he can speak for himself. Now, it's easy to lie to a young girl. But sit there and lie to me, *sir*," he sarcastically echoed Medophae's honorific. "Lie to *my* face and make me trust you."

Mirolah's stomach clenched. Perhaps telling them the truth had been a mistake. She glanced at Medophae, but he was unruffled, as always. The man seemed to have three faces: royal, playful, or enraged-and-ready-to-kill. He had his royal face on now.

"Are you suggesting I do something Wildmane can do? In order to prove it to you?" Medophae asked.

"That's exactly what I'm saying."

"Sir—" he began.

"And stop calling me sir," Lawdon said. "I make tiles for a living. I'm not some lord from Buravar. My name is Lawdon. Don't try to pull down my pants with flattery."

"Lawdon!" Tiffienne gasped.

Medophae said, "No."

Lawdon raised his eyebrows. "Excuse me?"

"No, sir."

Lawdon darkened to purple.

"I'm not going to do something to prove to you that I'm Wildmane," Medophae said. "Oedandus isn't a parlor trick."

"Then you admit you're lying to my daughter," Lawdon said.

"I doubt I could lie to her if I wanted to. You want the truth?"

"If you're capable," Lawdon said. Tiffienne put a hand to her mouth, but kept herself from saying anything.

Medophae suppressed a smile. Mirolah doubted anyone else saw it, but she knew him well enough now to see the signs. She suddenly realized he was actually enjoying this. Medophae liked Lawdon and his straightforward protectiveness.

"What I am," Medophae said, "is a man from the island of Dandere. I came to Amarion and was infused with the remains of the god Oedandus. I can summon a sword of my god's rage in my hand. I can summon the strength to rip the roof off this house. I could cut my own throat with this knife." He picked up the steak knife from the table. "And Oedandus would heal the wound." He paused, setting the knife gently back down. "But I can't make you trust me. Not with a parlor trick."

"That's rubbish," Lawdon said. He opened his mouth to say something, but instead forced his pipe between his teeth. A tense silence settled over the table.

Cisly stood up and started collecting plates.

Locke spoke up. "Mirolah, what you've told us sounds... Well, it sounds like you're making it up. And not just the part about Wildmane. It makes us worry that... Well, that..."

"That I'm not right in the head?" Mirolah said.

Locke held her hands up helplessly.

"I don't understand what I'm hearing from all of you," Tiffienne blurted. She gestured angrily at Lawdon and Mirolah's sisters. "Our girl comes back from the dead, and you treat her like this!"

Lawdon glared at Medophae, not giving any ground. Medophae held her foster father's gaze, appearing serious.

"Promise me you won't be afraid," Mirolah said softly.

That drew Lawdon's attention. "What?"

"I love you," she said. "I don't want you to hate me."

"Hate you?" Tiffienne seemed stunned. "That you could even think that... Dear girl, we love you," Tiffienne said.

"What do you mean?" Lawdon asked.

"Watch." She let out a breath, and opened the bright bridge to her threadweaver sight. She felt the GodSpill in the wooden walls and floor, in the table, in the bodies of her beloved family.

She pulled a few small threads.

The dirty plates rose into the air and floated across the table, depositing uneaten food upon the great platter and stacking themselves neatly in front of Cisly's empty seat.

Cisly screamed and dropped the two dishes she had been carrying. Mirolah caught them, and they floated back to stack on top of the others.

"Oh goodness," Tiffienne breathed. There were several other gasps. Mirolah picked up on all of their emotions, and she was relieved to know that each one of them was more awed than afraid. All save Cisly.

"By the gods..." Lawdon mumbled, his pipe slipping from his mouth and clattering on the floor.

"Every bit of it is true," Mirolah said.

4

MIROLAH

AFTER MIROLAH'S DISPLAY, Lawdon relented on his interrogation of Medophae, and he charmed the rest of the family. Dederi asked for a story, and Medophae obliged. He sat at the hearth, and the girls gathered around at his feet as he told a story about Vlacar the Paladin and his search for the goddess Natra. Mirolah had seen Medophae as a gruff protector, a furious warrior, even a grudging patient. It shouldn't surprise her to see him slip into the role of entertainer so easily, but it did. She stood in the doorway of the kitchen, listening to his rich voice rise and dip to the suspense of the story.

She felt Lawdon approach from behind, and he touched her on the shoulder.

"Can we..." he nodded toward the back door, which led to the tile yard, "talk?"

"Of course."

They left the house and stepped into the well-tiled back yard. The two open bays of Lawdon's workshop stood off to the left, like dark caves. Two neat stacks of wood stood on the left side of the workshop, and more than a dozen pillars of tiles, also neatly stacked, stood in rows.

The stars were bright above, and the crescent moon cast a slippery sheen of silver over everything. Three cobble birds had gathered on the far fence. Their square-ish heads swiveled to check the sky every now and then, but always refocused on her. They spoke to her, cooing softly, in a language she didn't understand. A few squirrels had gathered behind them on the roof. They chittered and scooted nervously to the edge, looking down at her.

Lawdon paused in the yard, packing a pinch of tobacco into his pipe, then set it between his teeth and lit it. "I'm not good with words," he said. "But I've got something to say, and I want you to hear me."

"Of course."

"I wasn't always a tile maker. Back before I met Tiffienne, I traveled around a lot. Fell in with some bad people, time to time." He cleared his throats. "Anyway, there's people out there, Mirolah, who can make lies seem real. They'd tell you the sun was the moon, and you'd want to believe 'em. This Medophae is one of them. He uses fancy words to dance around the truth. When I'm around him, I want to trust him for no reason, want to believe what he says without no proof as to why. That's dangerous. I see everyone, including Tiffienne, doing the same. All you have to do is take one look in there, with all of them gathered around him, to see what I mean. It isn't right, what he does. And I refuse to believe one word that comes out of his mouth. I feel like if I believe even one of his words, I'll believe 'em all. And I just want to warn you, because you don't seem to see—"

"It's a glamour," she said.

"What?"

"It's the aura of his god around him. It does that to people. He can't help it."

That silenced him for a moment. He chewed on his pipe. "I feel like you've been taken in by him, Mira. I feel like you can't see what he really is."

"Honestly, it's amazing that you picked up on his glamour without knowing what a glamour is. I admire that you sensed it and don't trust it. But if you can't trust him, can you at least trust me?"

"Not if you've been taken in by him."

"I haven't. Can you trust me?"

He sighed, puffed on his pipe and let the smoke leak out the side of his mouth.

"I saw it all," she said. "The fiery sword. The healing of wounds. It's real."

He shook his head. "I..." he started. "Maybe I just don't want to believe any of this nonsense. You went away, and then the whole world changed. I felt it. Everybody felt it. They're calling it 'The Wave' in Buravar. It was like someone poured water all over me and inside me, but there wasn't anything to be seen. Things changed since, a thousand small things. The grass was still green, but...greener, you know? The sky bluer. It even seemed easier for me to make tiles I've made the same way for years, like the tiles knew what I wanted them to be, and cooperated more than...before." He frowned. "But I talked to Old Man Baelin and his daughter who work the fields.... I talked with some of the other farmers. They say that since The Wave came, everything has been growing like mad. The harvest just came in, and some crops grew back in just a few days. Giller Black, best hunter in Rith, says the forests are chock-full of animals now, not like before. He says he can't walk three paces without stumbling across something new and strange, something he never saw in the forest before. He says sometimes he's afraid to go out there. Imagine that. Giller Black afraid of the forest."

Mirolah knew very well that there were things to fear in the lands now, and maybe even in the forests around Rith. She could not blame Giller Black for being wary. A darkling would happily turn the tables and hunt him.

"And you..." He paused, searching for the right words. He

shook his head and plowed forward. "You claim you did this? You made The Wave?" he asked softly, turned to look at her. He puffed his pipe, lighting the bottom of his face in orange.

"This is the way the lands used to be."

"During the time of the rot bringers—?" he stopped, glanced at her. "I'm sorry. The, uh, the threadweavers?"

She put a hand on his arm. "It's okay. It's a lot to think about. But no, the Age of Ascendance was when the threadweavers ruled and created their vast cities. That was different, and what brought about the GodSpill Wars and eventually the Devastation Years. I'm talking about before, during the Age of Awakening."

"I don't know anything about that."

"Before Daylan's Fountain even existed in the first place, the lands were filled with GodSpill like now, but learning to harness it, to be a threadweaver, took many years of study."

Inside, Medophae's voice rose to a powerful boom as he punctuated his story. The girls screamed with delight.

"You want to know the truth?" she said. "I'm a little scared myself. I'm not the girl I was when I left. I sometimes have a hard time remembering what it was like to be that girl."

"What's different?" he asked.

She nodded to the cobble birds on the fence. "Do you see those?"

He squinted. "The birds?"

"They don't come out at night," she said.

"I'll be skewered," he whispered. "You're right. That's the oddest damned thing...."

"They're here to see me," she said. "I think. But I don't know why. And there are some squirrels up on the roof, too. I think they're here for the same reason. And a weasel behind that stack of tiles." She pointed. "And a few rats over by the wood stack."

Lawdon tensed, looking around like a person in a dark forest who suddenly sees dozens of eyes gleaming back at him. "How do you know? I see the birds, but..."

"I feel them. They speak in a language I feel like I should know. And they think I should know it, too. The cobble birds coo as though I should understand. The squirrels chitter."

Lawdon let out a breath. "How do you...feel 'em?"

"Threadweavers can make a bridge to the tapestry the gods created."

"Tapestry?"

"The gods created the world. They did it by weaving together an incredibly complex tapestry. You're part of that tapestry. Your body is made of threads, some so small you can't even imagine them. They're woven into each other, making up your body, and also woven into the air around you. You're connected to the ground." She pointed down, then to the roof. "To the squirrels, the tiles on the roof. Everything. It's all woven together, and I can see the threads. It's where the name 'threadweaver' comes from. So the fact that there are tiles that block my normal eyes from seeing the rats doesn't stop me from seeing them with my threadweaver vision."

She admired him so much; she always had. She knew how difficult it was to have one's life turned upside down, to be told that everything you knew might not be right.

Finally, he sighed. "I'm not going to pretend to understand what you just said. But I came out her to warn you, and now you've heard me. If you're sure this Medophae is the one you want, then I'm not going to make trouble. I just want to make sure you know what you're getting into. You're a grown woman. You can make your own choices."

"I love you, Lawdon." She put her arms around him and hugged him tight. "Father..." she said more softly.

He patted her on the back. "You'll stay with us for a while, won't you? You and your young man?"

"I would like to. For a few days, at least."

He released her. "Well then, let's get you set up. We don't have an extra room, but for now, we'll just curtain off the living room."

Mirolah knew the routine. They'd had guests before. And now she was the guest. More than anything else, it drew a line between her and the girl she had been. This was no longer her home; she was a visitor. The knowledge was bittersweet.

They returned to the living room to find that Tiffienne had already cordoned off the northern side of the living room with a rope, and a sheet hung down from it. Fresh hay lay evenly under two soft blankets. Mirolah smiled.

Medophae had just finished his tale, and Tiffienne ushered Mirolah's sisters upstairs amidst loud complaints from Casra and Shera. They, of course, weren't tired in the least and wanted another story.

"I'm sure he's had enough of the likes of you, fawning all over him with your big doe eyes," Tiffienne said. "Off to bed with you!"

The girls protested that she was so unfair as they reluctantly ascended the steps. Lawdon and Tiffienne retired shortly thereafter, leaving Mirolah and Medophae alone in their little half room.

A lone candle burned, sitting on a chair taken from the dinner table, and Tiffienne had laid out one of Mirolah's old nightgowns on the bed.

Medophae pulled off his loose shirt and folded it, set it on the floor. She pulled her own shirt over her head and tossed it on top of his.

"This seems familiar," he said. He looked left and right, as though checking for intruders. "Are you sure it's safe?"

"I'll protect you," she murmured. She pulled a tiny thread, and the candle winked out.

5

ZILOK MORTH

ZILOK MORTH FLOATED FAR OUT over the True Ocean, so high that the waves were nothing but a white-capped floor of blue below. The gray maw of the Godgate swirled overhead. It hungered for him, groaning with its need because it had nearly had him. That seething, sucking terminus had almost gotten what it wanted when Zilok made his colossal mistake.

Almost. But almost was not enough. It was never enough. The Godgate almost devoured his soul. Zilok almost killed the Wildmane. That ironic sting quivered in his soul like needles stuck into skin.

I failed, he thought for the thousandth time. He repeated the words over and over in his mind. He would continue repeating them until they didn't hurt anymore.

I lived for hundreds of years, and yet still I'm a foolish boy. I had him. I had Medophae on his knees, and, in my glee, I rushed to the prize too quickly. I overlooked details. I was blind to my danger.

He had thought of everything. The plan had worked. He had stripped the god Oedandus from Medophae, turning him mortal, killable. The arrogant bastard had not even known what had hit him in the middle of Ethiel's palace, but then he'd somehow slipped through Zilok's fingers, running away before he reached his quarry.

Then again, with the spine horse upon them, Medophae and his little bitch of a threadweaver squeezed through that portal. Both escapes were so small, so seemingly inconsequential, so easily remedied. Finding and killing a fledgling threadweaver and mortal swordsman was child's play. Zilok had done that over and over again in his long, undead life.

There should have been no need to rush, but he had anyway. Zilok had heedlessly chased after, terrified that if he did not find and slay Medophae quickly, the dullard would slip away again or, worse, find a way to reclaim his god.

And Zilok blinded himself to his true danger: Vaerdaro.

Zilok had underestimated the feral god's bond to the Sunrider. Zilok hadn't imagined Oedandus possessed enough intelligence to reveal secrets to the Sunrider that would give him an advantage. That was stupid. Arrogant. Short-sighted.

I failed, he said to himself again.

The Godgate pulled at him like never before. The part of Zilok's mind that wallowed in the catastrophe wanted to give up. This pitiful lack of will caused the hooks in his chest to tighten as though lashed to a team of draft horses, dragging him upward toward the Godgate.

But Zilok refused to be foolish twice in such a short time. He fought his depression, called upon his years of experience to remember that failures brought wisdom. Failures sharpened the blade. Every stroke of stone on steel was a failure until the edge was, at least, deadly.

Zilok's nemesis remained. Medophae was a murderous splotch of injustice on Zilok's life, and that, by itself, allowed him to resist the Godgate's pull. Zilok would catch Medophae, would punish him. He would make Medophae confess each of his offenses and beg for forgiveness with blood and screams.

That would be how Zilok's story ended, with victory, not a

whimper of failure. This loss was just one more stroke, one more scrape of stone on steel.

Now say it again. Say it one more time, and then be done.

I have failed.

He felt the metaphorical stone grind to a stop against the edge of his plan.

Below him, after his long flight, he saw the tiny island of Dandere. Medophae's birthplace.

It was a speck of a thing, far out here where even the great whales and the goddess Saraphazia did not bother the humans who lived here.

This was his mighty, sharpened blade. These people, plucked from the mainland thousands of years ago by Oedandus himself, were ruled by a royal line that possessed the god's own blood. This was how Oedandus had recaptured a bit of his sentience within Medophae when he arrived on the mainland, by burning into this royal blood.

The Dandenes were simple folk, with a tidy society ruled by a tidy king. The island was bountiful, and gave her people all of their necessary food. They had no natural adversaries. Life was peaceful, and they occupied themselves with architecture and art, discovering culinary diversions, crafting buildings for the beauty of it, painting with pigments drawn from the island's flowers and coral reefs. These people were imbued with none of the powers rampant on Amarion. There were no threadweavers here, and there was no damned Wildmane. The GodSpill in the tapestry of the island was rich, perhaps secretly the reason for the Dandenes' need to create and build, but none had guessed that the power could be tapped to create the wondrous.

And most importantly, this was a place where Oedandus, in his threadbare state, could not reach. The god had been stretched and bound over the entire continent of Amarion by his enemies long ago, and he could not reach beyond it more than a dozen miles from the shore.

Zilok smiled inwardly. This place was holy, to him at least, as it would never be tainted by Oedandus. And when he brought Medophae here, there would be no escape for him.

But before he focused on Medophae, Zilok must remove every trace of Medophae's own tainted blood on Amarion, and that meant gutting every descendant of the Three Mothers of the Sunriders. Then, he would bring Medophae to this place. And once Medophae's corpse decorated the shore of his homeland, there would be no more Oedandus. The god would once again be reduced to a blithering idiot, with no more power than an angry wind.

Where you were born, Medophae, so shall you die. The last strike will be mine, and I will finally ram this sharpened sword through your guts.

6

STAVARK

THE SUN TOUCHED the tip of the great peak of Karak-Kin. What the humans called the Spine Mountains loomed over Sylikkayrn. Slashes of orange streaked across the sky. They would deepen soon to red, then purple. Stavark loved sunsets. He always had. He remembered far back into his childhood. Before he could even walk, Stavark had waited and watched as the sunsets bloomed and faded.

He took the moment. The elders taught that one should start within the present and radiate outward, like the ripples from a finger touching water. It was a tenet at the heart of his people's spirituality, but it was something they so rarely did. Stavark liked to imagine that the syvihrk once believed in it and followed it religiously, but the Riddak Kira—when the foolish human thread-weavers had stolen the maehka from the lands—had changed the syvihrk. In the end, these spiritual practices had given way to anger and resentment in the face of hardship.

But Stavark believed that remembering the wisdom of his ancestors was the most important during hardship. It was not the time to abandon wisdom. While his people had forgotten this, Stavark would remember. He could do that.

He put his concerns aside and took the sunrise into himself. He let the image soak into his mind so that he might call it forward during the times when he was not so strong. He paused for beauty, praised it, saved it.

The smells of the forest filled him. The quiet sounds of his people going about their business felt warm within him. He loved them beyond measure, even though they did not understand him, even though perhaps some of them truly hated him.

He reached out and touched the maehka, which now filled everything. It tingled in his fingertips, urging him to use the silverland that gave him his speed. He could not feel it as the Maehka vik Kalik did, of course. He did not see the tapestry of the gods, but if he concentrated, he could feel the tingle of the maehka that had been released. It rose to a crescendo, and he began to shake. That familiar ache began behind his eyes, and he blinked and looked at the sunset once more. Glorious crimsons and rich purples filled the sky. The land around him magnified. Colors jumped forth with startling brilliance.

This was what he had always wanted. This was what Orem had promised after he had stumbled into Sylikkayrn, injured, close to death. Reluctantly, Stavark's parents nursed him back to health and when they did, Orem told of the frightful creatures he had seen. He told of how maehka was returning, thin and sickly. He told of how the syvihrk must help return the balance, else all the lands would be lost.

And Orem kept his promise. Though Stavark had not been there to see his plan's culmination, the maehka had been released. He had felt The Wave as he struggled back to Sylikkayrn from Denema's Valley. Everyone had felt it.

Now it was Stavark's turn to keep faith with his companions. He had returned home to heal, and to keep his promise to his parents. He had fulfilled that obligation, reporting to his mother and the council. The syvihrk were now more informed than all of the humans in Amarion, but now Stavark must leave again.

When Stavark left with Orem the first time, his parents shunned Orem as the cause, said he was no longer welcome among the syvihrk. They said he had abused his welcome, filled their son with poisoned ideas. Since Orem was the first human allowed in Sylikkayrn in more than a hundred years, his betrayal weighed heavy. It made many of the syvihrk feel that they had been right about humans all along, that humans were faithless betrayers.

His parents had ordered Stavark not to go, and when that had failed, they had pleaded. But Orem's quest was what Stavark had been born to do. And now they had succeeded.

But it wasn't over. He could not celebrate while he did not know the fate of his companions. Orem, the Maehka vik Kalik, even the Rabasyvihrk, they might all be in danger. Now that Stavark was healed, he must return to the human lands and find out what had become of them.

These were his debts, and he must pay them. A true syvihrk always left more than he took.

He heard a light footstep behind him, and his reflective moment ended. He wrapped the picture of the sunset, the feel of the trees, the richness of the newly returned maehka, into his heart and kept it safe.

If the newcomer had been a human, Stavark would have assumed the person was trying to sneak up on him, but the syvihrk moved elegantly, quiet as a breeze. Without turning, he could guess who it was. She had followed him around since he had returned to Sylikkayrn.

"You will not obey your mother," Elekkena said. "She begs you to stay, but you will leave anyway."

"I have a debt." He turned and looked into Elekkena's dark silver eyes. Her jaw was low and square, unusual for a syvihrk, though common for a human. Her thick silver hair fell in waves down the sides of her face, hiding that wide jawline unless she pushed it behind her ear, which she did frequently.

Elekkena and Stavark had many things in common. She held moments, like he did. One-on-one or in groups, she was mostly quiet, then all at once she could be jarringly outspoken. Both of them had been on long journeys recently, and both had returned at almost exactly same time. All of these things made them oddities. Outcasts.

She had gone on a day hunt one year ago, just before Stavark had left with Orem, and she'd never returned until now. Her parents had thought her dead. She did not talk about what had happened on her two-year odyssey, but there was a story there.

Her silver eyes—so dark for a quicksilver—never left him. He liked that about her. She looked at him as though she had nothing to hide. Most syvihrk did not hold Stavark's gaze for long. Humans looked away even quicker.

Except Orem. He had never looked away. He had always looked everything in the face.

"And your debt is more important than your mother's wishes?" she pressed.

"Only when my mother's wishes are unworthy of her."

She arched an eyebrow. "That is boldly said."

He sighed. "I don't mean to be bold with it. It is simply true. She hides, but it is not the time for the syvihrk to hide."

They spent a long moment staring at one another. He was calm. She was calm.

"I will come with you," she said.

"No. It is my debt, not yours."

"We are syvihrk. Our debts are shared."

"No," he said.

"Now whose wishes are unworthy of him?"

He opened his mouth to speak, but right words did not come to him, so he said nothing. He waited for them.

"You will need help," she said.

It was a lie to say he would not need help, and lies were seeds that blossomed into self-deception.

"Not from you," he said, trying the words, but they didn't feel right, either.

"How do you know?"

He felt the need to break eye-contact, and it was like a breeze that ruffled his shame. In that instant, he knew she held the wisdom. Pride controlled him. He saw it clearly, and was angry with himself.

He let both emotions slip away. They flowed into the maehka all around him and dissipated. He returned to the moment and set his pride aside. Right actions radiated from the center. When the center was agitated, right actions fled.

"Very well," he said.

"You are leaving today?" she asked.

"Yes."

"You will talk to your mother again?"

"Yes."

"I will wait here."

He nodded and left her there in the trees. As he neared Sylikkayrn, several syvihrk watched him. He was the rebellious, human-loving son of Syvihrk Sallark. His mother was foremost among the elder syvihrk who made decisions, when there were decisions to be made.

Sylikkayrn was not like the human villages Stavark had spent so much time in over the last year. Humans felt the need to push the living land away from them when they established their spaces. He had never understood that. Why push the lands away when you could coexist with other living creatures? They chopped down trees to make space for their square houses or their mighty square castles. They beat ground flat and lifeless to make way for their wagons and horses.

Syvihrk cities were different. An unaware human could walk straight through the middle of Sylikkayrn without ever realizing he was among the syvihrk. Several hardy human adventurers had done this over the years since the Riddak Kira. The syvihrk, hidden by their rapport with the trees surrounding them, often gathered to watch when a human came through.

Soon, Stavark came to a brief meadow. On the western edge of the meadow, moss covered the crags of a great cliff that rose into the sky, higher than any human castle. A thin waterfall cascaded down the cliff, birthing a brook that meandered through the forest. The sky was dim now, and the shadows deepened. In the day, this place filled with light. Stavark had climbed that cliff countless times and splashed through that brook as a child. This place was the entire world when he was a youth. Now it seemed like a very small corner of life.

At the northern edge of the meadow, if one had the eyes of the syvihrk, one could see Stavark's home, and immense killik tree. Fully thirty feet in diameter, it rose almost as high as the cliff to the west. When Stavark was a child, he made a game of climbing to the highest branches and jumping to the cliff. Given the choice, any syvihrk would live within a killik tree. Before the maehka had been taken from the lands, syvihrk and killik trees cared for one another. The syvihrk made sure nothing harmed the trees, ensuring they had all the sunlight and water they could want, and the trees made room within their bole for the syvihrk to live.

But when the maehka left, the killik trees died, as did most of the syvihrk. Almost all of the great trees rotted away and sank into the ground within the first few years. A few still stood, smooth husks of their previous grandeur. Only the wisest and most important of the syvihrk were allowed to live within them.

Stavark closed his eyes and took another moment for himself. As before when he left with Orem, there was a good chance he was going to die on his coming journey. Also as before, he knew deep within himself that no other decision could be made. Stavark's life was bound to Orem's, to the Maehka via Kalik's, even to the Rabasyvihrk's. He must part with them in knowing agreement, or know for certain that they were dead. That was the way of the syvihrk.

As always, it saddened him that his mother failed to see this.

But he took his moment and memorized his home.

As he approached the darkened archway, a sliver of green caught his eye. At the crest of the arch, a tiny bud had sprouted. He paused, stunned.

"So," Stavark whispered, "like the syvihrk, you have waited for the maehka to return." He reached out and put a hand against the smooth wood. "Like the syvihrk, you will live again. Thrive, beautiful tree. Thrive..."

Stavark took the moment, then went inside.

His mother, Sallark, sat in the community room, waiting for him. Mother often entertained large groups of syvihrk in his house. There was a raised dais in the center of the room so that she could be seen and heard by those encircling her. She sat upon that dais now. Her long braid of silver hair curved down one shoulder and piled in her lap like a coiled rope. Her eyes were a dark black. When one of the syvihrk went blind, the silver of their eyes faded to night. Stavark's mother had been blind as long as Stavark could remember. There were many rumors of how she had lost her sight. Stavark had heard them all. He wasn't sure he believed any of them, and Sallark never talked about it.

They paused like that, Stavark watching his mother calmly from the entrance, his mother facing the doorway. Stavark knew that his father was nearby, but he would not show himself, not until his mother had spoken her peace. The bole was intensely quiet. Stavark did not shift, did not proceed further, and he did not sit down. His welcome here was conditional, and he would not dishonor himself or his parents by pretending that he belonged.

"You do not have the feel of one who intends to stay," his mother said at long last.

"I must go again. I have debts."

"You have more debt to your people than you do to humans. Some would question whether you consider the humans more important than the syvihrk."

In the quicksilver language, syvihrk meant "the people who love beauty." It was the word they used to refer to themselves, as all syvihrk bore an intense love of beauty and harmony. It shamed Stavark that his people did not believe this extended beyond their own race. Once, they had.

"There are syvihrk among humans. They are rare, but they are there."

"And you do not find syvihrk in Sylikkayrn? Do you not feel it is your debt to serve us?"

As always when he had these conversations with his mother, Stavark felt his anger rising. "I am serving them by going upon these journeys. I told you the first time that I would help return maehka to the lands. It has returned, and still you doubt me."

"Humans lie. They murder their own. They steal. They can only offer that which we do not want: suffering."

"And what of Orem?" Stavark asked. He let his anger slip into the threads all around him.

"Orem is the worst of all," his mother said. "He spoke gentle lies that anyone would want to believe, and then he stole my son."

"The maehka is back because of Orem, his bravery, his persistence—"

"Humans stole the maehka in the first place! And Orem did not do this thing for us, but for his own selfish purposes. Returning maehka was the very least the humans could do to make up for their hubris and their greed."

Stavark waited, feeling for the right within him. Finally, he said, "Orem was my companion. If he is dead, I must know. If he lives, I must help. Now that I am healthy, I can do nothing else and remain in the right."

"You people must come first."

"This debt was drawn in service to my people," Stavark said.

"My heart bleeds as I hear his words come from your mouth."

"I chose to go," Stavark repeated.

"You had barely completed your test of passing when you left. His seductive words poisoned your mind!" His mother's anger leaked out, then she fell silent.

Anger was the cousin of hatred, and hatred was never of the right. Those who did not show serenity in their words did not have clarity within. His mother's white features pinkened with embarrassment at her outburst.

"Is that not what the test of passing is for, mother? To choose my own path from that moment forward?" he asked quietly.

His mother was silent.

"I only wish that you would understand," he said.

When his mother spoke, it was in a cold, distant tone. "Your father awaits you in the garden."

That was all. It was over. Stavark wondered how someone could be as blind in their mind as they were in their eyes. And yet he loved her. Perhaps that is why it hurt so much.

Without another word, he walked quietly past the dais and through the archway that led to the garden.

7

MERSHAYN

Dark gray clouds slid across the half moon, giving just enough light to climb by. Mershayn's fingers and toes navigated the grooves between the blocks of gray stone that made up the palace wall. His boots lay across one shoulder, connected together by their buckles. The ocean rumbled far below, withdrawing and crashing. He soaked in all of the sounds and sights—a swordsman was always aware of his surroundings—but his focus was on the wall. One slip and he was a dead man.

But a climb like this wasn't as difficult as some Mershayn had attempted. The palace of Teni'sia had stood for centuries against coastal weather. The mortar between the stones had receded, giving easy handholds for a man of his skills. Mershayn reached the Northern Walk of the palace smoothly, and he dropped onto the stones.

Now he could revel in his victory, so sweet. He turned to look back at the balcony to the south, where he had come from. Ari'-cyiane was silhouetted there, her glorious curves wrapped in a thin sheet that rippled in the breeze. She blew him a kiss. She always watched him until he was safe. He surmised it was half because she was worried he would fall, and half because it gave her a thrill to see him do something so dangerous.

He had already tested himself by climbing to some of the taller towers. The architects of Teni'sia were brilliant. It was as though the palace had naturally grown from the cliff. In some places it was difficult to see where the mountain ended and the castle began.

Of course, Collus had no idea about Mershayn's climbing adventures. It would make the king angry to hear that Mershayn had risked his life a half a dozen times already while they had been here. Collus was petrified of being left alone to deal with this kingdom, and Mershayn's friendship was his only solace.

And Collus would be especially angry to know that a few of those climbing adventures were to woo the wife of Teni'sia's most powerful noble. It was a disaster waiting to happen, politically. But personally, Mershayn liked to think that Collus would hide a wry smile and approve. After all, chasing beautiful maidens was what the two of them spent most of their time doing before they came north to this stodgy castle.

Mershayn undid the buckles connecting his boots and sat down upon the neatly fitted stones of the Northern Walk. The guards on the walk came by every fifteen minutes, and he had it timed perfectly.

The interval used to be every thirty minutes, according to Captain Lo'gan, but the death of Queen Tyndiria had been a crushing blow to the morale of the royal guard. When Collus arrived, they had already set up a system to redouble their protection.

As they damn well should.

As Royal Arms Inspector, a new title that Collus had granted him, Mershayn's first self-imposed task had been to inspect each and every one of the guard posts. His new title elevated him to the status of a lord and gave him the right to inspect anything having to do with the royal guard or the military. Of course, what it really meant was that he had no obligations other than what he felt like doing, which was the perfect job for him. And, it was fun to see sourpusses like Giri'Mar have to call him lord.

Not that Mershayn wanted any sort of political power. Erg. He'd rather be chained to a wall than bow and scrape at court. They could have it all. Mershayn only wanted to keep his brother safe. That was the sole reason he was here in Teni'sia.

When he had arrived, he expected to have his hands full reworking the entire royal guard to suit him. After all, what kind of incompetent guards let an assassin walk right into the queen's study and brutally murder her?

Of course, Mershayn still didn't know exactly what happened there. The official story was that enemies of Teni'sia had murdered her. Nobody believed that one. The other stories were wild and inconsistent. Everyone had a different version. Some said that a supernatural creature had killed her, some bogeyman from legend. This was the version the royal guards told the most. Mershayn supposed it made them feel better about their failure if they could blame it on the supernatural.

The supernatural... What a bucket of horse dung.

When the story was told by the common folk in the lower levels of the city, it came out different. Like Mershayn, they thought the queen was killed by her lover. This rogue Medophae person, former Captain of the Royal Guard, had apparently given a tearful speech at Tyndiria's funeral, then vanished. That was highly suspicious. Mershayn was well acquainted with the blood rage that came over a person at a lover's betrayal. It took about ten seconds for some men to go from surprise to murder when they found their wife in bed with another man. He had experienced that firsthand on two different occasions. So without any better evidence than Captain Lo'gan's word, Mershayn had to believe that Tyndiria had been caught with a young man—or maybe a woman—in her bed. This Medophae person had slain them both, hidden the body of the queen's lover, and made up some story of bakkarals and vampires.

So Mershayn had gone looking for every flaw in Lo'gan's guarding strategy. To his disappointment, he found no holes at all. Lo'gan ran a tight ship. When Mershayn questioned him, Lo'gan answered every question succinctly. Also, he claimed no credit for the systems in place, said they were crafted by Captain Medophae. This missing man was also said to be spectacular with a blade. None of the guardsmen had ever bested him on the practice field, and Lo'gan had said that he surmised Medophae had never even unleashed his full skill.

Damned hero worship. Captain Medophae this. Captain Medophae that. Mershayn would like to test this Medophae's mettle for real, see just how "brilliant" with a blade he was. It was more likely he was a dullard with a blade and a genius at drinking. The obviously charismatic man had probably frequently tipped a brew with all of his guards. So because they liked him, they assigned sterling attributes to him.

But even if it was true, and this Medophae was a peerless swordsman, it made it that much more likely that he was the murderer. The bakkaral they claimed killed the queen had also slain four guards in the royal wing just beforehand. Someone cold-blooded and brilliant with a blade could have pulled that off.

With his boots firmly back on his feet, Mershayn swung his sword belt off his shoulder and buckled it around his waist. He was only halfway through the motion when a familiar voice startled him.

"Looking for weaknesses in the guard pattern?"

The torch flickering over the archway that led into the castle cast deep shadows around the owner of the voice. It was a woman's voice, but Mershayn could not see her.

Deni'tri, one of the royal guards, emerged from the dark.

Mershayn had noted her skill in the practice yard early on. She was a fearsome fighter, and big. She stood nearly six feet tall, about the same height as Mershayn himself, and she was one of the few who had agreed to spar with him when he'd arrived. He had bested her, of course, but she was good. She almost tagged him by capitalizing on the fact that she was ambidextrous. When he'd smacked her right hand with his practice blade, causing her to drop her sword, she had shifted fluidly to her left hand and continued the attack. He'd complimented her on that.

There weren't many women in the royal guard, and he had known in the first meeting with her that he should never approach her sexually. There were rumors about the three deep scars that marred her cheeks and forehead. It was said she did those to herself and shaved her head regularly to discourage suitors.

That was a special kind of crazy, and Mershayn had liked her immediately.

He wasn't sure how much he liked her now, though, with her right arm cocked back, a throwing hatchet read to fly. She held a short sword in her left, pointed straight at his head as though marking the spot.

Mershayn's hands were still tangled in the buckle of his sword belt. He slowly began to remove them.

"Leave them, Lord Mershayn," she said. "I like them where they are."

Mershayn had a sense for when people were serious and when there was room to talk. Deni'tri was serious, so he stopped. He smiled and shrugged. "You caught me," he said simply.

Her eyes flicked to his hands during his shrug, to make sure it wasn't a misdirection to free himself up. Mershayn admired the way she thought, and he made a mental note to commend her to Lo'gan for her instincts...as long as she didn't injure him tonight.

"The question is, what did I catch you at?" She looked around, and instantly noticed the lighted balcony from which he'd come. Ari'cyiane blew out the lantern, but her curvy silhouette was still visible against the night sky before she vanished inside. Deni'tri turned her eyes back to him, but he could see her thinking. Who lived in those rooms?

She seemed to come up with the answer, because she slowly eased out of her battle-ready posture. She was no longer on the edge of killing him. She sheathed the short sword. The hatchet came down, and she flipped it lazily in one hand, catching the haft and flipping it again.

"Can I move now?" Mershayn asked.

She eyed his hands, caught at the buckle draped over his groin. A flicker of a smile ran across her lips. When she spoke again, her serious tone had gone. "It seems an odd job for two swords," she said.

"Clever," he said. "I never go anywhere without my sword." He buckled the belt and let his hands rest at his sides. With his sword safely on, he felt far more relaxed. He'd bet on himself every day of the week to be able to pull that weapon quickly enough to block her hatchet, if it came to that.

"What does Lord Vullieth think about your midnight sword-carrying?" she asked.

"I doubt he gives it a thought." He leaned back against the stone wall and studied her. She flipped the hatchet again.

She looked at the dark balcony. "It is quite a risk for her. I wonder that she would bother with you."

"Some women go out of their way for a thrill."

"I bet you have a good sense for that."

He held his hands helplessly. He changed the subject. "How is the watch tonight?"

"Quiet, until I found you. I was hoping I'd get to kill someone," she said.

"Sorry to disappoint."

"It is probably best if I don't kill the king's beloved brother."

"You have keen political acumen."

"But yours is horrible." She nodded again at the balcony. "Ari'-

cyiane has much to lose, but you have more. Or rather, the king does."

A long silence ensued as she watched him. He didn't feel relaxed anymore.

"I have a hard time understanding politics," he joked.

"No, you'd just rather play with your sword than shoulder responsibility."

That was damned saucy talk for a guard, talking to a lord.

He was of half a mind to put her in her place, but he didn't. She was right about him, and when Collus gave Mershayn his lordly title, he'd promised himself he'd never abuse it. By the gods, he'd promised himself he'd never believe he somehow *deserved* it, unlike the rest of the royal and lordly. In truth, Mershayn didn't believe in hierarchy. That was why he did things like dally with the wife of a powerful noble. During his entire life, pure-born nobles had rubbed his nose in the fact that he was a bastard. Stealing a night with their wives was his revenge. So, despite the fact that Deni'tri had needled him, Mershayn was going to respect her courage and her honesty.

"Some things are worth the risk," he said carefully.

She pursed her lips. "I think you may actually believe that."

He shrugged.

"In that case, I can't fault your taste," she said, and to his surprise, she smiled.

He raised an eyebrow. "Ah, so the fierce warrior facade comes together a little clearer. You prefer to rest your head on a softer chest?"

"I rest my head wherever I choose. But I wouldn't kick the Lady Ari'cyiane out of bed."

He laughed. "You're an odd duck, Deni'tri."

"I'll take that as a compliment, coming from you."

He gestured down the Northern Walk. "Shall we keep going?" he asked. "I wouldn't want to make you late for your rounds."

They fell in step together.

"So, do you enjoy the midnight duty, Deni'tri?" he asked.

She stopped in her tracks, looked at him sharply.

"What is it?" he asked.

"I enjoy all the duties," she murmured, as if she had said it before. She stowed her hatchet on the hook at her waist and went to the stone rail. "That is chilling," she said to herself.

He followed her. That was odd. "What is it?"

"I've marched this walk a thousand times, but this is only the second conversation I've ever had here. The last time I was asked the exact same question. Three days later, the queen was dead." She glanced up at the cloudy sky. Moonlight hit the cliff castle in patches. "I pray it is not an omen."

"Who asked you if you liked the night shift? Lo'gan?"

"Captain Medophae," she said with the same kind of reverence everyone else did. "He led the royal guard before Tyndiria's death—"

"Yes, I've heard of him." Mershayn wanted to roll his eyes. "It seems like everyone has something to say about Captain Medophae." He leaned his back against the rail, facing her. "You don't strike me as the type of person to exaggerate, Deni'tri, so maybe I can get a straight answer out of you. Everyone here holds this Captain Medophae in a kind of awe. I want to know more about him. Truthful things, not exaggerated stories. Did you know him well?"

"Not really. I sometimes think that no one really knew him well, except the queen."

"And do you revere him as the others do?" Mershayn asked.

It took a moment before she replied. "We all did," she murmured. "He was different, unlike anyone else I've ever met. He was young, but he had a steadiness. He knew things, saw things that others missed." She frowned, seemingly disappointed with her description, then tried again. "When he looked at you, he didn't see another guard, or a chef, or a stable boy, or a bastard from the south. He saw the importance of you. You could feel it.

It made you feel as though you were his friend already, that you had been for years, even though it was the first time you'd met him."

"And that is what impressed everyone about him?"

She thought about that for a moment, then shook her head. "No. That was what made you like him."

"Then what was so impressive?" Mershayn kept his tone light, but he was exasperated. Would anyone ever tell him what was so special about this ghost Captain?

She smiled. "If you'd met him, you'd know."

He snorted. He couldn't help it. "That's the kind of answer I was hoping I wouldn't get from you."

"Well, it's a difficult question to answer," she said simply. "It would be easier to ask what was *not* impressive about him. He was amazing with a blade. He was always certain and, frankly, always right. His assessments of everything from guard rotation to swordplay style to the nuances of a fisherman's net to the economics of the kingdom, all of them were insightful and accurate. It was as though he had been a king himself, sometime before. And a sailor. And anything he seemed to turn his hand to. He had compassion for those beneath his station, and absolutely no fear. Of anything. I've never met a man who had no fear. He would happily train with real swords or wooden. He was so confident, it was as though he believed he could not be hurt."

"I doubt you caught him at midnight at hatchet-point with his pants down."

She smiled. "It would not have mattered. I assure you that if I caught Captain Medophae in your position, I would have been the uncomfortable one. I would have felt out of place, not him. Wherever he was, it was exactly where he should be, and no one could deny it." Then, she dropped her voice so low he almost couldn't hear her. "I wish he would return...."

"You miss him."

"Teni'sia lost its two greatest assets in one moment. Perhaps the two greatest leaders we ever had or shall ever have. The entire country changed when the queen died, though the kingdom won't feel it right away. I think eventually Medophae and the queen would have married."

"And you would have been okay with that? Some lowborn ruling over you?"

She chuckled. "You wouldn't say that if you had met him. So many of us longed for their marriage. This Wave, as everyone calls it, this thing that has washed over the lands, pushing vitality into the plants and animals, it has brought Teni'sia only misery. Many believe that The Wave is connected to our queen's death. The supernatural creature that killed her preceded The Wave by a matter of days. It is too great a coincidence."

"You don't think Collus will make a good king here?" Mershayn asked, irritated.

She turned to him, also irritated. "Would you rather I not speak plainly?"

He sighed. By Thalius, the woman knew who she was talking to. Mershayn would rather bite off his own tongue than encourage a convenient lie over the truth. "No, I'm sorry. Please continue."

"I do not mean to disparage His Majesty. He has fine qualities, and I know he is your brother, so you know him better than I. He may become an excellent ruler in Teni'sia, but he is not Queen Tyndiria." She took a deep breath and hung her head. "We loved her."

Mershayn kept silent. He liked Deni'tri, but even he could see that there were some subjects that shouldn't be discussed with a common guard.

She pushed away from the rail. "Pardon me, my lord," she said, seemingly troubled by her thoughts, "But I must continue my sweep. I enjoyed talking with you."

"I..." The departure was so abrupt, but he could think of nothing to say to stop her, and he wasn't sure he wanted to. "Thank you. Good night."

"Good luck with your...swordplay." She gave him a wry smile over her shoulder, then continued along the North Walk. As she disappeared into the night, he saw her hand drift down, unhook her hatchet and begin flipping it again.

He turned—

—and came face to face with a tall, thin albino. His skin and hair were the color of fresh snow... But no. He wasn't an albino, for his eyes weren't pink. They had pupils and a black ring around the white iris. He was something else. Something...other.

He was at least a head and a half taller than Mershayn. Tight-fitting white scale mail wrapped his torso, and a thick, black belt wrapped his waist. His leather breeches were white as well, and his knee-high black boots glinted in the torchlight. A wicked dagger protruded from his belt, hooked and curved as though it was a flicker of flame turned to steel. Mershayn had never seen a dagger like that. It sent a swift chill through him, and his first impression was that this was an assassin, perhaps the supernatural creature that had killed Tyndiria. Neither Deni'tri nor Mershayn had heard him approach.

His long, thin nose wrinkled at the sides, as though Mershayn smelled like week-old fish. His derision was plain as he stared at Mershayn, like he was a piece of dung about to be scraped off a boot.

Mershayn sucked in a breath and stepped back into stance. He pulled his sword—

The stranger spoke in a tongue that sounded like thick oil poured between rough rocks. Mershayn's sword stopped halfway out of its sheath; he couldn't move his arm.

He opened his mouth to yell for help, but the man spoke again, quickly, and Mershayn's voice froze.

The stranger's cold eyes regarded him. "Where is the man you call Medophae?" he asked.

Mershayn suddenly found he could talk again. "He was here,"

he was surprised to hear himself say. He hadn't meant to say anything. "He's gone."

"Gone where, human?"

The disdain in the man's voice when he said "human" made Mershayn feel like dung being scraped off the man's boot. "No one knows," Mershayn answered. And why did he just keep answering? Mershayn wanted to tell the man to jump into the ocean, but his lips just kept forming the words, and his voice kept telling what he knew as though he had no control over it.

"Where is Randorus Ak-nin Ackli Forckandor?" the stranger asked.

"What?"

The man sneered. "The one you call Bands." He said the name in the same tone as he'd said *human*.

That name sounded familiar, but it certainly wasn't anyone in Teni'sia, not that he knew. He tried to dig it out of his memory. Was this someone he'd met before?

"I don't know who that is," he said.

The stranger rumbled, and the sound seemed like it was coming from the belly of an enormous beast. His fists shook at his sides, like he was trying to hold something in, but his voice came out as cold and smooth as ever. "This place is beloved of Medophae?"

"Beloved? I don't know. I guess," Mershayn said. "The people here love him, that's sure."

"She will come here," the stranger concluded, to himself rather than to Mershayn. "She will come here looking for him." He glanced at Mershayn again, and in the stranger's white eyes, Mershayn saw himself as a corpse, cold on the flagstones of the Northern Walk. He saw Teni'sia burning. The blood of her soldiers dripped from her walls. Babies wailed at the sky, their mothers slain.

"I would kill you now," the stranger whispered, conspiratorially. "But my lord commands me not to, so I shall have to save that joy for when I return. You will forget you saw me."

𝒢𝒮

MERSHAYN FOUND himself back by the southern edge of the walk, heading into the hallway that led into the castle proper, that led eventually to his chambers. His head felt thick. Where was he going? He stopped, trying to remember....

Ah yes, to his chambers. He smiled at the thought of Lady Ari'cyiane. That was something worth staying up for.

Then he frowned. Why did he feel so befuddled?

There was something he desperately needed to remember.... Yes, something of great importance. Something...white. It was... The thought floated away from him like dandelion fluff. He looked at his hands. Red marks slowly faded from his sword hand, as though he had just gripped it very hard. He looked at his sword.

A foreboding worse than he had ever known hovered around him. But then it was gone. He spun around and looked behind him. There was no one there.

Mershayn paused in the hallway for many long moments. His heart thundered in his chest, but he didn't know why.

8

MEDOPHAE

WIDE LEAVES DROOPED *from the branches of thick-trunked trees, and bushes huddled at the edge of the forest. It took a second glance to realize that a city began there, but once Medophae saw it, he recognized it in an instant. Only Denema's Valley had such unlikely overgrowth. He turned and surveyed the moss-covered buildings. He moved slowly, as though his muscles wouldn't respond normally. Wasn't he... Wasn't he in Rith? He and Mirolah had just arrived and...*

He didn't remember the journey from there to here, and he immediately wondered if he'd had a memory lapse. He used to have them all the time when he lived in his cave, before Orem brought him to Teni'sia. But he hadn't had one since The Wave, since Mirolah had freed the GodSpill, since Zilok stripped Oedandus from him and made him mortal for a short time again, since Mirolah had loved him and pulled him back into the land of the living.

He looked to his left, expecting to see her, but she wasn't there. She wasn't anywhere.

Movement caught his attention, and he spun, looking down the green sward of the street.

An enormous red dragon rose above the buildings, crushing them under its talons as it moved forward. The dragon's long, serpentine neck rose overhead, as tall as a castle, looking down on Medophae.

Medophae's body went tight, and he could barely breathe. He frantically searched for Mirolah, but he could not see her. Where was she? She couldn't be here! This wasn't a threat that a mortal, even one as powerful as Mirolah, could survive.

He took a step back, then forced himself to stand firm. The presence of the dragon washed over him in waves, tearing at his sanity, ripping at his courage. Medophae had only felt this kind of fear once before, when he had braced Dervon the Diseased.

The force of Oedandus surrounded Medophae always, even when he wasn't wreathed in golden fire. That godly force created a glamour around him that made people like him, even love him. But there were other ways to use that presence, and Dervon had transformed it into terror. Rather than attracting and beguiling mortals, it horrified them. Anyone who looked upon Dervon would cringe into a babbling ball of insanity or flee screaming.

That was happening to Medophae now. It was like facing Dervon all over again. He knew who his dragon was, who he had to be.

This was Avakketh, god of dragons.

"Medophae," Avakketh said, his voice shaking the buildings. Even the ground trembled.

Medophae wanted to run the other direction, to get away from him, but he clenched his teeth and stood his ground. Oedandus stoked within him, and golden fire flared across his arms. As a mortal, he could never resist the fear spilling off Avakketh. But with Oedandus, he could, if only barely.

"What do you want?" Medophae didn't call the godsword. It was possible Avakketh only wanted to talk, possible that the fear pouring off him was incidental, much like Medophae's own glamour.

"I know your secret," Avakketh said. "I was there."

"You were where?"

"When you killed Dervon."

"Dervon."

"You braced him. You fought him. But you did not win. The thin little human legends say you destroyed him, but they lie."

Medophae remembered that horrible, excruciating moment. Dervon had him pinned like a butterfly to a board, sickly claws of black stuck through him in a hundred places, down from the sky, up from the stone below. Oedandus healed the flesh around the punctures, keeping Medophae's body alive as he screamed. Dervon had been too strong for him, for all of them. Even with Tarithalius and Bands helping him, the god had held them all at bay until...

Until Zilok intervened.

"Your threadweaver friend set Oedandus free," Avakketh said, as though reading Medophae's mind.

Zilok had done something to Medophae's mind, had opened a door, and Oedandus came raging through it like never before. The god took over Medophae's body, shot like an arrow into Dervon, consuming him with golden fire. That was how the battle was won. Medophae had been crushed. He, actually, had lost. It was Oedandus who prevailed.

Afterward, Zilok had described what he'd done, that he'd pushed Medophae's personality to the back of his mind where it wouldn't go insane from the twisting warp of Dervon's presence and the inhuman pain that coursed through him, a place where Medophae's mortal weakness wouldn't get in the way.

When Oedandus emerged, Medophae had been smothered in his own body, crushed under the weight of his god's rage. Medophae had almost been erased, and for an eternal moment—when Dervon's body lay in a smoking ruin—Medophae thought Oedandus would keep his body.

"You lost that battle," Avakketh said. "The humans call you a god, but you are not."

"I never claimed to be a god."

"You never denied it."

"What do you want?"

"I want you gone."

"What?"

"I've come to offer you mercy," Avakketh said. "An apocalypse comes *for all humankind. Amarion will be destroyed. Because you are the care-taker of my brother Oedandus, I have chosen to aid you."*

"What are you talking about? Amarion destroyed? What apocalypse?"

"As a favor to you, you may also warn a few of your chosen. You may take them with you when you go. And lastly, I will give you that which you most desire." His giant claw came forward, large as a house, and it opened. Inside was Bands. She was curled up in her dragon form, and her head rose. The dark green bands that gave rise to her nickname encircled her neck up to her chin.

Medophae's knees felt watery. "Bands!"

"My love," Bands said, but she seemed sad.

Avakketh closed his fist, and Bands was gone once more.

The sight of her twisted inside him. He had cast her away. He'd thrown her into the ocean, and she was still alive after all. He could save her...

Suddenly, it struck him. This was a dream, some threadweaver mind trick, like Ethiel had used on him. He wasn't really here.

"Bands is gone," he said. "She is beyond anyone's reach."

"Love," Avakketh whispered. Buildings crunched and crumbled as he turned, resettling himself on his haunches. His black gaze never left Medophae.

"What?"

"The answer to the Red Weaver's riddle is Tarithalius's grand trick upon your entire species. 'Love' is the answer you missed for centuries. But now, apparently, you have fulfilled the riddle, and Bands was freed."

Ethiel's words rang in his head: You must give to someone that which you have already given away. And you must cast away what now sustains you.

Love...

His mind raced, putting that word into the riddle. Avakketh was right. It fit. For over four hundred years, he had tried everything, but he'd never fallen in love with anyone the way he had loved Bands. Not until Tyndiria. He had loved Tyndiria, but he still couldn't cast Bands away.

He'd kept her close, and the enchantment remained. Tyndiria had put a crack in his soul, but Mirolah had shoved her way through.

Love...

That was exactly the kind of thing Ethiel would do. She knew falling in love with someone other than Bands was impossible for Medophae. Even if he tried. Especially if he tried.

But then came Mirolah, and he had cast Bands's gem into the Sara Sea.

"No..." he said.

"Bands is free," Avakketh said. "You two can have each other. But you must leave Amarion forever. This is my gift to you."

Gift...

Bands had rarely talked about Avakketh. Unlike the capricious "sometimes here, sometimes gone" nature of the human god, Tarithalius, Avakketh was like a stern father to his dragons, present and demanding. And Bands had not left Irgakth under easy circumstances. She had been banished. Or, more accurate to say, she had banished herself due to her curiosity about humans, and she had once confided to him that the reason Avakketh reviled Bands was because he hated all humans....

"You're the apocalypse," Medophae whispered, putting the pieces together. "You want to destroy Amarion."

Avakketh rumbled, shifting again, grinding stone beneath his tail, his scaled belly, and his talons.

"I won't let you," Medophae said, but he felt a weak flutter in his stomach, like he had no substance inside, like he had no strength.

"Leave and be rewarded," Avakketh growled. "Or stay and be destroyed. You may take your favorite twenty humans with you. The humans you care for. I will even let you take my rogue daughter. Randorus can fly these chosen few far over the ocean to Dandere, back where you came from."

Medophae swallowed hard. "No."

Avakketh lowered his head. "Resist me, and everything you love will die in torment. I will strip the flesh from your beloved one bloody rope at a time, and she will scream for you to help her. She will scream your name as she dies."

Oedandus responded to Medophae's anger, flaring gold fire across his skin.

Avakketh smiled, scaly lips pulling back from teeth as tall as Medophae. "Little godling, you are a fool. We will meet soon again, and I will have your answer. For if we meet a third time, I will consider your choice made, and my offer will be gone."

Avakketh moved so quickly Medophae didn't have time to react. His enormous talon whipped out, slamming down, crushing Medophae's body, smashing the breath from his lungs, cracking his bones...

The god's voice thundered in his mind as he died.

"A sweet reward, or bitter devastation. Choose well, godling..."

GS

MEDOPHAE THRASHED AWAKE, trying to escape the deadly talon. His breath came quickly, but he wasn't in Denema's Valley. No trees leaned over moss-covered buildings. No verdant streets. His aura crackled and spit, throwing golden light into the dark. He was in a house, sleeping on a pallet on a wooden floor, a woman lying next to him. A blanket had been stretched across a rope in front of him to his right. To his left were wooden walls and a window.

"Medophae?" the woman said. He shifted quickly. Her name. What was her name?

"Are you okay?" she asked. Her warm fingers pressed into his shoulder. "What's the matter?"

"Mirolah," he gasped, remembering her name.

"You're shaking," she said, concern in her voice.

"Just a dream," he managed, but the cold reality pressed into him. It hadn't just been a dream. Avakketh had been here. Medophae could still feel the overpowering presence of the god.

Mirolah encircled him with her arms and laid her head on his shoulder. "A nightmare for Wildmane," she said. "Who would have thought?" The concern gave way to playfulness as she whispered in his ear. "Shall I sing you a lullaby?"

If a spell had been cast on him, Mirolah might have been able to detect it if she looked. And he didn't want her looking. She was naturally curious and incurably impetuous. Nothing would hold her back if she sensed something. She'd trace it back to its source, and if the god of dragons found a human snooping about his threadweaving, he'd kill her. He'd snuff her out like a candle.

He didn't respond to her suggestion, and she rubbed his back softly, around in a circle. It was a nice gesture, and under most circumstances, Medophae would have welcomed it, but when she touched him...

He thought of Bands.

Stop it. You're with Mirolah. She is your beloved now.

But even as he thought it, it felt wrong. To use that term for any other than Bands felt like a betrayal.

What if Avakketh isn't lying? What if Bands has returned?

Mirolah stopped rubbing his back and laid her hand on his waist.

"Do you want to talk about it?" she asked.

"No."

She went silent, and he realized he'd stung her.

"I'm sorry. I just... I need to clear my head."

"Do you need to take a walk?" she murmured into his shoulder. "Clear the dreams away?"

He smiled his reassuring smile. "Are you sure you can't read my mind anymore?" He tried to sound light-hearted.

An acutely painful memory of Tyndiria came to him then. He saw his balcony at Teni'sia. He saw the young queen, her long ringlets framing her face. Curling red vines. He felt her come up behind him and wrap her arms around him.

He had betrayed Bands with Tyndiria. He was betraying Bands with Mirolah. He closed his eyes and banished the image.

"Yes," he said. "I think I will, for just a while."

"I'll be here," she said, releasing him.

He sat up. He felt the urge to lean over, kiss her again, but he didn't.

The dream... It wasn't a dream. It was an attack, the first of more to come. Avakketh was coming south. That was more important than Mirolah or Bands, more important than anything personal Medophae might have wanted. Avakketh was going to destroy Amarion.

He got up, began dressing quietly. "I'll be back by sunrise."

"Take your time," she said. "The sun is almost here."

He looked at her, about to ask how she knew that, but he didn't. This was Mirolah. If she said she could sense when the sun would rise, then she could.

"Okay."

"Remember, though, that Tiffienne will be cooking her miraculous eggy hash for breakfast, in honor of our visit. You'll regret it if you miss it."

"I'll be back in time." He hesitated, then leaned over and kissed her on the forehead.

He quietly left through the front door and wended his way through the squat buildings, trying to tamp down his emotions, that gutless fear that turned his courage to water, and the flare of hope that Bands had returned. He had put her to rest, clinging to Mirolah in his sorrow. But now, was it possible Bands not only survived the gem, but had emerged? If she had—if there was even the slightest chance she was alive—could he really just ignore it? What if Bands was looking for him right now?

His boots splashed through puddles as he turned down one street after another. He didn't pay attention to where he was going. He just needed to keep walking.

Love.

It was the answer to the riddle. Of course it was. How could he never have seen that?

Because it was exactly the kind of insidious thing Ethiel would do.

You can have your beloved back, just as soon as you cast her aside and love someone else.

Ethiel knew he'd never do that, so she knew she had him. Medophae couldn't have seen the answer because seeing the answer meant he had to give up Bands anyway. There had never been a chance for him to solve it.

For a brief moment in Calsinac after they had destroyed Zilok, and then here in Rith with Mirolah's family, he'd been happy again. He had moved on to a new life. He had found joy in simple things; he'd found humor again. Now he felt like he was betraying Bands by being in Rith. And he felt like he was betraying Mirolah by thinking of Bands.

He stopped walking, put his fists to his head. When he finally looked up, he realized he was standing next to the hacked and marred base of a blue tower. The sun was beginning to rise in the distance, as promised.

The tower loomed high, its pointed top catching the first rays of light. Deep grooves cut away at the blue marble base, back and forth, crosshatching each other. The years had smoothed the scars, depositing dirt into them, making them dark brown scabs. It was as though a beast with steel claws had attacked the tower. Why? What could be so offensive as to...

He looked up where the destruction ended, some ten feet high. There had been a mosaic on the blue marble, and just out of reach of the vandals' axes, sleek green dragon wings spread wide, gliding toward a setting sun. Astride the dragon was Medophae with flying golden hair. This mosaic was of him and Bands. The bottom half of Bands's body had been obliterated, but the vandals couldn't reach higher than that. The Wildmane and Bands in the picture were oblivious to their half-destruction, flying blithely into a brilliant sunset of oranges, reds and purples.

He remembered when he had crossed that ocean with Bands.

She was unfathomable back then. He hadn't even known if she was male or female. Dragons had not even been part of the lore of his people on Dandere. No one had ever seen one before, save his mother. She had crossed that same ocean in the opposite direction and found her future with Medophae's father on the island.

Bands had watched Medophae all throughout his childhood, unbeknownst to him. She protected him. It dizzied him, how long ago that had been. His life had changed a hundred times since then. The entire lands of Amarion had changed. The time of his childhood was an era that seemed like fragments of a dream.

He entered the tower, taking the steps seven at a time as he launched himself to the top. He emerged onto the turret and looked out over the city.

"Historia," he murmured, remembering the name and looking at grand spiral below him that had once told the history of the lands from the goddess Natra, who had made the world. Once there had been a great statue of Natra in the center with mist flying out all about, looking out over the unfolding of human history. The statue had been one of the wonders of the Age of Ascendance, and though Medophae had only seen it once in all its grandeur, he had always meant to return.

There were many things I meant to do, he thought, looking away from the sad little lake in the center of the spiral. *There were many times I stood at a crossroads, not knowing which way to go. And I have made more bad decisions than good.*

Do I believe a hateful god who claims to be doing me a favor? Do I throw away all else and dance to Avakketh's tune?

Or do I stay true to my companions, continue my search for Orem and Stavark?

The answer was simple. Medophae didn't trust the gods, even Tarithalius. He certainly wouldn't trust the god who hated humans above all. There was no reason for Avakketh to do Medophae any favors.

He started back down the stairs, winding around and around.

He would go to Denema's Valley with Mirolah. They would find their friends. That was what mattered most.

And Bands...

He reached the base of the tower, went through the doorway and turned, staring at the nearly-obliterated mosaic.

Bands was irretrievably locked in a gem. She was beyond his reach. Either that, or she had died centuries ago in that prison.

9

MIROLAH

MIROLAH WOKE before the sunrise and helped her sisters with their chores as though she'd never left. Ignoring the GodSpill or any attempt at threadweaving, she carried the wood in for the fire. She swept the dining room floor and helped with breakfast. For a glorious hour, she returned her to her childhood. She was that young girl again, the girl she had left behind, that girl who only transcribed letters for other people, who did not hear the lands breathing, the animals speaking.

But simply because she imagined it did not make it true. As Mirolah diced a cucumber for the morning salad, she felt the tapestry move, felt the breeze outside the door of the little house, felt five men approaching.

She set the knife down next to the half cucumber on the cutting board and ran a finger down one of the deep grooves in the wood, feeling the texture of it.

She memorized the kitchen, the sturdy wooden walls and the sturdy wooden counters, the matching cupboards perched at head height.

Tiffienne and Casra worked together over the stove, their backs to Mirolah, preparing to transform the eggs into a masterpiece. She could hear Mi'Gan arguing with Lawdon in the tile yard. She closed her eyes and took a deep breath.

I love you. I love you all.

She walked into the dining room and waited. The men outside arranged themselves cautiously, and she could feel their fear. When Mirolah had escaped the jail, the jailors had been beaten unconscious by Stavark in a flash of silver light. The magistrate and his men were going to be more aggressive this time.

The door boomed as the men hammered on it. The kitchen went silent, and Tiffienne hurried through the doorway, followed by Casra. Her foster mother glanced worriedly at Mirolah. She could feel Tiffienne's protectiveness, a palpable presence.

"It's okay," Mirolah said. Medophae hadn't returned from his walk. That was one small relief, at least. She wondered how much patience he would have for these men who had beaten her foster father and imprisoned her. The last thing Rith needed was an enraged Wildmane.

"Casra, go get Lawdon," Tiffienne said. Casra nodded and leapt for the back door, but she pulled up short as Lawdon entered the kitchen.

The door thundered again. "Open immediately, in the name of the magistrate!" came a loud voice.

"Go, Mirolah. Out the back," Lawdon said, coming into the living room. "I will deal with these men."

"No," she said. "I'm okay."

The door thundered again, as though they were done knocking and were going to break it down.

"They'll not have you this time," Lawdon said, starting forward. He held that big metal tiling tool again.

Mirolah held up a hand to Lawdon, stopping him, then pulled a thread and opened the door.

The magistrate stood tall and still outside, just as Mirolah had expected. Four men formed a semi-circle behind him. The magistrate, not waiting to be invited, stooped slightly and entered, his triangular hat brushing the top of the doorway.

"So." He gave Lawdon a cursory glance before focusing on Mirolah. "It's true. I doubted her when Selene told me her wild story. She said the rotbringer had returned in the night." The magistrate shook his head. "You should not have come back. We thought you dead in the forest, eaten by animals. How did you survive?"

Mirolah just watched him, waiting.

"If you like, Deitran," Lawdon said. "We will come visit you tomorrow and tell you the entire story."

The magistrate shook his head, his lips pressed together so hard they were white. "I am wroth with you, Lawdon," he said, not looking at him. "You have always been a pillar of our community, but you are harboring a murderer. That is a crime."

"She's no murderer."

"She killed Fillen," the magistrate said. "A girl entrusted to your protection. How can stand in the way of justice? Does she have you under some spell?"

"There's no spell over me, Deitran. I know my daughters, every one. You know none of them. Did you give Mirolah a chance to explain? Did you listen to anything she told you about the monster? No, you blamed her and shoved her into a cell and then lied to everyone about what happened. You're a poor magistrate and a liar on top of it."

"You're being foolish. She summoned that monster. We all know about her brother!"

"And what did he do? From how Mirolah tells it, he made some lights float around. That's worth killing a child?"

"Listen to you! That makes him a rotbringer, and rotbringers are poison. It's worth killing every single one of them to keep us safe. They destroyed the world. I'm not going to stand by and let one destroy our city." He pointed at Mirolah. "Men, take her to the jail. Lawdon, I pray you'll stand aside, but if you choose to interfere again, we will deal with you as you choose."

The four men filed into the room, and Lawdon lifted the sharp tiling tool like a short sword. Mirolah let out a low breath and—

"What's going on here?" Medophae's powerful voice cut through the tension in the room. Everyone, including the magistrate, stopped what they were doing and turned. Medophae filled the doorway, looming like a nightmare behind the magistrate's thugs. She remembered him as he stood in front of the darklings in Denema's Valley. He had seemed to grow when he was angry, as though the presence of Oedandus turned him into a giant.

"Who are you?" Medophae demanded.

The magistrate winced under Medophae's gaze and almost answered. "I am—" But he caught himself and regained his composure. He drew himself up, pointed a finger at Medophae as though to emphasize his authority. "I caution you, stranger, go back about your own concerns. This is official city business. We are apprehending a murderer."

Lawdon stayed tense, steel raised in case the magistrate's men should suddenly attack. Tiffienne waited silently, clasping her wooden spoon. Casra had gone to the kitchen and returned with an iron skillet. The rest of her sisters appeared like mice, clinging to corners of the rooms.

"Ah, you must be the magistrate," Medophae said, relaxing a little. "I was warned you were mighty and fearsome. I see every bit of it is true." Mirolah could see a slight smile at the corner of his mouth, but she doubted the magistrate or his men noticed.

"That girl, there," the magistrate turned his finger on Mirolah, "killed her sister and escaped the justice due her."

"Ah, of course. Was it a knife?"

The magistrate looked confused. "What?"

"The murder weapon. Was it a knife?"

"No."

"An axe?"

"No."

"Are you going to keep me guessing? What was it? What weapon did she use? Surely not a sword. She doesn't look like a swordsman."

The magistrate sputtered. "There was no weapon—"

"No weapon? Did the girl *strangle* her sister?" He glanced at Mirolah dismissively and rolled his eyes.

Now Mirolah had to hide her smile. He was playing with the magistrate. She wanted to tell him that, once again, he wasn't being funny, but this time it was, seeing the magistrate as the butt of the joke.

"No," the magistrate stated clearly. "She summoned a monster that slew her sister."

Medophae paused. "Summoned..." he said. "Oh. I see. She's a threadweaver."

"Yes!"

"And you are a threadweaver as well."

The magistrate hissed. "Of course not! *She* is a threadweaver! A rotbringer!"

"You're not a threadweaver?'

"No."

"So you're a sensitive."

"A what?" the magistrate asked.

"A sensitive. Someone who is sensitive to the workings of the GodSpill. Someone who cannot wield GodSpill but who can see it happening."

"I—I'm not... You circle me with phrases I am unfamiliar with, stranger, but it does not change the fact that she is a murderer."

"So you're *not* a sensitive."

"No!"

Medophae looked skeptical, playing the role like he was a born actor. Mirolah stifled a giggle. "Let me make sure I understand," he said. "So you are telling me that you aren't a sensitive, and you're not a threadweaver. Which essentially means you know nothing about GodSpill—except, of course, that it is a method of summoning monsters. Tell me then how you saw her summon this creature that committed the murder?"

"I did not see her do it," the magistrate said.

Medophae paused, incredulous. After a long, silent moment, he said, "I'm sorry?"

"There were other witnesses. Eleven, to be precise."

"Ah," Medophae said, seeming relieved. "And *they* were threadweavers?"

The magistrate had begun to understand that Medophae was making fun of him, and his face darkened. "Enough of this farce. This is none of your business, stranger. I am the dispenser of justice in this town."

"A particularly blind style of justice, by your own account."

"Stand in our way at your peril! The girl goes to jail, and we will determine her sentence there. "

"If I may interrupt again—"

"You may not," The magistrate said. "Men, Take her."

The men closed about Mirolah, and Lawdon stepped forward. One of the men cocked back to hit him, but she pulled a thread. The man spun away and hit the wall, fell to the ground, and she bound him there, deftly tying his threads to the floorboards.

Another swung at Lawdon. Mirolah sent him spinning after the other man before he could land the blow. Without waiting for anyone else to attempt another attack, she lifted the remaining two men and threw them onto the heap, binding them all to the floor and each other.

The magistrate gaped.

"I did not hurt them," Mirolah said. "But I won't let them hurt Lawdon, either." She came forward and stopped, looking up at the tall magistrate. Everyone else had gone completely silent. Casra's iron skillet slowly descended until it slipped from her fingers and *thunked* on the floor. Medophae leaned against the doorjamb, smiling.

The magistrate held his chin high, like a man readying himself to be hit. A few of the men in the pile grunted as they struggled against the bonds she'd created.

"I *am* a threadweaver," Mirolah said to the rigid magistrate. "But that is not the evil you think it to be. If I was the murderer you claim, I'd kill you all right now. But I'm not. You were wrong about me, and if I'd had the power then that I have now, Fillen would still be alive." She drew a deep breath. "There are many things to fear in the lands now, magistrate. And yes, there are evil threadweavers, but I am not one of them. I am not the enemy you try so hard to see when you look at me. I would never hurt you or your men unless you forced me to do so." She paused and held the magistrate with her gaze. "I did not kill my sister. You have falsely accused me."

He swallowed. She felt the magistrate's fear in waves. He struggled to keep the stern expression on his face.

"But I forgive you," she said. "The real murderer is a threadweaver named Ethiel. She sent the darkling. I have since brought justice to her. Rith need not worry about her again."

She let the magistrate's men loose. They tumbled across one another trying to gain their feet, then slammed against the wall, terrified of her. Each one of them looked at her as though she was the darkling who'd claimed Fillen.

"I am a citizen of Rith," she said. "I live here, and I'm not about to let you kick me out of my home—"

A strange noise outside caught Mirolah's attention, distant, like rocks clacking together in the wind. She spun to look at Medophae.

"Did you hear it?" she said.

He spun, looking out the doorway.

The clacking wind sound broke the silence again, much closer now.

"How could it find us?" She leapt to stand beside him. "There's no trail to follow. We used a portal."

"It's what they do," Medophae said.

The rapacious sound came again, unmistakable. It was the spine horse. Shocked screams followed.

Medophae charged into the street.

10

MIROLAH

MIROLAH LEAPT through the doorway and skidded to a halt next to Medophae. The spine horse stood at the end of the street. Its legs were as long as she was tall, and its rocky head hung low. The spines along its back stuck high into the air, and lava dripped from its toothy jaws, sizzling as it hit the packed earth. One burning eye fixed on Medophae, the other a dark, crusty wound where Medophae's sword had stabbed it the last time they met.

Villagers ran, screaming and covering their heads as the heat washed over them. A little boy at the back of the pack tripped, tumbling to the ground before the monster.

The spine horse paused as it looked at Medophae. Its windy, clacking roar shook the buildings. The little boy curled into himself, screaming as his clothes caught fire.

"No!" Mirolah's breath caught in her throat. It was Fillen all over again. She had returned to Rith. A monstrosity had followed her.

Medophae sprinted toward the creature like a charging bull.

Mellic's cobbler shop burst into flame as the creature crouched, readying to attack.

Medophae reached the boy just as the horse opened its

mouth. With the speed of a striking snake, he shielded the boy with his own body, then flung him high into the air.

"Mirolah!" he shouted.

The boy sailed towards Lawdon's house. Mirolah pulled threads, caught him in midair and lowered him gently to her side. He was horribly burned, down to the bone in some places. "Oh, gods," she whispered. "Oh, please no."

The horse bit at Medophae, but its teeth chomped dirt. Medophae rolled away, came to his feet, and the godsword erupted in his hand, a shaft of raging fire. The horse's clacking howl shattered the windows of nearby shops. Medophae's clothes and hair caught fire.

Mirolah tore her gaze away from Medophae. *He'll survive. I can't help him, but I can help the boy.*

The little boy seized, his back arching.

No. No no no.

Movement overhead drew her attention, and she looked up, gasped.

Above her, devouring the sky, was a giant, swirling gray funnel. She'd had never seen anything like it before. A tendril of light blue smoke curled upward from the boy. The highest wisp of it twisted into that gray maelstrom, and she suddenly realized that was the boy's spirit. He was dying. She felt his emotion—fear and confusion—slither past her.

She suddenly realized what that swirling maw had to be. That was the Godgate, where the spirits of the dead went, returning to the original place where the gods created the world.

"No!" she shouted. She thickened the threads in the air between the boy's smoky soul and the churning gray storm. It stopped his departure like a net. But the swirling grew more distinct. It demanded the boy, and she could even feel it tug at her now.

She heard people talking near her, in the real world outside her threadweaver's sight. They were muffled, rising as if from a deep well, and they threatened to distract her. The magistrate argued vehemently with Lawdon. Casra screamed.

She shut them out, focusing on the bright bridge, the threads, and she sent herself into the boy's body. He was weak, so weak. She had watched Medophae during his sickness in Gnedrin's Post, when he was close to death. She had watched the colors of Medophae's threads dim over those grueling days, and that's what this boy's threads were doing, except they were winking out quickly. He was at death's door.

Mirolah could pull from GodSpill from the lands to move things, to assemble things, but that type of GodSpill couldn't heal human beings. It was wild, too strong. She'd tried with Medophae, and it nearly killed him before she realized the secret to healing. A human body needed GodSpill from another human body, the living spirit of another's life. The GodSpill inside a person was softer, more...compatible.

But taking from her body to give to the boy was dangerous. It could kill her. She'd also learned that with Medophae. What she gave from him took a ferocious toll on her as well.

She had to be careful.

She found a small part of the bottom of the boy's foot that was not burned. She split her attention into a thousand threads. She became that foot and analyzed his blood, skin, muscle, and bone. Her threadweaver eyes searched out all the charred body parts. Those threads had been altered to new forms that were not useful for life. So she changed them to match the unharmed flesh and infused them with GodSpill pulled from the threads of her own body.

Live, she thought to them. *Live!*

Her attention raced through his bloodstream, across his flesh, healing. She sewed him back together using threads pulled from her own body, methodically undoing herself to add to him. With each thread she felt weaker.

But the boy's blisters shrank. His melted skin reformed. The burned holes knit together.

She glanced up at the Godgate overhead. It was closer now, and it hungered for her, not the boy. A dozen invisible hooks pulled in her chest, her arms and legs. They suddenly yanked tight, and she gasped.

She looked back at the unmoving boy, and found that she was high above him. With a chill horror, she realized she was now a curl of rainbow-colored smoke, and she was floating upward! The smoky tendril of the boy's soul had descended to hover over the body, questing, uncertain, but it hadn't reentered yet.

Mirolah's threadweaver vision began to fade. The bright bridge vanished, and the threads that comprised everything flickered in her sight, becoming common buildings, regular air, moving people.

"Mirolah!" Lawdon yelled, grabbing her limp body below. Even though she hovered over herself, she felt his hands, like he was touching her arms through five layers of clothes.

I've killed myself, she thought in horror.

She'd used all of the GodSpill in her body to save the boy, like she had poured the water of herself from one bucket into another.

She had to replenish herself somehow. She had to pull the GodSpill back into herself! She reached out, trying to connect to the GodSpill in the threads, trying to open the bright bridge again. Her questing fingers reached into the threads of the air, the packed street, the trees of the forest—

And they caught her, like hands closing over her wrists. They tightened, pulling her away from the Godgate in a tug-of-war.

You belong with us. It was the same voice that had whispered to her when she stood on the rise overlooking Rith.

"Thank you!" she said to it.

We are one.

She suddenly realized she knew that voice. This was the same voice from the GodSpill in Daylan's Glass! It was the voice of the force that had taken her apart thread by thread, then reassembled her and put her back into her body so that she could free it.

The GodSpill, the mystic creative force that saturated the lands, that enabled threadweavers to create wonders, tugged her away from the Godgate. But it didn't put her back in her body like last time. Like it had in Daylan's Glass, it absorbed her. She became a tiny drop falling into its vast sea.

"No!" she cried out.

This GodSpill, once a raging storm within the prison of Daylan's Glass, was now free. It was a part of everything. There was no conquering it, no subjugating it. It wanted her, and she had nothing with which to tempt it this time.

I upheld my part of the bargain, she screamed at it. *I set you free. This is my life. I'm not you, I'm Mirolah!*

The GodSpill pulled her away from her body like the tide pulls a bit of sea foam. She soaked into the wall, the packed earth, the air, the fields and forest. The GodSpill flowed throughout the lands of Amarion, rejoicing in its freedom like a little child, and it took her along with it. She was no longer the small, mortal human she had been; she was a living map of the human lands. She was the water of the Inland Ocean, the stone towers of Buravar, the moss-covered streets of Denema's Valley. She flowed through the bodies of a dozen new threadweavers that had newly discovered their power. To her, they looked like sparks on the huge tapestry of Amarion.

She breathed in, expanded to contain everything, forever inhaling without the need to exhale. She was everything, and everything lived within her.

"Mirolah!" A man's voice called to her, an annoyance, though that name seemed familiar to her. It was important somehow. Where was that voice coming from?

She turned her attention from the vastness of the lands to

pinpoint the single mortal voice. It came from a tiny village called Rith along the southern peninsula.

That, there, said a different voice, not the mortal man's voice, but a voice within her vast self. *Go back there.*

She focused her attention on that town, that street, that man who spoke to a dying female woman as he held her in his thin, ropey arms.

Heal her, the voice said, so she filled the threads of the woman's body with vibrant colors, bringing the vigor back to her dying flesh.

Yes... the voice within her said. *Thank you...*

ᛟ

MIROLAH SAT UPRIGHT, sucking in a huge breath that, thankfully, did have an end. Vigor poured back into her limbs. She breathed out, and looked all around her. She was in Rith. The wooden houses and shops. The dirt street. The blue sky overhead. She wasn't a map of the great tapestry. She wasn't a vast everything. She was Mirolah, warm and alive and human. She put her hands to her breast, to her stomach, to her head.

"I'm back in my own body," she gasped, and she ached with the joy of it.

"Mirolah," Lawdon said. "By the gods, I thought you were dead!"

She looked upward. The Godgate was still there, but it was distant, faded. Its gray swirl continued, superimposed over the sky, as though waiting for her. She could feel the hooks, pulling gently.

Legends told that only the dead could see the Godgate.

"No!" she whispered harshly. *I am Mirolah, threadweaver. Lawdon's foster daughter. Medophae's lover. I am not the GodSpill itself.*

Lawdon hugged her. "It's okay. You're okay," he said.

She was so scared, so confused, that for a moment she didn't know what had just happened, how she had ended up tumbled into the GodSpill's vastness. She couldn't remember anything before that terrifying fall into that flowing ocean of power.

Her gaze fell on the still boy next to her, and it all came back.

"No..." she said.

His little body was burnt beyond recognition. He was dead.

"No! I healed him!" she said, picking him up in her arms.

"You did what you could," Lawdon said. "You tried. It just...it wasn't enough."

Her heart thundered. His flesh had mended. She'd invigorated him with her own threads, but...

I took it back. I panicked, and I took it back to keep myself alive.

"Oh, gods..." she said.

She searched frantically for his little light blue wisp of a spirit. She could do it again. She could bring him back. She had to. Please...

But his spirit was gone, sucked into the Godgate.

"No!" she wailed, curling over his body.

"What did you do?" the magistrate yelled, towering her, his tall form casting a shadow. "What new monster have you brought down upon us?"

She tried to get her bearings, squinting up at the angry magistrate, blurry through her tears.

"Medophae," she said. "Where's Medophae?" She craned her neck to look back up the street.

Medophae rose from the burning corpse of the spine horse. One of its legs lay a few yards from the rest of its body. Yellow blood like molten gold splattered the road. The beast's head had fallen where the godsword had severed it.

The intense heat was dying down with its owner, and Medophae staggered away, his arm twisted and broken where the spine horse's teeth had chomped it. He was blind, bald, and burned down to the muscle. Blood flowed freely down his savaged arm, covering his hand and dotting the dirt.

Golden fire crackled fiercely around him, and the charred skin receded under the onslaught of new, bronze skin. His eyes healed, and he blinked. His arm twisted about, righting itself. Bones popped into place and mended. Hair sprouted from his head and flowed down to his shoulders.

"You are every bit the horror we thought you to be," the magistrate shouted.

"Shut up, Deitran!" Lawdon shoved him back. "She tried to save the boy!"

"And yet he is dead!" the magistrate roared. "Look!"

"She—"

The magistrate struck Lawdon across the cheek. He fell to the street, and the magistrate lunged at Mirolah. She didn't even see the dagger until he stabbed her. His snarling face came close to hers. "Die, rotbringer," he said. "Die! A curse upon you!"

The man suddenly flew backward, yanking the dagger from Mirolah's belly. Medophae, wreathed in golden flame, held the magistrate up in the air by the neck. His lips pulled back in a snarl.

"Don't!" Mirolah said, pushing her palm against the searing pain in her side. "Please. Don't hurt him. I..."

Medophae looked at her wound, and a low growl came from him. Golden fire spat and fell to the ground in flecks, and his biceps trembled. The magistrate dropped the dagger to grapple with Medophae's steel-like arm, unable to breath.

"Please!" she shouted.

He threw the magistrate to the ground.

Medophae turned, cowing the villagers who had gathered close. "She came here peacefully," he said. "She tried to heal this boy, and your magistrate stabbed her. If anyone else comes close, I'll kill you. I swear it."

"Medophae—"

He picked her up and walked through the crowd.

11

MIROLAH

THE MOON WAS large when they rode out, and Mirolah was heart-sick. She should be dead. That boy should be alive.

Medophae had stopped long enough to get their horses. He hadn't bothered with saddles or supplies; he didn't even pause to replace the clothes the spine horse had burned off his body. He just pushed the bits into the horses' mouths and fastened the bridles, helped her mount, then got on the horse stark naked. They rode out straight away, Mirolah holding her side. The wound was jagged, and pain lanced through her with every move-ment, but she didn't heal it. The pain reminded her of her failure. She wanted to feel it.

Medophae led them until they were miles away from Rith. He kept looking back at her, then finally pulled to the side of the road.

She leaned over her horse's neck. Blood leaked onto her thigh, onto her horse's flanks. The horse snorted, its ears twitching as it smelled the blood.

"What are you doing?" Medophae said, dismounting.

He helped her down, and she slumped against him.

"I've seen you heal worse than this. Fix it."

"I killed him," she whispered. "I killed that boy."

"The boy was dead before you could stop it."

"No. I healed him and then I...I took it back."

"What?"

"I was dying. I saved myself instead of him."

He knelt to the ground, his arms around her, and she went with him. He just held her.

"You can't blame yourself for that," he finally said. "I told you healing is dangerous. What you tried has killed other thread-weavers."

"He could be alive instead of me. We brought that thing to Rith. It chased us down."

He bowed his head.

"We should never have come," she whispered.

"Maybe."

"We should have faced that spine horse where no one could get hurt."

"You didn't know the spine horse was going to be there, Mirolah."

"You think we aren't at fault?"

"We didn't choose to bring that monster to Rith. We didn't ensorcel it in the first place to chase us. When it came, we dealt with it."

She curled forward and hugged her knees. The tear in her side lanced through her, and she clenched her teeth.

"Heal yourself," he said. "You're going to bleed out."

So she did. She reached inside and mended the wound, pulling on her own life, changing the shape and color of the threads. But she left a scar on her belly, long and ragged. She wanted to remember this feeling. Medophae was right about everything he had said. They didn't intentionally do harm, but it didn't change the fact that the spine horse came, that it killed that little boy. She and Medophae were different. Their mere presence could be a deadly threat to normal people. She couldn't ever forget that. She kept seeing the face of the little boy.

"This has happened to you before," she said. "Where someone died that you tried to save."

He stood up, let out a long breath. "We are to blame. You're right. We always are. Dying is a lesser evil than living when others die because of you. It's the curse of having power. It's the curse for...being what we are."

"How do you live with it?"

"You try to save the next person," he said without hesitating. "It's the only way. There will always be monsters in the dark, and they'll always be ravenous. When we can, we stop them. That's enough."

She looked up at him, but he stared at the horizon, solemn. "Is it?" she asked in a small voice?

"It has to be," he said softly.

"Why?"

"Because otherwise there's nothing. And we're evil just for existing. I can't believe that."

"Maybe I could have given him most of my life," she whispered. "Maybe I could have saved just enough, but I got scared." She didn't tell him why. She didn't tell him the GodSpill was alive, and that it wanted her to become one with it.

"Maybe. Remember this. You can't change it. Do it better next time."

"It's cold comfort."

"Yes."

She let out a long breath, shook away the thoughts. He was right. The best way to serve that poor dead boy was to make sure the next person who needed healing stayed alive.

"Come on." He extended his hand. She took it, and he lifted her to her feet. She looked him up and down.

"You know, you're naked," she said.

"Yeah. I thought it was more important to get away from

there than get clothes. I have experience with mobs, and that one was close to making a stupid decision." He shrugged. "I've ridden naked before."

"Have you?"

"Crossed the entire Red Desert."

"Without clothes?"

"It's a story."

"I'll bet." She unlaced her short skirt, worn over her tight riding breeches, and handed it to him. "Here," she said.

He wrapped it around his waist. "Thank you."

They rode west to Pindish in silence, where they got clothes for him, supplies for the road, and saddles for the horses, then started south on the Old Sea Road towards the Bracer.

They made camp that night in the forest, far enough from the road that no one could hear or see them. They slept close, but not together. Mirolah didn't want to be touched, and he seemed to understand.

When he fell asleep, she stared at the stars overhead. Despite the day, she was wide-awake. After another hour of simply lying there, she rose and walked into the woods. The whispers of the trees, the grass, and the ground were a constant babble in the back of her mind, though the voice from Daylan's Fountain hadn't spoken again.

I failed. I could have saved the boy, but I didn't. I won't make that mistake twice. I won't save myself at the expense of another.

She knelt on the ground and put her fists against the soft, wet leaves.

Take me to Orem and Stavark, she thought, speaking to the voice from Daylan's Fountain. *Whoever you are, heed me. I don't know how to find them, but you could. You're everywhere. Show me where they are.*

Whenever she had manipulated the threads before, she saw what she wanted in her mind's eye, and she crafted it step by step. She looked deeply, analyzed exactly, and twisted or colored specific threads to a specific effect. But this time, she didn't know what to do. How could she bring something to her that she couldn't see? How could she grab hold of something that wasn't there? She didn't know how to start looking for Stavark and Orem except by going back to the last place she'd seen them—Denema's Valley. She didn't even know if they were dead or alive. So she sent her demand into the GodSpill as a plea. The GodSpill was everywhere. If she could send her message into it, perhaps it could find what she was looking for.

Show me! She pushed her will into the threads like she had when fighting Ethiel, when she'd infected the Red Weaver with her own colors.

A ripple radiated outward on the threads like she was a stone thrown into a pool. The air shimmered, then the shimmer was gone.

Perhaps a lighted pathway would lead to Orem like the bright bridge opened her threadweaver's sight. Perhaps a ghostly string, invisible to all but her, would wind through the trees or even across the Inland Ocean, eventually linking to one or both of her companions at the far side. Perhaps it would just be a compulsion, a driving need to walk in one direction over another.

Nothing happened.

Please, she sent again. *Tell me what I need to know. Help me find them!*

The voice didn't answer her, and this time there wasn't even a ripple in the threads.

She fell to her knees, pushed her face into her hands, and cried. She cried for the little boy in Rith, burned to death. She cried for her mentor, Orem, who was almost certainly a corpse lying face down on the streets of Denema's Valley. She cried for Stavark. She cried for those she couldn't help, and because, even with her newfound power, there would be others in the future she would fail. She felt that horror and wept.

When she had spent her tears, she went back to their little camp. Medophae slept peacefully, curled into his blanket. She lay down and stared up at the starry sky. It was a long time before she closed her eyes.

𝒢𝒮

SHE AWOKE WITH A START. Clarity brightened her mind, like she'd never been asleep, like her brain had been working while she was unconscious. The last time she'd snapped out of a sleep like this, it was because Ethiel had mind-warped her and bid her to sleepwalk into a pack of darklings.

A tentative touch brushed across the threads of her mind, bidding them to change color, just a subtle shift. Panic blossomed inside her. The touch hadn't tried to dominate her, not yet. It was almost ephemeral.

The threadweaver probed her long enough that followed it back to the source. The being was close, hidden in the nearby trees.

Not this time.

She took hold of those seeking feelers and saturated them with her own colors.

Her domination was quick and complete. The threadweaver's defenses were glass and she was a hammer. A yelp came from the nearby trees. This threadweaver was nowhere near as powerful as Ethiel. The fight was over in an instant, and she had control of the creature.

She pushed her blanket away and stood up. "Come out," she said.

The creature slinked out of the dark. It was no threadweaver at all, but a giant, impossibly skinny yellow dog. He did not wish to come into the clearing, but she made him.

He was perhaps five feet tall at the shoulder and as hairless as a human. His ribs stood out starkly along his side. His sallow skin was so thin as to be transparent. She could see blue veins beneath and every strand of muscle strapped from hip to knee,

knee to ankle, neck to shoulder, and along its bony spine. The dog's shoulders rippled as it moved closer. He had thin eyes and an incredibly long muzzle. While his ribcage was large and round, his waist was barely the width of a pole. He looked starved almost to death, and yet the way he moved was lithe, graceful.

"What are you doing here?" she demanded.

He opened his long jaws, lined with crooked, pointy teeth, and he whined. Miraculously, there were words in that sound.

"This one felt you near," the dog said. "This one looked for you."

"You tried to bend me to your will," she said. "I felt you invade my threads."

The dog cringed, trying to withdraw, but she commanded its body to halt. The wretched thing's bony tail curled between its legs.

"No," it whined. "This one did not."

At the second whine, Medophae woke and rolled to his feet. Golden fire crackled lightly about his sword arm. The skinny dog whined louder, straining against Mirolah's control, trying to get back to the safety of the forest.

"What's going on?" Medophae asked.

"We have a visitor," she said. "I have it in hand."

Medophae crossed his arms over his chest.

"You tried to take control of me as I have now taken control of you," she said to the dog. "I want to know why. Were you looking for a meal?"

"No!" The words mixed with the whine. "This one was sniffing you, only. The land points to you. The land breathes of you. This one came to see the truth. Was only sniffing. Only sniffing." The dog had buried itself in the long grass, it was so low to the ground.

"You sniff with GodSpill?" Mirolah asked.

The whine was just a whine this time. There were no words. Mirolah cocked her head and listened closer. "What?" she asked.

"Don't you? Don't you sniff the GodSpill?" The dog whined more clearly.

"You're saying you followed me here because I'm a threadweaver?"

"Yes." The word was a bark.

"Okay. I'm going to release you. If you run, I'll have to stop you again."

"Yes." Another bark.

She released him. He shook, then shoved the side of his muzzle against the grass and pushed himself along, as though he were trying to rub a bad smell from his nose. Standing up, he shook again, then repeated the same with the other side of its muzzle. Finally, he stood before her, his bony tail up and wagging.

"The land whispers of you," the dog said with a yip.

"What does it whisper?" she asked.

"That you are the Thread. The Threadwoman."

"What does that mean?"

"This one came looking for the Threadwoman," the dog barked again.

"I don't know what that means," she pressed.

"The Threadwoman," he yipped quietly.

"That doesn't tell me anything," she said, annoyed.

The dog's happy posture contracted. His tail stopped wagging and dipped between his legs. He crouched low, as though she was raising a club over his head. "The Threadwoman... The Thread..." he whined. He eyed the forest, prepared for flight.

"It's all right," she waved a hand. "I'm not angry. I just...don't understand."

"Do you know what that is?" Medophae asked her, watching their exchange.

"A big skinny dog?" she said.

"It's a vyrkiz," he said. "That's the quicksilver word, anyway. They're also called skin dogs. Don't be deceived by its emaciated look. That thing is strong enough to bring down a bear, or a trained war horse. They're vicious hunters. In the Age of Ascendance, they were trained for war by those who could manage it. Only certain handlers could get them to submit. They're highly intelligent."

The skin dog did not protest its innocence. It looked at Medophae as though it could not understand what he was saying.

"Like darklings?" she asked.

"No. Skin dogs are not children of Dervon, though they were...made. Much like the quicksilvers or the spine horses or the darklings. They were often used to sniff out traps in the GodSpill Wars."

"But you think he's dangerous?"

"Oh, I know he's dangerous. But not duplicitous. They're very much like actual dogs in most respects. You've cowed him. From what I remember, that's not easy to do. But once they submit, they're loyal. They're pack animals, and they'll follow their pack leader, even if it's a human."

"Must go," the skin dog barked. "This one is hungry," he yipped, turning a brief glance to the nervous horses. "Must hunt."

"No. Those horses are under my protection," she said sternly.

He whined again and lowered himself to the ground as though she was about to strike him. "No. No. They are yours. They are pack. Cannot hunt pack."

"Okay, then."

The skin dog rose, his tail wagging. He gave one last glance to Medophae, then to her, then sprang into the forest, clearing ten feet with one leap and vanishing into the dark.

Medophae stared where the skin dog had gone, then looked over at her. "You just keep the surprises coming," he said.

"How so?"

"You were talking to it."

"Yes."

"Well, when did you learn skin dog speak?"

A chill scampered across her arms. "You didn't hear? He was talking out loud."

"No, he was whining and barking out loud."

Her heart thundered. "He spoke in words," she murmured. "To me." She sat down on her rumpled blanket. "I thought he just... I thought he could speak."

"Are you okay?" he asked.

No, I'm not okay.

She remembered feeling like she was dying in Daylan's Glass, tossed about, then unraveled by the tempest of GodSpill. But she'd convinced it to let her live. It had reconstructed her and put her back in her body. She thought that meant she would be normal again, but more unusual things happened to her with every day that passed.

Animals talked to her. The GodSpill hungered for her, as though it owned her.

What would it be tomorrow? And at the end, would there be anything left of the girl named Mirolah?

12

MEDOPHAE

MEDOPHAE COULDN'T STOP THINKING about the dream.

Going with Mirolah to Denema's Valley was the right thing to do. He knew that. He couldn't just forget about Orem and Stavark. He couldn't just pick up where he had left off a hundred years ago, searching the countryside for clues to rescue his beloved, but ever since Avakketh had so casually given him the answer to the riddle, ever since Medophae had realized what a perfect torture device Ethiel had crafted if love really was the answer, he couldn't stop thinking about Bands.

He tried to believe she was dead. He tried to make himself believe that was the end of it.

But if she was out there... Somewhere...

He thought about the magistrate in Rith, about how close Medophae had been to killing the man. Oedandus had raged through him, had wanted violence against an unjust ruler.

Bands had always tempered that rage in him. It was she who reminded Medophae to stay human, even as he slowly grew beyond humanity. It was always Bands's voice in his head when he tamed the raging god.

During his days in that cave near Belshra, Medophae had

lost himself in memories of his times with Bands. It had been the only salve to his raw soul, and he'd lived in the past in his mind.

He hadn't done that intentionally since Orem pulled him back into the world of humans, but he had to feel her again.

So, as Mirolah slept peacefully, Medophae closed his eyes and took himself back. He indulged in a reminiscence, just one. Only one...

$\mathcal{GS}$

MEDOPHAE SHAVED *another hank of hair from his scalp and nicked himself again, this time badly. A trickle of blood ran down his ear. Oedandus awoke, sending a rush of prickles to the site. The wound vanished.*

"By Thalius, it's like you've been in a battle," Bands said, holding out a white cloth for him to wipe the blood. "Let me do it."

"I never get to shave," he said. The last time he'd needed to shave was the morning Oedandus found him. From that moment forward, Medophae's physical form hadn't changed; Oedandus kept reconstructing him exactly as he had been.

"She's dead," Bands said softly, serious this time. If someone had been standing in the little room with them, they might have assumed Bands was reminding him why they were here in Korvander, but she wasn't. She was reminding Medophae to keep his temper.

"They killed her," he said.

King Horonid of Korvander and his advisors had created an elaborate list of laws in the last year, from the lowest type of law—such as meting out consequences for spitting on the street near the palace—to the increasingly popular champion challenges, where one could prove one's innocence —even of a serious crime—through trial by combat. Those accused by the crown could utilize a champion to prove their innocence and, if their champion won, they would be absolved of the accusation.

In fact, any of the king's subjects could accuse another of breaking the law. If you had a sword and a grievance, you could gain "justice" in the king's dueling arena.

King Horonid's champion was said to be unbeatable, and the king was using that power to bludgeon his subjects. The duels were becoming more frequent, sometimes as many as six in a day. They had transformed into a grisly kind of entertainment for the noble classes.

Oedandus bubbled up, heightening Medophae's anger. He wanted to run straight to the palace and tear Horonid apart.

He nicked himself again on the other side of his head.

Bands's hand closed over his. "Give me that. You're missing spots all over the place, and we're running out of cloths to mop up your blood. They're going to think you killed a cat in here." She took the straight razor. Smoothly and methodically, she finished the job without a single nick.

"He killed her because she was a quicksilver," Medophae said. "No other reason."

"It is against the law for a Korvandish noble to consort with someone so far below his caste."

"Caste is crap," Medophae said.

She didn't say anything. She never talked when he let his anger speak for him.

"If he loves her," he said. "That's all that matters."

"It would still be against the law."

"I want to kill him."

She smoothed her hands across his shoulders. "You could be a tyrant so easily, Medophae," she said. "So much power. Such passion when you believe you are right. Mix them together, and who could stop you?"

"You could," he said.

"Not if you saw me as an enemy. You would walk right through me."

Whenever they came to a kingdom to try to see justice done, Bands advocated for the other side. It was a frustrating dance they did. She'd come with him because she thought he was right. She helped him because she thought he was right. But she always did this.

He sighed. "Stop it."

"What are you here to do?" she asked.

"End this king."

"And this will prove your point."

"He won't kill any more innocent..." He sighed. *"They just wanted to love each other."*

He ran a hand over his smooth scalp and raised the mirror. His telltale golden mane was gone, and his head looked tiny with no hair.

He had wanted to charge into Korvander and remove King Horonid by force, but Bands had prevailed upon him to legally remove the king using his own laws—such that they were—with everyone else looking on.

"I'm in disguise," he said, smirking at the mirror, trying to lighten the mood.

She raised a dubious eyebrow.

"You don't like it? I'm thinking this may be my new haircut," he said.

"I'd love you even if you looked like a scaly-headed dragon," she said.

Her analogy struck him, reminded him that she was on his side. She was a dragon. He was a human.

He turned and stood, looking down into her emerald eyes. *"I keep seeing that quicksilver woman.... I keep seeing her with your face."*

"I know. And if it had been me—"

"I'd punish every single one of them. I'd kill them all. The king and anyone who stood by and let it happen."

"Medophae—"

He kissed her, and she wrapped her arms around his neck. She smelled like rose petals. Her dove-blond hair was like running his fingers through silken strands.

"It's time to go," she said.

They left the inn and started up the sparkling clean street. One of the temporary benefits of having such strict laws was an orderly, clean city. There were no crooked signs or grimy windows in Korvander. Every shop was tidy, with perfectly arranged wares set out to purchase.

They strode up the street until they reached the palace. The guards nodded at them, and let them in.

Korvander's throne room was an open-air arcade, with two galleries on either side filled with nobles. Tall columns supported the square gallery roofs, and at the end of the long aisle was a circular dais, four steps high. In the center of the dais, underneath a huge stone awning that looked like a clamshell, was a large throne, upon which was King Horonid. He sat ramrod straight, eyes cold as he surveyed the assemblage. His royal thread-weaver sat to his left, and two advisors sat to his right. At the base of the steps was Horonid's champion of justice. He was big in every way. He was probably the same height as Medophae, but his arms were tree trunks and his legs even larger. He was encased in plate armor, head to toe, and stared forward.

"So that's him, huh?" Medophae said.

"Wyrn Korvander," Bands said. "The champion of justice."

"He named himself after the kingdom?"

"Maybe he couldn't think of anything else."

"He looks twice my weight."

"Scared?"

He let out a breath. "How can this king believe that who a person chooses to love makes them lower somehow? What has to twist in your mind to think that a human loving a quicksilver is wrong?"

"You see it," she said. "And you shine brightly enough to show it to everyone else."

"All I want to do is kill him."

"I know."

He looked at the Den of the Accused, a ten-foot-square spot underneath the edge of the left-hand gallery, closest to the royal dais. There were no bars for the accused, but four executioners surrounded the man who had been caught in bed with a quicksilver woman, spears pointed at him. He sat forlornly on the cobblestone floor, his left leg bent at the knee, his right leg twisted and broken. He looked like he was clenching his teeth to keep from crying out, and his cheeks were stained with tears.

Medophae felt his anger rising, and Oedandus rose with it. He pushed it down.

"Gorvun Dandere," he said.

"Grovun Deneer," Bands corrected him. "Like Meetris Deneer, with the floating sword from the legends."

"*Grovun Deneer,*" Medophae repeated. "*Look what they've done to him.*"

"*He was caught by the king's justicers. His lover, Estakketh, used her flashpowers to attack them. They stabbed her to death and broke Grovun's knee.*"

Medophae started toward him, but Bands put a cool hand on his arm.

"*Why are you here?*" *she reminded him.*

"*Justice.*"

"*They'll make a call for final words to the accused,*" *she said.* "*Wait for it.*"

As though the king had heard Bands, he stood up.

"*Loyal subjects of Korvander,*" *he said, his voice booming down the wide aisle.* "*This man, Grovun Deneer, is accused of filth and consorting with a female below his caste. He has been sentenced to death. Before the sentence is passed, are there any who wish to speak their last words to the accused?*"

"*I will have words with the accused,*" *Medophae replied. A rush of quiet discussion rippled through the assemblage as Medophae made his way to the Den of the Accused. The two front executioners stepped aside, stone-faced, and Medophae knelt next to Grovun.*

The pain in the man's eyes drove a dagger into Medophae's heart. Both of Grovun's hands held his leg above the knee.

"*I'm so sorry,*" *Medophae said.*

"*Who are you?*" *Grovun asked through clenched teeth.*

"*Your champion, if you'll have me.*"

"*What?*"

"*I'm going to fight for you.*"

Grovun looked at Wyrn Korvander in his shining steel plate, then back at Medophae. "*Why?*"

"*Because it's what I do. Because I can.*"

"*I don't understand.*"

"*Will you take me as your champion?*"

"*That man will kill you.*"

"No. I don't think so." Medophae smiled grimly. "Say you'll accept me as your champion, and I will make things right here."

"How can you?" the man asked, his face twisted up. "They killed Estey." He began to cry, big, quiet sobs that wracked his bent back. "She's gone."

"Then I will make sure it doesn't happen to anyone else," he said. "Help me."

"How?"

"When they ask you, just say I'm your champion."

The man held his hands up helplessly. "Okay."

Medophae stood up.

"Is there anyone else who wishes to speak with the accused?" King Horonid demanded. None other came forward. "Very well," he said. "Grovun Deneer, you may choose a champion now to face Korvandish justice. Should your champion prevail, it will show Thalius's favor and prove your innocence. Do you have a champion?"

Grovun looked at Medophae, still confused, still in excruciating pain, then back at the king. "I...I do. He is my champion." He pointed at Medophae.

Gasps went up from the assemblage. King Horonid's eyes widened. Even the stoic form of Wyrn Korvander shifted, his armor creaking.

King Horonid looked Medophae up and down. "Do you accept this burden, stranger?"

"I do," Medophae said.

"And do you realize that this is a fight to the death?"

"I do."

King Horonid spoke quietly with his two advisors. The closest replied, still in a voice too low to hear, and she made small gestures with her hands. The king looked back at Medophae.

"As you wish, stranger." King Horonid nodded to Wyrn Korvander. The king's champion drew his sword and started toward Medophae. No preamble. No further ceremony.

Good. Medophae drew his own sword and moved forward, stopping just out of range of Wyrn's enormous blade.

"How many people have you killed for that man?" Medophae asked Wyrn.

"One more than before, in a moment," Wyrn replied in a low, gravelly voice.

"Did you give a thought to it? To all this killing? To those you slay? Do you have remorse for any of them?" Medophae asked.

"No," Wyrn said. "They were destined to die. As are you." He charged, sweeping his sword so fast it was a blur. He was a smart fighter. His lunge was so quick he crossed the distance in a blink, and his blade was too long for a normal man to leap back out of range. It was a lateral swing, placed just high enough it could not be jumped—even if an opponent were fast enough to try—and too low for an opponent to crouch beneath.

The godsword erupted, sheathing Medophae's blade in fire. With Oedandus's strength, he met the blinding charge, slamming the godsword against Wyrn's sword, shearing through it. Still, the broken blade sliced into Medophae's belly. Oedandus's golden fire went to work on the ghastly wound even as Medophae sidestepped and thrust the godsword through the side of Wyrn's chest.

Wyrn clattered to the ground, steel ringing as he tried to suck a breath through two punctured lungs. Medophae wrenched him onto his back and yanked the helm off the man's head. His eyes were wide, and he gaped like a fish on land.

"Good," Medophae said. "Then I will have no remorse for you, either."

King Horonid's champion of justice died, his last breath leaking out through his teeth. His eyes went glassy.

Medophae yanked his sword out, turned, and walked toward the dais, blade dripping blood.

"King Horonid," he said in a loud voice. "I accuse you of murdering an innocent woman." He pointed at Grovun. "By the laws of Korvander, Thalius has decreed that Grovun Deneer is innocent through trial by combat. As this is true, then you killed the quicksilver woman Estakketh outside the law. That makes you a murderer. Do you deny it?"

King Horonid spluttered, still staring wide-eyed at his dead champion.

Medophae leapt to the top of the dais before any of the king's guard could react. "Stop!" Horonid shrieked.

Medophae grabbed Horonid by the neck and lifted him into the air. His advisors shouted and fell over each other trying to get away from the flaming madman. The threadweaver on Horonid's other side closed his eyes, hands weaving in front of him as he tried to attack Medophae with GodSpill. He opened his eyes a moment later in shock as he realized it wasn't working.

Medophae pulled the horrified Horonid close to his face. "By Thalius's own decree, your champion has fallen, condemning you to death."

"No!" Horonid shrieked. "This is not the law! I make the law—"

"I am Wildmane!" Medophae shouted over the blubbering king, his voice thundering across the assemblage. "And anywhere I see injustice like I have seen here today, I will come. Anywhere the lives of some are crushed by the whims of others, I will come. And I will leave the guilty as corpses in my wake." He stared down at the guards; he stared down at the nobles. "So think well, any of you who would step up to take Horonid's place. You may put yourself above the law, but you will never be above my vengeance."

Medophae walked down the dais, the king in hand. Two dozen royal guards surrounded him, but none attacked.

Bands walked out of the Den of the Accused with Grovun, who was staring down at his leg, which she had just healed. Medophae threw the king into the spot that Grovun had recently occupied. The four executioners with their spears stared, open-mouthed.

"Loyal subjects of Korvander," Medophae repeated what King Horonid had said before. "This man, King Vinteer Horonid, is accused of murder beneath the eyes of Thalius. He has been sentenced to death. Before the sentence is passed, are there any who wish to speak their last words to the accused?"

Whispers ran through the assemblage, but none stepped forward.

"This is a farce!" King Horonid shrieked.

"Very well," Medophae spoke over him. "King Horonid, you may choose a champion now to face Korvandish justice. Should your champion *prevail, it will show Thalius's favor and prove your innocence. Do you have a champion?"*

The rattled king looked up at his threadweaver, standing on the dais. "Threadweaver Bemestis! You are my champion!" The threadweaver looked at Medophae, eyes wide, and shook his head.

The king whirled, looking at the tallest of the spear-bearing executioners. "You will be—"

"By the law," Medophae said, "an executioner cannot be a champion." He turned to the group of royal guards, fixing them with his stare. "Are there any who would champion the accused?"

"Captain Felks!" King Horonid shouted, and spittle flecked his lips. "You will be my champion. I order you to be my champion!"

Captain Felks looked at King Horonid, then at Medophae. He, too, shook his head.

"This is an outrage!" the king shouted.

"If there are no others," Medophae boomed, "the judgment has been rendered." He turned his gaze back to the executioners. "Do your duty."

"I'll have you all killed for this!" Horonid said. "I'll have you all—"

The spear took him in the throat. King Horonid toppled backward. The other three executioners stepped forward, each with a fierce stab to the king's chest.

Medophae turned away and walked to where Bands stood. Next to her, Grovun kept feeling his knee, looking back and forth between it and Bands.

"Nice speech," she said. "They will remember you. They'll remember what you said."

"If they don't, we'll come back," he said.

"And you didn't kill the king." She smiled. "Nicely done. How do you feel?"

"Cheated."

She touched his arm, and he felt better. "Let's go."

Together, they walked past the stunned assemblage.

"Do it," he said. "Come on."

She sighed.

"Impressions make a difference," he said. "One act can be buried and forgotten. A legend lives forever. Do it."

"You're incorrigible."

"But I promise to love your scaly dragon head," he said.

As they walked, she transformed into her natural state, growing long, scaly arms. Her tail sprouted and slithered out behind her, and her sinuous neck rose into the air. She beat her wings, sending hurricane gusts at the people of Korvander. They screamed in fear and shielded their heads.

He leapt onto her back, and she leapt into the sky.

13

ZILOK MORTH

"How do you kill a god?" Zilok asked Orem, looking out over the Inland Ocean as Orem, his anchor to this mortal life, stood politely at a distance.

"I do not know, my master."

It was a question Zilok had pondered more than any other human in history, he was sure, and he had never come up with the solution. He had trapped and tortured Medophae. He had held Medophae's friends hostage. He had even stripped away the power of Oedandus and given it to another, but through all that, the answer to that question had remained the same. You couldn't kill a god. Not if you were a mortal. Not even if you were an immortal spirit.

"To kill a god, you must *be* a god," Zilok said.

"Yes, my master."

No human could hope to overwhelm a god. Humans were spawned from Natra's tapestry. The gods lived outside the tapestry. They were forces beyond nature, and one had to be beyond nature to undo them.

It had only happened twice in history. Vaisha the Changer, daughter of Saraphazia and Tarithalius, had died giving birth to

White Tuana, who sucked the life from her. Dervon the Diseased had been killed by Medophae, Zilok, Bands, and Tarithalius combined. Thalius jauntily called him "Dervon the Dead" afterward, and the moniker stuck.

Zilok moved to the very edge of the open archway, seeing the play of the threads on the breeze, feeling the threads of the stone beneath him, above him, to the left and right, feeling the reassuring threads that connected him to Orem, that allowed him to dominate Orem's mind and secure his connection to the mortal plane. As always, far above, the Godgate swirled in different shades of gray, waiting for him, hungering for him.

Zilok had been there at the beginning of Medophae's journey, or near enough to know every detail. He had met Medophae shortly after his arrival in Amarion. Zilok had heard the story straight from Medophae's own lips, how Oedandus had been attacked by no less than three gods—Dervon the Diseased, Zetu the Ancient, and White Tuana—all three of whom still could not overwhelm him enough to destroy him. Aside from the absent Natra, the goddess who had created the world, Oedandus was the most powerful of them all. The best Dervon, Zetu, and Tuana could manage was to stretch Oedandus's life force over the continent of Amarion and reduce him to a barely sentient being. They had done little to reduce his potency, only his focus.

Even now, in the formational stages of his latest plan, Zilok knew it was all for naught if he could not succeed where those three gods had failed. Zilok had to best Oedandus. Medophae, in desperation or rage, would inevitably turn Oedandus loose, and Zilok would be overwhelmed. He had to face the god's full power and defeat it, something no human could possibly do, something Zilok had never done in fourteen centuries.

The new plan was to remove Medophae from Amarion, out of Oedandus's reach, far across the True Ocean to Dandere. Once Medophae stood helplessly on those shores, a true mortal once more, Zilok could dispose of him, and Oedandus would have no champion. Of course, Oedandus would never willingly let that undeserving, preening eagle loose. It was why he healed Medophae, why he kept the man immortal. Oedandus didn't want to return to what he had been after Dervon, Zetu, and White Tuana had finished with him: a vague, meandering force, lacking focus or even the comprehension of his plight.

But before that plan could come to fruition, Zilok had to surmount the walls in his way.

First, he needed strength enough to transport a mortal of Medophae's size through the threads, over the True Ocean to Dandere. Even an accomplished threadweaver like Zilok didn't have the ability to make a transport gate outside of Amarion. The threads of Amarion itself were soaked with GodSpill, especially during the Age of Ascendance, but the saturation of GodSpill over the True Ocean was low, and on the faraway isle of Dandere even less. Zilok could not construct such a portal.

Second, he needed to turn aside the power of a god. Zilok could not use ordinary threadweaving on Medophae. Oedandus would simply bat it aside. In fact, even if Zilok managed to steal the power of, say, Avakketh, he might not be able to blunt Oedandus's power. Three gods working in concert hadn't been able to do it. Who was to say that Avakketh was more powerful than Oedandus?

"Only Oedandus's own power is sure to be strong enough to best Oedandus himself, Orem," Zilok said.

"Yes, my master."

The idea came to Zilok swiftly, sending twin jolts of exhilaration and fear through him.

The solution to the first problem was the solution of the second. Zilok needed to turn the power of a god back upon itself. He needed the Natra's Crown.

Once upon a time, Natra was the most powerful of the world's deities, the goddess who created the great tapestry. The rest of the gods circled her like sycophants, either serving her or birthed by her. Zetu was her father and Avakketh her brother. Dervon, Saraphazia, and Tarithalius were her children. Oedandus had been her consort.

Most humans didn't know the history of the gods, but Zilok did. Natra left long ago. None knew where. None knew why. And almost no one knew she had left behind a secret place called the Coreworld, where she kept a map of the destinies of all living things...as well as the tools of her creation. One of those tools was Natra's Crown.

And this was the key to Zilok's plan.

Through torture of one in possession of many secrets, Zilok had discovered the crown was what had enabled Natra to keep peace among the gods. She mediated them with it. She ruled them with it, and none dared strike back against her because...

The crown had the power to turn any god's power back upon them.

The spell simmered in Zilok's mind. He would tempt Medophae to rage, a brilliantly easy task. It was Medophae's fall-back emotion. Whenever the going got tough, Medophae relied on the trick Zilok had taught him, back when they had been allies and fought to destroy Dervon together. Let Oedandus loose, and he'll make sure you win the day.

And then, when Oedandus burst forth in Medophae's time of need, Zilok would turn that power back on him like a mirror turned back sunlight, using Natra's Crown. He would push Oedandus out of Medophae, and, during that instant, he would use Oedandus's own power to shove Medophae through the threads, all the way across the True Ocean, all the way to Dandere.

"Natra's Crown, Orem," Zilok said.

"Yes, my master."

"That is how you kill a god."

"Yes, my master."

14

MIROLAH

MEDOPHAE STEPPED OVER THE CRACKED, flat stone. It was late afternoon. The sun was low in the sky, and long grasses rippled over the ruins of the city of Keleera like a green sea. It reminded Mirolah of Denema's Valley, except not a single building had been left standing. The shells of stone structures jutted from the ground like cracked teeth. Denema's Valley had teemed with life, as if it had a secret poised on its lips. This place had been forgotten by humans and nature alike.

But this was the place Medophae said they could find another portal. They had destroyed the portal from Calsinac to Denema's Valley, and the one they'd taken to Buravar only went between Buravar and Calsinac. But Medophae thought there had once been a portal in Keleera that connected to Denema's Valley. If they found it working, it would shorten their journey by days.

Medophae wended his way through the stones with Mirolah behind, and she looked over her shoulder, seeing a flash of the skin dog behind a broken wall. Ever since that night outside of Pindish, he had followed them. She sensed no malice from him, but his persistence worried her. Yesterday, they'd passed through the gates of the Bracer, an immense wall manned by soldiers from kingdoms and cities of the southern peninsula, and she had no idea how the skin dog had managed to get around it. The Bracer's formidability was what had kept the Sunriders from invading the southern peninsula during this last decade.

No one entered or left the southern peninsula by land without getting past the Bracer. She guessed the skin dog must have swum in the Inland Ocean to circumvent it. That took phenomenal persistence and stamina. The waves that crashed against the Bracer along that rocky shoal were one of the natural barriers that kept invaders out.

As though reading her thoughts, the skin dog climbed up onto a pile of jumbled stones and sniffed the air. His tongue lolled out happily, and he looked at her. He barked and, spinning about, launched himself into the tall grass.

"You made a friend," Medophae said, giving a glance to the retreating skin dog before bending over a fallen wall.

"I'm not sure he's a friend," she returned.

Medophae walked to the edge of the fallen wall and squatted at what must once have been the top. "I think this is it." Before Mirolah could say anything, he wedged his fingers under the wall. Golden fire crackled about him, and his muscles corded tight. The wall began to rise, but when Medophae had it halfway up, it cracked in half.

Stone blocks tumbled down and dust billowed into the air. Mirolah danced backward, avoiding the crash. He emerged from the cloud, coughing.

"Are you all right?" he asked, clearing his throat.

She waved a hand in front of her face. "Did you find it?"

"I thought the wall would hold." He was covered from head to foot in rock dust. "We'll have to look when the dust settles."

She wiped a spot from his cheek across his lips, then kissed him. He was hesitant, stiff at first, then finally kissed her.

That was odd.

He moved back over to the dusty wreckage and tossed square stones away one by one until he reached the floor level of a once-standing structure. He swiped at the flat floor stones, prying them up until he reached the packed earth underneath.

"You all right?" she asked, wondering about the strange kiss.

He looked back at her and smiled. "I just thought it would be there." He pursed his lips and looked around. For the first time since Medophae had regained the power of Oedandus, she wished she could read his emotions. He'd been an open book since he had cast Bands's gem into the Sara Sea, and it suddenly felt like that book had shut again. "I've only been to this portal once." He eyed another mostly standing building and started toward it. "It belonged to the threadweaver Hephylyzt. He was awed by the portals Bands built, studied them. He finally made one of his own. He had a vision of making Keleera a hub of threadweaver travel, much like Calsinac was—"

He was interrupted by a bark.

Both he and Mirolah turned to see the skin dog standing on a small hillock at the edge of the city.

"Sniffing?" the skin dog barked again. "You are sniffing?" He stood with his thin head low. His shoulder muscles twitched.

She realized that, to a dog, "sniffing" was exactly what they were doing.

"Yes." She wended her way through the debris. "We're sniffing." The skin dog was enormous. His shoulders were the same height as hers, his eyes at a level with hers. She remembered Medophae saying that skin dogs could be vicious. As she neared, he hunched down, elbows on the ground, his exaggerated chest touching while his thin middle was still a foot off the ground. His face was like a skull with a thin layer of sallow skin stretched over it, with spikes jutting up from the thin jaw. His lips pulled back, baring those crooked teeth even more, each as long as her pinky finger. A beast like this could move fast enough to chomp the head from her body before she could even shriek. She would have been terrified if it didn't seem so eager to please her.

She kept the bright bridge glowing and her threadweaving ready to use.

But the dog did not leap from the mound to attack her. "Sniffing GodSpill?" he asked again. His lips twitched nervously.

"We're looking for a portal, something built by a threadweaver long ago."

"GodSpill?" he barked. Every time he did that, it looked like he was going to take a bite out of her.

"Yes."

"Here," he yipped. He lunged at her, and his great front paws tore at the ground. She jumped back, reaching into the dog's threads, ready to—

He fell as though she'd gutted him. Whining, he rolled onto his back, showing his belly.

"No!" he whined. "No danger. Just helping. Helping sniff." He scratched tentatively at the air. It looked ridiculous, this enormous creature flailing his skinny legs in the air.

She calmed her beating heart and gathered her wits. "You found something?"

"Yes!" The dog flipped to his feet startlingly fast. His short, bony tail wagged.

She looked over her shoulder. Medophae stood at a respectful distance. "The skin dog says there's something underneath this mound," she said.

"That's probably it." He came forward. "If anything in this city has lasted for centuries, it would be the portal."

"Dig?" the dog barked, scratching hesitantly at the dirt, his slitted eyes looking at her warily. He bared his teeth again. The dog was so fearsome-looking that everything he did looked threatening, and she hadn't spent much time around dogs. She'd seen Giller Black's hunting hounds in Rith, but only from a distance. Still, she was beginning to suspect that bared teeth didn't always mean a dog was going to bite. She held her hand toward him. His lips twitched, still pulled back, but he moved under her hand and pushed his flat head into her palm. His tail wagged.

"No," Mirolah said. "Medophae and I will dig."

The dog cocked his head. "Medophae?" he said, not recognizing the word.

She pointed. "The big man."

"Medophae. Big man. Much GodSpill."

"Come down," she said, leaving the mound. The skin dog followed obediently and stood by her side, alternately looked up at her and back at the mound.

She raised her arms, closed her eyes, and sent her attention into the threads. She touched all of the many colors of the grass, the dirt, the jumbled pile of stones beneath, then lower and lower until she found open air, a corridor.

There you are....

There was no connection between the surface and the underground corridor, so she would have to make one. She closed her eyes and opened the bright bridge of her threadweaver sight. Pulling and changing the colors of thousands of threads of dirt, stone, and air, she created a pathway.

She opened her eyes to the transformed hillock. It now conformed to the vision she'd had in her mind. Two thick walls of solid stone flanked a ten-foot-square opening into the ground. Atop each wall were three wide pots filled with dirt and the flowing brown grasses. Tall stone steps descended sharply into the darkness between the walls.

She double-checked everything that she had bent to her will. The grasses grew happily in their pots. The stone felt strong and immovable in its new form.

"Wow," Medophae murmured, coming up alongside her. "Did you uncover that stairway or make it?"

"Made it."

He gave her an appreciative glance.

The skin dog approached, watching Medophae with what seemed like a hostile stare, but Mirolah wasn't sure. The dog had done nothing hostile yet; he just looked hostile. Still, there wasn't any subservience to the skin dog as he approached Medophae, not like there had been with Mirolah. He stood tall, body stiff, and he was nearly eye-level with Medophae. Medophae glanced at him, then ignored him, looking down the wide stairway.

"Big man," The dog said to Mirolah. "Medophae."

"He's a friend," Mirolah stressed.

"Pack?"

"Yes, he's part of our pack."

Slowly, the skin dog lowered his butt until he was sitting, and he seemed to relax. After a moment, his tail thumped on the ground.

"I'll bring the horses closer. There are torches in the saddlebags."

When Medophae returned with a torch, Mirolah turned to the dog. "If I leave you here to guard the horses, will you?" she asked.

The skin dog turned those narrow black eyes to look at the horses. "Protect?" he said.

"Yes."

"Protect," he said, then laid down, his tiny waist creating an arch over the ground between his powerful haunches and his deep chest. He put his head between his paws, eyes on the horses.

"Nicely done," Medophae said.

"He seems eager to please me."

Medophae smirked and shook his head, but he didn't say anything.

They lit the torch and descended into the darkness. The

corridor was constructed of polished granite, each block covered in designs inlaid with gold. Mirolah didn't recognize any of the symbols. Every now and then, the smaller stones would give way to one that was ten feet wide and as large as the corridor was tall. Great scenes were painted upon these larger stones. Perhaps the entire thing was a story?

Mirolah stopped at one, brushing away some of the ancient dust. The colors were still vivid. It portrayed a long-bearded man before a crowd of robed figures. The long-bearded man appeared to be explaining something. His hands curved around one another as though holding a sphere or some circular object. A table stood between him and the spectators, and upon it sat an open tome. She wiped away more dust. Crimson-smeared clouds heralded the sunset behind the speaking man.

Medophae didn't notice she'd stopped, and the torchlight bobbed away down the corridor, throwing long shadows. Making a note to return to this place and explore it further once they had found Orem and Stavark, she left the picture and followed him.

The corridor soon became a labyrinth of tunnels. At first, Medophae seemed not to know where he was going. They went down one passage only to double back and take another. At one point, he stopped and looked at one of the large picture stones. Tossing the torch from one hand to the other, he reached out and cleared off the dust. With an optimistic grunt, he turned and continued ahead more quickly.

After two more turns, they came to a locked iron door.

Holding the torch high, he looked back at her. "This is it."

With her threadweaver's senses, Mirolah reached through the door and felt on the other side. Yes, there was something there. The threads were lively and brightly colored.

Medophae put his shoulder against the steel door. "Well, stand back and I'll—"

She touched his arm. "Let me. I promise less dust."

He bowed and stepped away from the door. "As you wish."

She reached into the threads of the iron latch and changed their color. Their cohesion loosened, and they became the iron ore they had once been. All the mechanisms of the lock sifted out of the keyhole like sand. She pushed at it. It didn't move. She pushed harder. It screeched loudly, moving only an inch before stopping.

"Rusty hinges," Medophae said, stepping up. "My turn?"

He shoved the door open, and the screech reverberated off the walls. They went inside.

The portal arched to a point on the left-hand wall. It looked similar, but not identical, to the portals in Calsinac. The arch was made of simple stones with the same symbols. The center of the portal shimmered like moonlit lake water. The room was empty except for the portal and some centuries-old torches on the walls. Medophae lit them one by one.

"It's working. Let's get our gear and come back," he said.

They wended their way through the maze and retrieved the horses. True to his word, the skin dog had not hurt them. He remained exactly where he had laid down before they entered the corridor.

"Found GodSpill?" he barked.

"Yes," she said. "Thank you for your help."

"This one is glad," the dog barked, watching them as they led the horses down the steps.

In a few minutes, she and Medophae again stood before the portal. He tapped the sequence on the stones that would take them to Denema's Valley.

"Ready?" He looked at her.

"Let's go get them back."

"Orem may not be there," he warned. "Or Stavark. They may not even be alive. We have to be prepared for that."

"But they might."

He nodded and led his horse through the portal. It swallowed them, and they vanished. She followed, calming her mount with sweet words and a pat on the neck. But just as she crossed the threshold, the horse whinnied in fear, tossing her head. Mirolah pulled on the reins, trying to control the horse, but it yanked her through the portal—

—just as the enormous skin dog slipped through next to them.

15

MERSHAYN

MERSHAYN STOOD at attention beside Collus's throne. Collus drummed his fingers quietly on the stone arm inlaid with gold. The last of the common folk, obviously dissatisfied—and possibly confused—took one hesitant look over his shoulder at Collus, then left the audience chamber. Two of the royal guard closed the tall doors behind him.

The audience chamber was beautiful. Tall, square columns of the dark gray Teni'sian stone held up the vaulted ceiling. A royal purple carpet led from the throne down the middle of the room to the great double doors. The chamber was circular, and twelve long, thin windows let light in from all angles. Brightly colored banners hung from poles between each window, showing the coat of arms for each of the twelve noble houses from each of the twelve parts of the kingdom. The banner of sovereignty draped down from the center of the vaulted ceiling, as though binding the twelve other banners together. It created a colorful, powerful atmosphere. The colors would have been festive if they were not in such an imposing chamber.

Twenty-four seats flanked the king, twelve on each side of the purple carpet. Each seat provided a space for the noble lords and their ladies. After that came the minor nobles, other powerful men and women within the major nobles' service, the military men, and lastly the courtiers. Today was a busy day. They had all been busy since Collus had first arrived. All of the primary seats were filled save five. Lord Kari'dar of Seacrest had no wife or consort, so the seat next to him was empty. Kari'dar had brought his son for a time, to familiarize him with the proceedings of the court, but he left three days ago. Lord Baerst was also absent. It was whispered that his stomach flu had worsened. His wife, the Lady Ti'shiria, sat in his place. She was a shrewd woman and always had something useful to say when she spoke, which was rarely. She spoke even less since her husband had fallen ill. Her face was drawn, and she looked tired.

The seats for Lord Grimbresht and Lady Mae'lith were also empty, of course, since the accident. Lady Mae'lith was still in mourning for her husband who drowned last week on the Inland Ocean.

The doublets of the lords and the dresses of the ladies were worth seeing. More colorful than the banners of their homelands, the nobles were arrayed in the finest cloth that gold could buy. It was as much a fashion parade as a room of politics.

Mershayn might have enjoyed the parade of pretties once upon a time. He remembered the stories he'd heard as a child in his father's house. The Teni'sian court was where the lords and ladies of the realm met to discuss the future of the kingdom. It was a place of power, intrigue, and romance where the noble of heart rose to defend the downtrodden.

All lies, of course, but he hadn't known that at age seven.

Mershayn wished he could go back to those childhood days. He wished he could believe that again, but the noble of heart rarely wore titles. Lords and ladies were ambitious people who, rather than taking care of those who relied on them, only exploited them for their own enrichment and comfort.

He unconsciously flicked a glance at Grendis Sym, who wasn't in his seat as he should have been, but stood on Collus's other side, like Mershayn. It indicated his status as a valuable advisor. Mershayn could be described as the king's right hand, but if that were true, then Sym was the king's left.

He should never have been allowed so close. And that's my fault.

If he had involved himself in these distasteful meetings earlier, and actually paid attention, perhaps he could have stopped the slippery viper from gaining Collus's trust.

"Then that is that," Grendis Sym said as the doors closed behind last petitioner, a farmer from the north, who had come to hear the king's wisdom about his sister, who had been imprisoned because she had made a bucket of water float through the air.

Entertaining the requests of the common folk was a custom that Queen Tyndiria had begun. It was something that had made her beloved to the common folk, but under Collus's rule, it had become an opportunity for most of the nobles to disparage the very people who came seeking their help. Each day sparked new conversations about how the lower classes simply didn't understand what was best for them, and couldn't understand the many challenges that the nobles faced. Mershayn had a hard time believing that these audiences had ended in such a fashion when Tyndiria ruled.

Unfortunately, Collus let these remarks pass unchallenged. He believed he had bigger problems to handle, but Mershayn felt the sour attitude of the nobles was more important than it seemed. Anyone who would make fun of disparage common folk once they left the room would certainly show the same lack of respect to the king when he wasn't around. Mershayn thought he might be imagining it, but the most vocal grumblers seemed to traffic a great deal with Grendis Sym.

"Perhaps we could move along to matters of import now." Sym smiled at the various chuckles from the assemblage. "I believe it is almost time for the midday meal."

More laughter.

"Our people who are exhibiting these strange new powers is of vital import, I think," Mershayn said, berating himself for having forgotten the farmer's name already. *I am a poor opponent for Sym here. I'm a swordsman, not a statesman. I am not trained in these weapons of the court.*

But he had to say something. The smug look on Sym's face was insufferable. What if it were Sym's sister who had been quarantined for exhibiting strange powers? He might sing a different tune then. But then, Sym had no sisters, nor any brothers. He'd probably eaten them as they'd come out of his mother's womb.

Sym turned a tolerant glance upon Mershayn, like he would to a slow-witted little brother. "I'm not certain what you mean, Royal Arms Inspector. Do you think we should impose even more guards upon those we have quarantined for study?"

As always, Mershayn felt uncomfortable as every eye turned to watch him. Sym had a way of responding that made him seem like an idiot.

"No, I didn't mean that," Mershayn said. "What I meant was that it..." He paused, his tongue tumbling over his thoughts. "Perhaps we were wrong in quarantining them in the first place. The...the, uh, farmer's sister has been detained for some weeks now. She and many others. Are we any closer to finding out what we must do to assure their safety and the safety of those they come in contact with?"

"We cannot simply let them loose!" Lord Framden boomed in his heavy voice. He shot Mershayn a contemptuous look. "It would be better to put them to the sword than to let them loose."

Mershayn wanted to put Lord Framden to the sword. His fear-mongering had already made half the kingdom paranoid about people who had been changed by The Wave.

"We are working as fast as we might to determine the nature of their freakish abilities," Lord Balis said in his soft voice. "We care for them well. They are fed and housed. They have all they need."

"They're not animals," Mershayn said. That gained him a sour expression from Lord Balis. Mershayn tried not to be daunted. He certainly was making enemies fast. "You say they have everything they need. They need freedom. They need their families, and their families wonder what the crown will do with them. It's creating fear where fear isn't necessary. Could we not simply check up on them from time to time? Let them go back to their homes?"

"Did you know that the sister you speak of started a fire merely by touching a thatch of dry straw?" Lord Framden growled.

Mershayn had not heard that. He'd heard she'd lofted a bucket. It was possible he got the story mixed up, but he couldn't help wondering if the fire was a fiction made up by Lord Framden.

"If we let her loose, half the city could be in ashes by tomorrow night," Lord Framden finished.

"Mershayn," Collus turned to his half-brother. "This is something that—"

"Allow me, your majesty," Sym interrupted Collus smoothly, then faced Mershayn. "This is something we all debated at length a long time ago, Royal Arms Inspector. I think you may have been absent that day."

Mershayn seethed at the condescending tone. Of course Mershayn had been absent. Sym *knew* Mershayn had been absent. He'd only begun attending these meetings recently.

"The king decided it would be best to quarantine these aberrations until we could determine how dangerous they are to the rest of the populace," Sym continued. "And now we have moved on to other issues. We cannot dwell so long upon one small problem. There are many challenges we face in Teni'sia. Sometimes we do not even have enough time to attend properly to the greater issues." Sym turned from Mershayn as though the conversation was over. "Your Majesty," he said. "You must be famished. Let us break for our midday meal, shall we?"

Collus seemed about to say something. He looked at Mershayn, but then nodded. "Of course," he said in a strong voice. "Let us eat."

Mershayn stood rigidly as Collus rose to leave. Every moment in this chamber made him feel like he'd eaten rotten meat. Watching Collus fumble and flounder made him feel ashamed for his brother, but watching him dismiss Mershayn's counsel in favor of Lord Sym's pushed a cold dread into his stomach. Mershayn couldn't stay away. Collus was failing, revealing his weakness more with each passing day, and the wolves were gathered to devour him. Mershayn longed to forego these meetings and go back to his swordplay, drinking, and wenching...

His gaze fell upon Lady Ari'cyiane, who watched him. Her curly, strawberry-blond hair fancifully framed her oval face. Her blue eyes glittered, and she gave him a dimpled smile. Her husband, Lord Vullieth, was oblivious to the flirtatious glance. He rose from his seat, his black cape swirling about him, and she stood with him. They were a mismatched pair—Vullieth tall and slender, Ari'cyiane barely as tall as his shoulder, rounded with delicious curves Mershayn longed to touch again.

With an effort, he put his libido back in its drawer and focused on the politics of the situation. Vullieth had not said a word during the entire audience. Mershayn had only heard him speak once, during one of the first meetings Mershayn had attended, back when he hadn't been paying attention at all. He remembered thinking Vullieth was pompous and needed to pull the stick out of his posterior. The more Collus fumbled, the less Vullieth spoke, as though he were as ashamed for the king as Mershayn was. Mershayn wondered if Vullieth would have been an ally for the king, a lord who could have offered real counsel, if he could just get through the ring of wolves surrounding the king. Ironically, Lord Vullieth seemed like a man Mershayn could have respected, if he had paid more attention. In fact, the few lords and ladies who seemed the most thoughtful spoke less and less at court.

That was a horrible sign.

Vullieth and Ari'cyiane walked down the aisle toward the door with the rest of the nobles, and Ari'cyiane turned her gaze casually away from Mershayn.

Mershayn watched the pair for a second and then turned away...

...to find Sym staring at him from just beyond the throne. He glanced purposefully at Ari'cyiane's retreating backside as though appraising it, then purposefully looked at Mershayn. He nodded in approval as though congratulating Mershayn.

Then he smiled the thin smile of a lizard.

16

MERSHAYN

MERSHAYN KEPT his features stoic and left the throne room. He hurried to catch up with his brother and drew alongside him as they passed an antechamber. Two royal guards followed them and posted themselves at either side of the door as Mershayn closed it.

Collus set the crown down upon the table and sighed.

"Don't say it, Mershayn," he said, leaning heavily on the thick oak table and rubbing his closed eyes with two fingers.

"If I do not, then who will?" he said.

"Sym is right. That issue was dealt with weeks ago." Collus turned, and his eyes flashed. "You remember? Weeks ago? When I was struggling to find my place here and you didn't want to come to those meetings because they were 'tragically boring.'"

"Well, they're tragically *something*," Mershayn countered, trying to keep his voice even.

"Meaning what?"

"Meaning that I am your brother, Collus. You allowed Sym to dismiss what I said in there. You let him get away with that. Whose side do you think I am on? I'm trying to help you here, and you let him cut me off at the knees!"

"You make too much of it, Mershayn. Sym was right. Everyone knew it. And time is so precious. It seems to become ever more precious with every day that passes. We cannot go over the same problem again and again. Sym knows that."

"He is *not* right." Mershayn growled. "But he wants to make you *believe* he is right, and he is succeeding! I told you to be careful of him. And yet you bend to his whim like a reed bends in the wind."

"You go too far, Mershayn—"

"No, you do not go far enough. Did you hear what you just said as we began speaking? That you are 'struggling to find your place' here?" Mershayn threw his hands into the air. "You are king! If you do not know your place, then no one else does. If you say that the quarantined peasants are to be released, then they shall be released. Sym does not dictate this to you. You dictate to him. If you tell Sym to shut up, he will shut up."

"His counsel is invaluable. You do not understand—"

"I cannot believe my ears. Has he ensorcelled you? We grew up together, you and I. And I'm telling you this greasy noble is a rat. I tell you again and again, and it is as though you cannot hear me."

"He knows more about Teni'sia than you do," Collus said.

"You are locking up your own people—good people—who have only the misfortune to have been altered by The Wave. You should be courting these people as allies. They can help us understand this new world. Instead, you're making them enemies. We have enough guards. Post them and watch these people. Interview them. Help them understand what has happened to them, and they will help you. Do you think it is right that they be separated from their families though they have done nothing wrong?"

"It is more complicated than that. Sym says that—"

"Damn Sym! I want to know what *you* say. Is it right to keep these people against their will?"

"Of course not, Mershayn, but there are more variables than that. Lord Framden is correct. They could be dangerous."

"Traveling to Buravar is dangerous. Sailing the Inland Ocean is dangerous. There are dangers everywhere we look. But we don't stand by injustice because we're afraid. That's exactly what a king should *not* do. You have to stand for something, Collus. What do you stand for?"

Collus slammed his fist on the table. "I stand for keeping this kingdom together!"

"Well, you are failing," Mershayn blurted. "Do you watch the faces of your nobles? They do not trust you. They do not believe in you—"

"And how would you know?" Collus growled.

"Because I watch them."

"Lord Framden and Lord Balis support me. Ry'lyrio and Mekenest. And see how you treat them? You angered both of them with no more than three sentences today. You work against what I have been working for. As you say, the power in the realm begins with the nobles. I have been striving to make inroads with these people."

Mershayn shook his head. "These men... These ones you pick as your supporters... Don't you see that they belong to Sym? By Thalius, I have only been watching them for a matter of days, and it is obvious to me."

"You say that as though there is a plot against me. These are men who want to see the kingdom mended as much as I do."

"So you say. Will you do me a favor?"

Collus threw his hands up and marched to the other side of the room. "Oh, certainly. Whatever you wish. I'm chock-full of favors, you know. I'm king, after all."

"Remove Sym from the court."

Collus threw him a withering glance and opened his mouth to speak.

Mershayn held his hands up beseechingly. "Just as a fantasy. Imagine in your mind that Sym was not at court."

"Mershayn—"

"And imagine all those who agree wholeheartedly with his ideas and take them away as well. Take Balis and Framden, Ry'lyrio and Mekenest, Cayriol and Kuh'ter. Remove them in your mind."

"Wonderful. You have just hacked off half the court."

"Yes. Who is left?"

"Is this a test, Mershayn? I know who the major nobles are, for Thalius's sake."

"Who is left?" Mershayn pressed.

"Lord Vullieth, Lord Kari'Dar, Lord Baerst, Lord Giri'Mar, and Lady Mae'lith."

"These are the nobles you should befriend," Mershayn said quietly. "These and any of the minor nobles who do not sleep in Sym's pocket."

Collus squinted at Mershayn. "Where does this venom for Sym come from?" he asked incredulously. "Is it because he made some quip about you being the court fool when you first arrived? It was a joke."

"It's because he undermines your power."

"He aids me with volumes of information about the kingdom, information I have no other means to acquire."

"No doubt he tells you this."

"Stop it!" Collus boomed.

"It didn't bother you that he cut you off today, when you were about to address me? Did you even notice?"

"He was only trying to help you understand why the Wave-altered must be kept quarantined."

"As if I could not understand if you explained it? Nobody should interrupt the king, yet he does it to you regularly, in the guise of 'assisting' you. Don't you see how that makes you appear?

You seem as though you cannot answer the simplest questions by yourself."

"Sym is a loyal servant to the crown."

Mershayn closed his eyes and let out a long breath. How could Collus be so blind?

"I am not the only one who dislikes Sym," he said.

"Oh?" Collus said.

"Lord Grimbresht despised him. And Lord Baerst, jolly as he seemed, never agreed with Sym."

"I don't like where this is going," Collus warned him.

"Well you don't get to look only at what you like. You're the king. You have to face all challenges head-on."

"Are you saying that Grimbresht's death was murder? That Baerst's illness is premeditated? You're concocting conspiracies to suit your ire. It's madness! Grimbresht's vessel was overturned by a freak storm. Baerst is notorious for slumming in the seedy areas of the city and eating whatever pleases him. Sym says it's not the first time he's been poisoned by bad meat."

"Sym says. Sym says..." Mershayn clenched his teeth. "They were Sym's greatest opponents. And now they have been removed from court."

"My brother, the great and brave swordsman, jumping at shadows." Collus gave a bark of ugly laughter. "It is a good thing I am king and not you. You'd have half our nobles hanging from the gibbet by now, and the kingdom in open war."

Mershayn clenched his fists and concentrated on breathing evenly.

Collus picked up his crown and set it upon his head once more. "I am going to the dining hall. I am famished, and I would like to eat before I fall over."

Mershayn hesitated, then dutifully bowed. "Of course, Your Majesty."

"Oh stop it," Collus said. "By the gods, I thought I was the worrier of the two of us. Shouldn't you be tempting me to debauchery, not finding more worries to pile on my head?" Collus moved past him. "Things are not so bad as you say." He left the room with his guards in tow.

You're right. They're worse.

17

MERSHAYN

MERSHAYN SNAPPED the twig in two and tossed one piece into the lightly cascading fountain. A sculpture of a young woman stood in the pool of the main tier, balancing the second tier on one hand while holding some kind of sea flower in the other. She looked determined, strong. Ari'cyiane explained to him that the woman's name was Teni'sia, who supposedly walked out of the Inland Ocean one day and founded the kingdom. The craftsmanship was as fine as any Mershayn had seen, but he didn't like it much at the moment, because it reminded him of one of his three problems.

He snapped the remaining bit of twig in two again, tossed half of it into the fountain. A bird sitting on the rim chirped and hopped skittishly to the far side, cocking its head and eyeing Mershayn warily.

Nothing was simple anymore. At Bendeller Keep, it had all been simple. Until his father passed away recently, Mershayn had lived happily there, adventuring with his half-brother, and staying away from any official functions. When Collus became lord four months ago, he had settled into the slightly new role of trying to tempt Collus away from any and all official duties. Mershayn sharpened his swordsmanship on the Bendeller soldiers, his wit on any visiting nobles—in his brother's name, of course—and visited the nearby villages for drink and companionship. Once in a while, he would sneak into the lands of Lord Framden, visit his villages, sometimes even his keep, to sample different pleasures. Simple. He never left the practice ring without paying for his excellence in sweat and pain. And he never left the ladies without a smile.

But the rules had changed. Everything in Teni'sia was complicated. He didn't know the rules, and suddenly he was at odds with his brother. Before, he was easily a match for each of his pursuits; now he found himself pitifully inadequate. These nobles at court did not consider him an ineffectual bystander, as they had at Bendeller Keep. He was dangerous, an enemy with the ear of the king. He could not disarm them with a charming smile. They assumed he was after something, because that's the way they were. That was the way they lived at court.

He snapped the twig again and tossed half of it directly at the woman on the fountain. It thwacked against her head and fell into the water. She didn't notice, and continued looking toward the horizon with determination, holding her seaweed.

"Mershayn?" came the light whisper through the hedge behind him.

He pressed his lips together in resignation. "Yes, my lady," he said.

"Are we alone?" she whispered.

"Yes, my lady."

He heard a slight rustling of satin. Her footsteps were soft, and he tracked her movement around the hedge wall. She rounded the corner, and her smile filled him with a flush of excitement. Tall and slender, she stood with her long gown flowing down her curves. Her cloak brushed the smooth white pebbles of the path as she glided toward him. Her lustrous black hair tumbled out of the edges of her hood. He wondered if she wore the hood for the fetching effect, or if she actually believed she was hiding her identity. The ensemble was alluring, and his heart pounded faster.

He rose and bowed low with a flourish of his hand. It was a custom in Bendeller Keep, and a novelty in Teni'sia. She loved it, probably saw it as part of his provincial charm. When he brought his eyes up, her hand was there. He took it and led her to the bench he'd been sitting on.

"You wished to speak with me?" she said, and then her voice dropped conspiratorially. "Or was there some other, more dangerous purpose for summoning me?" She leaned close and nipped his ear gently with her teeth. "I could not stop thinking about you today," she whispered. "After watching you wrangle with that wretch, Grendis Sym. He is vile."

"We're agreed on that," he said, drinking in the sight of her. It suddenly seemed so unlikely, that a woman like this would agree to take a man like him to her bed.

What a stunning mess I have made.

She leaned her head against his, and spoke in a breathy tone. "I know of a place here, in the garden, that we could go. The risk is high, but I would take it." She looked up at him through long lashes, half-lidded eyes.

He swallowed. This would be so easy. Why should he worry about politics? This was what he really wanted. This was what set his imagination aflame. This was what he was good at. Why shouldn't he do what he always had? She was highborn and charming, smart and adventurous, and she wanted him. What could be wrong with stealing another moment right now, right here in the garden?

He shivered at the thought of it. She knew of a place to go, she said, some place secluded. But her gaze dared him to do more. She *wanted* him to do more. He could hike that gown right here by the fountain. She would only gasp in surprise, but she wouldn't stop him. She wanted him to do it.

His hand moved the cloak aside, and he touched the small of her back, moved up between her shoulder blades. His fingers deftly slipped into the tightly tied lace, found the bow. He pulled one long, silken strand. She drew a quick breath.

Unbidden, his mind flew back to just a few hours ago when Grendis Sym smiled at him in the throne room. He remembered the man's smug satisfaction.

He leaned back from Ari'cyiane so that he might look into her dark eyes, glazed with desire. Her lips parted as he started to speak, stalling him. Dark pink lips, so kissable.

He shook his head and looked at her hands instead. He took one in his own. "Ari'cyiane—" he began.

She closed her eyes. Her fingers caressed his. "Say my name again."

He sighed. "Ari'cyiane, I—"

"Yes..." she cooed. "It gives me shivers. Again."

"We must talk," he said. "About our...association."

"Such a cold word for two people who have been so...warm together."

All at once, Mershayn had the wild idea that Ari'cyiane had been sent by Grendis Sym to entrap him in a scandal. Why would such a highborn lady be so interested in him? Why pursue him so single-mindedly?

But that was simply the poison of court living. The intrigue drove a person to paranoia until you didn't know whom to trust. The court made upright men jumpy, constantly turning their head to look for attack. Ari'cyiane was no spy.

"We have to end this," he said, reluctantly dragging the words out.

Her hand, which had made its way to his thigh, froze. She looked around the garden. "Someone has discovered us?" she asked.

"I think so. I think...Grendis Sym."

The desire fled from her eyes, and she looked stricken. "How do you know?"

"I don't. Not for certain, but I have a feeling. Sym has never liked me, yet today in court he was practically beaming as I left. I can think of only one reason for that. I think...he saw the way I looked at you. And...the way you looked at me."

"My husband cannot know," she whispered. "Not ever."

"No." They were agreed on that, at least.

If Sym knew about Ari'cyiane, he could—and would—make Mershayn pay for it. Or worse, he would make Collus pay for it. He'd make sure Vullieth knew. Mershayn could see it now, Lord Vullieth standing before Collus, demanding that he execute his half-brother for the grave insult dealt to him. Collus would refuse, of course, and then Vullieth would leave, taking his entire retinue with him. Militarily, Lord Vullieth was the mightiest lord in Teni'sia. His lands stretched from the borders of the castle almost all the way to Clete. It was fully one-quarter of the entire king-dom. If he opposed the king, others would follow. Collus's rule would collapse. Teni'sia would fall into civil war.

All because Mershayn couldn't do what needed to be done. Why did he have to pick Ari'cyiane?

Because of his monumental ego, that's why. Because it was a challenge. Because it still rankled that Mershayn was not really a noble himself.

Stupid! Lord Vullieth could make a bid for the throne if he wanted. And he would get it. His standing army was twice the size of any other lord's, and infinitely larger than the amount of soldiers loyal to Collus. Many nobles and their sworn men would swing to Vullieth's banner if he called them. They were not impressed by Collus's hesitant rule. By the gods, *Mershayn* was not impressed by Collus's rule! Why would these strangers support him? A coup might be in the making right now. What was surprising was that one hadn't been tried already.

There was probably only one reason a coup had not been

tried, and that was Lord Vullieth himself. He did not stand with Sym, and Sym must clench his teeth at that. To overthrow the kingdom, Vullieth either had to be a co-conspirator, or he had to be eliminated. Vullieth was a man of stiff principles, and he believed in rightful succession. Whether he liked Collus or not, he would support the rightful king by blood.

Unless, of course, he fell into a mindless rage because he discovered the king's bastard brother made him a cuckold.

"Mershayn?" Ari'cyiane said, bringing him out of his horrifying fantasy. Wrinkles of worry danced the edges of her eyes. Gone was the bedroom stare she had fixed upon him. She looked like a wary rabbit, and she kept her voice hushed. "What should we do?" she asked.

"We must stop. From this moment forward, we do not see one another. We do not talk, except as public decorum dictates. We must act as though nothing has ever happened. We become acquaintances, as we would have been if we had not... If we hadn't ever met before except in public."

Her hand tightened on his. "Yes...of course."

He nodded.

"But tell me, my lord, how I am to accomplish that? These times with you... It has been as though I can fly, after years of scuttling upon the ground. My lord, I think that I—"

"No," he cut her off quickly. "Don't say that. You don't love me, so don't say it. You don't even know me. I'm not some dashing, shadowy prince. I'm a selfish, wenching fool. I've stepped somewhere I should not have, and now it could cost...everything."

"If you are so ignoble, then why would you try to stop? Why would you care about what happens to me, to my marriage?" she said softly.

Because I don't care. I care about my brother.

"Ari'cyiane, you are a wonderful woman. But there is more going on here than just you and I."

"I understand that. I know why we must stop," she said. "Sym and his serpents coil around the king, and my husband despises them. But will he support your brother if he catches us?" She shook her head. "I think not."

So she did understand. He felt a surge of respect for her, and with it came an even greater desire. He tamped it down.

"But how can I see you at court," she said, "and know that I can never touch you again? Love you again?"

"Don't use that word. What we have is lust. Easily started and easily ended," he said in a monotone.

"Not so easily," she whispered. She brushed her hand across his forehead, tucking his long hair behind his ear.

His gaze dropped to her knees. "It must be so. For all our sakes."

"Very well," she breathed. She closed her eyes and delicately wiped tears away with one slender finger. "We must do what is right. For the kingdom."

He held her hands tight in his. "Thank you, Ari'cyiane."

She blinked her eyes open, gave a bittersweet smile. "You have been a fire in my life, Mershayn of Bendeller. I thought my days were numbered before you came, each day to resemble the last. You reminded me what it was like to be alive again, vital and passionate."

"I'm sorry," he said, "I'm sorry that I—"

"Don't. Please. I am thanking you in the only way I can. You brought something to me I didn't know I was missing." She leaned forward and kissed him. Her hands went into his hair, and the kiss turned passionate.

She finally pulled away. Her breath was sweet upon his face, and that desire glowed in her eyes again. "Could it be so wrong?" she whispered. "For us to love each other one last time? The place I spoke of, no one knows of it."

"Ari'cyiane, I think it best if we just—"

"Let us say goodbye properly, without the weight of a kingdom on our shoulders."

His heart thundered in his chest. They had made the break. He should just return to the castle, return to Collus, but...

But they were alone. They would never be alone together again.

His blood rushed hot, and he stood, then bowed low. "As you say, my lady. Let us caress this guilt from our bodies one last time."

She beamed, took his hand in both of hers, and pulled him down the path.

He laughed. *This* he knew. *This*, he was good at. The rules were simple, and the joy was certain.

She pulled him around a tight corner in the hedge maze—

—and froze.

Lord Vullieth stood in the middle of the garden pathway, and Grendis Sym stood behind him.

18

MERSHAYN

ARI'CYIANE DROPPED Mershayn's hand like a hot coal. Lord Vullieth stared at her. He did not move. The skin around his eyes tightened, and his lips pressed into a hard, thin line.

Lord Vullieth was a good deal taller than Mershayn, and though he was thin, his shoulders were broad. A black cloak swept down from wide, black enameled shoulder clasps. His long red hair was pulled back tightly against his scalp. That carrot color blended with his complexion such that he almost looked bald. His eyebrows were so slight that he almost had none. It gave his black eyes a piercing quality. Vullieth's black and silver doublet, flared at the shoulders, made him look even larger than he was.

"M—My lord..." Ari'cyiane dipped a quick courtesy, bringing a courtly formality to the shocking awkwardness. But despite her grace, it looked comical. She realized this as soon as she finished, and blushed. Her tongue stumbled, and she stopped talking.

The silence hung in the air like a frosty breath.

"My lady," Lord Vullieth finally said in his deep voice. "Will you come with me?" He extended his hand, and it shook as though he was barely in control of his rage. She walked forward and took it. Her head began to turn, as though she would look back at Mershayn, but she stopped herself.

Thank the gods for that, at least.

Once Ari'cyiane's hand was in Vullieth's, the lord snapped a brief, powerful look at Mershayn. He couldn't tell if Vullieth was more angry or disappointed. Both emotions waged war on his face. Mershayn dropped his gaze to Vullieth's polished black boots, unable to meet the stare. He had no practice at hiding guilt. He'd never had any guilt before this. He'd always been proud of his dalliances, proud to flaunt his advantage over every noble he could. But Vullieth might be the only Teni'sian lord who could save Collus's reign from being subsumed by Sym. Mershayn had just shot an arrow into Collus's heart.

Lord and lady turned and left the garden without a word. Mershayn watched them go, wishing there was something he could say, something he could do. But none of his charming banter could change what had just happened. No cynical humor about nobles would aid him. What he required was honesty and integrity, and he had none. How did one apologize to a man for sleeping with his wife? He'd never even contemplated such an absurdity before. What could he possibly say that would make anything better?

"That is a shame," Sym said. The slithery lord watched Vullieth and Ari'cyiane turn a corner in the labyrinthine garden as though he was watching a pleasant sunset. His white and green doublet was tucked neatly into his golden belt, and he rested his hands there.

"You brought him here," Mershayn growled.

"Of course not," Sym said. "I simply had business to discuss with Lord Vullieth. I thought the fresh air might be nice. How was I to know that you would be sinking your claws into the noble Lady Ari'cyiane in such a public place?"

"You knew..." Mershayn growled.

"How would I know?"

"Because you're a rat sneak and a spy."

Sym took a small cloth from the sleeve of his shirt and held it up to his nose as though he didn't like what he smelled. "Do not blame your immoral choices on me, bastard. One does not need to follow the droppings of a fox to know that he can be found in the henhouse. And you are not a very cunning fox, to be out here in the open. Not very cunning at all."

"Better a careless fox than a dead rat." Mershayn lunged across the distance, batting aside Sym's hasty block, and grabbed the lord by his perfect doublet. Sym shoved at Mershayn, but he used the momentum, spun around, and threw the lord to the white gravel path.

Sym went down flailing, and rolled onto his back. He lurched upright to a sitting position. "You insolent swine! I'll—"

Mershayn drew his sword and tucked the point underneath Sym's chin.

"You'll do what, Sym?" he whispered. "What will you do before I carve your lying head off?" He bared his teeth. "Did you think I would not draw upon you because you have no weapon? The crown executes traitors. I'll be doing Collus a favor."

"You won't k-kill me." Sym said, trying to sound brave, but his hands were stiff and unmoving at his sides, as though he didn't dare move lest the blade accidentally slit his throat.

Mershayn spat on his white-and-green doublet. "I'm a bastard, remember? Uncouth. Uncontrollable. Who knows what I might do in a fit of rage?"

"This will be seen as an act of war," Sym said, his voice high-pitched.

Mershayn shrugged. "It's all so complicated, you and your courtly ways," he said. "A lie here, a truth there. Build trust, then undermine. I confess I don't understand it all..." He spun the hilt in his hand perfectly, twisting the blade like a corkscrew. That drew a nick of blood from the lord's neck. "But I understand that when a sword goes into a man's throat, that man dies."

Mershayn stepped forward, pushing gently with the blade and forcing Sym to scrabble backward like a crab until he hit the stone bench.

"I think you underestimate what I'm capable of," Mershayn hissed, and he struggled with himself. The swordsman in him told him to kill Sym. Now. That was simple. That was swordplay. In swordplay, you fought your enemy, you killed your enemy, and then the fight was over. But it wasn't the same in politics. If he killed Sym, he'd have to run.

Would it be worth it? It might. It was the honest man's path, not this indecipherable political muddle. If someone attacked you, you attacked him back. You didn't give him a second chance to hurt you or the ones you loved. Did it matter that Sym's attack wasn't with a sword, but a devious machination instead? Did it matter that—

Mershayn heard the quiet footstep a split second too late. He dropped low, but a splitting pain exploded in the back of his head. He heard his own sword clatter to the gravel.

Then, nothing.

19

MERSHAYN

MERSHAYN OPENED his eyes to darkness. He wondered for a moment if the blow to the back of his head had blinded him. The seconds rolled by. His ears focused on a steady drip of water somewhere. Slowly, a vague outline of bars became apparent. So he could still see. He was simply in a dark place. He let out a sigh of relief and thanked the gods for that much good fortune.

Then the rage came, like a pail of hot water pouring onto his head. Rage at himself.

He should have killed Sym when he had the chance. One second was all it would have taken. He had disobeyed the first rule of swordsmanship: the enemy means to kill you. When you have the advantage, do not hesitate. Strike hard and strike sure. He'd gotten bound up in his head, and it had cost him.

Still, he wasn't dead.

He reached up and gingerly felt the lump just behind his ear. Whoever had struck him knew exactly where to hit.

He slowly rose to his feet and went to the bars. Why hadn't Sym just killed him? The answer had to be that this was part of some plan. But Collus would note Mershayn's absence almost immediately; he'd come looking for him.

He rubbed his temples. He had a difficult enough time second-guessing Sym's deviousness without a throbbing headache. Sym never did anything that didn't serve his own purposes. If Mershayn was still alive, it was good for Sym somehow. How did Mershayn decipher what that was and stop that plan?

Well, he could kill himself. That would certainly undo any leverage his life might give to Sym.

His bitter laugh echoed in the cell.

Yes. That's a good idea.

Perhaps it would have been a better idea to have done it before Vullieth discovered Mershayn was bedding his wife.

He looked around as best as he was able in the black cell. There was nothing in it. No rocks or bowls or anything from which to make a weapon. "I wish I *could* kill myself," he muttered.

A quiet voice came out of the darkness. "Such a dark wish, lord of Bendeller."

Mershayn spun around and tripped over the uneven rock floor. He stumbled and slammed back against the wall.

"Where are you?" he whispered hoarsely.

"Right in front of you."

He strained to see, but all he could make out were the slight silhouettes of the bars. Then, a white face appeared from the inky blackness, as if floating. Two white hands appeared, fingers wrapping around the iron rods that separated them. They were as pale as snow.

"Ari'cyiane?" he asked incredulously.

"No," the woman said.

"Who are you?"

"My name is Silasa."

"How did you get in here? Who sent you?"

"A friend."

Mershayn had a difficult time tracking her in the darkness. Her hands vanished and reappeared several times as she worked at the lock. She wore a black cowl, and when she turned, her face vanished.

The click of metal on metal drew his attention, then the rusty lock screeched and gave way with a *clunk*.

She opened the door.

"Follow me."

"I can't see," he replied, squinting and moving forward with a hand out in front of him, questing for obstructions.

Strong, slender fingers closed over his. They were cold.

A shiver ran up Mershayn's spine. "Who are you?"

"I'm good in the dark," she said, leading him down the corridor. Mershayn stumbled along behind her. He could see torchlight ahead, illuminating the musty stone walls from somewhere around the corner. The cowled woman in front of him began to come clearer. She was dressed all in black, with a long, thick black braid of hair that trailed out of her cowl.

She let go of his hand, motioning him to stay put. She crept up to the corner and around.

She must be a thief of some kind, to move so quietly. Who do I know who's friendly with thieves?

She returned, and this time he could see her from the front. Her black skirt swished as she appeared around the corner. She motioned him to follow.

What kind of a thief wore a skirt? And...

He froze, looking at her eyes. They were white, save a thin circle of black that told where the irises of her eyes ought to have begun.

She cocked her head, waiting to see if he would say anything. His mouth hung open.

With a wry smile, she put a finger against her lips, then turned and vanished into the dark in front of him.

He hurried to keep up, using all of his prowess to stay silent, but compared to her, he was a clumsy oaf. She made no sound, but his boots scraped lightly on the stone floor, sounding loud in his ears. He rounded the corner as quickly as he could without sounding like a galloping herd of horses.

There were three torches burning in sconces on the walls, and he shielded his eyes from the harsh light.

"You can speak again," the woman said. "We're safe for now."

"Who are you?" he asked. She wasn't normal. Was she one of the Wave-altered, escaped from some prison down here where they were being quarantined?

He looked around the room. It was a guard room. A table in the center of the room held two plates of half-eaten food and a scattered game of bones. One guard lay prone on the floor half under the table. The second guard looked as though he had fallen asleep in his chair while playing.

"Are they—" Mershayn began.

"Yes," she interrupted him, lifting a ring of keys from the wall and unlocking the huge wooden door on the far side of the room. She pulled it open as though it were made of paper.

"Did you—"

"Yes," she said. "Come, Mershayn."

"How do you know me?" He suddenly wondered if he was safer back in that black hole of a cell than he was with this woman.

She stopped by the door and turned to face him. He glanced at the body of the seated guard. The dead man had a short sword. He could reach it with one lunge.

She followed his gaze. Her lips curved in a brief smile. "I'm not your enemy, Lord Mershayn," she said.

"Are you one of the Wave-altered?"

She raised an eyebrow.

"Changed by The Wave?"

"No."

"Then what are you?" he asked.

"Take it." She nodded at the sword. "You may need it before this night is done."

Mershayn went to the man, unbuckled the belt, and pulled the sword away. The man showed no signs of a fight, and no signs of violence except maybe a broken wrist. What had killed him? Certainly not a sword or dagger.

He belted the sword around his waist, drew it, tested the balance, then sheathed it again. He felt much better.

"Come," she said. "Let us try to be away before they change the guard."

"Silasa?" he said, testing out the name. "That's what you said, yes? Silasa?"

"That's right."

"I want to know...something."

She waited, the large cowl covering the top half of her face, keeping those eerie white eyes in shadow.

He swallowed. "How did you... How did you kill them?"

"Does it matter?"

He couldn't say why he asked her that, but some instinct deep within him screamed to know. Why were there no marks upon their bodies? It made his skin crawl.

"No," he said. "I guess not."

"Then come," she said, and disappeared through the doorway.

Mershayn kept up with her as she climbed the stairs, though only barely. She moved with a speed that made him feel slow and clumsy.

Where was she from—?

Suddenly, she pulled him into a darkened alcove and wrapped him in the shadow of her cloak. Long moments crawled past, and he listened intently. Just as he was about to ask her what was happening, he heard the footsteps. Seconds later, three guards descended the stairs past them. She waited until they had gone, then slid silently into the hallway again.

He tensed and followed, trying with every bit of his training to be as silent as she was. He failed, but the guards tromping down the rough-hewn steps did not hear them. Their torchlight faded and finally disappeared.

When Mershayn made his first inspection of Teni'sia, he had explored the entire castle. He had visited the cells where lawbreakers were held, but he'd never seen these carved dungeons. He shuddered at the thought that others had been locked down there with him, and he just hadn't heard them. How extensive was it? How many cells?

They climbed and climbed. The staircase began like a dried-up riverbed, rough and artless, twisting to the left sometimes and then switching back upon itself and twisting right. Soon, it smoothed out and became a spiral staircase leading ever upward and to the right. Mershayn could barely see anything. Sometimes Silasa even disappeared from his view. But she always returned, a ghost with a white face, silent and eerie.

He trailed his fingers against the rock and was happy to note when the rough stone became mortar and blocks. His fingers eventually fumbled across a door, but Silasa did not stop and he let it go by. If he survived this adventure, he was coming back here to find out exactly what this place was.

They passed several more doors, and finally Silasa opened one of them. They passed through, and she closed it quietly behind him. A lone torch spread its orange light onto the walls. At the far end, a staircase climbed upward and disappeared into the gloom. The passageway looked more conventional than the rough-hewn walls of the spiral staircase or the solid rock of the cave-like jails. There were two thick doors on each side of the passage. This was the castle proper, or at least very close. It frustrated him that he still didn't recognize it. How many secret passages were there in Teni'sia?

"Where are—?"

Her cold hand pressed quickly and firmly over his mouth, like cold iron wrapped in thin leather.

One of the doors opened. A robed and hooded figure stepped

out and turned, facing back the way he'd come. A strange voice followed him. It was the oddest voice Mershayn had ever heard. It filled the hallway as though it was oozing out from the walls, down from the ceiling, up from the floor. It sank into Mershayn's flesh like fish hooks. Soft and compelling, it spoke to the hooded man.

"Then the coup has begun," the voice said. He sounded young, but his manner of speaking reminded Mershayn of his grandfather. "Sym is tragically lacking in patience. But one cannot expect too much from such a man."

"Yes, my master," the hooded man replied in a toneless voice.

"Still, it will serve. A few more weeks, and the nobles would have thrown that spineless boy from the royal balcony. Now there will be fighting. Go then. Convey my displeasure to Lord Sym and make him understand that I will not tolerate more of this recklessness. Tell him I do not make plans so that he might abandon them at a whim."

"Yes, my master."

"And allow him to know my mind concerning what must be done next."

"Yes, my master."

The door closed and the hooded figure turned. He walked up the stairway and disappeared into the darkness.

Silasa slowly withdrew her cold hand and turned a fierce look upon him. She pressed her long, white finger to her lips. She motioned him to stay, and she moved back to the door where they'd come from, rather than the hallway where the hooded man had left.

He started to follow, but she pointed a silent finger at him and gave one emphatic shake of her head. He froze. On those same silent feet, she crossed the distance to him. He stifled a gasp as she lifted him in her arms like a baby and took him through the door.

She set him down, closed the door. The sudden absence of the torchlight plunged the stairway into darkness. He couldn't see her. He took a clumsy step backward, scuffing the rock step. He held his clammy palms in front of himself as if to ward her off, but she caught him, hands like steel tongs. Her cold lips brushed his ear.

"Not a sound." She spoke so softly that he could barely hear her. "If you make a sound, we become the playthings of a monster. I can move faster than you can, and silently, so I will carry you until we are safe. Do not struggle. I will be quick."

Without another word, she scooped him off his feet, turned and lunged up the stairwell as if she could fly.

20

MERSHAYN

SILASA OPENED the door and closed it behind them. She set Mershayn on his feet.

He backed a step away from her. "By the gods, what are you?" he managed to say, staring at her in the torchlight. She wasn't human. She couldn't be. No one was that strong.

The corners of her lips turned down.

"How can you simply pick me up as though I weigh nothing?" he said. "How can you leap ten steps at a time? Why are you not out of breath?"

"You are safe now. That is all that is important—"

"I believe I have a right to know."

"Do you? And what gives you this right? That I opened the door to your cage, led you out of the dungeons? That I hid you from the guards? Or was it when I saved you from an undead threadweaver and carried you here? Which of my actions entitles you to an explanation of 'what' I am?"

"I—I am the Royal Arms Inspector for Teni'sia." He fumbled with the words, trying to find some authority. "It is my responsibility to—"

"You are the bastard brother of a king who is losing his kingdom."

"But you're not human," he blurted.

"And you are an uncouth ingrate," she said sternly.

"I—I—" he stuttered. His heart was beating so fast. This had to be some kind of dream. He squinched his eyes shut and held up one hand. "I'm sorry," he murmured, trying to gain some control of his whirling thoughts. "I apologize. Please... It is only that I...I am far afield here. Too many things have happened. I don't understand what is going on."

"If you will listen, I will tell you what you need to know. There isn't much time. We are safe here, but only for the moment. Those guards we passed in the stairway were coming to kill you. By now, they have discovered your absence and are on their way to report to their master, and he will hasten his timetable."

"Their master?"

"Grendis Sym is making his bid for the throne of Teni'sia. He has powerful allies, and he will succeed. If he finds you, he will kill you, and I have been asked to make sure that you live. You must flee."

"Flee? And where is my brother?"

"Sym has sent assassins to deal with the king."

"No!"

"Quiet," she whispered harshly. "There is nothing you can do about that, but you must survive. There are many battles to this war. There will be other fields upon which to fight and you must choose yours better than you chose this one."

"I didn't choose anything," he said.

"Exactly so. That must change, or you'll lose more than your half-brother."

"I have to get him out."

"It is too late for that."

"It's never too late." He ran toward the staircase at the far end of the hall.

"Mershayn, wait!"

He turned at the base of the staircase, feeling the waste of every second. "Come with me," he beseeched her. "Please help me."

"I have helped you as much as I dare."

"Just once more, and I will ask nothing more of you."

She shook her head. "I was instructed to lead you out. I was specifically told to do nothing more than that, even if you chose to go after your brother."

"What? By whom?"

"Will you come?" she pressed.

"Not without Collus."

"Mershayn—"

"Help me!"

"No."

He turned and ran up the staircase, left the supernatural woman below in the flickering torchlight.

Rage drove him forward. The hallway extended into the darkness on his left and on his right. He stopped and looked both ways, thinking. He knew this place. He had been here before. The kitchens. He sprinted to the right. After a hundred paces, he opened a door on his left and ran down the next hallway, then opened the door at the end of it.

The heat of the room washed over him. Two women stood around a large pot upon an iron stove. A wide, walled fire pit dominated the center of the room. A stout man turned an entire spitted deer around and around. He stopped when Mershayn entered the room.

The two women stared at him.

"M'lord Mershayn," one of them said hastily and ducked into a courtesy. The woman beside her quickly followed suit. The cook at the pit looked at them, looked at Mershayn, then dropped to a knee.

It suddenly occurred to Mershayn that he had no plan. If he

rushed headlong into an assassination attempt, he might only add his body to the count. He needed an ally, but who could he trust? If he had been swept under the rug so easily, who would come to his aid? Certainly he could trust none of the nobles. The only ones he was certain would block Sym's plot were either sick, dead, or had just discovered Mershayn having an affair with his wife.

He cursed himself again. He had made no friends here. A few times he had thrown the bones with the guardsmen, but any of them could be in league with Sym. He had caroused incognito in a few taverns down in the city below, but there was no help to be found there.

"M'lord," the woman who had identified him said. "Is there aught we might do for ye?"

He realized then that he had been standing there for some time while they kept their obeisance.

"My apologies," he said, waving a hand. "Please continue with your duties. I was merely lost in thought." He jogged across the room and through the far door.

He knew where he was now, and he kept to the back ways, rising higher and higher through the castle. If he could have no allies, he must somehow obtain the element of surprise. In this, he had two advantages. First, he was free, and no one was likely to know that for the next several minutes. The dungeon guards who would find their fellows dead would certainly not be able to climb those stairs as fast as Silasa had. They were ten minutes away from reporting to Sym, at best. That meant Mershayn had at least fifteen minutes before Sym could mobilize anything against him. Second, he knew of the assassination attempt. It was happening right now, or very soon. Together, these two things might be enough.

He tried not to think about how Collus might already be dead. But if there had already been an assassination this day, then there would be at least two before the day ended. Mershayn would see to that.

As he ascended the stairwell of one of the many thin turrets in Castle Teni'sia, he glanced out through one of the tiny slits that served as windows. The sky was dark, but he had no idea how deep into the night it was.

His legs burned by the time he reached the Northern Walk. It would take a great deal of skillful climbing, but the only way to surprise Collus's assassin was to come in through a route that even an assassin would hesitate to take.

Mershayn adjusted his belt so that the sword hung behind him, removed his boots and left them, then jumped upon the thick stone wall that served as a rail to the Northern Walk. He looked down. Jagged rocks and crashing surf looked back at him from far below. He must calm himself. He'd never tried to climb to Collus's chambers before. They were in the highest part of the castle and intentionally difficult to reach this way. He would have to be at his best.

Letting out a slow breath and closing his eyes, he mentally prepared himself. It was going to be a long climb. He must do it quickly and calmly—

"Isn't it a little early for sword-carrying?" Deni'tri's familiar voice broke his concentration.

Mershayn dropped to the stone rail. He spun himself and his belt at the same time, drew the short sword, and jumped to the walk.

Deni'tri stepped backward in surprise. As before when she had met him on the Northern Walk, she had her hatchet cocked back, and her sword out, but she obviously had not expected him to respond this way.

"What are you doing?" she said.

"I might ask the same of you," he replied. He tried to think about the guards' rotation. Was it really Deni'tri's turn to patrol the Northern Walk again? He didn't think so.

She narrowed her eyes. "Sheathe your sword, Lord Mershayn. I'm a royal guard. It is my job to patrol the Northern Walk."

"Not this week, it's not." He gambled on his memory.

"I'm taking a shift for Gri'stan," she said.

"Why this shift? Why tonight?" He kept his sword light and ready in front of him and began moving toward her. It was too much coincidence for this day.

Her mouth became a tight line. "Stop right there, Mershayn," she said. Her hatchet hand pulsed on the haft of the hatchet, no longer casual. "You're acting strangely, and I don't want you getting any closer."

"You're wise in that," he murmured, slowing but not stopping. "You'll get one throw. You had better hope it hits."

"You're talking mad," she said, and he saw her fear. "I'm not your enemy. What's going on? Why are you sneaking around at this hour?"

"I might ask you the same."

"For the love of the gods, I'm patrolling!"

"Not here. Not tonight. Where are you supposed to be? What is your normal shift?"

"My post was in the royal wing. Outside of the king's hall. It was to be Faykler and me. Gri'stan and Faykler are good friends, and I don't like Faykler." She frowned. "When Gri'stan suggested the switch, I agreed. Lo'gan approved it. I enjoy the Northern Walk."

Mershayn's suspicion fell away to be replaced by a foreboding. "You switched..." He knew Gri'stan and Faykler, too. They had sly eyes and never had much to say when Mershayn was around. And both of them were new in the last two weeks. Deni'tri was not the traitor. She was moved because she would have actually protected the king.

"By the gods..." He lowered his sword. "I am a puppet on strings," he murmured.

It is already too late... He heard Silasa's words in his head.

"What's happening, Mershayn?" Deni'tri asked, lowering her hatchet.

"Assassination." He sheathed his sword and moved to the wall again.

"No," she murmured.

"There isn't any time. I wish I could explain, but Collus might already be dead."

"Wait!"

He turned his head in annoyance.

"What can I do?" she asked.

"Keep quiet," he said. "Half the royal guard is likely paid by Sym. I wouldn't trust you except that I have no choice. If you raise the alarm, it may only bring allies to Sym's cause."

"And you are going to Collus's rooms?" She nodded toward the highest balcony.

"Yes."

He started up. "If you know any prayers, send them to Tarithalius."

She turned and sprinted back down the Northern Walk, to alert enemies or friends, he didn't know, and he didn't care now. He climbed.

21

MERSHAYN

MERSHAYN REACHED THE BALCONY, arms burning. He wished he could haul himself over, flop to the ground, and simply breathe for a day or two. Instead, muscles quivering, he hoisted himself silently over the rail and delicately set his feet down. His arms felt like sacks of sand. His legs shook, but he took the time to listen.

The sun lightened the sky, brushing the clouds with wisps of orange. Its presence cast the western side of the castle in deep shadow, which suited Mershayn perfectly. He waited until the burning in his arms and legs lessened and then slunk into the king's study. His eyes scanned the bookcases, the writing desk, the shadowy corners. Was the assassin here?

He didn't see anyone.

Now came the tricky part. This was the king's study; the king's sleeping chambers were across the hall. He would love to have climbed straight into Collus's room, but it faced east, not west, and the Northern Walk did not continue that far around the castle. He would have had to climb up from the very bottom. Even he could not have managed that without a rope.

He paused for a moment, trying to come up with some brilliant plan. Nothing surfaced in his mind. All he had was speed and surprise, and he was wasting speed by standing here.

He opened the door and entered the hallway. The two guards posted outside of Collus's doors saw him immediately. Two short swords rang from their sheaths. Could Mershayn be so lucky? Were these two guards loyal to Collus?

He tried to remember their names and managed to come up with them. Falamae and Cor'lior. Falamae was one of the best swordsmen in the royal guard. She'd made certain to stand out whenever Mershayn came to watch practice. Cor'lior was huge and fast. If he hit you, you went down, and you didn't get up.

Had they already let the killer into Collus's room?

"Identify yourself," Cor'lior said in a calm voice. He advanced, in complete balance. Falamae stayed at her post. They were good. Dealing with the threat was of great importance, but not as great as guarding the king's door. Mershayn wasn't nearly as worried about Cor'lior as he was about Falamae. Cor'lior had a weak spot. He wasn't very flexible, and if you stayed on his right side, he could be had.

Mershayn had not detected any glaring weaknesses in Falamae. That would be a good fight, if it came to that. And she had a long sword, while he only had a borrowed short sword. He hoped he didn't have to test her mettle here.

"Don't you recognize me, Cor'lior?" Mershayn said. "I am the Royal Arms Inspector. Put your sword down."

Cor'lior's eyes narrowed, but he didn't lower his sword. He looked as if he were deciding something in his mind. He chose wisely and saved his life. Slowly, he let his sword dip, but he didn't sheathe it.

"It is very unusual, sir, for you to come to inspect us in the middle of the night, and to emerge from the study," he said.

Falamae watched Mershayn.

"Have you come to see the king?" Cor'lior said.

"I have." Mershayn stepped forward, forcing himself to act

casual. Falamae studied his dirty clothes. Cor'lior had submitted to his authority, however, and stood aside. Mershayn walked forward, and he wondered for a moment if Falamae would move or if she would challenge him. He passed Cor'lior and—

Mershayn's intuition screamed at him. With reflexes born from a lifetime of fighting, he threw himself sideways as Cor'lior's sword bit into his ribs. He heard the crack of bone and he stumbled away. That strike had been meant for his heart.

His sword whipped up in front of him, but Cor'lior did not move in for the kill. Falamae slammed against the king's door, choking. It took Mershayn a moment to see Cor'lior's slim dagger sticking out of her throat.

Cor'lior turned his attention back on Mershayn.

"Goddamned bastard," he growled, advancing on Mershayn.

Falamae's sword clanged to the floor. She yanked the dagger from her throat even as her legs folded underneath her. Her eyes were wide with shock. Blood spurted from the wound.

Mershayn's anger burned as he heard Falamae's death gurgles. She kicked her leg against the wall, as though it might somehow stop her life's blood from draining out of her neck.

Mershayn retreated. Cor'lior followed.

That's right. The fast kill. That's all you're good at. And you missed.

Cor'lior widened his stance, preventing escape. Mershayn limped over and leaned heavily against the wall.

"You going...to kill the king!" he said, feigning shock.

"Not yet, bastard. You first." He lunged, quick as a snake.

Mershayn spun. This was combat. This, he knew. Simple, straightforward. His ribs screamed as he pivoted, but the wound was not nearly as bad as he had let on. Cor'lior's sword flashed past his right ear. He gave it no thought. He knew where the sword was. He knew how fast it came and how far it would go.

Stone chips flew as the blade crunched into the wall. Mershayn finished his spin, crouched low, and severed the big man's meaty calf. He roared in pain. His knee crashed to the ground, and he slumped forward. Mershayn stepped between his legs and plunged his sword into Cor'lior's lower back.

Cor'lior's roar twisted into a scream of anguish. Mershayn did not stop. He leapt back and kicked the guardsman's hip. As Cor'lior toppled, Mershayn stepped forward again and speared his sword arm to the ground. Cor'lior's strength was impressive. Only when Mershayn give a vicious twist did the big man drop the blade.

The guardsman was beaten. That was obvious. Some swordsmen might stop and gloat before the final strike, but Mershayn had seen a man die doing that. *Never underestimate the opponent. Continue until the fight is finished.* He dropped one knee onto Cor'lior's stomach and plunged his sword into the man's chest.

Cor'lior's scream stopped. His eyes bugged out, and he stared at Mershayn in stupefaction. Mershayn leaned over and breathed into his ear. "No more backstabbing for you, not on this day or any other, you stinking pile of offal."

The big man gave his last breath and died.

Mershayn moved quickly to Falamae, but she was already gone. The door to the king's chambers suddenly opened.

Mershayn stepped back smoothly and rose, pointing his short sword up.

"Collus!" he exclaimed. "Thank the gods." His brother was disheveled in a hastily drawn robe. He brandished an ornate long sword, and he looked at the dead guards incredulously.

"Who—?" he began, then said. "Mershayn! Dervon's breath, what is going on—?" He choked on the words. "Falamae, no!" He started to crouch, then stopped, as though something had just occurred to him. He brought his sword up again, pointing it at Mershayn. "What did you do? These are my royal guards!"

"It's not as it looks. I assure you, brother."

"Are you mad?" he repeated.

"No," Mershayn said. "Cor'lior is an assassin. I came to stop him. Falamae knew nothing of this plot, and paid for her ignorance. You will see that the dagger is not mine."

"I've been looking for you for more than a day. You just vanished," Collus said.

The double doors at the end of the hall crashed open. Gri'stan and Faykler entered, swords drawn.

"Your majesty, is all well?" They saw the bodies and continued forward quickly.

They were traitors. Mershayn could see it in the way they advanced, in the fact that they had not seemed surprised to see the dead bodies. They did not look at the king in concern, but rather as cunning predators, trying to get closer. And they frowned when they saw Mershayn.

"I—I don't know..." Collus said shakily.

"Stand back, assassin," Faykler said to Mershayn. To Collus, he said, "Back into your room and close the door, Your Majesty. We shall deal with this one."

"They've come to kill you," Mershayn said. "Don't listen to them."

Collus was not grasping the situation quickly enough. He doubted Mershayn. How could that be? Why in the world would Mershayn want to kill him? To his horror, Mershayn saw three more guards rush through the double doors, out of breath.

"Collus, if I'd wanted to kill you, I could have done it any day of a thousand before now! Quit quaking and help me with these traitors, else we will both be dead. I'm your brother, for Thalius's sake."

Collus's jaw set and nodded. He moved into the hallway at Mershayn's side, and Mershayn took a thankful breath.

"Then you were right," Collus said. "All along, Sym was...he wanted what his father wanted."

Gri'stan and Faykler slowed their advance now that it appeared Collus would fight by Mershayn's side. They didn't back off, though.

"Throw down your weapons," Collus commanded. "There is no threat here, unless you have brought it." Neither of them obeyed. For the first time that morning, Collus did not seem surprised. He let out a long breath. "I have been a fool..." he murmured. His eyes narrowed. When he spoke, his voice lashed them like a flame of rage. "Come then, dogs, and taste a king's steel."

Gri'stan and Faykler paused long enough for their three fellows to join them.

"Like old times, eh, Collus?" Mershayn said as they advanced. The odds were bad, worse than the two of them had ever faced before, and never had they faced opponents so bent on ending them. But Mershayn felt relaxed for the first time since yesterday at court. If he died here, at least it would be a good death.

"I am almost relieved," Collus said, as though reading Mershayn's mind. "At least this makes sense. I will not wonder whether I did a good job or bad when this business is finished."

Mershayn grinned, and he began to feel the battle thrill that filled him when fighting. "Let us show these cravens how men of Bendeller carve their way out of trouble."

Mershayn and Collus moved slowly forward, but the traitorous guards did not wait. With a battle cry, Gri'stan and Faykler rushed. The three traitors behind them, who Mershayn did not recognize, charged as well.

King and brother met the five head-on. Collus was not as talented a swordsman as Mershayn, but he knew how to handle a blade. He and Mershayn had spent almost the same amount of time practicing.

Faykler lunged at Mershayn, aiming for his middle. Mershayn twisted, barely dodging the blade. The point ripped through his tunic. Mershayn stepped forward, grabbing Faykler's throat and jamming his short sword into the guard's side. Thick leather armor under Faykler's tunic turned the blade. Mershayn growled. He could not afford to make mistakes like that.

He ducked low and spun as another guard cut down at him. The guard almost cut off Faykler's hand in his rush to get to Mershayn. Faykler stumbled backward, cursing as he lost his balance and his chance at a follow-up strike.

Mershayn rose, his sword flicking out like the tongue of a snake. The nameless guard clutched his throat and gurgled blood. He died with a mighty cough, spraying red. The hallway was wide, and the long swords the guards used had an advantage on Mershayn. He had to get close and stay close.

Faykler moved in again while the other three concentrated on Collus. Steel clashed as Mershayn met Faykler sword to sword. He used all of his strength and tried to hit at an angle that would shatter Faykler's sword, but the guardsman was too good for that. He kept the correct slant to his weapon and pushed Mershayn's smaller blade to the side.

Three more guards poured into the hallway, and Mershayn's hopes sank. For a moment, he thought that he and Collus might escape this trap, but Collus was already retreating under the onslaught of three. They would have him soon.

With a shout of rage, Mershayn blocked Faykler's next strike and lunged. The guardsman's sword whistled over his head, clipping off a lock of flying brown hair. Mershayn came up within Faykler's guard and drove the short sword into his armpit. There was no armor there.

Faykler grunted, then slid noiselessly off Mershayn's sword and crumpled to the ground.

Collus suddenly cried out as a blade weaved past his guard and took him in the side.

With a shout of anguish, Mershayn batted away the swords of the two guards who turned to meet his rush. One of the swords grazed his leg, but he ignored it and slammed headlong into the third of Collus's adversaries. Mershayn drove the guardsman into the wall, blasting the air from his lungs, and yanking the guardsman's dagger from his belt.

Mershayn stood up straight, ramming his head into the guard's chin beneath his helmet, then raked up with the dagger, slashing the man's neck. The guard dropped, clawing at his throat.

Mershayn twisted around just in time to parry a sword away from Collus.

His brother stumbled, and fell to the cobblestones, huffing and clenching his teeth. He held his side with one hand and feebly tried to hold up his sword with the other. Red blood covered his hands.

Mershayn's heart thumped wildly and he made two quick, threatening feints. Respectful of his skill, the two guards stepped back, buying a moment's time.

The three latecomers arrived then. It was five to two again. Mershayn was injured and Collus was out of the fight. Mershayn kept his back against the wall, straddling the legs of his wounded brother. He prepared to make the walk to the Godgate.

The first two guards closed in, heartened by the arrival of their fellows. Mershayn saw two more guards sprint through the door into the hallway. Now it was seven to one.

"Dervon grind your bones in his teeth!" he shouted. He would not wait for them to come to him. He lunged forward, blocking a sword strike with his stolen dagger. The point of the man's blade shot past his ear, and Mershayn shoved his short sword into the nearest man's stomach, punching through the thick leather. He gurgled and slumped over, dragging Mershayn off balance. The second guard swung at Mershayn's head. The blade cracked into his cheek, and his right eye went blurry.

Mershayn shouted anew, screaming at them. Another sword came down. He threw himself to the side, barely caring whether it hit him or not. Somehow, it missed. One of the guards howled in pain.

He found himself in the center of a throng of bodies, and he struck out in one direction at a time, methodically seeking the soft spots. His blade found a meaty thigh. The guard cried out and fell. He spun, blocking another blade and getting inside the man's parry. He plunged his dagger into the guard's armpit. The guard screamed and fell backward.

Mershayn slipped on the blood-slicked stones and went down. He rolled to the side, knowing that a blade must be descending upon him. He heard it clang on the stones. He lashed out, but only hit the ground.

Another guard screamed. Mershayn turned in time to see him fall. He blinked his good eye and tried to bring the fallen guard into focus. That was a hatchet in his chest.

He pushed on the slick stones, scrambling jerkily to his knees, trying to get to his feet. There were two guards left. He managed to get upright and lunged at the woman. She hastily blocked him and backed up.

"Mershayn, don't!" she said. Blood began to run into his good eye. He blinked it away and pressed his attack, but it was too late. The final guard stepped in and batted his blade down.

Mershayn turned on him, bringing his sword up and attacking, but his vision was fading. His arms were full of sand. And the guard he now fought was good. Mershayn pressed him with every ounce of strength he could muster, but the guard's blade was there again and again. The man backed up smoothly one step at a time, drawing out the attack, dictating the terms, wearing Mershayn out. But he wasn't attacking. Why wasn't he attacking...?

Suddenly, Mershayn realized that the man was talking to him.

"My lord..." he said in a steady, coaxing voice. "Mershayn, listen to me. We haven't much time. The king is hurt. Mershayn—"

Mershayn stumbled back, somehow managing to keep his feet. He lowered his sword. The guard did not attack. Neither did the other guard, the woman, who stood behind him. He suddenly realized that she could have spitted him at any time. He peered intently through his blood-covered eye at the man. "Lo'gan?"

Captain Lo'gan let out a quiet breath. "Yes. Thank the gods, Mershayn. I thought they'd chopped into your brain."

"They might have," he said, staggering. The woman behind him moved forward and supported his weight.

"Deni'tri?"

"Yes, my lord."

"You went for help. I told you not to... Not to...tell anyone."

"Lo'gan would never betray the true king," she said simply. "And we arrived just in time."

Mershayn suddenly remembered Collus.

"Collus!" He spun about, but his legs gave out. Deni'tri groaned as she took his weight and hauled him upright. "Enough of that, my lord. Hold still."

"I will help the king," Lo'gan said, kneeling before Collus. He paused for a long time.

Mershayn felt his consciousness ebbing, but he held onto it fiercely. "Is he alive?" he demanded.

Lo'gan had never been one to mince words. He turned, and with that same stoic expression he always wore, said, "Barely. I hesitate to move him, but we cannot stay here. We don't know how deep this betrayal goes. Others may arrive shortly."

Lo'gan let out a brief sigh, then hefted Collus onto his shoulders. The king groaned, as if in his sleep, but made no other sound. "Come," Lo'gan said, stepping carefully among the dead bodies and slick stones. "This way."

Mershayn began to feel the pain of his wounds. His head felt like it was being slowly crushed between two great stones. He sagged in Deni'tri's arms.

"No," she said sternly. "Stay awake, my lord. I cannot carry you. I have not the strength."

"Gods, the pain!" he whispered, trying to control it. But it overwhelmed him. All he wanted to do was lie down and fade into unconsciousness.

"Up, my lord!" she barked, dragging him after the retreating Lo'gan. "If you fall, you are a dead man. Help me."

Mershayn reached down for his dagger, but he could not find it.

"Give me your dagger!"

She hesitated, then unsheathed her dirk and handed it to him. With shaky fingers, he put the leather-bound handle between his teeth and bit down. He nodded. Pain fired through his head, and he almost fell again, but he recovered just in time to be dragged forward.

Deni'tri followed Lo'gan down the hall. He staggered along with her, fighting to stay awake.

22

STAVARK

STAVARK PAUSED on the ridge above of Denema's Valley. It was still the greenest valley he had ever seen. Even before GodSpill returned to the lands, the greenery of Denema's Valley had seemed unnatural, as though a small bit of the Age of Ascendance had remained.

He saw the cluster of shops surrounding the city circle and the fountain, where the darklings had taken the Rabasyvihrk and the Maehka vik Kalik, where they'd nearly killed him, and where...

He could not find his calm when thinking about what the darklings had done to Orem.

This moment...cut short by violence, the end unknown, it must be returned to. It must, or it will hold my spirit prisoner forever.

Elekkena came up behind him. She was as much an enigma now as she had been before they left Sylikkayrn, but she was a good companion. She did not speak, except when there was something important to say, and she was a superlative hunter, even better than Stavark himself. They traded nights where one would hunt and the other would make the fire and forage for vegetables. She always brought back meat, and quickly. He would like to have gone with her on one of her hunts, but to travel fast, it was best to alternate hunting duties.

Elekkena never offered anything about her past, specifically about her two-year journey, and Stavark did not pry.

"Have you been to the human lands before?" he said to her.

"Yes," she said, but did not say more.

"Have you been to Denema's Valley?" Stavark asked, surprised.

"Yes." He continued to watch her, and she raised an eyebrow. "Did you think you were the only syvihrk to travel the human lands, Stavark, son of Sallark?"

He searched within himself. Why was it surprising she had been here? Was he so judgmental that he assumed all of the syvihrk were like his mother, enclosed by fear, unwilling to venture into the human lands? That was a shortcoming. He must be wary. Wisdom was found in resilience.

He spoke the truth. "Yes, I did."

She smiled. Another surprise. He had never seen her smile before.

"It appears that you do not know everything," she said.

He didn't answer that. "Come," he said. "This city is where it happened."

He slipped around the boulder and down the trail. Elekkena fell in silently behind him. He hadn't gone more than twenty paces when he heard something to their right near the cliff face of the ridge. With a quick signal, he dropped to a squat. Elekkena did the same.

There were people in that direction, a flash of light between the trees, the sound of horses. He felt the air ripple, as though someone was using GodSpill. This was not something every syvihrk could do, but Stavark tried to be at one with the land. He could tell when a threadweaver was working.

He nodded to Elekkena and triggered that place deep within himself that was the birthright of all syvihrk. He flicked his gaze to a specific tree.

Silver burst within him. It began in his eyes, expanding outward through his head and body. He could taste it, smell it, feel it in his skin. It lit up his arms and legs like dry leaves touched by a torch. The forest around him became silver. The slope became silver. The rocks and the grass and the sky, all of it. The lands stopped moving, as though they had been cast in molten silver.

He did not have time to ponder it. He could not stay long within the silverland. His people told stories of unwary syvihrk who did. They never returned, living on only as flickering glimmers of silver light in the real world.

Within the silverland, Stavark scampered to the tree he had chosen before triggering his gift, hid behind it, then left the silverland. Everything around him began to move again. A breeze whispered through the forest, leaves rustled, and the noise ahead returned.

Elekkena stood beside him, her head hung low, and she breathed as though she'd run all the way from the True Ocean. Stavark knew that feeling, but the gift of the syvihrk flowed strongly in him. Even without maehka in the lands, he had been able to use it, something almost no one else in Sylikkayrn could do. During that time, he reacted exactly as she was reacting now, exhausted just by the smallest use of his power.

But since the Maehka vik Kalik had freed the maehka, it was as though Stavark was a bird whose wings had finally been unbound. He could enter and leave the silverland at will. It still tired him, but not nearly as much as before. He could go further, last longer, than ever before.

"What is it?" Elekkena asked.

Stavark held up a hand. "Threadweaver," he mouthed, and his heart caught between hope and dread. The Maehka vik Kalik wasn't the only threadweaver who'd returned with the destruction of Daylan's Fountain. So far as Stavark could tell, all of the others were creatures of nightmare.

He took a moment to release his fear. Fear was the knife whose handle was a blade. Useless and damaging.

"We must wait," he whispered. "We must be ready to run."

Between the shadows of the trees, leading horses, were two people. One man, tall and powerful with golden hair. One woman, shorter, wearing breeches and a short skirt.

For the first time in weeks, Stavark smiled.

23

MIROLAH

Just as the previous two times Mirolah traveled through the teleportation gates, she felt like she was walking through a vertical lake. The surface was like water closing about her face, except there was no wetness, no heat or cold. Reality rippled for an abrupt, threadless moment outside the tapestry.

Then she was through. The gate delivered them to the leafy slope near Denema's Valley, descending steeply away from the rock face where the gate had been built.

She shook her head, bewildered, and the soft light of the gate faded behind them. The skin dog, just ahead of her, lunged sideways and dove into the tall brush. She barely caught a glimpse of him before he vanished.

Medophae shook away his disorientation, then looked at her.

"He followed us?" he asked.

She stared where the skin dog had gone, though there was no sight of him. She thought of the cobble birds in Lawdon's tile yard, the weasel, and the squirrels. They'd all watched her intently. She had thought the skin dog was the same, but none of the others had followed her, or not far, at least. She remembered a fox that had paced her from the tree line as she approached the city of Rith, but he hadn't followed her into the city, nor when she left.

"He wants to be close to me," she said.

"Did you bond with him?"

"Bond? No."

"Did you name him?"

"I didn't 'bond' with him. He's just following me."

"Maybe you bonded with him and you didn't know it. You should name him, if he's going to be your anchor."

"Anchor? Like Zilok Morth?" she asked sharply. She hated the idea of what Zilok did, enslaving Sef to serve his needs. "That's ridiculous!"

"Calm down. Not like Zilok Morth. That's not what I mean. Zilok's anchor keeps his spirit bound to life. A threadweaver's anchor is about binding her attention to her body, like a string that always leads home. It's similar, but not the same. You see, before the Age of Ascendance when threadweaving became easy enough for everyone to do, threadweavers would sometimes bind themselves to an animal to anchor them while threadweaving. Nearly every threadweaver I ever met had some kind of affectation like that, an object that served as their anchor: a staff or wand they carried, fancy robes with symbols stitched into the cuffs. One threadweaver constantly stroked his long beard every time he threadweaved. Piercing was also used, an earring or nose ring. The physical weight of the object through their flesh reminded them of their physical body while their mind was working in the threads. Others used throwaway components, attaching the significance of the threadweaving to the components, rather than seeing themselves as the spell. Some would talk while they threadweaved, letting the words flow into the GodSpill like verbal components. Threadweaving requires so much focus. It's why most people couldn't do it before Daylan's Fountain. Bands said..." He trailed off at her name, then cleared his throat. "That it's easy to get lost in the GodSpill."

Lost in the GodSpill.

"Did you ever know anyone who did?" she asked, her heart in her throat.

"Got lost? A few. I actually visited an infirmary in Belshra once—"

"What happened to them?" she demanded, cutting off his sentence. She calmed herself, breathing deeply.

"Mirolah, is something wrong?" He cocked his head, concerned.

"I just want to know," she said.

"Did you lose your focus with the boy? Is that what happened—?"

"Just tell me," she said.

"Well, they sat there. Their focus, their...minds, never returned to their bodies."

"They died."

"Starved to death. You could get them to drink. They'd swallow reflexively if forced. But you couldn't get them to chew food. Their minds were lost somewhere in the GodSpill."

By the Gods...

"I'll never bind anyone to me," she whispered. "Not a person and not an animal, either."

"The dog seems to want to serve you. You're not enslaving him if he wants to be your familiar. He would make an intimidating ally. Most familiars are small animals. I've never seen one as big as a skin dog."

"Familiar?"

"That's what they called them, the animal anchors. Something familiar to guide you back to your body, in case you got lost."

"I don't need one," she said adamantly.

He paused. "Mirolah, did you lose focus in Rith—?"

"No," she stopped him. "I'm fine." But the GodSpill had lifted her out of her body and stolen her away. She had almost died. Except it wasn't the same. She knew where her body was. She knew how to get back. She hadn't been lost, she'd been...everything. It was more that she hadn't *wanted* to come back. Or that she had become part of something larger that didn't want her to come back.

"Mirolah—"

"Please," she said. "Just...give me time to think about it." She didn't want to tell him about the voice. She didn't...want him to know.

"Okay."

"Let's just go."

He hesitated, then nodded and led his horse down the slope. She followed.

She let the thought of anchors, components, and familiars flow out of her mind. That wasn't her. She didn't need to lean on such things. She hadn't flowed into the GodSpill because she was weak. She'd gone because it yanked her away. It wasn't incompetence. She didn't need a crutch. It was a fight. The GodSpill was her ally...and maybe her enemy.

We are one....

They descended into Denema's Valley, the city where Stavark and Orem had faced their fate, where Ethiel had stolen Medophae and Mirolah and left her companions to die, torn apart by darklings. They might have been devoured seconds after Kikirian took her, or they might have somehow escaped.

Please let them be alive. Somehow, please. This was my fault. When the challenge came, I wasn't ready. And my companions suffered for it.

But her spell in Pindish, her appeal to the GodSpill to find them, had done nothing. Obviously begging the voice was useless—

She sensed movement in the threads, someone hiding close by. Was it the skin dog, trailing them? She opened the bright bridge, feeling the threads, feeling—

"Stavark!" She let out a joyful squeak, dropped the reins of her horse and ran down the slope.

"Mirolah!" Medophae called.

Stavark and another quicksilver girl emerged from the trees. Stavark smiled. He bowed his head to her respectfully, but she slid to her knees and threw her arms around him, hugging him. Stunned, he was stiff for a moment, then slowly closed his arms about her back. She held on for a long time. She didn't want to let go.

"My heart is joyous to find you well, Maehka vik Kalik," he said calmly.

"'Your heart is joyous?'" she mimicked him, drawing back to look at his silver eyes, then laughed and hugged him again. "By the gods, Stavark, we thought you were dead! All we found was your blood on the door of a shop near the attack."

"Yes."

She finally let go of him, and he stood with his hands at his sides, watching her with his eternally serious little-boy expression. What in the lands made him so serious? "But you survived," she said.

"And you brought Orem's dream to life," he said. "You freed the maehka to live in the lands again."

"We all did," she said. "Now it's time to make sure we all can celebrate together. Is Orem with you?"

He paused, then shook his head. "No, Maehka vik Kalik."

Her heart sank. She had hoped to find them together. "What...what happened to him?"

"I do not know. Like you, I have come to find that out," he said. "I...could not protect him. We were separated. When I returned to where we were attacked, he was gone."

"Did they eat him?" Medophae asked the question Mirolah dreaded. Her stomach fluttered. It made her sick just to think about it.

"I think not, Rabasyvihrk," Stavark said. "There would have been...something left. There was nothing."

"Do you think they took him?" Medophae pressed.

"I do not know."

"We will find him," Mirolah said.

"Yes, Maehka vik Kalik."

"Please call me Mirolah," she said.

He paused, then nodded slowly. "If you wish. I will do that."

"I wish," she said.

Medophae chuckled. They both turned to look at him. "I knew you could work miracles, but taking the formality out of Stavark, that is a feat. Stavark, who is your friend?"

The girl quicksilver, taller than Stavark, maybe a few years older, stood respectfully at a distance, hands at her sides. She was a willowy thing, with long, slender arms and legs. She wore nearly the same type of clothing as Stavark: an ash-gray and green shirt belted at the waist, loose pants good for running through the forest, and soft boots. Her hair was waist-length and shimmering silver. The angles of her chin and cheeks were softer compared to Stavark's sharp features, though still far sharper than that of a human, and her pointed ears were nearly as tall as the top of her head. Her eyes were huge. Mirolah didn't know much about quicksilvers, but she'd be willing to bet Elekkena's eyes were larger than average for a quicksilver. They were certainly larger than Stavark's, and they were much darker, almost a graphite color.

"Rabasyvihrk, Maehka..." Stavark paused, then corrected himself. "Mirolah, this is Elekkena."

Mirolah said, "She is your sister—?"

"No," Stavark interrupted. "She is a syvihrk who chose to accompany me."

"Stavark does not like me to be here," Elekkena said. "He is brave, and he wishes to show his courage by pretending he is an island, connected to—and needing—no one. He feels this will prove to our people, especially his mother, that he is worthy. He does not realize that his legend is already large." She paused. "In this alone he is shortsighted, but such a quality is found in the best leaders. It is an honor to assist him."

Stavark looked at Elekkena, his mouth open. Mirolah had never seen him stunned before. She glanced at Medophae, feeling like she had walked into the middle of something deeply private. "Uh." She struggled to find words.

"You are welcome among us, Elekkena," Medophae cut in smoothly. He came forward, towering over her, almost twice her height, and extended his hand.

"Stavark's legend is large among the syvihrk," she repeated. "But everyone knows of the Rabasyvihrk." She didn't take his hand, but instead descended into a graceful curtsey. "It honors me to be filled with your presence."

Medophae hesitated, which wasn't typical of him. He was usually as graceful as a king in these kinds of situations. She wondered what he was thinking.

"The pleasure is mine," he said, hesitating again, then bowing.

Elekkena turned to Mirolah. "Stavark speaks nothing but bright truths about you, Maehka vik Kalik. He says life trails behind the tread of your feet. I am honored to meet you." She dipped into that curtsey again, like a graceful reed bending forward in a breeze.

Mirolah couldn't read Elekkena's emotions. Of course, Stavark had been difficult to read in the beginning, but he was much more transparent now. She saw his desire to find Orem like a firebrand in the dark, a twin to her own desire. She saw his excitement at Medophae's presence, masked by diffidence to ensure Medophae didn't know how important he was to Stavark. She felt Stavark's surprise and newfound curiosity when he looked at his Elekkena. That, perhaps more than anything else, aroused Mirolah's own curiosity. Stavark did not know his companion well. She wondered how they had met.

Elekkena's aura danced with silvery rainbow colors like Stavark's, but it danced with something more. Mirolah could not put her finger on it, but the girl was different. Could it be that all quicksilvers looked different? This was only the second one she'd ever met.

"It's good to meet you," Mirolah said.

"You'll want to visit the library," Elekkena said.

Mirolah glanced at Medophae, then back at Elekkena. Was mind-reading something that quicksilvers did? Except Mirolah had been mind-probed, mind-controlled and mind-read before, and there was no invasion of her threads at the moment. "Well...yes," she said. "You know Denema's Valley?"

"I have been here before," Elekkena said.

"Why the library?" Medophae asked.

"If Orem survived and wanted to leave a message for me he would leave it there. It was the first place I'd intended to check." Orem would know that. But Elekkena wouldn't.

She looked at the quicksilver girl. Mirolah ached to probe that strange silver-and-rainbow aura, but the girl was watching her. She sensed that if she tried to sneak into Elekkena's threads and figure out what was different about her, the girl would know. It also smacked of something Ethiel would do. Mirolah's curiosity was eating her alive, but taking from another—even something as innocent as knowledge—was a violation of privacy. She kept her threadweaver "fingers" to herself.

Stavark trusts her. I will, too.

"Why don't Stavark and I inspect the site of the darkling battle," Medophae said. "It was the last place we saw him; there might be something there. You and Elekkena check the library."

"Okay," Mirolah said.

Elekkena nodded as though there was no other possible outcome.

24

MIROLAH

MIROLAH STEPPED into the old library. The memories flowed over her like a river. She stood a long time in the doorway, then called the bright bridge and connected herself to the threads running throughout each object in the room. At a glance, nothing had been moved, but the place danced with GodSpill. When she had first come here with Orem weeks ago, all she had seen was books, a broken ceiling, moss on the walls and water on the floor. Now thin strands of gold and blue, red and green streaked across the room.

Orem had wanted to see the world this way, with the vision of a threadweaver.

Where are you, my friend?

She thrust away from the doorjamb and walked into the center of the room. Elekkena followed her like a ghost.

Mirolah stepped into the puddles without a care. She knew now why nothing had ever decayed here. She knew why the moss had only eaten through certain books. She had discovered many things since her rebirth at Daylan's Fountain. So many things about Daylan Morth, Harleath Markin, and the Great Dying had come clear.

GodSpill had never completely left the lands; it was a raging river that had been dammed, leaving only a few sad mud puddles remaining. Life and GodSpill were intertwined. It was the force of creation from which the gods had made everything. For life to exist at all, there had to be traces of GodSpill. One could not exist without the other.

That was why this library and this city had not completely crumbled. The spells laid on this place pulled from the scant, remaining puddles of GodSpill, enough to keep some of the books safe through the ravages of time. Every tome in this great library of Denema's Valley had some kind of preservation spell laid on it. The books with lesser spells had fallen to the ravages of time, but not the greater ones.

She drew a finger down one of the books. How that must have confounded Orem. To know there was a supernatural reason why the books stayed, but to be unable to see it, to explain it. She closed her eyes and pressed her palm against the spine of the book. She could almost feel him here, watching her study, forcing her to study.

The tears came then, and she let her hand drop as she cried.

That was when she saw it.

The tiny orb, clutched in a silver claw that tapered to a needle point, hovered several inches above a nearby table. An open book lay beneath the orb. The memories flooded back to her. That was Harleath Markin's journal and that strange artifact she'd found with it the night Medophae arrived.

She moved closer, studying the subtle threads that swirled about the item. They were primarily blue and green. A few thin tendrils of red wound through like veins. The orb had called to her back then. She awoke from a deep sleep to its whispers in her mind, but she never had a chance to study it. Medophae had arrived that same night, at almost that same instant. Then the darklings. Then Ethiel. Her life turned upside down and the thought of some relic from the GodSpill Wars was forgotten.

She lifted the orb from its place, and it went heavy in her hand. Holding it over another part of the table, she let it go. It fell, slowed, and righted itself, hovering a few inches above the wood.

She didn't know how to create something so intricate. Certainly Mirolah could create things, but they were huge, crude things, like the stairway down to the portal in Keleera. She could reform something that already existed easily enough, but something like this orb wasn't just formed, it was filled with purpose. It protected itself and served a function, though she didn't know what that function was.

Mirolah touched the book next to Harleath's journal. *The Ways of GodSpill* by Dessil Corvayn. It was the last book he'd been reading. Orem had wanted her to read this book so badly when she first arrived. Now she knew more about the threads than Dessil Corvayn had ever learned. She flipped through each page meticulously, looking for anything that indicated Orem had been here after the darkling attack. She looked for loose notes, revisited the two chapters Orem had made her memorize.

There was nothing in the book, no handwritten notes in the margins or slips of paper tucked between the pages. She gently shelved it, but she kept Harleath's journal and took the orb in hand. She suspected Harleath's ghost had vanished once his horrible mistake had been rectified, but if she ever met him again, she would give him back his musings.

She looked at Elekkena, who had respectfully kept her distance, studying shelves on the far side of the library. The lanky quicksilver girl never made any noise at all, moving along the floor like she was floating. Mirolah wondered what it must be like to be so graceful.

Seeming to sense her stare, Elekkena turned. "Did he leave anything for you?" she asked, moving toward Mirolah.

"Nothing to solve the mystery of what happened to him."

"We will keep looking."

"I don't do well with mysteries," Mirolah said. "An unanswered question is like an itch between my shoulder blades that I can't reach."

"The curse of the threadweaver," Elekkena said.

"So you've heard of it," Mirolah said. Orem had said almost the same thing to her.

"Yes."

"You know, talking with Stavark, I find that he is unfamiliar with many common sayings and phrases that humans use. You aren't."

Elekkena paused on the other side of the table. Her dark silver gaze held Mirolah's.

"I have traveled."

"A lot, apparently. You've been to this library before?" Mirolah asked.

"Yes."

The girl's silver and rainbow aura reminded Mirolah of Medophae's golden fire of protection. Except that with Oedandus, the protection was just sheer power, a wall she couldn't push through with all the GodSpill in the world. With this girl, it was like the threads shifted and moved in rotation, creating and recreating a net, holding in the girl's emotions that would otherwise leak out, and...distracting Mirolah's threadweaver vision. Mirolah found she didn't actually *want* to look at it for long, like it was somehow repulsive, like it was convincing her to look away.

That was odd. She itched to dig into it and understand it. Without putting her threadweaver "fingers" on it, Mirolah would guess it was some highly complicated threadweaver spell. Was the girl ensorcelled?

Elekkena's sharp cheekbones drew shadows across her jaw line in the singular torchlight. "What I told you was true," she said. "Stavark will be a great leader of the syvihrk someday. He must be protected. I came with him to help him find his way, to be a companion to him. But there is more to my truth..." She paused. "I came to help myself, too."

"What do you mean?"

"I came to find you," Elekkena said.

Mirolah opened her mouth to respond, then found she didn't have any words to respond to that. "We...we haven't met before," she said.

"You are the Maehka vik Kalik."

The Maehka vik Kalik... No. Could it be that this girl was...

Mirolah reached through the threads and took a book from the high shelves behind Elekkena. She made the book float toward Elekkena's back, slowly and steadily.

When it had almost reached the quicksilver, Mirolah felt another tug on the threads. She let the book go, and it floated behind Elekkena. Ponderously, it floated around her, then dropped onto the table with a thump.

"You're a threadweaver!" Mirolah exclaimed.

"Yes."

Mirolah moved around the table and wrapped the quicksilver girl in a hug. Elekkena went stiff, skittish as a rabbit, but Mirolah held on. After a moment, Elekkena accepted the embrace and hugged her back, just like Stavark had.

"Humans are strange," she murmured against Mirolah's shoulder. "This custom of grasping another... It is like beasts trying to dominate each other."

Mirolah laughed softly and released her. "It is meant to be comforting."

"It is alarming," she said bluntly.

"I won't do it again."

"No," she said. "It is okay. It is important to...embrace the unknown." She smiled briefly.

"Have you told Stavark?"

She shook her head. "I would prefer if only you knew."

"Please, sit," Mirolah said. Elekkena looked at the chair, then sat down. Mirolah joined her. "Tell me what has been happening to you. Tell me what you see."

"I see colors sometimes," Elekkena said. "I noticed this library. It has colors every now and then. And sometimes, when I reach out, I can see a bright tunnel between me and other objects. And through that bright tunnel, I can...touch the colors. Or, well, not actually touch them, but touch what makes the object. There are smaller parts within an object. Smaller...colors."

"Those are its threads."

She drew in a quick breath. "This is why we are called thread-weavers! Those smaller colors are threads."

Elekkena couldn't see them, but she could still make a book float. That seemed so strange to Mirolah. The first time she could do anything with the GodSpill was after she'd seen the threads for the first time. "How do you move things, then?" Mirolah asked.

"I tell them where to go, but I can only move basic things. Just holding onto the book was difficult. I could make it float, and I could drop it, but I couldn't make it spin in place. I could not open it and move the pages."

"I brought it from behind you so you could not see it. When did you notice the book was floating toward you?"

She reached out her arm behind her head. "About here."

So her range was not nearly as long as Mirolah's, and she saw the bright bridge, but not the threads, though she sensed that she was manipulating smaller pieces within the objects.

"And sometimes," Elekkena said. "I can see what others feel. Especially for those whose feelings trample over them. Those are easiest to see. But you, I cannot see. You have shifting colors, but no feelings that sneak out. And the Rabasyvihrk, I cannot see. A golden flame surrounds him."

That was why Mirolah couldn't read the girl's emotions. It wasn't some complicated spell. It was what another threadweaver looked like!

"Well, with Medophae," Mirolah said, smiling, "just try looking at his face. What he feels is usually right there."

Elekkena gave a ghost of a smile in return. "Maehka vik Kalik, will you teach me how to use the maehka?"

"On one condition," she said.

Elekkena regarded her seriously.

"Stop calling me Maehka vik Kalik and call me Mirolah."

Elekkena hesitated, then nodded. "I would be honored to do so...Mirolah."

"Then I'm happy to help you."

"Thank you, Mirolah."

"Good. Let's start tonight, a brief lesson right now, yes?" Having a friendly threadweaver around was exciting. Every threadweaver she'd ever met, besides the ghost of Harleath Markin, had tried to kill her. There was so much Mirolah could learn from Elekkena, even as Elekkena learned from her.

"Okay, let's just start with—"

A whine cut her off, and she looked up to see the skin dog standing in the doorway.

25

MIROLAH

MIROLAH STOOD UP, and Elekkena slid fluidly from her chair to stand with her. The skin dog's huge frame darkened the doorway, but he did not come inside.

"A vyrkiz," Elekkena said.

"It's okay. He's with us," Mirolah said. "I think."

"He is following you?"

"Yes."

"He has not attacked you."

"No. He seems...almost afraid of me," Mirolah said.

"He can smell the GodSpill on you," Elekkena said. "It is fearsome to him. Are you bonded?"

"Medophae asked the same thing. No," Mirolah said. "We aren't bonded."

"Interesting," she said.

"That we're not bonded?"

"No, you *are* bonded. It is interesting that you don't know it."

"He's just trailing us. I think he's curious about me. I haven't done any bonding of anything."

"A vyrkiz isn't curious. You never see one unless you are pack or prey." Elekkena spoke a short rhyme:

If vyrkiz hunts
And bond is true
The vyrkiz never hunts for you

If vyrkiz comes
With no bond laid
From vyrkiz teeth your grave is made

"A quicksilver nursery rhyme?" Mirolah asked, wrinkling her brow at the gruesome poem.

Elekkena gave a polite smile. "No. It is a human rhyme. A caution on the nature of the vyrkiz, to remind the unwary that, for these beasts, it is one or the other."

"Sniff the GodSpill," the dog whined. "Bad GodSpill. Dark GodSpill." The skinny dog shivered as though cold. He raised his head and lowered it but always kept his gaze on Mirolah.

"Come in," Mirolah beckoned the skin dog. "You are safe here."

The skin dog whined and shifted on his thin legs but did not enter the library. He looked nervously around, then back at Mirolah, lowered his head and whined again.

It took Mirolah a second to understand. The library was full of GodSpill. Perhaps it "smelled" too strong to him. She crossed the room and touched the skin dog gently on his flat head. It was warm and hard, skin over muscle and bone.

He snapped his long jaws three times, and she jumped, startled. He cringed, dropping to press his chest against the ground.

"This one greets," he whined. "This one greets. No harm! No bite!"

"That's how you say hello?" Mirolah asked.

"Yes," he yipped quietly, glancing up from where he groveled on the ground. "Snap teeth. This one greets."

"Okay."

Slowly, the skin dog rose again. His tail came up and wagged.

He pressed his bony head against her leg. She felt his bramble of teeth through her skirt and breeches.

"Won't do again," the skin dog said. "Not scare you."

"No, I like it. I'll know next time," she said. She looked down at the dog and clacked her own teeth together.

The skin dog gave a bark, and his bony tail wagged hard.

Mirolah turned to see Elekkena watching her curiously. "You're talking to him?" she asked.

"It's... Well, yes."

Elekkena bowed her head in reverence. "Maehka vik Kalik."

"Stop it," Mirolah said. "We had a deal."

"Yes, Mirolah," Elekkena said, but the way she said it had the same reverence as the quicksilver title. And she bowed her head.

"And no bowing," Mirolah said. "Don't do that."

"Have you named him?" Elekkena asked.

"I...no. We're not bonded. I just—"

"You should name him."

"Look, he probably already has a name." Mirolah looked back at the skin dog. "Do you have a name?"

"I sniff the GodSpill," he yipped.

"But do you have a name?"

"Sniff the GodSpill," he whined. His tail stopped wagging.

"No," Mirolah said. "An actual *name*."

The skin dog cringed. "Sniff the GodSpill," he whimpered.

"It's okay. It's okay," she said. It was like talking to a four-year-old child with giant teeth. "You sniff the GodSpill. Look, I'm just going to call you Sniff. You can choose your own name when you want to. I mean, if you want to."

The skin dog's tail came up and wagged again. "Sniff the GodSpill," he assured her. He raised his head and sniffed the air. "You come. Human house," Sniff barked. "Bad GodSpill."

Excitement thrilled through her belly. Bad GodSpill. That could mean darklings. It could mean Orem.

"Yes," she said. She glanced over her shoulder at Elekkena. "Let's get the boys first."

Mirolah and Elekkena stopped by the city circle where the darkling corpses still littered the street. The bodies were stiff where they had fallen, dried but not decaying, as though nature wouldn't touch them. Medophae and Stavark looked up as they arrived. Sniff barked, and Stavark raised his silver eyebrows.

"Sniff found something," Mirolah said.

"Who?" Medophae glanced over at the huge skin dog. "Oh. You *named* him." He raised an eyebrow.

"Shut up."

He gave an insufferably smug smile and held his hands up in a pacifying gesture. "I didn't say anything."

"Let's go," Mirolah said. Sniff started up the street, and they all jogged after him.

They soon arrived at a large, low building. Sniff stopped in front of the closed door and barked.

"He says he has found bad GodSpill inside," Mirolah translated. And now she could see it. From a distance, it would have seemed like just another house, but now that she stood close, she could see the threads inside the house. It was like they had been yanked open, twisted around, then left that way, rent unnaturally wide.

Elekkena spoke quietly to Stavark in the tongue of the quicksilvers.

"This is a bad place," Stavark said, and he moved toward the door. Sniff whined, as if in agreement.

"Wait," Medophae said. "I'll go first."

26

MEDOPHAE

"ARE YOU SURE?" Mirolah asked. "If there's a spell upon this place—"

"Then I'm the one best equipped to survive. Stay back until I cross the threshold."

Medophae put his hand on the door, expecting any moment for something to trigger, a blast of flame, an attack on his mind.

He opened it and entered, peering around. It was exactly what he expected. He'd seen lairs like this before. This was a house for dead things. Decay rode the air.

Charred ropes dangled like dead snakes from a burnt bed. A wide, oak table carried disparate objects. Spell components. A dagger lay next to a bunch of herbs tied together with twine. A pot of dirt hunkered in the right-hand corner of the table. There were fleshy lumps on the table that he could not make out.

He moved closer, following the smell of decay. The rotting lumps had once been animals. Some kind of fish and...was that a rockfire toad? Dried blood on the dagger told the story, and Medophae felt a twist in his guts. Zilok had been here.

He heard Mirolah's footstep on the threshold.

"Be careful," he said. "This was where Zilok worked his spell on me."

Stavark and Elekkena slipped in behind her.

"I've seen his workshops before. This is what they look like."

"He was here? In Denema's Valley?" Mirolah asked. "While we were here?"

"That is exactly the kind of thing Zilok does. He finds himself particularly clever when he's hiding in plain sight."

She looked at the table, her brow wrinkled and her mouth open. "He killed these animals?" She touched the rotting, half-charred rockfire toad. "Why would he do that?"

"Zilok is the kind of threadweaver who uses components to guide his thoughts. To steady his mind. To keep the picture of what he wants firmly focused. These were his components."

"Living things? Why not use objects?"

"Lives *are* objects to Zilok. It's all the same to him. He spent a long time learning to view the world differently. What appalls you comforts him."

"That's disgusting," she whispered.

"He's not really a person anymore."

"Look," Elekkena said. She had gone to the far side of the room, a shadowed little corner with a steel ring bolted into the floor. Empty manacles lay in a pile. Elekkena stepped aside, and they looked at a small cache of two pouches and a wide, thick book bag.

"Orem!" Mirolah raced around the table and dropped to her knees next to the book bag.

She flipped open the leather flap and pulled out a book. "It's *52 Ways to Threadweave* by Beverid Lorz," she said. "He was here." She closed her eyes, and Medophae recognized that type of trance. She was searching the threads, looking for Orem. Or Orem's body.

"The only corpses in this room are the ones on the table," she said a moment later, opening her eyes. "But he was here. He was alive. For at least a little while."

Medophae put two and two together. "Zilok drove away the darklings. For some reason, he decided to save Orem."

"Why?" Mirolah asked.

"To use him," Medophae said. "Zilok always has a purpose."

"But why would Zilok need..." She stopped in mid-sentence.

"What is it?" Medophae asked.

"By the gods..." she murmured.

"Mirolah—"

"Anchor," she said.

A cold chill ran up Medophae's spine. "Sef was Zilok's anchor," he murmured.

"And Vaerdaro killed him," she said.

"Oh gods..." Medophae said.

"Zilok Morth isn't gone," she spoke his dread. "He's not dead. Orem is Zilok's new anchor."

27

ZILOK MORTH

ZILOK MORTH COALESCED in the Coreworld, obsidian walls glistening with moisture that looked like diamonds. Everything sparkled when he was this full of GodSpill. It roiled within him, stolen from the Godgate only moments before. He needed it. If his calculations were correct, this overwhelming amount of GodSpill would deliver victory today.

Though there was no obvious source of light, he could see as though it was dusk, as though some illumination oozed from the black walls themselves. The floor, ceiling, and walls were smooth and flat. There were miles of hallways and rooms, twisting and turning for no apparent reason, all empty. Or so it seemed.

At first glance, one might wonder who made this place, and why? Had it been abandoned? Why was it empty?

But it wasn't empty. There were cracks all over this flat floor, in these walls, in the smooth ceiling. These cracks, invisible to Zilok, represented the life and destiny of every mortal. He reached out with his threadweaver sight and tried to see them, but he couldn't. He never could.

The goddess Natra, maker of the world, had created this place, and she had set protections around it such that none could tamper with it. Anyone who might manage to find this place would be summarily killed. Immortal, obsidian guardians came out of the walls for any disturbance. Even the slightest touch on the invisible waters within those invisible cracks would bring the guardians, and they were immune to threadweaving.

The entire labyrinth was made of some unearthly obsidian, and it did not have threads. Zilok couldn't manipulate it no matter what he did. To even arrive in this place was a harrowing journey, like squeezing himself through the eye of a needle.

The Coreworld intrigued him...and frightened him. His curiosity harried him to understand it, but he was nearly helpless here. There was no GodSpill from which to draw, which meant he'd had to bring a reserve with him, and every moment he stayed, his reserves slowly bled away, and he became weaker. If he stayed too long, he simply wouldn't have the ability to push his way out again, and that would be the end of him.

But the Coreworld was important somehow, integral to the great tapestry Natra had woven. Even if he didn't understand how it worked, he knew that much. He could feel the magnitude of power all around him. Here, if you were one of the few who could see the invisible cracks—the flows of destiny—you could predict the future.

So far as Zilok knew, only unicorns could see the cracks and the flows of destiny within.

As a spirit, Zilok Morth could travel the threads to wherever he wanted. The threads of the world, everything the gods had created—except this place—were imbued with GodSpill. When Zilok had first lashed himself to an anchor, denying death, he had discovered his ability to travel great distances at will. He could sink into the very GodSpill that saturated the threads, and travel along them like oil down a string.

He had experimented. He had traveled to all the places that would be dangerous to a mortal man. He went to the top of the Spine Mountains, to the center of the Sunrider culture. He braved the perils of the dragonlands, Irgakth. He even went across the sea to Dandere, the island where his once best friend and now immortal enemy, Medophae, had been born.

And he had stumbled across the Coreworld, a place so secret that almost no one knew it existed. Even, he suspected, the other gods.

He had found unicorns here the first time he'd come here. At first, he had thought they were the guardians, but he soon came to learn that they were interlopers like him. They hid from the real guardians, viewing the cracks of destiny, playing with the future, influencing events with their knowledge.

Of course, Zilok had not discovered this information until after he had captured one of them. While the obsidian guardians were immune to threadweaving, the unicorns were not. So he had taken one, tortured it, and learned from it.

The unicorn's name had been Lynvarion, and under the right pressure, he had revealed everything: how the Coreworld came to be, that it was Natra who created it, that it bore deep secrets and power and finally, unforgivably, that these unicorns had been aiding the Wildmane in his arrogant endeavors. These unicorns had been instrumental in ensuring the Wildmane prevailed, over and over again. So many times Zilok had thought that the Wild-mane had some unseen, unfair advantage, and finally he knew it was true.

Zilok returned to the Coreworld and killed every unicorn.

Or so he had thought.

The first thing he'd done when he had returned to sentience after Daylan's Fountain began leaking was to plan to destroy the Wildmane. The second thing he did was return to the Coreworld to see if, by some unlikely chance, there were any unicorns remaining that might thwart him by reading the future and moving events. Sure enough, he had found one, and he'd made sure the obsidian guardians destroyed her. There would be no more stacking the deck in favor of the Wildmane.

But then something new had arisen. That damned thread-weaver from Rith had interfered and changed the balance of things just enough that Zilok had once again failed. Zilok intended to pull that thorn before he and Medophae faced one another. The Threadweaver of Rith was talented, but Zilok had dealt with talented threadweavers before.

He flowed through the granite hallways, carefully watching. Touching the invisible waters of destiny inside the invisible cracks brought the guardians like falling anvils, so he stayed well away from the walls, ceilings, and floors.

Lynvarion the unicorn had rambled about many things during his torture. He'd been hard to break. It had taken Zilok two weeks and, toward the end, creative techniques before the unicorn began to spill his knowledge. But once he snapped, he babbled as if in a trance.

Zilok had learned about the guardians, the cracks and the water of destiny within them. He'd learned that the unicorns had been created by Saraphazia's daughter, Vaisha the Changer, and Vaisha had gifted the unicorns with her ability to see possibilities, including possible futures.

And he'd learned about Natra's treasure room. Within it were implements that Natra had used to create the world, and she left them behind when she had departed. Lynvarion had described a scythe, three books, a tall staff, two spheres, a short wooden stick, and a crown made of green vines grasping upright crystals.

The last was Natra's Crown, imbued with the power to destroy a god, mentioned only in the oldest recorded human text, a journal written by a woman named Shev Lek. Shev Lek recorded a conversation with the goddess Natra, back when the great goddess would sometimes take walks with certain mortals of the different sentient races. Shev Lek described a crown that Natra wore, and Natra had said the crown was the reason none of the other gods would challenge her. The crown could redirect any god's power, enabling the wearer to utilize that power in any way she saw fit, to even redirect it at the god from whence it had come.

Natra's Crown was a god-killer. It was Natra's insurance that none of her unruly children or siblings ever turned on her. And she had left it here in the Coreworld.

Zilok slowed as he neared the great archway. It was easily fifteen feet tall, a pointed arch with bordering black stones as wide as a human was tall, each lighter than the dark obsidian of the wall, each inscribed with a curse in white, flickering sigils.

Zilok had known about Natra's treasure room since he had first come to the Coreworld a millennium ago, but he had never entered. The goddess who had birthed all life had created those curses.

But Zilok had no choice. He had tried and failed too many times to cling to caution now. He needed the power of a god on his side. He couldn't continue to be this errant spirit, tied to the world only by his rage at the injustice that a person like Medophae could have the power of a god when he, Zilok, did not.

Beyond the threshold of the treasure room were artifacts that would elevate him to Medophae's level. Then, at long last, they would have their final battle.

The tall archway was beaded with moisture. The words weren't written in any language of humankind, but Zilok had studied the writing of the gods, and he could read it. The words were warnings from Natra to her fellow deities:

> My love, my dedicated bind, take these up and all
>   unwinds.
> Brother, leave these peaks untouched, or face the
>   fear you fear so much.
> Zetu, father, keep your place, it's not with these to
>   join the race.
> Dervon if, for greed's sweet sake, you wield my
>   tools, your soul will break.

Saraphazia, endless toil, touch these and your
  waters boil.
Thalius, my jaunty son, dance with these, your
  dancing's done.

Those who seek, please walk away, take your
  pleasure in the day.
I've made it, and it's free for you. A joyous life with
  simple truths.
But touch these items, flesh will rot. In decaying
  throes you're caught.
These, my children, let them be. Or lose all this
  that makes you free.

If these warnings you can't heed, if wisdom is
  subsumed by need,
Then breach the threshold, do not wait, and face
  the horror of your fate.

A warning to all. A rhyming fairy tale to turn away the faint of heart.

Zilok floated there for a moment. He could see the tools beyond, laying about the room like lounging prostitutes in a pleasure house. There was the scythe, flat on the floor. The three books were piled on a black stone table, and the gnarled oak staff leaned against the wall. Two floating spheres of different sizes—the small one clear, the large one filled with swirling blue smoke—hung in the middle of the room. An ancient wand lay next to a jeweled dagger on a shelf that stuck out from the wall. And there at the back of the room, on its own little pedestal, sat a crown made of green vines grasping upright crystals.

Natra's Crown.

This was it. Never step backward. Always step forward. It was time to play his gamble.

Zilok entered the room.

He heard a sigh in his mind, sad. The sigh passed through him like a breath.

The obsidian guardians fell from the ceiling and walls in the hallway behind him, black boulders thumping to the floor, unfurling into the humanoid obsidian guardians. These creatures weren't mortal, weren't natural, and their speed was not to be believed. They charged ahead even as Zilok flew at the crystal crown.

He felt the jerk as they severed the ethereal cord that led back to Orem, his anchor to this mortal plane. Zilok couldn't see the Godgate here in the Coreworld, but it yanked him upward immediately.

Zilok let loose all of the GodSpill he had brought with him, using it all to wrap himself up and push his spirit into those crystals. This was the moment. If Zilok had made a mistake, if the crown didn't do what he thought it did, then Medophae had won. There would be no final battle. The Godgate would pull Zilok upward, into its greedy maw, and he would die.

The crystals in the crown flickered a soft magenta light. They took hold of the GodSpill and it drew it in. The call of the Godgate was powerful, but it was nothing like this. Natra's Crown sucked in the GodSpill and Zilok with it. He swirled into those magenta crystals, which were as vast as a kingdom.

He lashed himself to the inside of the crown, creating a new anchor, and looked out onto Natra's treasure room through a magenta-tinged, crystal lens.

The obsidians turned, searching for him, then began making their way back to the hall outside, thinking their job was finished, thinking they had dispatched the invader. If Zilok had had breath, he would have laughed. The GodSpill he had brought swirled inside the crystals of the crown, holding his spirit.

Zilok lifted the crown into the air, and the obsidian guardians turned as one, stunned. He saw their essence clearly now, how this entire cavern was a solid construct of pure GodSpill, unbound by threads. It was why the obsidian guardians had so easily been able to sever his cord, why threadweavers could not even touch them. The obsidian rock was all one organism, and each humanoid "guardian" was like a tentacle.

They leapt at him.

He used the power of the crown, sucking the GodSpill from each of the humanoid guardians. They dropped like lumps of mud, no longer animate.

He raced back through the hallways, the crown floating behind him, until he reached the spot where he could escape to the mortal world, back to the tapestry Natra had created using this very crown.

Obsidian guardians plopped onto the ground and unfurled.

He expected them to run after him, to reach out toward him, try to swat him down, perhaps to drop from the ceiling on top of him, but they didn't. They only stood there, at attention, watching.

Zilok reached his arrival spot, that one area he'd discovered long ago, and pushed himself through the needle-thin portal out of the Coreworld. The crown bent with him, flattening, spiraling, and pouring through the portal as though it had as little form as he did.

He appeared on the grassy plain north of the ruins of Belshra. Floating next to him was Natra's Crown, the green vines writhing and moving about in a circlet, intertwining with the six tall, pointed crystals that formed the front of the crown.

He lifted it and put it on his insubstantial head, but he could feel the writhing of the vines as though he still had a mortal head. It touched him like it recognized him, settled onto his nonexistent brow as though it had been made for him.

There were entire mountains of caverns inside those crystals, waiting to be filled with the energy of a god.

Zilok formed the vision of his once-mortal body, black vest, and pants and boots, and he stood there, looking out over the plains.

No guardians chased him. Nothing came to challenge him.

And nothing ever would again.

He laughed.

28

YNISAAN

YNISAAN STOOD IN THE SHADOWS, aghast. It wasn't possible. It just wasn't possible.

She watched the Obsidians converge on Zilok Morth, and she felt joy at his foolishness. The Obsidians were immune to thread-weaving. They would crush him, and with Zilok Morth destroyed, shepherding Medophae would be easier.

Then she had watched Zilok reach Natra's Crown and use it to turn the Obsidians to mud. He fled, squeezing out of the Core-world into the mortal world.

With Natra's Crown.

She forced herself to control her breathing, but she couldn't put down her panic.

Natra's Crown was an unimaginably powerful weapon. Natra had ruled the other gods with it. She couldn't even conceive of what Zilok might do with it.

How had he made it past the Obsidians? Why hadn't the curse destroyed him?

Get yourself together. Move past your incredulity. Act. Somehow, he has done it. Now you must see what that means.

From the shadows, she breathed deeply and opened her

special unicorn's sight, viewing the possible destinies of those cracks beneath her feet, behind her on the wall, overhead on the ceiling. They appeared as ghost lines meandering ahead of each crack, showing her the destinies of those the cracks represented.

They had all changed.

By the gods...

Down the hallway and two rooms away was the crack that represented Medophae, intertwined with the crack that represented Mirolah, the threadweaver. Ynisaan longed to gallop to that room, to see what had changed, but she couldn't. She was an intruder here as surely as Zilok Morth. If the Obsidians caught her, they'd kill her, so she waited.

The Obsidians roamed about looking for Zilok, and Ynisaan stayed in her supernatural shadow, safe for the moment. She thought of the future she had seen just moments ago. Medophae and Mirolah's futures.

They would have braced Zilok Morth in the kingdom of Teni'sia, and there they would have defeated him. There had been dozens of possibilities for that outcome. Afterward, Medophae would have prepared the kingdom of Teni'sia for Avakketh's attack.

Ynisaan had seen the best scenario. Under the thread of unleashing Oedandus, Avakketh would have agreed to a parley, an agreement on set boundaries between the lands of Irgakth and Amarion. They could have avoided a war altogether.

After settling that, Medophae and Mirolah would have married. Mirolah would soon wrestle her overwhelming threadweaving talent under control, and the two of them would become stewards of Amarion's reconstruction, traveling from kingdom to kingdom with knowledge and assistance. They would make a lifetime of happy memories before Mirolah died at age eighty-seven.

After an hour of fruitless searching, the Obsidians finally curled into lumps. Some flew up and splatted against the ceiling, vanishing into the darkness. Some leapt into the walls and got reabsorbed. Some sank directly into the floor.

It was quiet in the Coreworld.

Ynisaan crept from her hiding place to the room with the two cracks that mattered above all others: Medophae's and Mirolah's. She stood over the many cracks in the room and looked at those two with her unicorn's vision...

No. Oh, no....

Every bright possibility was gone. Zilok Morth won the conflict at Teni'sia in every scenario. Ynisaan searched frantically, looking deeper. Sometimes, an unlikely future would appear if she searched the lives of the most unlikely people, finding a secret moment where, if they could just be nudged to help Medophae, things would change.

But all of it was gone, and Ynisaan searched frantically for the best possible scenario.

No matter how she followed the ghostly lines, all of them ended with Zilok Morth's victory, Medophae's elimination from the war, and humankind's subsequent destruction at the hands of Avakketh.

She strained, her brain reaching its breaking point, but she couldn't stop. Finding unlikely possibilities required that she hold all the other possibilities in her head while she searched. If she let go, they'd all vanish. She had to hold them until she found...until she found...

...a way through. There!

She paused, seeing it now, the grisly pathway through this horrible turn of events. There was one. Only one.

Ynisaan bowed her head. Not for the first time, she loathed who she was, that she knew who must be sacrificed so that humankind might survive.

Oh, Mirolah... Sweet girl. You're the best of them. It's not fair.

Ynisaan touched her obsidian horn to the dark walls and pulled back from the Coreworld, leaving the cracks and their water of life behind. But she kept the memory of what must happen.

To turn aside Avakketh's apocalypse, for humankind to have even a chance at survival, Mirolah must die. There wasn't a single ghost line, no possible future for the survival of Amarion, in which Mirolah lived.

29

MIROLAH

MIROLAH PULLED GodSpill from the threads outside the door, adding it to her body. It burned, filling her with vigor, but it also hurt. She could tame some of the wild GodSpill, but too much made her feel like she had needles on the inside of her skin, poking out.

She had spent hours analyzing every thread inside Zilok's lair. It had to be midnight now, and she hadn't found anything that told her where the vile spirit had taken Orem.

Again. Look again. There is a clue here. You just have to find it. Find the clue. Bridge the gap.

She drew a shaky breath. The GodSpill she had taken from the air and the street churned inside her. Her heart raced, and she couldn't think straight.

Concentrate. Try again.

She reached into the threads of Orem's manacles, seeking something else, perhaps the residue left behind by Zilok in this place. If she could catalogue it, identify it, memorize it, perhaps she could use it to track him, find him. But her threadweaver sight was fuzzy now. There was two of everything, and as she dove deeper into the tiny threads, and the fibers that made up those threads, and the fibers that made up those fibers, it just looked like a mass of writhing worms, all overlapped.

"Mirolah..."

No. She didn't have time for Medophae. He kept coming to talk to her. He wouldn't leave her alone.

Sniff, who lay unmoving at her side, raised his head and growled at Medophae. Sniff was the only one who understood how hard this was. Medophae came a step closer, and Sniff stood up, lowering his head and baring his teeth.

She forced herself to focus, to separate the different threads of the manacles. There was some clue she was overlooking. There had to be.

"There has to be..." she murmured. Because there was nothing else.

"Mirolah," Medophae said again. "Tell Sniff to back down."

The threads in the manacles, each doubled and blurry, began vibrating. She released them and let the bright bridge collapse. She slumped against the wall, put her hands to her face and sobbed.

Sniff whined and sat down, turning his head to look mournfully at Mirolah.

"I can't..." she said. "I can't find anything. There's nothing here that can help us know where to go next."

"You need to rest," he said, slipping past Sniff, who no longer growled. Medophae crouched next to her.

"He's out there right now," she said. "He needs us, and I can't find him."

He put his hands on her shoulders. "It's almost sunrise."

She looked despondently out the door, and saw light brightening the sky. She hadn't felt the coming of the sunrise. She'd thought it was midnight.

"Mirolah, you can't help him like this—"

"I can't help him at all!" she said.

"If you rest—"

"How long has that foul creature been using him, Medophae?" she said. "It's been a week since Vaerdaro killed Sef. And Orem has been under Zilok's thumb the whole time. I can only imagine..."

Sniff raised his head and howled. It started deep, in his belly, then stretched out into a high-pitched "Ooooooo..." as the dog ran out of breath.

"Zilok will keep him alive," Medophae said.

"And what torture is he suffering now, with every passing moment that I fail? I've been mind-controlled before," she said. "It's so awful.... Zilok has him, just like Ethiel had me, making him do whatever he likes. It's like having oil in your veins, slithering, sliding under your skin. It's a hand squeezing your brain where you can't reach it, where you can't make it let you go. Everything hurts. Everything is wrong. Every step she makes you take, every time she makes you raise your foot, it's like she's sticking her arm down your throat, choking you...."

"She?"

She shook her head. "I mean Zilok." But Mirolah could feel the Red Weaver inside her, saturating her threads, coating her insides with oil, making her dance like a marionette. She could feel it still, like it had just happened. It was the most horrible feeling she'd ever experienced.

Orem was feeling that same horror right now.

She lurched to her feet, lost her balance, and banged into the wall. Her head swam. "I just need to take a walk, clear my head." Sniff was suddenly there, and she put her hand on him. He was rock-steady, leaning into her, holding her upright.

"Mirolah—"

"What is the point of having all this power?" she shouted. "What is the point if I can't save the ones I love!"

She swayed off balance again, away from Sniff, and she stumbled into Medophae. "Dammit!"

He caught her. She tried to get away, to stand on her own, but he embraced her.

"You have to stop," he said.

"No!"

Sniff lowered his head and growled again.

"You can't help him like this," Medophae said softly. He lifted her up in his arms. She wanted to resist, but it felt so good to just lie there, to not move. She let out a breath, and Sniff stopped growling.

"We have to do something," she murmured. It was hard to keep her eyes open.

"We will," he said, leaving the house with Sniff following close behind. His nose was just a couple of holes on top of his toothy muzzle, but it came close, sniffing her hair. He whined.

"Attack?" he asked. "Where to attack?"

She felt his emotions flow into her. He was scared by her behavior. Angry at anyone who would stop her. He wanted to protect her. But he didn't know where the enemy was.

"I can't find him," she murmured to Sniff, and somehow her head was leaning against Medophae's shoulder now. His powerful strides were rhythmic, and they lulled her. Her eyes slid shut. "I can't protect him...."

"Find," Sniff said. "Protect."

And she fell asleep.

30

MEDOPHAE

MEDOPHAE LAID Mirolah down on her blankets by the river. The softly rushing water was natural and soothing. She'd rest well here; it had been a smart place to make camp. Once again, Stavark had proven to be exceptionally competent at everything he did.

Once Medophae had her covered, he started to rise, but Mirolah had hold of his hand. She murmured when he tried to remove it.

Stavark moved forward gracefully.

"You stay," he said. "Elekkena and I have rested."

"I don't need to sleep," Medophae said. "I can go for much longer than this without—"

"Rabasyvihrk," Elekkena interrupted. "Your strength is mighty. Everyone knows. But it is not necessary for you to be strong right now. It is necessary for you to make her stronger, and she will feel stronger with you near."

He looked down at Mirolah, then nodded. "Okay." He gave a tired chuckle, giving Elekkena a glance as he settled himself down beside Mirolah.

The quicksilver girl stood by Sniff, who whined and watched Mirolah with singular focus. Her eyelids fluttered, hearing words in the dog's noises. Elekkena put a hand on the skin dog's shoulder. The creature flinched, whipping his big, toothy head around to look at her. She kept her hand there, and slowly he turned his gaze back to Mirolah. He stopped whining.

"Thank you," Medophae said, watching her. "You're very good with..." He couldn't think of what he wanted to put at the end of that sentence. People? Animals? Everything? Elekkena was a calm presence in the background. She was like Bands in that way. His beloved had that same quality. Just her presence in a room made everyone feel secure.

"You remind me of..." he began, hesitating. "Of someone I once knew."

"Was he your friend?" she asked.

"She was. Yes."

"Was she wise?"

"Wise?" he said, smiling as he put his arms around Mirolah. "Beyond my ability to comprehend."

"Then I am honored."

"Is that what you want, Elekkena?" he asked. "To be wise?"

"It is what we all want," she said. "But only the wise know this, I think."

He gave a soft laugh and laid his head next to Mirolah's. "You even sound like her."

"Sleep, Rabasyvihrk."

It was good advice. So he did.

$$\sim$$

MEDOPHAE BEGGED FOR DEATH.

Dervon's appendages came from everywhere. Sharp, jagged spikes of black bone jutted up from the ground, lanced down from the sky. They stuck him through the belly, the chest, the neck, pinning him to the stone. They speared through his arms and legs. They speared through his head.

And yet he lived. Oedandus raged within him, healing his body, making those foul shards of bone part of him, healing his flesh around them.

During the short time Medophae had housed his god, he'd been stabbed, his arms broken. His throat had even been sliced and healed. Each of those wounds had been excruciating, but the spikes of Dervon's body burned like they had been coated in poison. And there were so many, piercing him everywhere, pinning him so he couldn't move. All he could do was scream at the pain. His mortal mind couldn't comprehend how he was alive and, as the excruciating seconds continued, he didn't want to.

He begged for death.

That was when he heard his friend's voice in his mind.

"Easy, my friend," Zilok said. "You are stopping him. You are holding him back."

"It hurts!"

"Bands is down. Tarithalius is losing. If you do not let Oedandus loose, we all die here," Zilok said.

"I can't move. I can't think. It hurts! Please, let me die."

"Not today, my friend." Zilok whispered something, and suddenly, Medophae couldn't feel his arms or his legs. He couldn't feel his cracked head or skewered chest. He was falling down a deep well away from the pains of his body. Above him was one circular hole of light, the last of what his remaining good eye could see, rising above him as he fell: Dervon's twisted, tentacled face hovering over him.

He didn't feel the pain anymore.

"What have you done?" he asked.

"You're safe now," Zilok's disembodied voice said. "You're safe. Stay there."

And Oedandus raged forth as though Zilok had unlocked a gate that the god had been trapped behind. Golden fire rushed past Medophae, shooting out of the narrow tunnel above him, shooting into Dervon's slimy, misshapen face. The dark god screamed, lurching backward as the fire roared into him, burning into his head.

No, *Medophae thought, shutting away the horrible vision.* This isn't happening. I already lived this. I already survived this.

"Yes," Avakketh said in his deep, rumbling voice. "You survived, but they had to save you. That weak mortal had to peel back your weak mind to let your true power free. Dervon would have peeled your flesh."

The blasted plateau of black rock vanished. Medophae wasn't pinned to the ground with Dervon's appendages anymore. He wasn't sunk deep down the well of his own soul. He stood on the docks of a harbor. Ships bobbed gently in their berths, waiting to take on cargo, or to offload.

A great crunching sound made him spin around, and Avakketh was there, looming just like Dervon had, but Avakketh's vast bulk was larger. He stood over the buildings of this familiar city. Medophae felt he should know this place, but he couldn't remember. He'd been in so many cities in his life, and he didn't know which this was.

Avakketh lowered himself down, crushing shops and houses. People screamed, dying beneath the falling stones and timber. Others ran.

Avakketh blew fire at them, and more people died screaming.

"Stop it!" Medophae leapt forward. The godsword burst to life in his hand.

Avakketh turned his enormous head, horns jutting from his brow and the top of his scaled head, and stopped breathing fire.

"This is your last chance," the dragon god said. "Save the ones you love. Leave the rest behind."

"I won't!"

"Then watch them die!" He swung his great head around. To his right, Bands perched gracefully on the top of a house in her dragon form, tiny compared to Avakketh, like a squirrel next to a horse. Avakketh leapt into the air, blasting her with fire. Bands roared, engulfed. She tried to get away, beat her wings to take to the air, but they burned up like paper. She crashed to the houses, and Avakketh leapt on her, raking her open her with his claws.

"Bands!" Medophae ran at the dragon god, but the fire turned toward him, burning into him. His flesh melted and healed as Oedandus kept him alive, and Medophae kept running, screaming through the pain. Avakketh flapped his great wings, rising higher, sending flames farther outward to

consume anything that would burn: wagons, houses, ships, horses, people...
Behind him, above the flames, Medophae saw the towers of Teni'sia.

Avakketh flew toward the palace, setting everything alight along the
way. Medophae tried to catch him, but he was too slow. The flames melted
him, and he fell to his knees, watching as Avakketh's claw cracked into the
side of the nearest tower.

A black horse with a curling black horn stood at the top of that crum-
bling tower, unafraid that it was about to plunge to its death. The unicorn
reared, and her dark hooves shone in the sun as she kicked and came back
down. She tossed her head, then pointed her horn at Medophae.

The castle crumbled, and the unicorn was lost. Fire rose over
Medophae's head as Teni'sia fell around him....

31

MIROLAH

MIROLAH JOLTED awake when Medophae thrashed in his sleep. She was disoriented for a moment. Then it all came to back to her. She had exhausted herself trying to find Orem last night. And now, the sun was high in the sky. It was close to noon, and they were still in Denema's Valley.

Medophae thrashed again, and she sat up. She shook him, but he wouldn't wake. His lips parted, his teeth clenched. Golden fire flickered across his chest. He growled, and his arms tensed.

"I won't!" Medophae murmured. "Bands!"

Bands...

Mirolah felt like the breath had been swept from her body. He was dreaming about *her*. She hesitated, then shook him.

"Wake up," she said.

He stopped breathing. His back arched, and the golden fire flared so that she had to shield her eyes. The flames, as ferocious as they looked, weren't hot. They didn't burn, but she could feel their power. The flames blotted out her ability to see the threads all around her.

He opened his mouth, but no sound came out. His hands

curled into claws, and he stayed that way, completely still, as if he'd died in this ghastly position.

"Medophae!" She shook him again.

He gasped and fell flat. His muscles relaxed. He drew a deep breath and suddenly sat up, blinking. He was sweating, and his eyes looked wild.

"What happened?" she asked.

"Where are we?"

"Denema's Valley."

"Denema's Valley," he whispered, blinking and looking around. "Yes. We're searching for Orem."

"Medophae, what happened? What..." she paused, then pushed forward. "What did you dream about?"

"Just...nothing," he said. "It was just a nightmare."

"Hardly nothing," she said.

She'd seen him face living nightmares without flinching. What could he possibly dream that would make him like this?

"You called out for Bands," she said softly.

"I..." he said. "I was...reliving something from the past."

"Okay," she said, and her heart hurt. The open book was closed. He was lying. She didn't need to feel his emotions to know it. He was hiding the dream from her, and it stung more deeply than she would have thought. He knew everything about her, but he was an immortal man who had seen more in his life than she could imagine. He couldn't possibly tell her everything about himself even if she had a year to listen. He had secrets, and some of those would haunt him. She had no right to expect him to tell her everything....

But he had called out Bands's name.

She had looked into his eyes on that beach in Calsinac, and he had seemed free of her. He had put her behind him, had acknowledged that she was gone forever. He'd turned to Mirolah while he cried. But now he was dreaming about Bands, and he wouldn't tell Mirolah why. If there was nothing to hide, why not just tell her?

You didn't tell him about the voice from Daylan's Glass. You didn't tell him about that, did you? Why don't you tell him about the voice?

Medophae stood up. Stavark waited a short distance away, watching them. Elekkena was on the beach, sleeping, but she roused.

What did you dream about? All unanswered questions were an itch she couldn't scratch. But this was far worse. This wasn't an itch, it was a bowel-twisting nausea. Medophae's love for Bands was legendary. Mirolah had been a fool to think he could let her go.

"I found!" Sniff barked.

Mirolah twisted to see the skin dog running toward her. He sent sand flying as he churned to a stop.

"I found!"

She jumped to her feet. "What did you find?"

"Mistress looks for bad GodSpill. Mistress looks and looks in house of bad GodSpill, but mistress cannot sniff," Sniff yipped.

"Sniff—"

"This one sniffs the GodSpill," he barked.

Hope wafted to her as she realized what he was trying to tell her. "You found a trail to Orem?"

"Bad GodSpill." He lunged away, spun back and crouched, butt in the air and head low over his front paws like he was ready to play.

"We must follow him right away," Elekkena said.

"You think he can track Zilok Morth?" Mirolah asked, daring to hope.

"That is what vyrkiz do," Elekkena said.

"That's what they were used for during the GodSpill Wars," Medophae said. "Quickly, let's pack everything up."

GS

THEY LEFT DENEMA'S VALLEY, following the skin dog east.

Stavark and Elekkena rode one horse, and Mirolah rode behind Medophae. According to Sniff, he had followed the path for a long distance, sorting out the vague scents while Mirolah and Medophae slept. Mirolah craved to know how the skin dog could do it. She couldn't find any trail at all.

She reached out and touched the GodSpill in the leaves and the grasses in front of Sniff, but she still couldn't see anything. After nearly thirty minutes of trying to find what he was "sniffing," she finally decided she had to look through his eyes.

Gently, softly, she pushed her attention into his threads, tried to feel what he was feeling, tried to see what he was seeing. For one flashing instant, she looked through his eyes, and on the air was the barest wisp of smoke, a thin, dark string that Sniff followed, barely the width of a human hair—

Sniff yelped and rolled onto the ground. He looked up at her, paws in the air, belly showing. "So sorry! How was this one bad? How was this one bad?"

"No," she said. "You're not bad, I was just—"

"So sorry!"

Mirolah dismounted and knelt next to Sniff, put a calming hand on his chest. He shivered, then went limp, turning his head to the side.

"What happened?" Medophae asked, hopping down. He looked around, trying to see the threat.

"I wanted to see how he was doing it, how he was following Zilok. So I probed him, and I...I think I hurt him."

"I was bad. How was I bad?" Sniff whined.

"I'm so sorry, Sniff." She put both hands on the pronounced ribs of his great chest, trying to soothe him. "I just wanted to see how you did it."

"Not bad?" he asked.

"No. You're doing great. It was my mistake."

He nudged her hand tentatively with his long, bramble-toothed muzzle. She patted the flat top of his head. "It's okay."

"Okay?"

"Yes."

He rolled to his feet. "Sniff the bad GodSpill?" he barked.

"Please."

He ducked his head, then turned and went to find the trail again.

"He's actually following something," she said to Medophae. "I don't know what it is, but it is there." It was odd that she could not track the GodSpill the way Sniff could. Seeing GodSpill and its effect had always come naturally to her, so why not this? Perhaps Sniff's special abilities were akin to the flashpowers of the quicksilvers. She couldn't do what Stavark did any more than she could do what Sniff did.

She and Medophae remounted their horses and continued on through the forest. After a time, she noticed a herd of deer following them. They were intensely curious, but they had smelled the big skin dog and kept their distance. Mirolah touched the light breeze that blew past her all the way to the deer. As a lark, she gently pulled the threads of the breeze, causing it to curve around the deer, then blow back this way, bringing a rush of wind that ruffled her hair.

"So," Medophae said to Stavark, "now that we've got some time, how did you escape the darklings?"

"Ah," Stavark said. "There were many. I tried to shield Orem, but they carried me away with their claws and teeth. I had to use the silverland many times to escape them. But finally, they caught me. They were about to eat me. I had many punctures from their teeth by then. But then they stopped and ran away."

"They ran?"

"I thought their master had called them back, but I realize now that perhaps it was this spirit that we are chasing. I think he scared them away."

Medophae nodded grimly.

"I was...hurt badly. But I had seen an old herb shop close by. I crawled to it," Stavark said. "I was dying, but I knew of one herb that might save me. I hoped to find it inside. It was my only chance." He paused. "But the door was locked. I could not get inside. I fought with the handle, but my strength had fled. I would have died, I think...." Stavark trailed off.

"What happened?" Medophae prompted him.

"I was saved by a vyrksikka," he said. "A hollowskin."

Medophae turned in his saddle. "A vampire?"

"You met a vampire?" Mirolah asked. She knew she shouldn't be surprised by the strange and unusual creatures that kept popping up, but she honestly thought vampires were a fiction. "Are they even real?"

"Oh, they're real," Medophae said.

"She arrived from nowhere," Stavark said. "I thought perhaps she had watched the battle, waited until she knew I could not fight her, then came to drain me of my blood."

"White eyes. Black hair in a braid."

"Yes," Stavark said.

"Silasa," Medophae murmured.

"How did you know her name?" Stavark said, incredulous.

"She is a friend. I visited her just before I came to Denema's Valley," Medophae said. "I had no idea she followed me. The question is: Why?"

"She was kind. There are no kind vyrksikkas, so say the elder syvihrk. Vyrksikkas live only to destroy," Stavark said.

"Most do." Medophae fell into deep thought.

Mirolah had never heard of Silasa. Was this one more secret that he had kept from her? Or was it simply one more experience in a long life that had no relevance to her before now?

"She acted as though she had been sent," Stavark said.

"Sent?" Medophae asked. "Sent by whom?"

32

SILASA

SILASA NEVER KNEW what woke her when night came. It was not the complete absence of sunlight. She had awoken often in time to see the purples and blues of the clouds at the end of a sunset. But never the sun. She never awoke in time to catch a glimpse of that blinding orb.

She looked down at her dirty clothes and frowned. She had bought new skirts and a new blouse only two nights ago, along with a new corset, and now they were ruined. Sleeping in caves was rough on clothing. Of course, she hadn't been expecting to sleep in caves. She let out a breath and put her hand against the rough, porous rock wall. This was her home, at least for the next few days. And who knew where she would be after that? Well, Ynisaan knew. She was in Teni'sia because of Ynisaan.

Protect Mershayn, she'd said.

But Ynisaan never said more than the absolute minimum.

Silasa plucked at the dark lace of her sleeve, pulling it to length and letting it dangle from her cuff just so.

She sighed. She lived a shadow's existence, a pale woman with black clothing slipping through the darkness, aiding those who could walk in the sun, who could have friends, who could laugh and talk and discuss their finery, which was not ruined from sleeping in a cave.

She walked to the cave's opening and stared out at the Inland Ocean. She was almost as high up as the castle turrets here. It was a good hiding place. No one would accidentally climb to this height and explore this cave, and few mortals could do it at all.

The tips of the waves flashed blue in the twilight. The rest of the water was deep and murky. In mere moments, even the tips of the waves would succumb to the darkness, and the Inland Ocean would become a sea of black. For her, it was always a sea of black. She remembered her childhood in Belshra, not very far from here. She remembered running along the sandy beach of the northern shore. She had splashed in the ocean in new dresses. Oh, how her warden had chastised her for that. Baelifa, her dear sweet warden. Baelifa, who had died protecting her when the vampire Darva came for her...

"Mershayn did not come with you," Ynisaan said quietly from behind her.

"He wouldn't," Silasa said as though she wasn't surprised that Ynisaan had just appeared again. "He insisted on saving his brother the king." Silasa continued to look at the ocean. Ynisaan never made a sound when she appeared or vanished. There were times when Silasa thought Ynisaan did not exist at all, that she just was some figment of Silasa's imagination created by loneliness. Of course, Silasa really didn't like the idea of being dead and insane at the same time.

"You bought new clothes," Ynisaan said.

A long silence fell between them, but Silasa was not in a mood to break it. Finally, she said, "Silly, isn't it? And now they're ruined after visiting the dungeons of Teni'sia and a few nights sleeping in a cave."

"It becomes you," Ynisaan said.

Silasa turned at last, looking into depthless black eyes of the strange woman who had appeared to her out of nowhere, talking about Medophae's certain death if Silasa didn't intervene. Ynisaan had black hair, black skin, and black eyes, all as dark as obsidian. The dark eyes held reservoirs of memory. They brimmed with knowledge and pain.

Silasa's problems flew away like paper-thin bits of ash on an updraft. This woman saw so many things, and she bore the burden alone except for Silasa. And Silasa complained about loneliness? At least she could venture within the gates of Teni'sia at night and buy clothing. Ynisaan could not even do that. According to the mysterious woman, each interaction with Silasa might mean death for Ynisaan. Silasa lived in a cave, but Ynisaan's home was, apparently, filled with creatures that would kill her if they found her.

"I am sorry," Silasa said. "I am wallowing in self-pity tonight." She crouched and leaned her back against the rock wall. Her flowing black skirts draped over the lip of the cave, fluttering in the sea breeze. She dangled one leg over the edge like a child. "I did not mean to burden you with my problems."

Ynisaan walked forward and took up a spot on the opposite wall. Studying Silasa's position for a moment, she sat down, imitating it. It was the first time Ynisaan had ever done something awkward. Her heel slipped, and she sat down hard. For a second, Silasa thought she would topple over the edge of the cliff. With a startled expression, Ynisaan looked up. "I have never done that before."

"Sat down?"

"On the floor of a cave, no."

"Well..." Silasa said. "Well done."

"I have heard that Tuana's Children are usually better liars," Ynisaan said.

"I didn't mean—"

"It is okay. There are many things I am not good at."

"The only other vampires I've known except for myself are horrible," Silasa admitted.

"You are unique," Ynisaan said. "The others of White Tuana's blood are petty, thieving killers. It is easy to lose compassion for mortals when you possess the blood of a god. Most vampires take the burden of their metamorphosis as an excuse to drop their humanity. And once they forget what it is to be human, it is nearly impossible to return to it."

Silasa had felt that compulsion so many times, the need to sink her teeth into someone she hated or loved, the need to destroy. Each time, she asked herself why not? She had no ties to the mortal world. Why shouldn't she simply give in to it? Why not run from kingdom to kingdom, taking what she wanted?

"It's why Medophae is so important to you, isn't it?" Silasa asked. "Because he's human still. Angry and sad and impetuous and mixed-up. But human. Oedandus hasn't claimed him."

"He is an example for all of us who have gods' blood," she said.

That surprised Silasa. "You have a god's blood?"

"Not like Medophae. Not even to the extent that you do. I cannot summon a sword of fire or heal my wounds. I do not live forever, and I do not have superhuman strength like you. But I can travel to the Coreworld, and I have Vaisha's vision. I can see...possibilities like she did."

"You have blood from Vaisha the Changer?"

"She was the one who made my kind." She paused. "It's hard to...keep from believing we are above mortals, because of the things we do. It's why I choose to serve. It's the only way to hold onto the value of all living things."

"You think that's why Medophae does it? Because he believes in the value of all living things?" Silasa had seen Medophae kill his fair share of people and beasts.

"No. He does it because he's in love," Ynisaan said.

"With Bands? Or Mirolah?"

"With humankind. Or rather, with the best of humankind. He fights so hard for them. Even in his attempt to detach from the human lands, even when he lived in a cave close to your home kingdom, he couldn't stop himself from saving Orem. He wants us to become better. Medophae is what the other gods should aspire to be."

"The gods don't care about mortals," Silasa said. "And they don't listen to Medophae, even if he would try talking to them. They don't see him as one of them."

Ynisaan paused, and her voice was barely audible. As a vampire, however, Silasa had exceptional hearing. "They fear him, though,," Ynisaan murmured.

They sat in silence after that, until Silasa said. "So what happens next with Mershayn? Did he die?"

"No. He lives."

"He walked straight into an ambush."

"For his brother, but not for him. They did not expect him to arrive. He swayed the battle."

"All by himself?"

"He had help."

Silasa raised an eyebrow. "Your doing?"

Ynisaan smiled. "Some things happen all by themselves. No, Mershayn is a resourceful man. He has made some friends in the castle of Teni'sia."

"Where is he now?"

"He and his allies are hidden in the village at the foot of the castle, within the walls of Teni'sia. As is the king."

"The king lives?" Silasa asked incredulously.

"He will not survive the night. There is no future for him that leads away from Teni'sia."

"And Mershayn?"

"Will also die tonight, most likely," Ynisaan said.

"Most likely?"

"Grendis Sym is tracking them. In a few hours, they will be found. They will fight bravely, but they will lose, unless you go to them."

Silasa said, "Zilok Morth is in Teni'sia. He almost caught

Mershayn and me when we escaped the dungeons. You didn't tell me he was here."

"You did well."

"A warning would be nice."

"I cannot see Zilok. He isn't alive, and so is difficult to predict. He has no cracks in the Coreworld, no flows that might predict his destiny. But he can alter them. If he had caught you, I would not have been able to save you."

"Good thing he didn't."

"Yes."

"Where is Medophae?"

"He is coming. But there are...many possible paths for him. Avakketh will lay traps for him."

"If you can see these traps, let's spring them before Medophae reaches them."

Ynisaan looked down. "We could. But every time we nudge events, it is a risk. If Avakketh discovers me and, through me, the Coreworld...he would use it to destroy this world Natra built. Every life form would be doomed, save dragons. Even Saraphazia, goddess of whales, could not fight Avakketh if he controlled the Coreworld. The more we allow events to unfold naturally, nudging only where we must, the more it seems natural, and the less attention it draws."

Silasa paused. "So Mershayn, then? For now?" She grabbed the hem of her skirts and gathered them, stood up, and tucked them into her belt. Her pale legs shone in the moonlight.

"Yes."

"Where is he?"

"He and his friends have hidden themselves in a run-down bait shop in The Barnacles."

The Barnacles was the wharf-side shantytown near the wharves of Teni'sia. "What is it called?"

"The Gutted Fish."

Silasa wrinkled her nose. "Pleasant." She crouched at the edge of the cave, preparing to climb down.

"Silasa," Ynisaan said.

Silasa stopped.

"Tonight, the kingdom will divide into two separate camps. Grendis Sym will make his move, and few will oppose him. Of those who do, even fewer will live, and those few are important. But these friends of Mershayn's will not be friendly to you. Everyone is suspicious. They will think you an enemy first."

"They always do," she said.

"Use Medophae's name. He still carries great influence in Teni'sia."

"Medophae carries great influence everywhere," she said, and began the climb down.

33

MIROLAH

THEY ALL STOPPED and stared into the darkened trees. It was afternoon, but within the forest, it was as though night had fallen. Sniff whined, moving forward toward the forest, then back. Obviously, the trail went in, but the dog balked. The threads of the ground, the trees, the air of this place were tainted, darkened as though they had been soaked in tar. The trees drooped and the grasses bent over in decay. Winter was coming, but this forest had not died because of a turn of the seasons. It had been transformed by powerful GodSpill.

They had been on the road for nearly four days, following Sniff's nose. For the last day they'd been traveling fairly swiftly across grasslands, but this was where they ended. Medophae said they were within a few hours of the ruins of Belshra, where his vampire friend hailed from.

Sniff whined and paced back and forth in front of the group. The horses flared their nostrils and neighed.

Medophae got off their horse and peered into the gloom. The sun hung low on the horizon, and twilight was not far off. Greasy mist swirled between the soft trunks of the trees. Mirolah dismounted as well and tethered the horse.

Elekkena hopped down from her horse and Stavark followed.

"This place is vakehk," Stavark said, and it sounded like he was spitting. His fists were clenched.

Medophae shook his head. "This wasn't here before," he said.

"This malevolence?" Mirolah asked.

"This forest. Not here before. I took this route to Denema's Valley when I came looking for Orem. By the gods, I've ridden this way a hundred times in my life. There was never a forest. I think there was a village near this place, but no forest. This happened with the Wave."

"You think this was created when we released the GodSpill?" Mirolah asked.

"GodSpill," Sniff whined. "Bad GodSpill." He paced back and forth, then sneezed, shaking his great head. "Trail goes in."

"Zilok went in there," Mirolah said. "This is his new lair." The thought of the freed GodSpill creating something so vile made Mirolah's stomach turn. The voice that spoke to her from the GodSpill seemed insistent, but not...malevolent. This had to be something Zilok created specifically for his own needs.

Stavark followed, unsheathing his curved sword. Sniff whined, pacing back and forth.

"Yes," Medophae said, unsheathing his own sword. A flicker of golden fire ran from his fist up the blade. "I think you're right."

The two of them moved into the trees with Mirolah and Elekkena behind. Sniff loped ahead of them, head down and looking around every tree.

The mist thickened. The air outside had been crisp, late fall awaiting winter. But inside the trees, it clung to Mirolah's skin like hot breath. She followed Elekkena, just able to see Stavark and Medophae ahead. The godsword crackled in his hand and lit the way.

"Let's stay close," Medophae said.

Mirolah's toe bumped into something, and she looked down at the ground. She recoiled. It was a dead squirrel, except it wasn't quite a squirrel anymore. Its head was three times the normal size, and its eyes bulged from their sockets. Its neck was a thin thread that connected the overlarge head to its shoulders, and yet it appeared to have grown that way. A ribbon of dried blood trailed from its mouth onto the grass.

Mirolah reached out to its threads to try to see what had happened to the poor creature, but the mist obscured her thread-weaver vision. She fought through it and touched the wretched creature's threads. Some of the squirrel's threads had gaps in them, some were shredded, and the frayed ends turned into mismatched colors.

Was this some aberration that had happened when the GodSpill had been released back into the lands? So many wondrous things had manifested since she tore down Daylan's Fountain, but there might be other effects, not so benevolent.

"You aren't happy with your creation?"

Zilok Morth's oozing presence soaked into her threads just as he spoke.

"No!" She jerked upright, ejecting his insidious influence, pushing the black color from her threads. "He's here!" She spun about—

But Sniff was no longer beside her. Elekkena was not in front of her. Medophae and Stavark were nowhere in sight. She heard someone calling her name, and she heard Sniff's howl.

"I'm here," she yelled. She tried to see them, but the greasy mist had thickened to an impenetrable fog. Now it blocked her regular vision as well as her threadweaver sight.

Zilok Morth materialized in the fog, and he bowed low. He wore the same tight black vest, the same white, high-collared shirt. He rubbed at his goatee.

"They can't hear you. These mists are an interesting creation. It took me an hour of studying them to discover how to manipulate the threads in this place while I was waiting for you."

"You didn't make this forest," she said.

"Please," he said. "Why would I?" He shook his head. "No, this is part of your great creation, Lady Rith. Did you think the GodSpill was some benevolent force in the world?"

"It's—" she began, but cut herself off. Zilok looked amused.

"No, Lady Rith, the GodSpill is not benevolent. It would as soon morph you into a tree as love you, whichever it chooses in that instant. This is the force of creation used by the gods. It cares nothing for the desires of mortals. It caresses and stabs at will. It is wild. You released something unpredictable into the lands. Where we stand, this used to be a village. There was no forest here."

She felt through the threads, but the fog was blocking her ability. The threads were faded, barely perceptible, but as she touched them, they grew brighter.

"You're lying," she said, trying to stall him until she, too, could figure out how to threadweave in this cursed place.

"I never lie to those who are about to die," Zilok said.

She felt the shiver in the threads a second before the air shoved her backward. It was a simple spell, meant to throw her off balance, but she kept her feet—

Something stabbed through the back of her thigh. Her thigh-bone snapped, and she screamed, falling onto her knees.

Fiery pain tore through her, and Zilok winnowed into her mind, infecting her threads with his oily tar.

She tried to shut him out, but the pain of the wound distracted her, and, in seconds, he had dominated her. It was just like Ethiel, all over again, except Zilok was far better at this.

"History never remembers," he whispered inside her head. "How kind I am. How many chances I give to my enemies. You could have lived, Lady Rith. But you will get no more chances from me."

A dozen new branches came at her from the tree behind her. They punctured her neck, her chest, her legs and arms. She gasped as blood flowed from the wounds.

She could heal herself. She could...

But Zilok held her mind, preventing her from doing anything. He waited, letting her blood flow, letting her life ebb. Her vision began to go blurry, and in the mist, she saw golden light flashing.

Medophae, she thought, but Zilok prevented her mouth from calling out to him.

"This is what happens to those who do not accept my generosity," Zilok whispered.

She let out a long last breath.

"Die, Lady Rith."

The greasy mists lifted and Mirolah could hear the voices of her friends once again. But she had no voice. She had no strength. Her body was cold, and she couldn't raise her arms. She slumped, held aloft by the branches that impaled her. Her vision turned dark. She looked down at her punctured body, wicked branches sticking out of it, pinning her to the ground.

Her spirit began floating upward toward that swirling gray maw overhead.

34

STAVARK

WHEN THE MIST thickened so abruptly, Stavark knew the attack would come.

The greasy mist was an offense. It was nature turned inside out. With every step, he longed to put an end to the forces that had twisted the trees and grasses. He looked back and saw the calm determination in Elekkena's eyes as well, that same revulsion that he felt. She glanced at him and, for a quick moment, Stavark saw inside her head. He saw her thoughts. Such a connection happened among syvihrk sometimes. According to the wisest of his people, it could only happen between two people who knew their heart's desire and followed it with clarity. It was called kihrkakis, or "the soul glimpse" in human. For that brief moment, Stavark was her and she was him.

Elekkena worried for Medophae, but she was not afraid. Her serenity was not a facade; it stretched far back into her soul. She would follow Medophae, Stavark, and Mirolah into any peril. She would never waver, but there was more. She had another reason for being here. She—

Elekkena shook her head and the kihrkakis ended. Stavark stared at her and slowed to a stop. She looked up at him with calm silver eyes. He tried to see inside her again, but the connection was gone.

"You..." Stavark started to say, but he could not put his thoughts into words. "You are more than you seem," he said in the language of the syvihrk.

"Everyone is more than they seem," she replied.

"How did you..." Again, words failed him.

Elekkena paused for a moment, as though deciding whether she would tell him or not. Finally, she said, "Much happened to me during my two-year journey, Stavark. More than I have told you. I will explain later, but now is not the time for this story."

"But how could you know these things that you know—" He cut himself off. "Where is the Maehka vik Kalik?" he said.

Elekkena spun around. The Maehka vik Kalik was gone.

"Rabasyvihrk," Stavark called, but the mists had swallowed the big man.

He could enter the silverland. In an instant, he could move forward and back, but he had taken his eyes off the Maehka vik Kalik and the Rabasyvihrk for a moment, and they were gone. It would be a mistake to lose Elekkena the same way.

"The Rabasyvihrk will be fine," Elekkena said, glancing back where they had come from. "We follow the Maehka vik Kalik." She flipped her silver hair over one shoulder and started back the way they had come, picking her way carefully.

The sickly mist closed in about them.

"Take my hand," Elekkena said, and Stavark grabbed it. Even then, it seemed as if the mist tugged at them, trying to pull them apart. At times, it was difficult to see his hand in front of his face, or the path at his feet, but Elekkena stepped with confidence, as though she could see what he could not. She called out for Mirolah, but the mist swallowed the shouts.

Ahead, they saw a flicker of golden light.

"The Rabasyvihrk," Stavark said.

They charged in that direction. The greasy gray mist slithered past them, but the golden light grew brighter. It flashed like lightning, and Stavark decided that now was the time.

He let go of Elekkena's hand, and the tortured forest became silver. Elekkena froze beside him. The mist stopped swirling. Stavark's legs and arms burned with joy. The golden light had become silver as well. Stavark sprinted through the silverland. He ducked around the waves and walls of mist, and suddenly he saw the Rabasyvihrk.

Medophae was in mid-air. A huge tree with thick branches like thinly muscled arms hunched over him. The tree was at least thirty feet tall, and a dark, shadowy silver. Tiny boles covered its diseased bark, and the gray mist poured out of them. A hundred of its menacing branches bent at angles to attack Medophae. He had been wrapped soundly in a dozen of them, but his fiery sword had shorn many of them apart. They lay on the ground at his feet. Several thin, tenacious branches held his ankles. Stavark aimed for them, slashing through one, two, three, four, five... Breathing hard, he stepped out of the silverland.

Color returned. Medophae's golden fire lit up the darkness. The black, twisted trunk of the tree shivered as its branches fell to the ground, severed by Stavark's blade. Medophae hit the ground with a wet thud. Three more branches launched out and attached to his arm and leg. Stavark stepped into the silverland again and severed them.

Medophae rolled to his feet, and they faced the tree together.

"I wondered where you had gone," Medophae said. "I turned and everyone had vanished. Then this monstrosity took me from behind. This is what is creating the mist. Do you see?"

"I see."

More branches came for them, but the Rabasyvihrk rolled low, avoiding the attack and clipping a few.

Stavark entered the silverland again and ran past the frozen branches. With small strokes, he severed bole after bole that leaked gray mist. He stepped in and out of the silverland, resting, then fighting, and he stayed ahead of the branches. He had never used the silverland this much, and he began to tire.

But with the branches trying frantically to kill Stavark, they left the Rabasyvihrk alone. Just as Stavark's strength began to fail, the Rabasyvihrk charged and cleaved halfway into the tree's trunk.

The tree shuddered and swayed. Thin, sharp branches shot at Medophae. Half a dozen of them pierced him through the arms and abdomen. Red blood flew. Medophae roared. A dozen other branches twined about his arms and legs. Stavark stepped again into the silverland. He sheared half of the branches away before he had to step out again, lest he collapse there and run the risk of remaining forever.

Though skewered by multiple branches, Medophae kept hacking at the tree. His fiery sword spit and hissed and he cut completely through the trunk. A great cracking groan filled the air, and the tree fell over backward. The wicked branches thrashed in every direction. Stavark entered the silverland, dodging the branches and retreating.

Medophae fell backward. He looked down at the gnarled spears that protruded from him. He grabbed hold of two in his gut and yanked them out together. He stood and staggered backward.

The tree's thrashing quieted. Black ichor oozed from the stump Medophae had created, but already the forest was beginning to clear.

Stavark helped Medophae pull the branches from himself, even as the golden fire healed him. He leaned on the slimy stump and levered himself to his feet. He stood unsteady on his bloody legs. The mist continued to clear. Stavark could see nearly fifteen feet distant.

Finally, the tree stopped moving altogether, and a slimy, pale seed slipped out of the severed top of the tree. Stavark jumped at it, but it floated upward into the sky.

He strained to see what it might have been, but it vanished into the mist overhead. The mist cleared even more, and Stavark could see two more figures. It was Elekkena, leaning over the Maehka vik Kalik.

"Mirolah," the Rabasyvihrk cried.

35

MIROLAH

You will come to us now. We are one.

The voice reverberated all around her. All Mirolah could see was white mist, and all she could hear was the frightening voice. In Daylan's Glass, that voice had barely noticed her. In Rith, it had invited her. Now it commanded her, angry.

She felt the GodSpill absorbing her again, pulling her back from the Godgate overhead, and she knew this time it wouldn't let her go, wouldn't let her come back to her body.

You will come now.

Then she heard a different voice, a chant. Behind the frightening demand of the GodSpill, a woman's voice murmured in a language Mirolah had never heard before. The voice was soft, but steady and unbending. Tiny threads formed a net around her, stopping her from being pulled into the GodSpill or up into the Godgate.

The steady chant seemed to say: *Come back. You are not yet done. Come back.*

We are one! the GodSpill shouted, a thunderclap of sound inside her mind as it felt her slipping away.

Agony flared through her from a dozen wounds, then the agony faded. Memories raced through her head. Zilok Morth, the mist, the branches stabbing her. Golden flashes of light in the murky mist.

The chant surrounded her, foreign and incomprehensible.

Mirolah sucked in a breath. The chanting stopped. She opened her eyes.

A fuzzy figure leaned over her, then Elekkena slowly came into focus.

"What happened?" Mirolah asked.

"You are within the forest still, Mirolah," Elekkena replied.

Mirolah squinched her eyes shut, opened them again and looked down at her body. She touched her stomach, her neck, her arms. She felt her chest, her legs with both hands. Her shirt, skirt, and breeches were a bloody mess, like she'd been run through with a dozen swords, but there were no wounds. Her gaze snapped to Elekkena.

"You healed me," Mirolah said.

The young quicksilver girl shook her head. "No, Mirolah."

"You were murmuring. I heard you as I woke. You stopped when I opened my eyes." Mirolah sought vainly to read her emotions. She received nothing. "I can barely do that."

"It was not me. It was you." Elekkena shook her head.

"I was unconscious."

"I tried to watch what you were doing," Elekkena said. "But I could not understand it all."

Mirolah tried to put it together, tried to remember if she had fragmented a part of her attention to save her body. It made a kind of sense, but she couldn't remember doing it. It felt like someone else was pulling her back into her body. Was it possible that she unconsciously fought to protect herself from dying?

"You...weren't murmuring? Maybe in your own language?"

"No. You were murmuring."

How could that be when she didn't even understand the words?

The doom descended on her again. It was the same feeling she'd had when she first realized that Sniff was not speaking the human tongue, but rather that she was speaking his. Now she was casting spells in her sleep? Was that even possible?

"I cut the tree. I pulled the branches from your body," Elekkena said.

She glanced past Elekkena to see the tree in its final thrashing stages. The mist faded, and she saw Medophae and Stavark beyond, by another tree that had been demolished. Medophae looked as though he'd been half-chewed by a spine horse. Stavark, in true quicksilver fashion, had not a scratch on him, but he drooped from exhaustion.

Just as Mirolah was about to call out to them, she saw something at the bottom of the fallen tree. It was faded, but it looked like a figure. She concentrated on her threadweaver sight, and the little ghost appeared with stark clarity.

"By the gods..." she murmured.

The ghost was a young girl. She crawled out of the tree's trunk and looked about herself as though she did not understand what was happening. She began to float upward. She looked at Medophae then at Stavark in confusion. Finally, her gaze found Mirolah's. Above her, the Godgate churned, superimposed over the mists. It pulled the girl, and she began to rise.

"Mirolah!" Medophae called to her in a hoarse voice.

Ignoring him, she wrapped the girl in the same kind of net she'd used on the boy in Rith. The girl opened her mouth in a silent scream, writhed and twisted. The swirling sky moved faster, becoming more insistent. It was more difficult than it had been in Rith. The maw was stronger. The girl looked as though she was being twisted apart.

What was she doing in the tree? This poor girl, what was she doing in the tree?

Mirolah doubled her efforts. The strain was incredible, and the girl thrashed as though Mirolah was ripping her heart out.

"Let her go," Elekkena said quietly. "You cannot help her." Elekkena's hand was gentle but firm on Mirolah's arm. "She is dead."

"But I can save her."

"You're torturing her," Elekkena insisted. "Release your spell. She has no body to return to."

With an anguished cry, Mirolah released the net and watched the girl's spirit fly upward. The swirling sky took her and withdrew higher into the sky, but did not vanish. Mirolah could always see it up there now, swirling at a distance.

She lowered her head.

"Are you all right?" Medophae asked, kneeling next to her. Golden fire crackled around him, healing him, but his clothes were a bloody mess like hers.

She hugged him, pressing her face against his neck. "No," she said. She wasn't all right. Was this insidious forest really of her making? Had this grown because of the GodSpill released into the lands?

"I fought Zilok," she said. "He knows we are tracking him. He nearly finished me."

"This is his lair?" he asked.

"No, I don't think so," she said. "I think he discovered we were following and chose this place for an ambush. But these mists inhibit my ability to see the threads." She didn't tell him that this horrible forest might be her fault. "The GodSpill is...angry here."

A long howl rose from the mists.

"Sniff," Mirolah said. "Where is Sniff?"

The howl rose again.

"Sniff!" she shouted. The mists had withdrawn from this area of the forest, with the two trees dead, but it was still thick some thirty feet away from their group. Mirolah wondered how many trees were in this place.

Sniff leapt through the mist to her right, churning turf as he landed. He raised his toothy head and spotted her.

"Mistress!" he yipped, jogged toward her, then lay down in front of her." He was covered with slashes and scrapes all over his skinny body. Bits of bark and wood chips stuck to his lips and between his bramble of teeth.

"What happened?" she asked.

"Bad trees," he said. "Could not find you. Mist is bad GodSpill. Bad trees make mist. Sniff hurt trees. Made path."

"You made a path?"

"Sniff kill tree mouths. They do not puff mist anymore. Come." He stood, ran to the edge of the mist, and she realized there was a thin break there, a pathway through the mists, slowly parting.

They all followed Stavark through the tunnel in the mist. It cleared more until they came upon another deadly tree. This one still had its branches pointed at them, ready to spear them, but they stayed clear. However, the boles on the center of the tree had been torn and chewed by Sniff.

"That's where the mist comes from." Medophae pointed. He glanced at Sniff with new appreciation. "How did he tear those apart without getting speared?"

"I have no idea," she said.

"Come," Sniff said, leading them quickly forward.

They passed two other trees that had been bitten and chewed like the first one, then the mist parted. The forest ended, and they emerged into the open air, the afternoon sky above them. They stood on a rise that sloped down into a valley that held the ruins of a harbor city by the Inland Ocean.

"That's Belshra," Medophae said.

"Trail goes this way," Sniff said, lifting his nose into the air. He started down the slope.

Mirolah looked back at the twisted forest. *Is this my creation? My fault? And if so, how many people died there?*

They continued on to the ruins of Belshra and made camp there for the night.

36

MERSHAYN

THE DRIP CONTINUED. *Drip drip drip*. Mershayn tried to ignore it, but it pounded in his ear like a blacksmith's hammer. *Tap tap tap*. He wanted to get away from it, but he couldn't move his head. The last time he'd tried, he'd thrown up. As long as he stayed completely still, the ground stayed where it should, and the hammer didn't get hit any harder. So he lay there in misery so it wouldn't get worse. *Drip drip drip*.

Deni'tri and Lo'gan argued in what they thought were quiet tones on the other side of the room. It was truly a miracle that they had managed to get them this far. In the rush from the castle, Lo'gan had grabbed three of his most trusted guards. They stood watch outside the small, crooked door. To what avail, Mershayn didn't know. He wasn't worried about death coming through that door. It was already inside the room.

Collus lay against the cold rock wall, right next to Mershayn. His breathing was shallow; it came in quick little huffs. Sweat glistened on his brow, and he moaned in his sleep. He hadn't been fully conscious since the attempted assassination.

Mershayn's last movement had been to roll over so that he could watch his brother. After they'd cleaned up Mershayn's vomit, he'd felt good about the effort for about half an hour. Now he realized all he'd done was give himself a prime view of his brother's impending death.

He wanted to be angry at the injustice of it. He would even have welcomed an aching despondency, but he didn't feel either of those things. He could barely think of anything except the pain in his head. His sole comfort was that he wouldn't be far behind his brother; Mershayn would pay for his mistake. King and bastard would leave this mortal life together.

"We cannot stay here long," Deni'tri insisted. She had been insisting that forever, it seemed. He wished she would stop insisting. He wished they would stop speaking altogether. Their words hurt almost as much as the accursed drip. *Drip drip drip. Tap tap tap.*

"Rumors have begun to fly. Two of the king's guard limping down the street with injured in tow... If we leave this place, we will gather a crowd in moments."

"Sym is searching for us. If we stay here, he'll find us."

"Where is a better place to hide?"

Deni'tri lowered her voice. "Out of the city," she said. "Any place be better." She paused. "I don't trust the owner of this establishment," she murmured.

"Who? Bi'sivus?"

"Yes, Bi'sivus. The man stinks of greed. He'll flip on us if enough gold is pressed into his palm. And he stinks of other things, too." She wrinkled her nose.

"He is overdue for a bath, I grant you that."

She shook her head. "He will sell us to Sym if pressed. By the gods, he may have already sent someone to contact Sym."

Lo'gan paused and lowered his voice. "Look at them. Let us imagine we had a place to go. They cannot be moved. We barely got them this far."

Just us die in peace. We tried. We failed. Mershayn the Idiot and Collus the Blind, that is what they will call us, if they call us anything at all. Grendis Sym proved himself the better man. The fight is over. The battle is lost. We're the losers. That is the way of things.

Deni'tri stopped insisting, thank the gods.

When they did not speak again, Mershayn craned his eyeballs downward, to view the door where they stood. Deni'tri looked on the verge of tears. Her head hung low and her fists were clenched. Lo'gan kept his back to the wall beside the door, watching the king and his bastard brother.

They will die, too. They took your side, and it was the wrong side. When Sym comes, he'll kill them.

Lo'gan saw Mershayn attempting to watch him and pushed away from the wall.

"Do you need anything, my lord?"

"A new head," he croaked. The sound of his own voice thudded inside his skull like a mallet. He winced. Suddenly, he was tired of lying on his side in the mud. The vertigo, which assailed him like waves, had withdrawn for a moment.

"Help me up, Lo'gan," he said, shutting out the pain that his own words created. Lo'gan and Deni'tri were beside him in an instant.

"Help me to sit. I cannot lie here anymore."

Deni'tri shot a worried glance at Lo'gan.

"Just do it," Mershayn said tersely, hating to spend the energy on convincing them.

Together, they eased him up. He clenched his teeth, and the ground swayed. The blurry walls danced about, but at least they did not spin. He closed his eyes and concentrated on his breathing. In a moment, the swaying stopped, and he realized his back was against the wall.

"Good," he grunted. He took a long moment to recover himself, then looked up at them as best he could. His good eye saw clearly enough, but mixed with his destroyed right eye, which he couldn't close, he only saw jumpy blurs of the two guards.

"You should leave," he said simply.

"My lord?"

Mershayn clenched his teeth. "Leave. If you are here when they find us, they'll kill you. And even if you did manage to fight them off, Collus and I are done. He cannot even wake, and I can't stand. My head is..." He didn't want to finish the thought, but it was cracked. This wasn't an injury one recovered from readily, certainly not while on the run. "No one knows yet that you helped us. Show me your steel and give Collus and me a merciful death. And take that shifty innkeeper Bi'sivus on the way out. Make good your escape, and I will piss on Sym from the Godgate."

Lo'gan and Deni'tri exchanged glances.

"That's an...order," he managed to say. "There is nothing more to protect here. You can see our condition as well as I."

"Do not say such things," Deni'tri said.

"An order," Mershayn restated. "A yard of sharp steel in the chest."

"I cannot do that, my lord," Lo'gan said in his captain's voice. Intransigent bastard.

"You are...useless," Mershayn said, then stopped speaking for the pain. He rallied and tried again. "I ask you for one thing, and you deny me. You will die for nothing."

"Not for nothing," Lo'gan murmured. "I will die for my king and his brother. I will die for my country. I will die with honor."

"Much good it may do you." Damned stiff-necked guards. Mershayn looked away from the pair of them, anywhere but at their loyal faces. Light leaked down through the wooden planks overhead. Every now and then, the booted feet of Bi'sivus or one of his family thunked overhead. There were no windows in this accursed tomb, only that crooked door on the far side of the room.

He closed his eyes, drifting, the silence and the dripping mixing in his head. He wanted to sleep. Maybe he did, riding waves of pain into the darkness, but he didn't go far. When he heard the voices, he opened his eye again.

Their "benefactor," Bi'sivus, was speaking to someone at his front door. The voices were hushed, muffled by the planking, but Mershayn could guess what was happening. The gold had arrived. Bi'sivus would make his fortune today by betraying a king. At least, that was what Bi'sivus dreamt.

More likely he would earn a dagger across his throat, and the throats of each of his family. Sym wouldn't want any witnesses to what happened here today.

Both Deni'tri and Lo'gan sensed the same thing. Lo'gan drew his short sword and whispered out the crooked door to his men, "Stand ready. We die here today for the king. But we will take them with us."

Deni'tri drew her own blade and unhooked her hatchet. She gave a meaningful look to Lo'gan that he ignored.

Then it began.

Like an avalanche of rocks, booted feet stormed across the planks overhead. The light in the small room danced as Sym's guards invaded The Gutted Fish.

Ironic. In moments, we'll all be gutted fish.

He watched the light that slipped through the slats. It was all fuzzy, but he imagined he could see the Godgate above him.

What would that be like?

Boots thundered down the stairwell and shouts went up from the two hapless guards stationed outside. Steel clashed against steel. Mershayn clenched his teeth against the nausea and drew his hand carefully close to his body, groped for the dagger at his waist.

But he didn't have a dagger anymore.

He let his hand go blessedly still once more and continued to stare forward. He did not want to watch Lo'gan and Deni'tri's deaths. They were stupid and stubborn, but they were good guards. He didn't want to witness their slaughter.

If I'd been with Collus in those early audiences, I could have stood in Sym's way. If I'd been a little less self-involved, this would have turned out differently. We could have taken steps together.

He could have. Collus would eventually have listened to Mershayn, if he had persisted. But Mershayn had wasted his time courting the wife of Collus's ally. No doubt Vullieth sat with Sym right now, waiting for Mershayn's head to be brought back to the palace.

A cry of pain arose from the conflict on the other side of the door. Lo'gan's men could not prevail. At least a dozen men had thundered across that floor and down those steps. Even Mershayn at his best couldn't stop that many.

Lo'gan and Deni'tri stood tense on either side of the door. They both looked as though they wished to fling it open and join the fray, but Lo'gan had assessed that hallway. Only two could fight efficiently. His two guards would do maximum damage before they fell, then Lo'gan and Deni'tri would pin their hopes to getting the rest as they tried to come through the door.

Another shadow passed over the planks overhead, silent. He wouldn't even have noticed it if he hadn't been looking upward. The figure crossed the room as though flying.

A cry of fear arose among the grunting melee. Then a cry of pain. And another.

Clashing swords faltered. More screams. A body thudded against the wall. Armor clanged against the stairwell. All sounds of swordplay ceased. Another death cry filled the air.

Then, silence....

"Wh—Who are you?" someone asked beyond the door, one of Lo'gan's guards.

"I am not your enemy. I have come to aid Mershayn," came a woman's voice. "And the king," she added.

By Thalius... It's that vampire woman. Silasa.

"You...how did you...? It's not possible..." the guard babbled.

"If Mershayn and the king are to live, they must be taken from this place," Silasa said. "More of Sym's soldiers are on the way."

"I—I can't let you in there," the guard said.

"You cannot stop me."

"Let her in," Mershayn said, but he wasn't sure Lo'gan or Deni'tri heard him.

"I—I... Captain Lo'gan?" the guard said in a plainly frightened voice. "I don't know what to do, sir."

"Let her in," Mershayn demanded, louder this time. Both Deni'tri and Lo'gan looked at him. Mershayn closed his eye and fought the urge to throw up.

Lo'gan hesitated, Mershayn heard the door unlatch. His nausea subsided, and he opened his eye.

Lo'gan had his sword at Silasa's throat. She came forward, flicking a glance at the sword, then ignoring it. Her long braid had come undone, and her black hair spilled over her shoulders. Her black skirts, shirt, and corset flowed down her like one long shadow. Her gaze fell upon Mershayn, and she smiled. "Well," she said. "You're alive."

"Silasa," he croaked.

"I told you not to go. This time, you are coming with me."

"The king cannot be moved," Lo'gan said. "He clings to life by a thin thread. Mershayn is not much better. He is stricken with vertigo. If you move him, he will vomit."

"Then he will puke all the way, but he's coming."

"And just who are you?" Deni'tri appeared from behind the door, her hatchet cocked back, her sword pointed at Silasa's back.

Silasa paused. She didn't turn, but she looked over her shoulder. "Calm yourself, guardswoman. If you would save this man, you'll help me. If you stay here, you will not survive the night."

"Some of us don't think we should survive the night," Mershayn mumbled.

Silasa's eyes flashed. "Some of you are idiots."

"Agreed," Mershayn said.

Lo'gan pushed his sword point against the flesh of Silasa's throat. "Why should we trust you?"

"Because I am the only one coming to help you tonight. Because I walked through Sym's thugs. Because I could walk through you just as easily," she said. "But if these three reasons do not satisfy you, then know that I am a friend of Medophae, sent to see you through this night."

Lo'gan looked astonished. "You know Captain Medophae?" he asked. "Has he returned?"

"No. But events are moving in Teni'sia, and Medophae always manages to be at the center of events that are moving. I would not be surprised to see him soon."

A small smile snuck its way onto Lo'gan's face, despite himself. "I, too, have noticed this about our young captain."

"Young indeed," Silasa said.

Lo'gan lowered his sword, and Deni'tri lowered hers as well. She rehooked her axe onto her belt.

Silasa moved past Lo'gan. Her dusty black skirts swished as she knelt next to Mershayn. He angled his head to meet her stare, and the vertigo seized him. The room spun.

Her cold fingers touched his good cheek, and he wanted to recoil, despite himself. With her other hand, she lifted the bandage away from his ruined cheek. "It is a bad wound," she murmured. "I am sorry that you must endure it."

"You are the soul of compassion," he grunted.

"But you will survive."

"The real question is: should I?"

"Self-pity?" she asked. She put his bandage back in place.

Mershayn closed his eyes. "Collus is dying. It is my fault. I will die with him." He looked up at her, hoping she would tell him that Collus would, in fact, live.

She did not.

"So you will die here with your king and let Sym have his way with Teni'sia?"

"What do I care about Teni'sia?"

"What indeed." She frowned. "Some wish their entire lives for the loyalty that surrounds you now. Be worthy of it. When the truth comes to light about the assassination, this will be a kingdom divided. Sym will make himself king unless someone stops him. Captain Lo'gan knows this. The young woman with the hatchet knows this. They will give their lives to serve their people. What will you give?"

"I did not ask them to drag me here," he growled.

"And I did not ask to be one of the damned."

"What would you have me do?" he growled and immediately regretted the volume of his voice. It ripped through his head.

"Topple Sym. Make him pay for what he has to your brother and to Teni'sia."

"Yes, I will simply march back up to the palace."

"No, you will come with me, and I will take you to a safe place."

"I am ruined," Mershayn breathed, feeling desolation wash over him. "I cannot see. I cannot fight. I cannot even stand."

"I will carry you."

"I will never hold a sword again. Tell me how I can bring this fight to Sym and his horde."

"A fast sword is not all you have to give."

He fell silent. *Drip drip drip.* The puddle behind him continued to collect its water.

"What of Collus?" he asked. "Do you have some supernatural cure to heal his wound?"

"No."

He clenched his teeth. His throat tightened, and he could not speak. His brother would die.

Fine.

A recklessness overcame him. He didn't care about the pain. He didn't care about anything. Let them drag him all over Amarion. Let the lands spin on a stick. Let him puke his guts over the cobblestones of The Barnacles. If Collus deserved to die, Mershayn deserved to suffer for it.

With a surge of strength, he pushed his heels against the mud floor. He braced his back against the wall and forced himself to stand up. The room danced into a frenzy. He grabbed for the rock wall, but he found nothing. The room spun. He fell—

Strong, cold fingers gripped his arms, held him upright.

"Hold your fury," Silasa said. "That is the strength you will need."

Mershayn vomited across her frilly black dress. She did not flinch, and she did not let him go.

"Carry the king," she said. "Follow me."

The room finally steadied, and Mershayn watched Deni'tri's blurry figure kneel beside Collus. She touched his cheek and withdrew her hand quickly. She craned her head about to look at Lo'gan.

"Captain..." Deni'tri's voice trailed off.

Mershayn stumbled forward with Silasa's help. The room bucked and spun. His stomach flipped, and he vomited to the side, but there was nothing left. The dry heave wracked his body. He fumbled to a kneeling position next to his brother.

Deni'tri's hands joined Silasa's in steadying him, and when the vertigo left him, he stared down at his dead brother. Mershayn closed his bad eye so he could see his brother clearly one last time.

The skin of his face was pale wax, and he wasn't breathing. His eyes did not dart beneath closed lids. Mershayn reached out one hand and touched Collus's cold cheek.

He bowed his head and ignored the spinning. He clenched Collus's cool hand and pressed it to his forehead. He did not know how long he stayed like that, but Silasa finally interrupted his mourning.

"We must leave," Silasa said. "Come. Buy the chance to avenge him. Stay here, and there will be no revenge against your brother's killer."

Mershayn let Collus's hand go and pressed his fingers into the packed earth floor. The light sheen of mud was cold on his fingers. He waited for another long moment, shaking with anger.

Finally, he reached out. Silasa gripped his hand. "I'll go. I'll fight Sym."

"Good—"

"On one condition."

Silasa paused. "Very well."

"You help me," he said.

"That is why I am here," she said.

"Not now. Later. Until Sym is dead. You help me. Swear it."

Silasa raised her chin, and Mershayn held her hand in a death grip. She'd hefted him like a bushel of wheat once, carried him up steep stairs as though he weighed nothing. But she did not pull her hand away. "Mershayn, I cannot promise—"

"Swear it! Or leave me here to die."

"My services are pledged to another. I cannot assure you that—"

He threw her hand away from himself. "Then leave. I belong here with my brother."

He waited, striving to stay upright in a room that insisted on leaning to one side, then another.

Softly, Silasa said, "Very well, Mershayn. I swear. I will help you as I can."

"No. You will come when I call."

She hesitated. "Very well."

"Don't be so dour, vampire," he said. "My death will free you from your vow. I wager your service will last a day, three at most."

"We shall see," she said, scooping him into her arms and leaping up the steps.

37

MIROLAH

THE SALT SPRAY flecked Mirolah's face. Clouds soared above her, and the late fall sky was as blue as a robin's egg. She gripped the rail of the bow and leaned into the wind. Another day of traveling had taken them to Corialis Port, a village east of the ruins of Belshra, and they'd hired a boat to take them south along the coast. Zilok's trail had turned south over the Inland Ocean, and Sniff stood next to her, nose to the air. He would yip to her, and she would tell the captain which way to go.

A seagull paced the boat, flying to starboard and keeping level with her. He squawked at her, and she touched him lightly with the fingers of her GodSpill. The seagull had followed them all the way from Corialis Port and Mirolah had become fond of him. He'd started alone, but now a dozen gulls swarmed around the small ship.

Though they still followed Sniff's nose, Medophae was sure now that they were going to Teni'sia. Zilok Morth had sent the bakkaral that had killed Tyndiria. The undead spirit knew there were others in Teni'sia that Medophae cared about. Medophae said Zilok was too strategic a thinker not to capitalize on that. If he was going to create a trap, he would do it there.

They'd been at sea all day, sailing toward a trap.

Sniff barked. "It goes a little left and farther south."

Straight toward Teni'sia.

Stavark made his way up from the back of the ship where he had been talking with Medophae. "Nature breathes easier when you are around," he said, looking at the seagulls.

And may well twist in torment because of me, she thought of the putrid forest with its deadly trees, but she didn't say it.

"You do not seem angry with him anymore," Mirolah said, glancing at Medophae.

Stavark watched the flat horizon. The sun would set in a few hours. "He is not the same as when I first met him. He was a frightened, curled creature, bent inward so that he could no longer see himself. A creature that fears its own nature is a dead thing that walks."

"And now?"

"He looks at the present with fire, and the future with hope. The legends tell of him this way, a sun that lights the way."

"Except we are not suns, Stavark."

"The Rabasyvihrk is."

"He is a man. If you expect too much of him, you will disappoint yourself."

"That is saying a tree is the same as a stick. It is a lie to expect the same from him as I would from another. He is not just a man."

"Then we do not see the same person when we look at him."

"No," the quicksilver answered softly.

Was Stavark right? He only said things because he felt they were true. And the truth was that Mirolah had hated the moment she'd first met Medophae in Denema's Valley because she realized just how far beyond her he was. She'd wanted him to be her equal because she wanted to love him. But Stavark was right. Medophae wasn't a god, but he was closer to being one than he was to being a man.

She cleared her throat and changed the subject. "When did you meet Elekkena?" she asked.

"Ah," he said. "I knew of her when we were children, but we were never friends. She was the girl who disappeared. But then she returned to us recently, shortly after I did. She arrived while I was recovering from the wounds of the darkling fight. When I told her of my quest to find Orem, she insisted she come along, to help."

"That is all you know? She is a bit of a mystery."

Mirolah knew why Elekkena had come. Unfortunately, the other answers she wanted wouldn't come from Stavark. He knew less than she did.

They both watched the water, but Stavark did not speak again. Eventually, he made his way back to his berth.

Soon after, she left as well. Sniff's yips indicated a straight line toward Teni'sia. She told him to stay at the bow and alert her if the trail took a turn.

Mirolah found Elekkena and invited her to the relative privacy of the bow, and they continued her threadweaver lessons. Elekkena struggled to see the threads, and the more Mirolah worked with her, the more she was sure Elekkena had not been the one to heal her. She remembered seeing the threads so quickly, then the smaller fibers, when she had begun training to learn threadweaving. She remembered devouring those lessons in mere hours, then working through more and more complex spells. She tried not to be frustrated as Elekkena tried and failed over and over again until the sky darkened from sunset to night. The sailors lit lamps and put them on hooks, two at the front of the boat and two at the back.

She and Elekkena were so engrossed in the lessons that Mirolah was surprised when Medophae interrupted them.

The lamp illuminated his handsome face in sharp relief. "We are nearly there," he said.

She and Elekkena rose, looking east. They could see the

hulking shadow of mountains against the midnight-blue sky. Below that jagged horizon, pinpricks of light dotted the shore.

Mirolah leaned against the rail. "That is Teni'sia?"

"Yes," Medophae said.

"Where you came from, before you joined Orem's quest."

"Yes."

"I'm sorry for what happened to Queen Tyndiria."

"Thank you." He was quiet for a moment. "I did not think I would return," he said. "Not in this lifetime. But now I find myself anxious to get there. If Zilok has taken up residence, the people of Teni'sia are in danger, and I made mistakes when I left. I should have stayed to see Tyndiria's cousin, Prince Collus, safely installed on the throne, but I...just left."

"It will be all right," she said.

He pursed his lips doubtfully. "Well, I simply came to tell you we'll be docking within the hour. Make certain everything is ready to take ashore. And be ready for what we discussed concerning Sniff, Stavark, and Elekkena. We can avoid a great many questions if they are not seen by the port authorities." He pulled his golden hair back into a ponytail and tied it, then tied an old kerchief around his head.

"That's fetching," she said.

"I'm in disguise." He returned to the helm, talked with the captain, pointed to the horizon.

Elekkena went to tend to the horses, but Mirolah lingered. The boat's lamplight streaked across the black water as though painting a path toward their destination.

38

MIROLAH

THE LIGHTS of Teni'sia pleased Mirolah. From a distance, they were like quiet fireflies, winking shyly. But as the ship came closer, she found the view breathtaking. Dark minarets pierced the night sky, rising out of the craggy cliffs as though they had been carved from the rock. It was difficult to tell where the cliffs ended and the castle began.

Mirolah remembered her first impression of Calsinac. She had never seen such mighty walls, such high towers. But though it was obvious that Teni'sia was barely a quarter the size of Calsinac, she found it more beautiful. Calsinac had died long ago. It was a hulking, beautiful husk, but Teni'sia teemed with life. It felt like safety, knowing that at least in this place, humanity had prevailed.

The ship pulled into an empty berth, and Mirolah went to work. Sniff, Stavark, and Elekkena slipped quietly over the rail of the ship, and she levitated them gently to shore. She made certain they hovered low to the water where the casual observer would never look for them. Both Stavark and Elekkena wore their cloaks and kept a dark blanket over Sniff. They were practically invisible under the night sky. They alighted on a shadowed landing and disappeared into the space between two dockside shacks.

No sooner had the ship's crew thrown a rope over a barnacled pylon than three dock officials marched down the creaky pier to meet them. They waited impatiently as the captain and his men lowered the gangplank.

"Something strange here," the wizened captain murmured to Medophae. "I don't see Slider."

"He is your usual port official?" Medophae asked.

The captain gave a quick nod. "And I never seen three officials watchin' the docks before. Two of them look like soldiers, or I'm a squid."

Medophae grunted agreement.

The captain walked calmly down the gangplank to meet the officials. Mirolah could not hear their words, but as they discussed, the captain became more and more animated. Soon he was making gestures with his hands, as though on the edge of fury. He kept pointing at his ship. She caught a couple of phrases such as "just passengers..." and "tired and wish to eat and sleep..." and "don't need to be bothered with such nonsense..."

The official firmly shook his head, and the two soldiers came alert, ready for trouble. Finally, the captain bowed his head tersely. He started up the gangplank. As he was halfway up, he said over his shoulder, "You'll cost me my bonus this day, I warrant."

The official remained stony-faced.

When the captain returned, he spoke in a normal tone, but made apologetic gestures, like he was breaking the bad news to them.

"It's as I thought. Something's amiss. They want to inspect you. They told me that they never get ships in this late, and that's a bucket of chum. I come in under the stars often enough. Slider knew me well. I asked where he was, and they didn't like that question one bit. I argued with 'em. Said you were paying customers, and that you wouldn't like the idea of someone prodding your personal items. But they're going to search you." He paused, looking at Medophae. "I tell you, something in Teni'sia stinks like low tide. What would you like to do?"

Medophae was thoughtful. "Let them aboard. Tell them we will submit to their inspection. We have nothing to hide."

Nothing that they will find, at any rate.

The boat creaked softly in the sway of the water as they led their horses out of the hold and down the gangplank. The crew of the ship watched with interest as they lined the horses up in front of the dock official. His two guards stood a measured distance away, watching them with hawk eyes.

The official looked them up and down. "And who are you, exactly?"

Medophae stepped forward. "I am Gorlior from Corialis Port. This is my wife," he indicated Mirolah.

"Remove your hood," he said to Mirolah. She did so. "You come from Corialis Port?"

"Yes. We are recently married."

The official grunted. "And what is your business here in Teni'sia?" he asked Medophae.

"A visit to my uncle," Medophae said, then put on a curious face. "I must confess I have never had such trouble entering the city before. Has something happened?"

"Nothing as concerns you," the official said and turned away.

He walked up to the saddlebags and Medophae went to help him. The two guards stepped forward, drawing their swords. Medophae stopped at the blades pointed at his neck. The official turned lazily, pursed his lips.

"Exactly where are you going?" the official asked.

Medophae's eyes narrowed, but he did not move. "To help you go through the bags, of course."

"Were you now?" the official said. "I think I can inspect a few bags on my own."

"Of course." Medophae stepped back. The official continued his search. He went through each bag thoroughly, dumping items on the dock as he dug to the bottom. He moved from bag to bag, throwing their belongings onto the wet wood. Something in Mirolah's belongings gave him pause. He withdrew the Harleath Markin's journal and thumbed through it. His eyes narrowed and he turned to Medophae again. "Who does this belong to?"

"My wife."

"You read books?" he asked.

"For the pictures, sir," she said.

"You can't read it?"

"Read? Of course not," she said.

He narrowed his eyes. "You get changed by The Wave?" he asked.

"What?"

"You do anything strange? Turn things other colors. Move things without touching 'em?"

He studied her, and she tried to keep the anger from her face as his emotions floated to her. He was hunting for threadweavers, and she felt his greasy hope float over to her. There was some reward for this thing he was doing, for finding anyone with unusual abilities. Something bad happened to threadweavers in Teni'sia.

She thought of the moment in Rith when she had become one of the GodSpill, had spread across the lands of Amarion and seen the sparks of new threadweavers like Elekkena. Mirolah had hidden her threadweaver abilities in Rith because of fearful men like this. It was men like this who had killed her brother. If Mirolah hadn't been so afraid to use her powers, if she'd begun learning in Rith like she had in Denema's Valley, she could have saved Fillen from that darkling. She could have saved them all in Denema's Valley, and Orem will still be with them.

She was tempted to grab the man's threads and fling him into the ocean, but Medophae had warned them to be careful. She glanced at him, then back at the official. "Move things?" she asked. "Without touching them?"

The official stared at her. "There are many dangers after The Wave, and we have to keep an eye on them. We keep these people in a safe place, so they can't hurt no one. They are dangerous to normal people."

"I see."

"Some can send a dagger flying 'cross the room without throwing it. I've seen it myself. One of them can light a piece of parchment on fire by pointing."

"I see." She tried to sound afraid, but she wasn't sure if that was coming across over her anger.

Medophae put a calming hand on her shoulder.

"You may enter the city," the official said, sounding bored now. His disappointment floated from him. There would be no reward for him this day. He turned on his heel and walked back up the dock.

The two guards waited a moment, then one of them turned and followed. The second remained, and his eyes opened a little wider. He turned and hurried to catch up with his fellows.

Medophae watched his back until he disappeared into the darkness.

"We should go now," Medophae said.

"That soldier—"

"Either he knew me, or he recognized something about me. If he doesn't already know who I am, it'll come to him shortly. We'll take rooms along the wharf tonight. I know a place."

They paid the captain and thanked him, then the three of them went to join Stavark, Elekkena, and Sniff. Medophae said he knew of an inn close to the docks where no one would recognize him. They would get some rest, then explore Teni'sia at first light.

39

ELEKKENA

ELEKKENA ROSE QUIETLY from the bed. She moved so softly that Stavark did not wake. He was a light sleeper, and she gave a brief smile for herself that she did not disturb him. Medophae had purchased two rooms for them in a run-down inn by the docks. She and Stavark slept in one while Medophae and Mirolah took the other.

She crept across the floor, grabbing her pants and her boots, and paused before the window. Across the street, a man in ragged clothes staggered, finally stopped and leaned against the stained shop wall, slid down to a sitting position and uncorked a bottle.

Elekkena found that nothing within herself had changed. She still loved them, every single one of them, from the poor and the drunken to haughty kings and queens. If she let herself, she could stop, just like this, and watch them for hours. She'd had to guard against that inclination while traveling with Medophae and his companions. She'd had to be careful not reveal too much of her true personality.

The man on the street drank a few more swigs before he passed out. His hand fell and the bottle cracked on the cobblestones.

She couldn't linger here. She had business.

She believed in destiny, not in coincidence. She'd lived long enough to see that strings of coincidences formed patterns. Of course, it was human nature to shrug and pass coincidence off as the unknowable, but that was only because they lived such short lives. One had to look beyond the seventy or so years of a human lifespan in order to see the patterns.

In her time, she had watched coincidences like beads on a string, leading to the great cruxes of history. And here in Teni'sia, tonight, she felt the fate of Amarion balancing on a precipice. A queen had fallen and a new king had been installed. The GodSpill had returned. Medophae had come out of exile, and Zilok had followed him. And they were all in this place. History would pivot here.

She murmured a few silent words and reached into the threads of the door latch. It opened as silent as still air. Once in the hall with the door closed behind her, she pulled her loose pants on, tied them and cinched the soft, braided rope belt with the thin wooden buckle favored by quicksilvers. She laced up her soft leather boots.

She looked at the two doors; behind one was the sweet and dedicated Stavark, behind the other the most powerful young threadweaver she'd ever seen, and Medophae, of course. She had grown quite fond of Mirolah, and the young woman's connection to the GodSpill was staggering. It was as though she bobbed on an endless wave of GodSpill. When Elekkena had healed her in the mist forest, the GodSpill had actually tried to wrench Miro-lah's soul away. That was the first time Elekkena had ever seen anything like that. Ever since, she had been keenly aware of how the lands paid heed to Mirolah as she walked by. The seagulls on the ocean. The skin dog. And it probably focused on her in other ways that Elekkena had not seen yet. Being so inexperienced a threadweaver, Mirolah simply assumed it was normal.

It wasn't.

The GodSpill never chose sides. Or...it never had before. The human lands had come to the brink of total destruction during the GodSpill Wars because the GodSpill didn't take sides. It was a resource, like water, occasionally deadly, but never benevolent or malicious. But the GodSpill fawned on Mirolah. It also made demands of her, as though they were in some kind of lover's quarrel.

The GodSpill had changed during its imprisonment in Daylan's Fountain. Either that, or Mirolah had somehow changed it when she destroyed the Fountain. She had somehow given it a personality. The idea was frightening.

She longed to ask Mirolah about it, to explore what had happened, but she certainly couldn't tonight. If they survived this knot in history, perhaps afterward the two of them could sit down for a long month and talk about GodSpill and nothing else. Perhaps Elekkena could stop pretending that she was an ignorant novice, and the two of them could create wonders that humanity had never before seen.

She bowed her head and looked at her boots.

Yes, and perhaps the sun would rise in the west and set in the south. Perhaps the dragons would come and live peacefully among humans. Perhaps Calsinac would burst into life once more.

Bitterness washed over her, and a desperate loneliness. So much had been taken from her, and it was sometimes hard to pretend otherwise. She drew an incautious breath that whispered in the hallway.

She found herself stepping toward Medophae and Mirolah's door. She even put her hand on the latch before she stopped herself.

Don't I deserve to see him once more before...?

She cut herself off mid-thought. No. It wasn't about what she deserved. It was about what she could give. It was about how she could help others. It was about how she could help them get what they deserved.

Mirolah had sacrificed much for one so young. She deserved this brief moment of happiness before history pivoted on her shoulders.

Slowly, Elekkena turned away from the door. With a scoop of one hand, she gathered her long, silver hair into a ponytail and bound it back. On silent feet, she descended the stairs and left the inn.

The moment she was out in the night air, she felt better, and every step she took away from the ramshackle inn eased the tightness in her chest. Her goal was the correct one: protect them. Help them.

She wound her way up the hill, through the streets and toward the palace like a shadow. Teni'sia was built on a slope, from the crest of the mighty castle towers down to the waters of the Inland Ocean.

It had been a long time since Elekkena had walked these streets. Much had changed, but the layout was the same, and she headed ever uphill as the broad shore of Teni'sia narrowed into the canyon that led to the castle. Once she neared the castle, she recognized what she used to call "Royal Row." She could not remember its actual name. It was probably changed by now anyway.

The expensive wares of the wealthiest merchants lined the cliffs just outside the castle. The nobles never needed to go far for their shopping, certainly not down to The Barnacles where she had just come from.

The road that wound up to the castle was a gully that had been lined on either side with shops, cliffs rising sharply behind them. A wall had been built into the cliffs, blocking the road and dividing the outer city from the inner city. No one could approach that wall without being seen. The guards had the high ground and total visibility. It could be held by a half dozen guards against an army, and the only way to get around the wall was to scale the cliffs on either side, which had been smoothed and polished fifty feet up. Even a lizard couldn't scale that.

But she had talents a lizard did not.

She paused in the deep shadows between two shops and contemplated the open gate. Two guards stood on either side, holding their long, steel spears straight up. Two more paced the wall above. They were all well protected with scale-mail shirts, greaves, and bracers. Short swords hung at each of their sides. The long nose guards of their helms hid their eyes in darkness and gave them a sinister, inhuman appearance.

No one could sneak close enough to those guards to surprise them. And these men were alert. They did not stand like they had taken this boring shift every night for the past three years. They stood as though they expected something to happen tonight.

For about twenty feet in front of the wall, there were no shops, just a clear cobblestone street with no place to hide. She crept along the buildings, pressing herself into the ever-decreasing shadows until she was as close as she dared.

Murmuring a few words, she closed her eyes and visualized her desire, touching the threads of the air on the far side of the street. A crouching, darkened figure emerged from the shadows and made a run for the gate. A shout went up from a guard on the top of the wall, and he rushed over to that side with his crossbow. The two gate guards moved forward to intercept, just as the shadowy figure turned left and dashed away from them.

While their attention was elsewhere, Elekkena jogged to the wall and laid her hand upon one of the huge blocks, murmuring. It shivered and crumbled as if made of dry sand. She shimmied her way into the newly made alcove, then did it again on the next block, then the next one, opening a hole through to the other side.

GodSpill coursed through her. It felt good to use it, and she wanted to do more, but she pushed down the feeling. Zilok was somewhere inside this castle, and while threadweavers typically could not sense the use of GodSpill unless they were looking for it, Zilok *would* be looking for it. The louder a "splash" she made with her threadweaving, the more likely he would notice. He knew that Medophae was coming. He was watching.

The risk of the guards catching her was barely important compared to being caught by Zilok. While the guards looked for her shadow man, who had doubled back and was now running away from the wall, Elekkena whispered again, replacing the missing block with a permanent illusion. No one would know she had created a hole here unless they put their hands on the illusion and pushed.

As the guards searched in vain for a person who was not there, she darted up the street, through the inner city to the castle proper, murmuring words as she went and creating a chameleon illusion about herself. If one of the guards happened to look her way—and if they looked closely—they might see a ripple in the terrain that was her moving body, but that was all.

She ran fast, past the royal stables and up the winding road. Thankfully, it was empty at this hour.

There were three ways to get into the Teni'sian castle. One to the south, one to the north, and the one she'd just entered from the west, which opened onto the city at the edge of the Inland Ocean. The castle was beautifully wrought and built up the side of the mountain like the spiral of a unicorn's horn, with smaller horns rising within. The highest towers flanked the north side of the city, some with a straight drop to the ocean below.

She wound her way around until she came to the great double doors. Two more guards stood at attention there. She paused, shielding herself behind a craggy protrusion of the mountain. She thought about her options. Teni'sia was almost perfectly designed against invasion. From this side of the mountain, there was only one door into the castle. There were no windows within reach, and even if she could climb to one of them, the guards would see her long before she reached it.

She let out a little breath. She would have to threadweave again, and if Zilok were watching, he would find her. But there was no help for it. She would have to play the odds and hope he was looking somewhere else. She spared a brief glance for the guards, then murmured a complicated string of words to guide her imagination.

She transformed from the small, pale-skinned quicksilver into a tall woman with short blond hair. Her loose pants and long shirt changed into a tight-fitting, sleeveless green dress with a white collar. It was the human form she had chosen more than a thousand years ago, a form that was more comfortable to her now than her real body.

Bands stepped out into the path and strode up to the guards, focusing her attention on each of them in turn so that neither would escape. She released a glamour at them like a gout of mist. The guard on her right moved quickly toward the side of the archway. A small rope dangled there. An alarm. But she kept her focus on him, and he slowed. His hand poised next to the rope, but he did not touch it.

She arrived, and the guard's hand dropped away. Glamours did not work as well at a distance as they did up close.

Both of their mouths hung open, and, as she drew up next to them, she reached out and touched each of their arms. "I wonder," she murmured. "Would you please open the door for me? I've spent a long night in the city, and I wish to go to my rooms."

The left guard grabbed for his keys. The right guard hesitated. His brow wrinkled, confused, as though someone had asked him an odd question, and he was trying to come up with the right answer. He opened his mouth to speak, and Bands traced a line on his cheek.

"I can't get into the castle, you see. I'm dreadfully tired," she said.

The right guard swallowed, and his confusion melted away.

"You heard her," he barked at his comrade. "Open the damn door. Can't you see she needs to get into the castle?"

"Yes, sir," the other guard said, fumbling with his keys. He produced the correct one, tried to put it into the lock, and dropped it. He scrambled to recover the keys and again managed to find the right one. This time, he inserted it and turned. Great tumblers clicked and ground, and the latch opened. He pulled the key out, managed to find the second, and inserted it into the lower lock with no mishaps. He opened the door.

"Oh," Bands breathed. "You've saved my life. Thank you."

They grinned at her like simpletons.

She passed through, and they watched her avidly.

"Oh," she said, turning. "One last favor."

"Yes, milady," they said in unison.

"I don't want anyone to know I've been in the city. Can you keep it a secret? Just between you and me."

They nodded vigorously.

"Of course, milady," the left guard said. "To the grave with your secret I'll go."

"Yes, milady," the right guard said.

"You serve your kingdom with poise and precision, gentlemen. Don't forget to close that door behind me."

They both nodded again.

"Goodbye," she said.

The door closed, and she heard the locks click. Bands moved close to the wall of the hallway. There was no one around, but she believed in being careful.

She crept along quietly. She had a scant few hours to explore what she could of the castle, find out what she might. If she was lucky, she would find evidence of Zilok and what he intended.

For more than an hour and a half, she snuck through the passageways and hallways of the castle. She explored the smaller, out-of-the-way places first. She considered it more likely that

Zilok would cling to darkened spaces than brightly lit halls. He always had before.

The sun would rise soon, and she needed to make good her escape before then. In each room, in every hallway, she searched for threadweaving of any kind.

She found none until she came to a room deep in the castle, but the door had a brisk draft coming underneath it. She paused, listening to see if anyone was inside, then opened the door. It looked like a forgotten room that no one had entered in years. On the far end was a giant opening in the side of the castle. A huge, circular platform extended out from it, and it was not a human balcony. It was wide and flat, and there were no rails.

Bands's heart beat faster. This was a dragon's balcony, a way to enter and leave the castle that no one would see. She stepped onto the balcony, which faced north so no one from the Inland Ocean would notice the hole in the side of the castle, but she could see the bay from the very tip.

Avakketh sent someone. They're here, right now, spying on Teni'sia. It's possible they're spying on every major human kingdom.

She went back inside, and, due to her preoccupation, she almost overlooked what she had been seeking throughout the entire castle.

It hovered above the door and slightly to the right, as large as a walnut. To normal eyes, it was invisible, and she'd passed right by it. But to those with a threadweaver's sight, it stood out like a slight glimmer on a moonlit pond. This was a node of concentrated GodSpill.

It was a trigger, a hanging spell, awaiting only the correct circumstance to let it loose. And it was made of GodSpill from Amarion. This was not something one of Avakketh's dragons would make.

Zilok Morth...

She came closer, but she dared not tamper with it. If she

played with one of Zilok's creations, he would be on her before she could take a breath.

However, if she could deduce even a small part of its purpose without disturbing it, that would be a triumph—

Footsteps thumped softly outside in the hall, coming toward this door. For an instant, she considered bolting through the door, but she stayed the impulse. Instead, she ran to the balcony and stood out of sight, just to the left of the opening, and she watched.

The door banged open. A very tall man entered, wearing white chain mail as tight as a second skin. A thick, black belt wrapped his waist, and he wore a dagger that looked like a frozen flame. His tight leather breeches were white, and his boots were black. His snow-white hair hung to shoulder-length, and his white eyes gave a quick scan of the room.

It was Zynder!

Bands drew in a slow, calm breath to still her heart. He had shape-changed. It was something most dragons could do if they wished, but it was frowned upon. Why pretend to be a lesser species when you were a dragon? It was one of the things Avakketh hated about Bands.

She concentrated every fiber of her being on shielding her thoughts, on being as small as she could be. If he noticed her, he would immediately attack, and there were too many lives in this castle. Zynder would happily wade through piles of human corpses to kill her.

And what if he wasn't alone?

Zynder-in-human-shape stood there, unmoving, staring at the hanging spell Zilok had left, as if deciding whether or not to tamper with it. At the end of an interminable minute, he turned on his heel and marched toward the balcony where she hid.

She kept as still as ice, holding her breath, waiting for him to see her, but he walked past her, his gaze on the horizon, and never once looked to his left where she pressed herself against the outside of the castle.

Zynder held his hands up to the sky and murmured a long string of words, calling his power from Avakketh far away.

He transformed. The white chain mail spread over his arms and legs, up his neck and over his head. His legs lengthened and his torso swelled. A tail sprouted from his lower back and lashed, just missing the side of the castle wall. The man's neck lengthened and widened. Huge muscles bunched at his shoulders and great white wings erupted from his back.

In seconds, Zynder perched on the edge of the stone balcony in his natural form, flexing his wings. He bared his teeth to the night and a wisp of smoke curled up from his mouth. His claws scraped into the stone at the platform's edge, and a trail of fine dust fell to the ocean below. His muscles bunched, and he launched himself into the air. He flapped his wings twice, then dove out of sight.

She walked to the edge of the balcony, her lips set in a grim line. Zynder looked like a dark bird against mountains below, and she watched his progress as he flew northward.

He was here for a reason, and now he is leaving, going back to Avakketh to report.

She couldn't just leave Medophae and his group. She was needed here. Zilok had a trap ready to spring, right in this room.

But Zynder was flying north. He had something to tell his god, and it wouldn't be something trivial. It would be something of vital importance, because you didn't go before the god of dragons with trivial matters. And whatever information he had, it would be bad for Amarion. She wouldn't have a better chance to stop him. And he was alone. She might be able to face Zynder alone.

She bowed her head.

"Forgive me, my love. You'll have to fight this battle on your own." She let out a small breath and released the spell that kept her in her human form.

Her dress became green scales and spread over her body. Her legs and arms lengthened. Her torso expanded, swelling to four times the width of a horse. Her neck snaked out, dark green with light green bands from her shoulders to her chin. Her tail slithered into a neat coil behind her.

Her dragon eyes saw perfectly in the moonlight, and Bands watched Zynder catch the updrafts along the edge of the Inland Ocean. With fear in her heart, she launched herself after him.

40

MEDOPHAE

MEDOPHAE AWOKE, and gently pushed back the covers, rolling to a sitting position. Mirolah slept peacefully next to him, still asleep, but as he got up and began to dress, she woke. The barest hint of the predawn light played off the single window in the small room. Bringing a hand up, she scratched her head. Her hair was a tumbled mess.

Medophae felt he should kiss her. A week ago, he would have, but now he didn't know what to do. The two dreams Avakketh sent to him haunted him. Would Avakketh really come south and destroy the human lands? And Avakketh's lie about Bands was clever enough to seem true, to make Medophae doubt himself. Once again, his heart was divided, dreaming of a Bands he could never reach. And suddenly, he didn't know where he stood with Mirolah.

"Another dream?" she asked.

"No."

"Come here," she said, patting the bed.

He hesitated a second—hoped she didn't see it—then he went and sat down.

"I'm eager to find out what changes have been wrought since I've been gone. I want to go take a look outside."

"Explore Teni'sia alone?"

"That's right."

"That's the dumbest thing I've ever heard," she said. "Even dumber than charging into a tainted forest without thinking it through. Zilok is here. He wants to catch you alone. The worst thing you can do is what he expects."

"We can't send Stavark."

"No," she said thoughtfully.

"And we can't do nothing."

"No..." she said, then smiled. "No, we'll send you. We'll just do it my way."

ᛡ

MEDOPHAE LEFT QUIETLY and made his way up the street to the castle gate. After witnessing his ridiculous kerchief cap, Mirolah had crafted a wide-brimmed hat for him. As the streets filled with people going about their business, he noticed a great many soldiers walking among them. The soldiers were stopping and inspecting people at random, and most were wearing the green and white livery of Sym's and the burgundy of Bordi'lis's. That made his stomach sink. Magal Sym had tried to overthrow the crown. Bordi'lis had been one of his allies.

Medophae proceeded along with the small influx of people. A few servants of the castle led donkey-driven carts full of wares.

The doors to the inner city were open, but passing through would be the test. He was certain one of the soldiers would ask him to remove his hat, and when he did, he gave himself good odds of being recognized by someone.

For that, though, he would rely on Mirolah. He didn't know where she was exactly, only that she was watching him from hiding, ready to threadweave. If he couldn't talk his way through, then the plan was to let the soldiers take him in as a prisoner. Once they were inside the castle, Mirolah would put them to sleep and they'd continue exploring.

Just as Medophae approached the guard house, however, he was intercepted. A child grabbed his sleeve.

"Please sir," the child said. Medophae could only see his chin beneath the wide cowl and cloak the child wore. "The cook says come quickly. They've made a mess of things, and she needs your help."

He was about to tell the child he was mistaken when he pulled back his cowl. "Please sir..."

It was Casur, his page when he was Captain of the Royal Guard!

"If you please, sir," Casur insisted. He turned and led Medophae into a nearby alley, where he threw his cowl off.

"Thank the gods I found you, Captain Medophae," the boy said. "They said you were back in the city. I didn't believe them at first, but they were right."

"Who said I was back in the city?"

"Orvin, sir," Casur said. "You never met him. Works for Lord Balis, he does, but he knew you. And he came to us." Casur shook his head. "Dark days here since you left, sir. Dark days. Those you'd trust is looking to betray. Those you don't trust is looking to help." He shook his head. "But if you'll come with me, I'll take you to the person that can tell you what's what."

"Who? Lo'gan?"

Casur looked at his feet, then back up at Medophae. "Please, sir. They asked me to bring you first, as quick as I could find you."

"Then lead the way." The clandestine behavior didn't bode well. He followed the boy.

They cut through darkened corridors, descending back down into the larger part of the outer city.

Finally, they arrived at a respectable inn halfway up the slope that led to the castle. Casur led him through the common room and to the rooms at the far back of the hallway on the ground floor.

He stopped in front of the door and indicated it with a wave of his hand. "Inside, my lord."

Medophae entered, closing the door behind him. Lit lanterns hung on the walls on either side, augmenting the natural light from outside the window. An old oak table, cracked and worn, stood in the center of the room. Lord Vullieth stood behind the table, flanked by two of his house guards. They held drawn short swords and watched Medophae carefully. He glanced over his shoulder and saw there were two other guards behind the door.

Lord Vullieth looked impressive, as always, in his floor-length black cloak. His carrot-colored hair was pulled back tightly, and his black eyes were pinpoints of night in his pale complexion.

"Please remove your hat," Lord Vullieth said in his quiet voice. "I would see your face."

Medophae took his hat off and let it drop.

A small smile played across Vullieth's stern features. He did not look so gaunt as he had a moment before.

"It is true, then. You have come in our hour of need," he said. "You seem to have a knack for that." Vullieth walked around the table and extended his hand.

Medophae took it. He had only met with Vullieth a handful of times, though he had been one of Tyndiria's favorite advisors. He was the most powerful of her nobles, and the most loyal.

"It is good to see you, Captain Medophae."

"And you, as well. What is happening here, Lord Vullieth? Why are we meeting secretly? Why are there so many of Sym's and Bordi'lis's soldiers in the city?"

"Please," he indicated one of the chairs at the table, "sit, and I will tell you all."

In his deep baritone, Vullieth told the story of the coup in Teni'sia. King Collus had vanished, and Grendis Sym had seized the throne. Of the ruling nobles, only those who supported Sym remained. The rest fled the castle, or they had been killed outright.

"Who?"

"Kari'Dar was slain. Grimbresht died in a sailing accident weeks ago, though he was a vocal opponent of Sym. I think it was no accident that he died. I do not know about Rol'if. Baerst has been sick and was not at court, but Lady Ti'shiria escaped, as did Lady Mae'lith."

Vullieth went on to describe how Sym had solidified his power in the past days. His guards were posted at every crucial post in the castle. Practically nothing happened in the castle that Sym was not privy to. He monitored the city, creating patrols or guard stations using the soldiers of his loyal nobles. Vullieth explained that it was blind luck that he discovered Medophae was back in the city. One of the soldiers accompanying the official that stopped them last night was Balis's man, but he didn't like Sym and didn't like what was happening in Teni'sia. He'd passed the word to Vullieth. He had served in the palace for a long time, and recognized Medophae.

"And Sym thinks you are one of his loyal nobles?" Medophae said.

"Yes."

"How? You opposed his father's coup."

Vullieth's face grew grim. "He believes that I am beside myself with rage at King Collus and his brother, the bastard of Bendeller."

"Are you?" Medophae asked, seeing the flush on that freckled face.

"Not enough to betray my country," Sym said. "He thinks me ruled by my emotions, and it is to my advantage to allow him to think this."

"Why didn't you fight him? Why didn't you stop the coup?"

"It was over before I knew it had happened," Vullieth said. "The king and his brother vanished, and Sym's attack on the others came quickly. If I had fought him outright, I would have lost. But inside the palace, I foresaw that I could consolidate the lords who fled, and strike later from a position of stealth and strength. And now you have returned, which I take as a good sign. Even some of Sym's lords might rally behind you. To many of us, you are an extension of the queen we dearly loved."

"I think you played it smart," Medophae said.

"And," he said, "there is something else. I think there is an advisor behind Sym, someone giving him orders."

Zilok. Medophae frowned. "I think you're right."

"The kingdom has been strange and tumultuous since you left. Have you heard of the Wave-altered?"

"The inspector at the dock mentioned something. Are you talking about threadweavers?"

Vullieth raised his chin at that, as though he didn't like hearing the word. "Is that what they are, captain?"

Medophae nodded. "The GodSpill has returned to the lands. With it comes threadweavers. Anyone exhibiting strange abilities is likely a threadweaver."

"Sym has quarantined an entire building for the Wave-altered."

"We'll deal with that next. But first, we need to put a new ruler on the throne. A legal ruler. Not Sym."

"We may have an advantage yet. I do not believe the king is dead."

Medophae leaned forward intently. "How do you know?"

"My intelligence reports that the king and a few of his loyal guards may have escaped into The Barnacles. Sym sent an entire troop of soldiers to recover them. I don't know what happened after, but Sym has been scouring the city, so I think he must have escaped.

"I wish to find the king and retake the throne for him," Vullieth added, and his hard black eyes smoldered. "And I wish to erase Sym's line from the Teni'sian royal scrolls. And from the lands, for that matter. Treason runs in their blood." He paused a long moment, searching Medophae's face. "Will you help me?"

"Of course. But if I find that you are false, Lord Vullieth... If you are playing the wrong side of this struggle, I'll see you pay for it."

Vullieth offered a thin smile.

The two men stood and shook hands.

"There are many within the city and the castle who are still loyal to Collus," Vullieth said. "Sym wants to close an iron fist on the populace, but there is a good deal of confusion. It is possible there are messengers who sneak out at night to report to the king. We may be able to get a message to him, and while I do not believe Collus will trust me out of hand as I have publicly declared for Sym, those who protect him will trust you. Captain Lo'gan vanished the night of the assassination attempt, as did several of the royal guard. I would like to believe they are with the king. If we could join forces with him and the nobles who fled, we could remove Sym from power."

"See if you can get a message to the king," Medophae said. "I will go to him."

Vullieth moved to the door and opened it. "I apologize that I must cut this short, but every moment I am away is dangerous. It would not take much for Sym to suspect me. I will send word to you tonight here at the inn."

Vullieth left, his long black cloak fluttering through the doorway behind him. The guards followed one after the other, leaving Medophae standing in the hallway with Casur.

"With your leave, sir, I'll get back about my duties," Casur said. "I've never been part of a revolution before."

"Go softly, Casur. Take care."

With a flash of white teeth, Casur ran off into the darkness.

41

MERSHAYN

MERSHAYN TRIED to get comfortable in the chair. It was late, and he wished he was lying down. Deni'tri had somehow managed to procure some cushions for him, but it didn't make a difference. Every position he sat in sent a spike of pain to his head. Even lying down did not help much, but it was better than this.

He right eye was still ruined, showing nothing but a light blur, and he tried to keep his eyes closed when he had no need for them. At least the vertigo was somewhat manageable. If he moved slowly and concentrated on keeping his head steady, the room only spun a little.

He coughed, resenting again the smoke from the torches. The cave only had two entrances. They could not very well install a chimney. At least there was something of a draft to keep the smoke from choking them all to death.

Deni'tri stood by his chair. It had been two nights since Collus died in that muddy basement, and she hadn't left his side. Apparently, Mershayn had been unconscious for a lot of that time, but he wondered if Deni'tri had slept at all. Surely she must have, but every time he bubbled to the surface, groping for a hand to steady him, she was there.

Mershayn felt like an old man, to need such constant attention. At moments, he found himself wanting to give up. He could not see himself storming the walls of the castle. He could barely walk from this chair to the distant mouth of the cave.

But something had changed in him when he took Silasa's hand and followed her to this place. When Collus died because of Mershayn's mistakes, it was as though his soul—a molten blob of metal—had suddenly been hammered into a sword. Mershayn had a purpose: To wreak vengeance upon Sym. He would not give up. He would not lie down to accept his fate. If need be, he would crawl back to fight Sym. He would die to bring that murderer down, and that was the only place he would die.

Even inside the constant pounding of his head, Mershayn saw what needed to be done, and he told Lo'gan what to do. Everyone seemed to sense his resolve, and they fed on it. Lo'gan stopped hesitating. He was back to his old self, taking Mershayn's orders and giving orders crisply and confidently down the line. At Mershayn's suggestion, he had been recruiting. For the last two days, many of Lo'gan's loyal guards had joined this fledgling resistance. He still had people in the city who reported to him, and he let no one know about this cave, save Deni'tri and the two guards who had stood with them at The Gutted Fish. But he had created a hidden camp north of the city, up in the mountains, far enough from the cave to be unconnected, far enough from Teni'sia to be undetected. It had already grown larger than they could support with more than fifty soldiers ready to fight. Local farmers aided them, sending food and supplies, but if they became any larger, they would be noticed. Despite Lo'gan's efforts, someone loyal to Sym was going to find the camp eventually. They needed to make their move soon.

And, as if destiny had heard them, they'd received a curious message today from Lord Vullieth. He had already tried to contact them twice, already offered to help them, but Mershayn did not trust Vullieth in the slightest. The uptight lord had been loyal to Collus, but Collus was dead. Once he discovered that Mershayn was the leader here, he would become an implacable enemy. How could the most powerful lord in Teni'sia support the bastard who had slept with his wife?

And according to Lo'gan, the lord had already publicly declared himself in support of Sym, who had now officially taken the throne.

So Vullieth's first two messages had been ignored. The third, however, contained something different. In today's message, Vullieth claimed that the legendary Captain Medophae had returned. The lord wanted to send Captain Medophae with a message, as he realized why Collus and Mershayn might not wish to trust him. Medophae would come with his companions and none of Vullieth's men. Lo'gan himself had gone to meet them, to see if it was, in fact, Medophae and not some imposter. Deni'tri argued with him, saying that she should be the one to go, but Lo'gan would have none of it. In the end, he'd ordered her to stay with Mershayn and rowed off with two other guards in a longboat.

Mershayn didn't think it wise to risk it, but he had agreed with the plan. He kept his mouth shut and waited for events to unfold. The bait of Captain Medophae's return was far too much for Lo'gan to resist. It was—very probably—the simplest trap in the world, and Lo'gan had rowed into the center of it. Even if this Medophae had returned, who was to say that he wouldn't side with Sym as the kingdom's rightful ruler?

In addition, the camp's scouts had reported strange sights during the night. No threats from Teni'sia to the south, but lights danced around the peaks of the Corialis Mountains to the north. They whispered that all of the lands were going to change again, that a second Wave was coming.

"Have you not thought that Medophae himself may surrender us to Sym?" Mershayn grumbled to Deni'tri.

"No, my lord," she said dismissively.

"The rightful king is dead. Sym's bloodline is the most pure after Collus's bloodline. If this Medophae knew that Collus is dead, he would back Sym."

"No," Deni'tri said adamantly.

"Excellent. A fine argument. Do you have anything factual to support this conclusion?" Mershayn asked.

"First, Medophae would never side with someone who took the throne by such a means. He is a fair man, if nothing else. You would know this if you had been here when Queen Tyndiria's parents died, when my queen claimed her rightful heritage. Grendis Sym's father, Magal Sym, tried to assassinate her. It was Medophae who saved her. It was Medophae who slew Magal Sym. He would not support this man's son under these exact same circumstances."

"If he knows that Collus is dead, he may look upon the situation differently than you do. He supported Tyndiria because she had the legitimate claim."

"No," Deni'tri said simply.

Mershayn clenched his teeth, then stopped because it made the throbbing in his head even worse. Instead, he focused on the mouth of the cave, staring into the darkness outside. It was only because of this that he noticed Silasa enter, silent as a shadow.

"Ah, the vampire has emerged at last," Mershayn said. "Why do you not come to see me except at night, I wonder? What do you do during the day?"

"Your humor is brittle," she said. "Give me something juicy."

Laughing would have been a bad idea, so he didn't, but he liked Silasa's dry wit. "We were having an argument about this phantom Captain Medophae and his supposed return—"

"Medophae *has* returned."

Deni'tri perked up at this. "It is true then? You know?"

"I have seen him."

"And how would you know him?" Mershayn drawled. "Teni'sia is not your home. You said so yourself." He closed his eyes. The strain of arguing with her sent wave after wave of pain into his right eye.

"I know Medophae from long ago," Silasa said.

"What, two years?"

"Much longer than that."

"Did you know him as a baby? Because Deni'tri says he is barely twenty years old."

"Cultivate patience, Mershayn of Bendeller. It will be worth the wait."

"Unless this is an ambush," Mershayn said. "I do not relish waiting for that."

To'miln came running to the back of the cave at that moment. He drew up short and bowed to Mershayn. Mershayn nodded to him and immediately regretted it.

"They are here, milord," the guard said. "Captain Lo'gan has returned. He comes with...strange company, my lord." He glanced nervously at Deni'tri. "But it *is* Captain Medophae. His hair is long and wild, but he stands as ever the Captain did. I would know him anywhere."

"How is his company strange?" Mershayn asked.

"There is a child with them. At least that is what I thought at first glance, but I doubt myself now. I think he may be...some other kind of creature. Perhaps a Wave-altered. He wore a hooded cloak, but pushed it back when they came close to the shore." He hesitated, looking back at the mouth of the cave, then turned back to Mershayn, his voice lowered. "He has silver hair, shiny as a coin. Silver eyes, and pointed ears. I've never seen the like."

"And that is all?"

"No, there is a woman. She seems normal enough, but she has a dog, if you can call it that. Nearly the size of a horse, and no fur at all. It's... I don't know what to say about it, sir, but I wouldn't turn *my* back on the thing."

Boots crunched up to the entrance, and Lo'gan appeared. He

came forward and knelt before Mershayn. As he did so, four figures hung back from the entrance of the cave—three people and the huge dog To'miln had described. The dog and the boy were too far away to see anything but silhouettes. The man was tall like Vullieth, well-muscled in the shoulders. The woman was covered by a cloak, and she wore her cowl.

Lo'gan stood again. "My lord, Captain Medophae is here with his companions."

"To'miln says they come with giant dogs and silver-haired boys."

"Yes, my lord."

"What do you think of that?"

"His companions are odd," Lo'gan said. "But I trust Captain Medophae with my life, and I would trust him with yours. Will you see him, my lord?"

"Is that not what I have waited up for?"

Lo'gan nodded smartly and returned to the cave's entrance. He conferred briefly with the huge man who must be Medophae. He and the woman came within the light of the torches, and at last Mershayn could see them with his good eye. Medophae moved like a fighter, and Mershayn realized that the stories of his prowess were likely true. He had golden hair that hung past his shoulders and almost seemed to float of its own accord. He gave Mershayn a respectful nod. As Deni'tri described, he was unbelievably young for how much power and respect he seemed to wield. Twenty years old? Hardly. This boy couldn't be to the end of his teens.

The most startling of the four were the boy and the dog, though. The boy clearly was not human. His tall, pointed ears would have been comical if not for the stern expression on his young face. His cheekbones were almost square and his chin was very long. His eyes were large and as silver as the boy's hair.

The woman removed her hood. She was also young, and beautiful in that country girl kind of way that he had found so alluring so many times in his past. She didn't flinch at his gaze, looked directly into his good eye as though studying him for a weakness.

"My lord Mershayn," Captain Medophae said, and he knelt as Lo'gan had knelt. "Thank you for agreeing to meet us. I realize that you are untrusting at the moment, but we are here to help you."

"So you are Captain Medophae?" Mershayn asked.

"I am."

"You are...younger than I imagined."

"I am often told that."

"You are as enigmatic as my mysterious protector, whom apparently you've known for 'a long time'." Mershayn said sourly.

"Your protector?" Medophae asked.

"She was behind me, somewhere in the shadows. Look long enough, and you may find her. If you can't see her, I don't blame you. I rarely can."

"I am here, Mershayn," Silasa said, stepping forward to stand next to him.

"Silasa!" Medophae blurted in obvious surprise.

"Hello again, Medophae. You look...better than when I last saw you," she said.

"You've been busy," he said.

"Belshra was a ruin. So I came here to help."

"It seems you've been helping all over the place." Medophae glanced back at the silver-haired boy, who watched Silasa with reverence. He put his fist over his chest, then knelt to her.

"It's a long story for another time," she said.

Medophae seemed about to say something more, but held his tongue. A strange smile flickered over his face, then he turned back to Mershayn. "Fate favors you, Mershayn," he said.

"All evidence to the contrary," he said. His head throbbed.

"Lord Vullieth is behind you and the king," Medophae said. "That's what I'm here to tell you. He sent me because he knew, at least, those who protect you would believe me, even if you do not."

"Vullieth has declared for Sym," Mershayn said.

"As a ruse. He believes he can best help Collus recover the throne by working from inside Teni'sia." Medophae paused. "Alas, Lo'gan informed me of what has befallen your brother. I am sorry, Lord Mershayn."

"As am I."

"But I am certain he would just as readily put his soldiers behind you instead of behind Sym. His offer still stands."

Mershayn gave half a laugh, then clenched his teeth as the room spun and he nearly lost his dinner. He swallowed hard, trying to regain his composure. "I would not be so certain of that," he managed to say. "And I am not king. I'm merely...orchestrating a way to bring Sym down. Once I've done that, the Teni'sians can choose their king. Lord Vullieth himself, perhaps."

"Aren't you his brother?" Medophae asked calmly.

"His bastard brother."

"It would not be the first time Teni'sia has seated bastard blood upon the throne. You are the closest claim after Collus."

"Sym is the closest claim. And Vullieth would never support me as king."

"No?"

"No."

"And why would that be?"

"Because I am no king," he said. "Ask Vullieth."

"Lord Vullieth would rather see you on the throne than Sym, I would wager."

"That's money you would lose," Mershayn said. A spike of pain went up Mershayn's spine into his right eye. He grit his teeth. "Besides, I do not wish to be king," Mershayn snarled. "I wish to avenge my brother and then die."

Medophae nodded as though he understood, and Mershayn wanted to spit at him. This overconfident pup didn't know what it was to love your brother more than your own life, then to watch him be cut down because of your shortcomings.

"Hmmm," Medophae said. "I suppose we shall see."

Another spike of pain went up his spine and into his head. Mershayn stifled a gasp. The room canted to one side and Mershayn closed his eyes a moment. He forced them open again. "I will welcome Vullieth's help to unseat Sym, but I do not think we will have it when you tell him Collus is dead."

The woman leaned over and whispered into Medophae's ear. Another spike of pain shot into Mershayn's head, and he feared his skull would crack open. This time he could not suppress a gasp.

"My lord, Mirolah says that your wounds are worsening. If you would—"

Mershayn did not hear the rest of what the young captain said. The room slanted to one side, and he couldn't stop it this time. It was as though everyone before him stood on the wall of the cave. His right eye went black. He could see nothing out of it, and it felt like someone had lit his brain on fire. Something hard smacked into his injured cheek, and he screamed. He saw the woman lunge forward.

Then, nothing....

GS

I WILL NOT LET you go.

Mershayn struggled in terror against the webs that held him. He must get away. He fought them with every ounce of strength he had, but they held him, immovable. Above him, a huge, gray-black swirl pulled at him. That was where he belonged. He had to get free, had to get to it. He pushed his face between the threads of the web, but could not force his head through.

"Let me go," he screamed. He felt the fabric of his being tearing. It was excruciating. It was as though he was being torn in half, starting with his eyelids and pulling down until all his flesh was parted. Why could he not get past this web? He needed to reach that swirl. That was where he belonged!

All will be well. The wound is complicated. I will be finished shortly.

"No!" Mershayn threw himself against the web. He bit, but his teeth were not sharp enough. He kicked, but he was not strong enough.

Suddenly, the pull of the vortex lessened. He considered the swirl in the sky and, for the first time, wondered what it was. The bonds of the web did not bind tightly against his skin anymore. Rather, he was floating down, away from it. He turned about and saw his body below him. It jolted him speechless.

The woman knelt over his body, her hands on his chin and his right cheek. As he floated closer, he saw tiny tendrils of light connecting her head to his own. There were hundreds of the light tendrils, wriggling into his chin and cheeks.

Then, all at once, she turned her head, and looked up at him. The tendrils slithered toward him. Mershayn threw his hands up in front of his face and rainbow lights flashed.

GS

HE OPENED his eyes and sucked in a breath. Straight brown hair shielded him in a shimmering curtain. The woman leaned over him, as though she had almost fallen on top of him. She smiled wearily, and it was as if the new day had risen from that smile. He had never seen anyone so lovely.

"By the gods..." he whispered. He saw her in perfect clarity now, through left and right eyes, and the pain in his head had vanished. "What did you do?"

"By Thalius, you fought me," she said, sounding exhausted. "But I wasn't going to let you go."

"You healed me?" She was so radiant he could barely speak. She glowed like a goddess. "I watched you from above myself," he said. "I was entangled in a web. It burned me, tried to tear me apart."

"I apologize for that."

"You made the web!"

"Your spirit had already left your body. There was no other way."

"That swirling gray above me..."

"The Godgate."

"The Godgate," he whispered again. "You are... You are..." He could think of nothing that could adequately describe the surge in his heart. He longed to stare forever into her eyes. He felt whole, but feared that feeling would vanish the moment he stopped looking at her.

She smiled self-consciously, as though she could read his thoughts. She shyly averted her eyes and stood up on shaky legs. "Come." She extended her hand, though she did not look at him directly. "You should be able to stand."

He took her hand and a shiver ran through him.

"What is your name?" he murmured.

"I am Mirolah," she said. Once she had helped him upright, she let go of his hand and went back to stand beside Medophae once more. When her hand slipped out of Mershayn's, he felt a loss. Without her near him, he felt...fragmented.

Somebody said something, but Mershayn continued to stare at her.

"My lord, I apologize," Medophae said. "Perhaps we should talk more later."

Mershayn shook his head, trying to clear it. "What?"

"Perhaps we could continue this conversation in the morning? I think a good night of rest will serve you well."

Mershayn's gaze strayed to Mirolah. She watched him curiously. He suddenly realized how strange he was acting, and snapped his attention back to Medophae.

"No, Medophae. Not at all. I feel as though I have just flown through the air. I feel...as if I have awoken from a nightmare to find..." He looked at Mirolah again, but the words he had been about to say died.

"Are you all right?" Deni'tri took his arm, looking with concern into his eyes. "Did she addle your brains, my lord?"

"In the best of ways. Give me a moment."

He reseated himself, trying to tamp down his unreasonable joy, though he could barely contain it. He felt as if he could take on all of Sym's soldiers single-handed.

Once he had rallied his thoughts and forced himself not to look at Mirolah, he got back to business. They would retake Teni'sia. They would do it as soon as possible.

They talked deep into the night, discussing strategy. The moon was high in the night sky by the time they finished. Medophae seemed as indefatigable as Mershayn, but the quicksilver—whose name was Stavark—and Mirolah were exhausted.

Their council ended, and it was with that same striking sense of loss that Mershayn watched Mirolah leave his cave. He desperately wished to come up with some reason why he should talk to her alone, but he could think of nothing.

"You should rest, milord," Deni'tri said.

"I cannot sleep. It is as if I have been reborn," he said. "Tonight, you sleep. I shall watch over you."

Her eyes were red-rimmed from fatigue, but she shook her head. "No, my lord."

"Consider it an order."

Her mouth set in a firm line.

"Come, Deni'tri. We attack Teni'sia tomorrow. I need you fresh, and I know you have slept but little. Do me this service. Allow me the privilege of protecting you as you have protected me."

She seemed about to refuse, then said, "Very well, Your Majesty."

Your Majesty. King. Of all the laughable, bizarre things.

Tomorrow they would attempt to retake Teni'sia. He didn't need to worry about something so silly as becoming king. His would be the first blade to cut into Grendis Sym, or he would die trying. That was his kingdom. That was all that mattered.

He leaned against the cave wall and settled in for his watch. Soon, Collus would be avenged, and they could both rest.

And it was all because of her. He knew he should be thinking about the upcoming attack, but he couldn't. His thoughts strayed to beautiful Mirolah, her brown eyes looking into his soul.

42

MEDOPHAE

COOL MOONLIGHT SHONE on the craggy rocks nearby Mershayn's hidden cave. Since the moment he saw her emerge from the shadows to the left of Mershayn's chair, Medophae knew Silasa would find a moment to talk tonight. He had made himself obvious, and she would find him.

She appeared around the fold of the cliff, her dark silhouette breaking the glimmering pattern of the waters behind her. The smooth roll and crash of the surf echoed quietly all around.

She was the same as ever, an affliction they shared. Her long black braid sloped over one shoulder, and her stance was that same equal-legged stance she'd always had. She did not cock her hips, lean one way or another. It was the stance of a young woman, open and receptive and unbruised by the lands.

The irony caught at Medophae's heart. Silasa had been more bruised than most, had suffered more hardship than a mortal could comprehend. She did not stand that way because she was innocent, but because her body had the muscle memory of a sixteen-year-old girl, because that was when Darva had infected her with the blood of White Tuana. Silasa would never hunch under the weight of age, feel the aches in her joints that would cause her to shift her weight when she stood too long. She would never swing her hips seductively to catch someone's eye.

"I always wonder what you are thinking when you look at me that way," she said. She hiked her black skirts and deftly navigated her way around the rocky ground. Not a single stone crunched under her advance. She moved as if she was walking on air.

"I was thinking about you during a younger time in your life," he returned.

"Before I became a vampire."

"I remember you running after a ball through your father's audience chamber."

"Much younger, then."

"I hadn't seen you for years when Darva snatched you. By the time I saw you again..."

"I was this," she finished for him.

He looked down at his hands that rested easily between his knees. "I'm sorry about that."

After a moment, she said, "It's not your fault that she took me."

He wondered if that was true. If he hadn't spent so much time talking with Darva, trying to find a peaceful solution... If he'd simply jumped straight to violence, would the outcome have been different?

"I found a log," he said. "Good for sitting."

She glanced at the piece of driftwood he had turned so that it made a passable—if short—bench, then looked at her dress, then sighed.

"Is that a new dress?" he asked, realizing she was reluctant to get it dirty.

"Mershayn vomited on my last outfit."

"We can stand."

"No, let's sit."

They sat in silence. After a moment, Silasa scooted closer and rested her head on his shoulder. He put his arm around her, and they looked out over the ocean, watched the waves lap against the shore.

"It is good to touch someone," she murmured. "Sometimes, I feel that I am not real because I do not touch. Not the way humans normally touch. I do not shake hands. I do not hug. The only time I touch another creature is when I kill it. I have no contact with those that I love…. It is easy to feel as if I am not real at all."

His arm tightened around her.

"I have missed you," she said with a sigh. "I miss the life I once had, broken as it was, when Belshra still existed. Even when my father and sister and nieces and nephews died of old age, I continued helping my grand-nieces and nephews. It wasn't much of a life, but I miss it fiercely now. My fringe existence near Belshra seemed small and lonely until it was taken away. Now I have no one."

"You have me."

"I cannot make a life from waiting for you to stop by every decade or so."

"I'm sorry," he said.

She took a deep breath. "Tell me of your journeys since last I saw you. Tell me of this Mirolah who you find so precious."

Medophae related the story of the destruction of Daylan's Fountain and the ensuing chase by Zilok Morth. He told of how he had lost Oedandus, and how Mirolah had healed something inside him he hadn't known was wounded. He told of how he had cast away the ruby containing Bands, and how he'd learned to be in love with another.

He didn't tell her about the dreams of Avakketh, or the answer to the riddle, or the notion that Bands might have been freed when he cast the gem into the Sara Sea.

Silasa wept, and Medophae wept with her.

"And how did you come to ally yourself with this Lord Mershayn?" he asked.

"I fill my nights how I can. There was a need. I helped. Who knows, perhaps Teni'sia will become my new Belshra."

"You have a right to do what you wish. So much has already been taken from you."

"Don't pity me, or I'll bite you," she warned.

He laughed. "Mershayn is lucky to have you at his side."

"And to have Wildmane. And a full-fledged threadweaver. I almost feel sorry for this Grendis Sym."

"I wouldn't go that far."

"You've already passed judgment on him, then?"

"You think me heartless." He raised an eyebrow and craned around to look at her.

"I think you implacable."

He let out a long breath. "I gave too much sympathy to Ethiel. It cost me everything."

"And you will never make that mistake again, will you?"

"You bait me," he said.

"Compassion isn't a failing."

He went silent. The truth was: he wanted to be fearsome to those who deserved it. He wanted evildoers to imagine the fiery rage of Oedandus coming for them. He wanted them to quiver at the thought of it. "Then I shall do better," he said.

She nodded. If someone like Silasa could find compassion, past the hunger inside her, after all that had been done to her, then he could strive to at least match that compassion.

He changed the subject. "So, Teni'sia is your new home, then?"

"There are many lightless corridors in the castle. I like it. It's easy to move about."

"So Denema's Valley was just a stop along the way?"

She glanced at him. "Stavark told you."

"It's not every day a quicksilver gets saved by a vampire. He thought you came to eat him."

"I *was* hungry," she said. "And I imagine quicksilver blood tastes like fresh snow."

He laughed, knowing Silasa would rather eat her own arm than feast on an innocent. "What were you doing there?" he asked.

"Protecting my one friend."

"You should have told me you intended to follow me," he said.

"And spoil the surprise?"

"Why do I feel like you're still not telling me everything?"

"Because you have wisdom." She stood up.

"Silasa—"

"The dawn is close," she said.

He sighed. "Will I see you tomorrow night?"

"If not, then soon."

"If you insist on being cryptic, then good hunting, princess."

She moved down the slope like a dancer, neatly managing her new dress, and disappeared into the night.

43

MIROLAH

WE ARE ONE, the voice whispered to her. *Come to us.*

It had never stopped since the insidious forest. She was constantly pushing it to the back of her mind. The voice was stronger, more aggressive.

She sat inside the cave, shielding herself, and waiting with Sniff next to her. He never left her side now, and he was a reassuring companion. He was content to sit still as long as needed, and he didn't interrupt her unless something was important. When he was hungry, he would hunt, but he never left for long. And he never complained when he had to sit still.

The cave was a good hiding place. She didn't want to interrupt Medophae and Silasa's reunion. The vampire seemed to have perfect night vision, but she couldn't see through stone. Mirolah could see them, though, with her threadweaver vision. While she sat in this cave, her attention lightly touched Sniff, almost as a reference point, and then meandered farther afield, weaving throughout the threads of the rocky ridge, the waves of the Inland Ocean, and the first breath of winter on the cold air. She also kept her attention on Medophae and Silasa.

Medophae, as always, was a golden bonfire. Silasa's aura was different. Instead of a fire, she was surrounded by a jumpy white flicker. It wasn't as overwhelming as Medophae's radiance, but she was obviously more than human. And less.

The white flicker was a net much like the one Mirolah had thrown over Mershayn to keep his spirit from floating up to the Godgate, but the woman's body was dead—its natural vibrancy was gone. A normal dead body would have begun to break down, ravaged by the elements, eaten by minuscule creatures that caused decay and eventual disintegration, but an endless network of white threads interwove throughout every part of Silasa: her lungs, heart, liver, intestines, skin, muscle, and bone—all of it, tying it tightly together, holding it still. Only her blood moved—at a much more sluggish pace than the blood of a living person—sprouting the white threads that bound her together. No creature, no matter how low, would instinctually touch Silasa's flesh, and so she could not suffer from sickness or decay. It was as though Silasa was sheathed in a repellent bubble. Even humans would instinctually recoil from touching her.

It was cruel, what White Tuana had done to Silasa. The goddess had given her supernatural abilities and a thirst for blood, then severed her from humanity. It was no wonder vampires were reputed to be rapacious villains. Humans, their own kind, instinctually reviled them. It would be hard not to become bitter about that and want to lash back. She wondered at Silasa's will to resist that compulsion. She wondered if it felt like the voice that hounded Mirolah, that demanded she leave her body and join the GodSpill. Did Silasa's own blood demand that she rip and tear and feast on people?

We are one....

Mirolah pushed the voice back, denying it, and she took a deep breath. She had lost her family—again—in Rith. She had lost her mentor in Denema's Valley. She'd lost her innocence in the battle against Ethiel, and she'd lost her entire identity in Daylan's Fountain. She had rebuilt herself, and she'd done it around Medophae. He'd been the only steady point around which she could rebuild. In a matter of days, he had become her entire world. But the more she saw Medophae interact with Silasa, with Lo'gan and Deni'tri, with the layers of his past, the more she realized what an infinitesimal part of his life she really was. He had lived for fourteen centuries. She had been with him for a few intense weeks. It was foolish to think he had not bonded with others the way he had bonded with her. It was foolish to think their connection was something unique to him. He didn't truly belong to her. He belonged to his angry god, to the very people of Amarion. He was their hero, and they would always need him.

Silasa and Medophae talked near the ocean, reminiscing about events that didn't include Mirolah, and never could. They talked of generations past and cities long fallen. Medophae had lived a hundred lifetimes, and Silasa had been part of many of them. Mirolah had only been part of the last few weeks. She had been his lover. She'd thought that meant they belonged to one another. She had seen it as a young woman sees such things, hopeful, as if her entire life was beginning with him at her side.

But did he see it that way? How could he possibly, with her only being a recent addition to his eternal life? How could he really belong to her?

And where did she belong?

We are one....

She pushed the voice back again, pushed down the slowly rising terror she had felt over the last few days. It was as if she had been standing securely on solid ground ever since Daylan's Fountain, assured of her safety, but all the while she was really standing with her back to a sharp drop-off, her heels almost over the edge. She simply hadn't seen it because she hadn't turned around.

Silasa stood up, giving Medophae a smile, then climbed the rocks and vanished into the darkness. He also stood, preparing to return to Mershayn's camp, so Mirolah left her hiding place, Sniff at her side.

Medophae looked up. "Mirolah," he said, surprised. "I didn't realize you were here."

"I didn't want to interrupt your conversation." She pulled a few threads, floating down to alight next to him.

He smiled, but it was hesitant. He didn't light up at her presence like he used to. Instead, she made him uneasy.

Last night in The Barnacles, she had cuddled up to him in their bed, and he had been reluctant to touch her. She had wanted to mark it up to everything that was happening to them, that he was just as preoccupied as her, but the question arose in her mind: What was wrong?

As always, she couldn't let go of a question once it bubbled up in her mind. That's when she began thinking about the last time he had actually been affectionate toward her as a lover and not just a companion. It took her a moment to trace it back, but it had been in Rith, that first evening in Lawdon and Tiffienne's house, before he woke up from his nightmare and went for a walk. Since then, so much had happened—the fight with the spine horse, the continuing search for Orem, and the increasingly demanding voice of the GodSpill—that she hadn't thought to quantify the difference in his behavior.

But something has happened. Something I've been too preoccupied to notice. This isn't a momentary distraction. Our relationship shifted while I wasn't watching.

"Are you okay?" she asked him, putting a hand on his shoulder.

He paused, then took her in his arms, hugging her and kissing her on top of her head. She felt his glamour wrap her up, making her feel wanted and loved, but she gently pushed it back with her own threadweaving. Usually, she enjoyed basking in that feeling, that warm, golden affection, but tonight, she needed to know the truth.

He had just kissed her on the forehead, not the lips. He'd kissed her like you would a friend or a sibling. Another sign.

Her heart beat faster, painfully, like her heels were shifting farther backward, out over the steep cliff.

She tried to rationalize his behavior. Tomorrow, they would begin an invasion of Teni'sia. He could be distracted by battle.

Or he could be distracted by seeing his friend Silasa again, or that Elekkena had mysteriously vanished. She told herself it could be any of a half dozen things.

But she wanted to come right out and ask him: *You called out Bands's name in your dream. Are you dreaming of her? Are you wishing you were with her, not me?*

"So the attack is tomorrow." She repeated the obvious, losing her nerve.

"Moving swiftly will take Sym by surprise. I'm still nervous about you going after Zilok."

"He thinks I'm dead. He won't be expecting me. You be the lightning rod. He'll come to you."

"Clever." He glanced sidelong at her. "It's what he expects. He'll believe it."

"Then I cut his anchor."

"He's going to keep Orem in a safe place. He was overconfident last time with Vaerdaro. He won't make the same mistake twice." Medophae paused. "Are you sure there's no way he might believe you survived?"

She shook her head. "I was dead. Zilok knew the job was done, and it would have been, but Elekkena healed me."

"I thought you healed yourself."

"So did I. That's what Elekkena said, and I believed her at the time. But now that she has vanished, I'm questioning everything she told me. When I was healed, I heard murmuring in a language I didn't understand. She said it was me. I marked it up to these strange powers that I'm still struggling to understand, but the more I think about it, the more ridiculous her story sounds. She lied to me, to all of us. *She* healed me."

"What? How?"

"She's a threadweaver," Mirolah said. "She kept it a secret from Stavark, from you. She said she wanted me to train her." She shook her head. "And I swallowed it because it was just close enough to the truth. It explained everything strange about her— her odd aura, her mystery, her aloof behavior. But she's not a novice threadweaver, Medophae. I think she's experienced. She healed me, something even I couldn't have done, I think. Zilok wouldn't think it was possible for me to heal myself like that."

"But you were the first threadweaver in centuries," he said.

"Actually, my brother was the first. It stands to reason there were others. I was just the one Orem found. What if Elekkena left her people when she discovered her powers, then began practicing them in seclusion? I have learned so much in just a handful of weeks. I can only imagine how much she might have learned in two years." She paused. "Remember at Zilok's lair in Denema's Valley? You said Zilok used objects and rituals to guide his mind when he threadweaves. You said others take anchors to help them threadweave, crutches to focus their minds. That seemed odd to me, because I don't do it that way. But what if Elekkena does? Except, instead of rituals, what if she murmurs words to hold her focus?"

Medophae stared at her, stunned, as though he'd just had a revelation.

"What?" she said. "What is it?"

"I..." He stumbled over the words, then apparently realized his emotions were an open book, and he turned away.

"Medophae, what?"

He shook his head. "Nothing," he said to the night. "I just... I mean, that's just so...unbelievable." He turned back around, and he had managed to clear the surprise from his face. He gave her a smile, and his glamour tried to invade her threads with its warmth and well-being. She pushed it away.

"There could..." he began. "Well, this could mean that there are a lot of threadweavers in Amarion, couldn't it?"

She felt ill, and she suddenly wanted to be anywhere but here, watching him fumble and try to lie to her. Medophae knew Elekkena's secret, whatever it was, or he knew something about it. That revelation on his face couldn't mean anything else. Medophae wasn't terribly sly in concealing his emotions. Yet he didn't want to tell her about it, and he didn't want to tell her about his dreams. One decision at a time, he was pushing her away.

"I wonder if she stumbled across Zilok," he continued, trying to reinforce the deception. "If she threadweaved near him, and he sensed her, he would have captured her," he said. "Or even killed her. I wonder if Elekkena went exploring Teni'sia."

"I wonder if she did," she said softly. Her lips felt numb.

"When we attack," he said in his confident, commander's voice, "you know you can't threadweave until we get close. Not until you're ready to look for Orem. Zilok will be watching for anyone using the GodSpill. If he senses you, our advantage diminishes."

"We don't want him to sense me," she repeated, trying to get a handle on her beating heart as she had her own revelation. Who was Elekkena? What kind of revelation could Medophae have had that would stun him so?

Then a single question bubbled up in her mind. It kept repeating over and over. She opened her mouth to ask him, then closed it again.

Did Bands murmur when she threadweaved? Was that her *anchor?*

44

SILASA

A STORM MUST HAVE SET in during the day, and snow had begun to fall. The caves and the coast were dusted in white. Silasa watched the boats line up along the sand. It was testament to this Captain Lo'gan's efficiency that he could organize so many boats in just a day and have them arrive in secret.

Medophae had told her the plan, and it was elegant in its simplicity. Wildmane, a threadweaver, a vampire, a quicksilver, and fifty soldiers to storm a castle. Grendis Sym didn't stand a chance. Medophae was an army unto himself. In fact, the upcoming battle would have been a forgone conclusion if not for Zilok Morth.

But Medophae's young threadweaver, Mirolah, had a plan to deal with the spirit. She claimed she could neutralize Zilok.

Apparently, Zilok believed Mirolah was dead. He had attacked her outside of Belshra and thought he'd killed her. To Zilok, fifty soldiers and a quicksilver was a laughable challenge. But Mirolah's perceived death was an advantage. Zilok would happily envision the battle between just himself and Medophae. He would easily believe Medophae would simply charge forward, relying solely on the power Oedandus to prevail, just like he always did.

And while Zilok was licking his chops, anticipating the moment he would spring his trap, Mirolah would lie in wait. When Zilok sprung his trap, she would attack, unraveling Zilok's scheme, and, if the young threadweaver was to be believed, Zilok as well. For good.

And that was something neither Bands nor Medophae had not been able to accomplish in a thousand years. The young thread-weaver seemed inordinately talented, and Silasa found herself beginning to believe her claims were not boasts.

However, Bands had always been the strategist in her and Medophae's legendary partnership. To see this spot so elegantly filled by this young threadweaver sat uneasily in Silasa's belly. Mirolah was not Bands. Yet Medophae seemed happy to let her slip into Bands's role.

Silasa dug her boot into the sand and watched the soldiers as they checked their equipment and began boarding the boats. She didn't relish the idea of sitting in a boat with them, sailing south to Teni'sia. Mortals didn't like being too close to her, and she could feel their revulsion.

She knew it was stupid, but she couldn't help caring what they thought. When they recoiled from her, she couldn't help but agree with them. How else should a mortal respond to a monster in their midst?

She waited, watching for the boat Medophae would board. She'd join him on that one.

The soft step behind her was surprising. It was nearly impossible to sneak up on Silasa, so she knew who it had to be. She looked over her shoulder.

Ynisaan stood there, wearing all black tonight. Her white hair was bound in a black scarf, and her midnight skin seemed a part of the shadows. Silasa was surprised to see her. Ynisaan didn't visit when there were other people around.

"Taking a risk, aren't you?" Silasa asked softly, facing the beach again so as not to draw attention.

Ynisaan let out a small breath. "Every moment of my life is a risk. I am used to it."

"What's wrong? Why did you come?"

She hesitated, then said, "Bands has returned."

Silasa felt like Ynisaan had poured a bucket of ice water over her. She swallowed, then backed into the deep shadows next to the mysterious woman. When she was out of sight of the soldiers on the beach, she turned, looking into Ynisaan's depthless eyes. "What are you talking about?"

"I don't have time to explain," Ynisaan said. "But Bands is free. She has been for many days. As always, she has put herself at the heart of things."

Silasa couldn't find her tongue. After all these years, Bands was alive. She was free. Giddy butterflies filled in her belly. To see her old friend again...

"Where?" Silasa asked.

"They fight near Galandel Peak, north in the Corialis Mountains."

"Who's they?"

"You saw the lights in the clouds?" Ynisaan asked.

"The unnatural storm. It's been the talk of the camp. That's her?"

"Dragon fire. She has been battling another dragon, all day yesterday and some of the previous night. I need you to go to her with all haste."

"And do what?"

"Make sure she survives."

Silasa paused. "Ynisaan, I...I can't fight a dragon. I wouldn't even know where to start."

Ynisaan said nothing.

"And what of Medophae's invasion?" Silasa asked. "They need me—"

"He doesn't need you. Bands might."

"Might? You don't see what will happen?"

"The ghost lines of dragons are harder to read than humans."

"Ghost lines?"

"There isn't much time, and you have very far to go. Will you help?"

Silasa hesitated.

"Medophae has Oedandus with him," Ynisaan said. "And Zilok will not take the god away this time." There was something odd in her tone. Almost...reluctance.

Silasa tried to guess what it was. "You don't mean to tell Medophae about Bands," she said.

"He must go to Teni'sia. He must defeat Zilok. If he does not..." She trailed off. "This invasion is paramount. Would you tell him right before this battle?"

Medophae would abandon everything if he knew Bands was back. "No, I wouldn't," she said, then shook her head. Silasa looked over her shoulder at the shore. Most of the soldiers were loaded up, and some of the boats had already pushed out into the gentle bay. Medophae was on the beach now, his yellow hair glowing in the moonlight. The young threadweaver and the huge skin dog stood next to him.

"Will you go?"

"Yes," she said. Mershayn wasn't going to like that. He wanted Silasa with him, but Silasa had come to trust Ynisaan. If she said this was best, then she would know. "Let me just tell Medophae."

Ynisaan's eyes widened.

"Not about Bands," Silasa amended at Ynisaan's expression. "About the fact that I won't be able to join the invasion."

"What will you say?"

"That my blood hungers. That I need to feed. That I can't be on a boat packed with other mortals right now. That I'll meet him later." She smiled, uncovering her pointed canine teeth. "All those vampire lies."

Silasa glanced at the beach again. Medophae's young thread-weaver was looking directly at her, curious.

"You'd better go," Silasa murmured to Ynisaan. Mirolah seemed to have extraordinary talent for a novice threadweaver. That she could spot Silasa in the shadows spoke of some kind of extrasensory ability. "The threadweaver is looking this way."

Silasa turned around, but Ynisaan was already gone.

45

STAVARK

AUTUMN HAD TURNED to winter in a day, and soft snow had begun to fall as they rowed up the coast. Everyone stayed silent at their work. The creak of the wood and the quiet splash of the waves were the only sounds. Stavark worked at the Rabasyvihrk's side, while two Teni'sians worked the opposite side of the boat. The oars dipped and raised, pulling them over the gentle waves of the Teni'sian harbor. The castle lights twinkled. Stavark watched the shoreline, and he wondered where Elekkena had gone. Somehow, she had snuck out of their inn the night before Captain Lo'gan found them, and she had vanished.

As with so many things surrounding Elekkena, this was a mystery. He had no idea where she might go, or why she would leave. He thought her connection to this quest was him, but obviously he had been mistaken. In what time he could spare before they came to Mershayn's cave, he had searched for her in Teni'sia, but he had found nothing.

He had barely known her. He hadn't wanted her to come with him in the first place, and yet he was angry she had left. He missed her. And it frustrated him that he had overlooked something about her personality. He would never have guessed she would simply abandon them without a word.

He pushed her out of his mind and glanced over his shoulder at the shoreline again, searching through the falling snow for any sign that an opposing force waited for them. The unexpected storm was a blessing to their attack. Visibility was short; it would be difficult for someone on the shore to see the approaching boats.

The other rowboats followed at a distance, carrying the human leader, Mershayn, the Maehka vik Kalik, and Silasa, the hollowskin who had saved Stavark's life.

The sun had risen and fallen only once since they'd first met with Mershayn, and now they were going to war. Captain Lo'gan and Lord Mershayn had argued about it. Lo'gan was cautious. Lord Mershayn was reckless. Lo'gan insisted that they take their time, gather more loyal soldiers to fight on their side. Mershayn said striking fast with a smaller force was the only way to win this conflict quickly and decisively, with the least amount of bloodshed. If they struck tonight, they could unseat him with a small attack force. If they waited and allowed Sym to secure his position, any attempt to take the crown by force would require large armies and, possibly, years of fighting.

Stavark let the moment flow over him. He was not a killer, and yet he had leaned upon his sword since the moment he entered Orem's service. He had hurt men in Rith, and he had slain darklings, but he had never taken the life of a human or a syvihrk. Tonight, he wouldn't be able to avoid it, and the thought hurt him. He knew the moment he killed someone, his heart would change forever.

To help his mind settle, he recalled the sunset he had captured before leaving Sylikkayrn. The oranges, the reds, the deep purples before the fading of the light. For a moment, he returned to that place and stood within the memory, absorbing the serenity he'd had. His muscles pulled at the oar, but his mind watched the sun settle itself peacefully behind the mighty Spine Mountains.

But his thoughts alighted on Elekkena. What if she hadn't left them? What if she'd been taken? Should they be looking for her? It was not unreasonable to think she'd slipped into Teni'sia during the night, the only time a quicksilver could safely explore a human city. What if she'd meant to come back, but couldn't?

Stavark set his mouth in a line, unable to unravel the tangled possibilities.

"All right," the Rabasyvihrk murmured, still leaning forward and back to the rhythm of his oar. "We're almost there. You know what to do. Look before you attack. Vullieth's men will wear his sigil on the right shoulder, a crested helm and a mallet."

Stavark nodded. He knew all of this already.

Their silent rowing brought them to the edge of the docks. At the Rabasyvihrk's nod, Stavark stowed his oar and stepped lightly to the bow. The lantern at this end of the docks was dark, as Vullieth had promised it would be.

They slipped in silently next to the old, weathered dock, which glistened with moisture and small patches of snow. Stavark leapt onto the planks and pressed himself against the cliff's shadows.

There were six guards down the wharf, double the amount there had been when they had sailed in just a few nights ago. All were wrapped in cloaks; some had taken their helms off. He must get them all.

He focused his eyes upon the closest trio and opened the silverland. The docks, the water, the dockside shacks all became silver.

Stavark ran lightly forward. He hit the first man on the back of the head with the pommel of his dagger, then did the same to the second man. The third man bore Vullieth's insignia on his right shoulder, and Stavark left him alone.

Stavark raced to the second group. Only the leader of this group lacked Vullieth's insignia. It was the dock official from when they'd first arrived. Stavark delivered another carefully placed blow to the back of his head, then he left the silverland.

The two guards and the dock official crumpled to the ground.

The three remaining guards of Vullieth's house jumped as if struck by a serpent, all of them jerking their heads to look at Stavark. All they would have seen was a silver flash streaking through the guards. He nodded to them.

The Rabasyvihrk and the other soldiers in the rowboat pulled up, and leapt onto the dock. The other rowboats drifted closer, docking in more obvious berths now that the guards had fallen.

Still shooting incredulous glances at Stavark, the nearest of Vullieth's guards met the Rabasyvihrk. They spoke in hushed tones, and Stavark breathed deeply, conserving his energy. The remaining two of Vullieth's guards kept flicking glances his way.

One at time, all of the boats docked, and Captain Lo'gan's soldiers disembarked and began jogging up the street between the dockside houses to wait for the rest. The vyrkiz, seemingly unaffected by the cold, padded quietly next to the Maehka vik Kalik. All of Lo'gan's soldiers gave Sniff plenty of room.

When everyone had disembarked, Stavark ranged ahead of the group. It only took him a few minutes to find the first guard patrol. They saw him, and one opened his mouth to give the alarm, but Stavark stepped into the silverland and dropped them all. By the time Mershayn's little army caught up with him, Stavark was bent over his knees, trying to regain his breath. The army moved as quietly as fifty men could move, but they still made a great deal of noise. The Rabasyvihrk sensed the same thing Stavark sensed, and he urged them to move faster. Once the alarm went up, this would become more difficult.

Soon, they reached the last curve in the road before they would come within sight of the wall and the gate that led up to the castle. Stavark stayed in the shadows and snuck around the curve, then returned and reported.

"The gate is closed, Rabasyvihrk. There are four guards. Two behind the gate. Two above on the wall."

"Okay," he murmured to Stavark. "As we practiced."

"Yes, Rabasyvihrk."

He put his hand up near his shoulder, as though he was going to hold a platter of food there. Stavark clambered up his back and put both his feet in the palm of the Rabasyvihrk's hand. Holding Stavark against his shoulder, the Rabasyvihrk ran around the corner in sight of the wall. He surged forward until the first guard saw him. The woman opened her mouth to shout, and Medophae burst with golden fire as he heaved Stavark toward the wall.

Stavark entered the silverland the moment he left the Rabasyvihrk's hand, just before the woman could shout. Silver buildings sailed beneath him, and he landed on the wall next to the first frozen guard. He lifted the man's helm and whacked the pommel of his dagger against the base of his head, then did the same to the next. Stavark dropped to the street inside the wall, then did the same to the guard who was reaching for a rope attached to a bell, and then to the final guard. The final guard had the keys, and Stavark took them, unlocked the gate, then let them fall to the ground as he left the silverland.

He sucked in a breath. There didn't seem to be enough air to fill his lungs. Leaning against the wall, he breathed hard and watched as the Rabasyvihrk ran to the gate.

Lord Mershayn, Captain Lo'gan, and their soldiers jogged after. Thank goodness for the snow, which cast a muffled quiet over their noises. Still, Stavark grimaced at the thumping feet, the creaking leather. Some of them even jingled. He shook his head.

It seemed far too long before they reached the gate with their creaking and jingling. Mershayn stopped at the entrance as the rest of the soldiers jogged through.

Once all of the soldiers were through, the Rabasyvihrk closed the huge doors behind them and went to Lord Mershayn.

"Headcount," the Rabasyvihrk said.

"All accounted for, sir," Captain Lo'gan answered.

"Good. Then you know what to do," Lord Mershayn said. "Remember, many of the guards serving Sym might still be loyal to Collus, just misinformed. There's been plenty of confusion in the castle these past few days; who knows what they have been told. Give them the chance to join us. If they won't, make captives, not corpses, if you can. A bloodless coup is our true victory. My group will make straight for Sym's chambers."

"We understand," Lo'gan finished.

The Rabasyvihrk nodded. "Lo'gan, you have Vullieth's medallion?"

"Yes, sir." He pulled the thick silver disk from his tunic. It bore the crested helm and mallet of Vullieth's house.

"With luck, your little army will grow quickly, and there will be no need for fighting," the Rabasyvihrk said.

"Yes, sir."

"Then let's go," Mershayn said. "For Collus."

"For Collus," Captain Lo'gan and his soldiers echoed. The little army jogged silently up the twisting road until they reached the last bend. As they came to a halt, the Rabasyvihrk motioned that they stay close to the cliff. The Rabasyvihrk nodded to Stavark, and he entered the silverland, jogging around the bend and making for the frozen silver statues of the guards who stood by the frozen door leading into the castle. They lasted no longer than the guards at the wall.

Lord Mershayn's army infiltrated the castle and went their separate ways. The Maehka vik Kalik, the Rabasyvihrk, Lord Mershayn, the vyrkiz and Stavark moved quietly up the right passageway while Lo'gan and the other soldiers went left.

Stavark brought up the rear now, trying to slow his breathing.

He had not used the silverland that much since the battle with the darklings. Then, he had been completely spent. Now, he was tired, but not debilitated.

The young quicksilver followed his companions into the lamp-lit corridors.

46

MIROLAH

As Mirolah followed Medophae and Mershayn deeper into the castle of Teni'sia, Mirolah's mind chewed on the question like a dog gnaws a bone: Was Elekkena Bands?

At first thought, it seemed ludicrous. She was just a slender quicksilver girl, respectful, innocent. How could such a girl actually be an ancient dragon in disguise?

But she couldn't let the notion go.

Medophae had tried to solve the riddle for so long that he had been certain she was dead. It was ridiculous to think that now, somehow, not only was she alive, but she'd somehow broken free without the riddle of the spell being solved. After all, Medophae hadn't done anything new to solve the riddle.

The little troupe that Medophae led up the slope to the castle of Teni'sia stopped, blending into the shadows as Stavark went ahead to deal with some soldiers.

She followed, deep in thought as she recalled the riddle, exactly as he'd told it to her in Calsinac.

You must give to someone that which you have already given away. And you must cast away what now sustains you.

A cold breeze of realization blew through her. Medophae *had* done something new. He'd thrown the ruby into the Sara Sea.

Cast away what now sustains you.

Did the ruby sustain him? How did the ruby...

Love.

Not the ruby, but what it represented. He was supposed to cast away his love for Bands. By the gods, that was the answer. The riddle required Medophae to love another, someone other than Bands, and he had to cast away the ruby in the bargain as proof of his commitment to another.

The pieces clicked together. Mirolah wasn't the first he'd loved, of course. He had told her stories of Tyndiria, the dead queen of Teni'sia. He'd loved her, too. But he hadn't cast away the gem.

"By the gods..." she whispered, reeling with the truth. Medophae had solved the riddle after all! Bands was free....

Medophae was intent on watching Stavark put the guards down, ready to jump in and help if the quicksilver couldn't manage it. He didn't hear her, but Mershayn turned his head.

"Something wrong, Lady Mirolah?" he asked.

"No," she said quickly. "Nothing."

Yes, everything.

The answer to the riddle was that Medophae had to fall in love with someone other than his epic, beloved Bands, and then he had to throw her away. It was Ethiel's perfect revenge. No matter the outcome, Medophae would lose.

The riddle was solved. The spell broken. The dragon freed. But why not come straight to Medophae? Why transform into a quicksilver and hide in plain sight?

Had she been with them even before? The ancient dragon was a shapeshifter. Had she taken some other shape, a passing deer or a rat, and watched them?

It made Mirolah ill to think that while she made love with

Medophae in the empty marble city of Calsinac, Bands was lurking somewhere nearby, watching.

If Bands had returned, it answered every question. Every piece fit. Click, click, click. Elekkena. Mirolah's miraculous healing in the insidious forest. Medophae's decrease in his affections...

He had suspected. Something tipped him off that Bands might be alive, out there somewhere. Had he known Elekkena was Bands?

The idea that they might have snuck off together while Mirolah was sleeping, or busy doing something else... It made her sick to her stomach.

No. No, he looked surprised when he considered Elekkena's murmuring. That was genuine shock. Elekkena was Bands, but Medophae hadn't known it.

Medophae was a good man. He wasn't always right; he didn't always make the best decisions, but he always tried to do good....

A cynical voice in the back of her mind said: *You have no idea what kind of man he is. He has lived for centuries, and you've only known him for weeks.*

But he loves me, she thought, fighting against that soul-sucking voice. *He would have to, to solve the riddle.*

But not like he loves her....

Stavark finished his business and they moved forward again, quietly, through the gate and up the winding path toward the side of the castle at the top of the hill.

Maybe Elekkena left because she knew the pieces were all there. Maybe she knew she was only one contemplative moment away from being discovered.

The small invading force jogged forward. Medophae dropped back to run next to her. "Do you know?" he asked.

She looked at him, stunned. "Know...?"

"Orem. Do you know where he is?"

She let out a big breath, her heart pounding. "No."

At her expression, his brow furrowed. "Are you okay?"

"I'm sorry," she said. "I was... I was thinking... I mean, Sniff lost the trail once we got to Teni'sia. I think Zilok erased his tracks somehow. And...I was waiting to get a bit closer to the castle before reaching into the GodSpill. Like you said, I didn't want to use it until I had to." She pulled her mind away from the puzzle. She needed to focus on her job here.

"Good."

To find him, she was going to have to tap into the GodSpill. She'd have to become part of the castle walls and the floors, just like she had in Ethiel's palace inside Daylan's Fountain. It frightened her. The demands of the voice became louder with every day that passed, it seemed, and she wondered if it was going to be dangerous for her to use its power. She was more than a little worried about that part of the plan.

We are one. Come to us.

She pushed the voice back down.

"Ah," Medophae said. "Do you want to wait until we're inside the castle—?"

"I'll do it when I'm ready," she snapped.

Mershayn turned at her outburst. Medophae looked surprised.

"I'm sorry," he said. "I didn't mean to—"

"Unless you want to do the threadweaving, I'll handle it."

"Mirolah, I—"

"I need to concentrate," she said.

He hesitated, then slowly turned and moved to the head of the group again.

They got through the next door using Stavark again. He became silver light and beat the guards senseless. Once they entered, Mirolah set one piece of her attention to walking. The rest, she fragmented and sent into the stones of the castle.

Sniff sensed her using the GodSpill, whined, and moved closer. She rested her arm on the top of his back. It felt good, touching him. He made her feel grounded, and she closed her eyes.

She split her attention again, and again, and again, becoming smaller fibers of threads throughout the castle, searching for anything.

We are one.... the voice said, excited, and louder now that she had put so much of herself into the threads. The voice tugged at her, wanting to yank her free of her body, but the largest portion of her focus stayed on where her arm rested on Sniff's back, where her hand touched his shoulders.

This is me. I am Mirolah.

In the time it took Medophae's troop to walk fifty feet up the hall, Mirolah spread herself throughout the stones of every room overhead, from the tallest minaret to the level they were on. She found nothing.

The soldiers turned a corner, climbed a staircase, and came to another long hallway. As they walked, she delved deeper into the castle. There were a few paths carved deep into the bedrock of the mountain, into the foundation upon which the castle had been built. She sent her attention down these tunnels and found what she was looking for.

In a room deep in the rock far below, an oily blackness covered the threads, just as it had in Zilok's lair in Denema's Valley. This was his new lair, and inside it...

"Orem..." she whispered.

As Zilok's presence covered the threads in an oily blackness, so too could she sense that Orem had been in this room recently, though he was not there now. Traces of his unique threads were there, covered in that same inky blackness.

"Mirolah?" Medophae whispered, keeping his voice down. "What is it?"

"I found him. Or rather, I found where he was recently."

Medophae's face went grim, and he looked around.

"And I don't think Zilok detected me snooping around."

As she talked to Medophae, she reached out to the threads of air in front of Sniff's nose and transformed them, duplicating the feel of the oily blackness of Zilok's lair with the hint of Orem's threads. He raised his head, sniffing, and she felt satisfaction flow from him. He had lost the trail before, but now he had Zilok's scent again.

He gave a low whine and padded forward. Lo'gan's soldiers shrank away from the giant skin dog, putting their backs against the wall as he slunk past them.

"He's got the scent," she said, following him to the head of the column and the point where the hallway forked.

"Sim's rooms will be this way," Medophae said, nodding to the right-hand path.

"I'll find him," Mirolah said. "Once I free Orem, Zilok goes through the Godgate. If he tries to latch onto something else, I'll stop him."

She turned to go, and he grabbed her arm. His face was conflicted.

"Mirolah..."

It's a good kissing moment. Do you feel like kissing me?

"Just...be careful." He squeezed her shoulder, and she had to swallow her heart back down.

"I will."

She turned and started up the hallway, following Sniff.

47

MIROLAH

Sniff led her down, and even though she trusted his nose, she reached out gently with her threadweaver's fingers, touching the stale air in the corridors, the rock of the walls.

"Soon, mistress," Sniff said. "It is soon."

The air became less stale, a crisp, cool draft coming from somewhere ahead. They turned down a long hallway, then again to the left. Mirolah slowed as they approached an open door. Beyond it was a huge hole in the side of the castle, big enough to fit a house.

"There." Sniff gave a low growl. "Big GodSpill. Dark GodSpill. Be careful, mistress."

She moved forward, reaching out and touching everything in the room. There were strange residues on the threads. Someone had been threadweaving here. And most prominent of all, there was a sweltering little dot, a hanging spell like a shimmering silver coin just inside the doorway.

In case it was triggered by threadweaving itself or the mere touch of a threadweaver, she kept clear of it.

"Stay here," she whispered to Sniff.

"Mistress—"

"I'm not kidding. If something happens, I'll be able to get away. I'm not sure I could get you away, too. If Zilok is here, you run like I told you."

He lowered his head, looking up at her with those slitted eyes. "Mistress..." He gave a quiet whine.

"If I start using GodSpill, you run. You go find Medophae."

He didn't say anything, but he hunched even lower, chest on the stone.

"Say it," she whispered.

"Yes, mistress."

"Okay then."

She went into the room. It was empty save the hanging spell, just rock walls and that weird, giant circular balcony with no rails.

Dammit!

She spun, feeling Zilok arrive. How had he known she was here?

His presence pushed the threads aside even as he formed his visible ghost of a body on the tip of the balcony, with its black hair, blue eyes, and neat goatee. He adjusted his black vest over his white shirt as though it was actually there, actually needed adjusting, and he "walked" toward her, his boots clicking on the stone. This time, he wore some kind of crystal crown, made of green cords. Were those vines? It was certainly not a part of his fashion statement, and she wondered why he wore it. Did he fancy himself the king of Teni'sia now? The king of forests?

She hadn't been able to sense him until this very moment. How did he do that? It was as though he could be far away, then suddenly close. She needed to know how he did that.

She had hoped to find Orem first. She had hoped to surprise him. But she had fought Ethiel in her own palace. She had fought Zilok before and survived, and she knew more now than she did then.

The GodSpill flowed all around her, through her, begging her to use it. This time, she was going to show him what she did to those who sent spine horses to kill little boys.

"You're clever," Zilok said, bowing.

"I work at it." She fragmented her attention into a thousand threads, looking for his connection to Orem.

In the hallway, Sniff whined.

She sent a third of her ethereal fingers searching outward, looking for Orem or for the connection Zilok had made to his anchor.

"The skin dog," Zilok said. "When he began tracking me from Denema's Valley, I thought it was an amusing trick, but the beast has talent."

"Where's Orem?"

"Learning. Absorbing. He is receiving the education he always wanted."

"Let him go."

He chuckled. "Lady Rith, you surprise me. The first time we met, I gave you respect and admiration. I gave you the tools you needed, and you eliminated the Red Weaver. The second time we met, you were stronger still and even more clever. Still, I did not underestimate you. What makes you think I will underestimate you now?"

"Because you already have."

His blue eyes narrowed. "Do you think I was fooled? Lady Rith, I knew you were in Teni'sia the moment you stepped onto the docks. I have hanging spells all over the city. In fact, there is one right behind you."

She saw the threads shiver next to him, rippling toward his hanging spell.

She froze those threads he was trying to affect. His thread-weaving never touched the hanging spell. It hovered where it was, an impotent little node of destruction.

No expression crossed Zilok's projected face, but she felt his surprise and anger.

She sank into the GodSpill. She *became* the GodSpill. He wasn't going to do anything in this room.

"You're an aberration," her mouth stated, even as her attention hovered all around him, a part of the very threads of the air and stone. "And you will not touch Medophae or Orem again." She pushed herself into every oily thread of his spirit, looking for his weakness, for that thin thread that, if cut, would send him hurtling upward into the Godgate.

But there was no cord. She couldn't see that ethereal cord that had once connected him to Sef. There was nothing. The threads of Zilok's spirit twisted only around themselves and that crown at his head.

It's the crown. He's bound to the crown. That is his anchor now!

She switched her focus, reaching up to slice through his many threads that clung to the crown—

Her questing "fingers" were suddenly seized and yanked up, toward the crown.

She gasped. Her threadweaver sight vanished. The walls became normal walls. She couldn't see any of the threads, couldn't feel the GodSpill at all. Even the voice was gone. Zilok Morth looked like a real man.

He made a gesture behind her, and the hanging spell triggered.

There was a loud *whack*, like someone had clapped their hands next to both her ears, then silence.

Suddenly, there was no air. She gasped, trying desperately to inhale. Zilok lifted her off the ground. She was inside an invisible sphere that he controlled. She flailed, trying to find the edges of it, but she fell forward, and her fall turned into a gentle spin in mid-air. She tried to right herself, but there was nothing to push against. She gaped, mouth opening and closing like a fish on land. How had he removed the GodSpill from this room? That was impossible!

"Yes, why you didn't die in that forest is a mystery to me, but it's a mystery I can live with. This is better. Come now, let's do what you're aching to do. Let's find your beloved Medophae."

He flew upward from the giant balcony, and the invisible sphere yanked her along.

Sniff leapt into the room, charging after her a second too late. His great jaws snapped shut just shy of her boot as she flew upward. She zoomed along the outside of the castle, and Sniff's mournful howl ripped through the night.

48

STAVARK

THE RABASYVIHRK LED them through the darkened hallways of the castle. They ascended a half-dozen staircases as they wound around, but everyone kept up with the quick pace. Lord Mershayn was energized, determination on his face. Mershayn did not wish to survive this mission. He longed to kill the other human leader, Grendis Sym. He wanted to give his life doing it. That was all. There was no future for Mershayn beyond this night.

The Rabasyvihrk stopped them just before a hallway intersection and held up his hand. Everyone did their best to slow their breathing.

"One more stairway," Mershayn said. "Sym's rooms are up ahead. We have to be quick. If Lo'gan hasn't been spotted yet, it won't be long."

"Remember, we capture Sym," the Rabasyvihrk said pointedly, perhaps seeing in Mershayn's face the same thing Stavark saw. "The kingdom benefits from seeing justice done, a trial and punishment meted out by the crown."

The muscles in Mershayn's jaw twitched. "He won't escape."

The Rabasyvihrk watched him. "Mershayn—"

"We're wasting time."

With a grunt, the Rabasyvihrk moved forward and turned the corner.

At the end of the hall stood Sym, dressed in his nightclothes as though they'd caught him sneaking out to the privy.

He shouted, recognizing Mershayn, then shouldered his way through the door. Mershayn roared and leapt forward, running down the long hallway, but Sym was gone.

Stavark entered the silverland, but even as he started forward, leaving his friends behind, he heard the Rabasyvihrk shout. He stopped, stepped out of the silverland to hear him.

"Stavark, no!" the Rabasyvihrk said, sprinting to keep up with Mershayn. "We stay together."

"I could catch him, Rabasyvihrk."

"I know it. But this whole thing is a trap. Let's spring it one step at a time. Let's spring it together."

They reached the end of the hall, burst through the door, then started down a flight of stairs. They could hear Sym's bare feet slapping the stones even as he reached the landing below and barreled through the door.

"That's the throne room," Mershayn said, leaping the last few steps and pushing through the door with the Rabasyvihrk and Stavark right behind him.

They entered the throne room, and it was filled with seemingly every soldier in Teni'sia. There had to be a hundred humans, weapons drawn, waiting for them.

"They knew we were coming," Mershayn said.

"Yes." The Rabasyvihrk stepped to the front, and golden fire crackled up his arms and across his chest. "Go back," he said to Mershayn. "Both of you. They can't kill me, and I won't risk you. From here, I continue alone."

"What—?" Mershayn protested, but Stavark laid a hand on his arm.

"The Rabasyvihrk can fight entire armies," Stavark said.

"Soldiers of Teni'sia," the Rabasyvihrk boomed. "I have no wish to kill you. Please lay down your swords. I would parlay with your leader."

"But they wish to fight you. Every single one of them." A man stood in the tall window that led outside to the open air. He was of medium height, with a white shirt and an expensive black vest, black breeches, and tall black boots. His hair was combed neatly, he had a goatee, and he wore a crown of crystals atop his head. "I have made sure of it."

That same voice suddenly slithered into Stavark's mind. Stavark tried to shove the voice out, but it was like pushing his fist into a bucket of oil. Everywhere he touched, it covered him, flowing over his entire head.

As a last desperate act, he entered the silverland, but the voice followed. Stavark opened his mouth to scream, but the voice told him not to.

So he didn't.

The man's voice oozed into Stavark's mind. Private. Intimate.

I am Zilok Morth, and I am your new master, the voice said.

"Yes, my master," Stavark replied.

Wait here, Zilok Morth said. *I will have need of you.*

Stavark shivered. He saw Mershayn shiver next to him, and he knew Mershayn was hearing the same voice.

Then Stavark no longer cared. He cared only about waiting until the voice told him what to do next.

"Just kill them," Sym yelled from across the room. "Don't play with them."

"You have made a dramath's bargain with Zilok Morth," the Rabasyvihrk said. "You'll lose much more than you will gain. At least send your soldiers away. Don't make them pay for your decision."

"You killed my father." Sym spat.

"This isn't going to be what you think..." The Rabasyvihrk trailed off as the Maehka vik Kalik floated through the window behind Stavark's new master. Her hands were wide, searching, and she gasped.

"Mirolah!"

She floated so close to the ground that her feet struggled to touch it, but couldn't. She bowed her head, and her hand went to her throat as she wilted.

"In the end, she's just a girl after all," the man in the black vest said.

The Rabasyvihrk charged, sword blazing fire, dropping flecks of golden flame on the floor as he ran. The soldiers in the room ran toward him, blocking him from the Maehka vik Kalik. The Rabasyvihrk knocked soldiers aside as they threw themselves at him.

"You gutless spirit! Fight me," the Rabasyvihrk shouted, killing soldiers left and right.

"No..." Zilok said, his voice low and full of venom. "This time, there will be no fight. You will simply lose. And I will watch you suffer." Zilok's laughter was soft in Stavark's mind.

One of Sym's soldiers lunged toward the Maehka vik Kalik, sword first. He would have driven it clean through her chest, but the Rabasyvihrk was faster. He caught the guard's steel on the godsword. The soldier's sword shattered. The Rabasyvihrk sidestepped and struck the soldier with his fist, knocking him away. He skidded across the polished stones and lay still.

I need you, the voice said to Stavark. *Kill the girl. Now.*

In the back of Stavark's mind, he heard his own voice begging him to resist. But his voice was small. His voice was weak.

He stepped into the silverland and ran toward the Maehka vik Kalik, weaving through the dozens of soldiers that were but statues to him, sidestepping the furious Rabasyvihrk. He reached the Maehka vik Kalik and stepped back into the real land. She saw him appear, and raised her head, her eyes half-lidded as she struggled to breathe.

Stavark, she mouthed, holding up a hand to him. She wanted him to grab it, to pull her away from whatever was stealing her breath.

Stavark drew his sword and stabbed her through the chest. She gaped, eyes flying open as the steel broke ribs and punched through her heart. He yanked his blade out and stabbed her again, then again, then again until she fell, face down, unmoving as she floated above the floor. Her glassy eyes looked at nothing.

"Stavark! No!" the Rabasyvihrk yelled. Golden flames erupted from him like a column, blowing a hole through the ceiling and incinerating the men grabbing onto him. His roar shook the throne room, and he directed the column of fire at Zilok Morth. The soldiers still tried to reach Medophae, driven by Zilok's command, and they burned as they got caught in the blast.

The fire engulfed Zilok, and for a moment it seemed as though he had been destroyed. But then Stavark could see him in the midst of the conflagration, laughing. The golden fire flowed upward into the crystals of his crown, vanishing before touching him.

Medophae ran forward, pouring all of his rage into that fire, but the crown took it all. The fire seemed never-ending, Medophae coming closer and closer to Zilok.

Then, suddenly, the golden fire slackened, turning from a giant column of flame to a bolt the width of a tree, then the width of a pole, then a spear, then it became a flickering trickle and died out.

Medophae fell to his knees in front of Mirolah, inches from Stavark's unmoving feet.

Golden fire flared from the crystals of Zilok's crown.

"Yes," he laughed. "Yes!" He pointed at Medophae. Inky blackness swirled with golden fire and spiraled toward the Rabasyvihrk. It plunged into him, turning his body black and gold. Medophae screamed, arching his back as the colored fire wrapped around him, chest, belly, neck, and finally his face. Medophae began to shrink.

He became smaller and smaller until he was the size of a fist, then he spun, curling into a ball of black and gold fire, then shot toward Zilok. Zilok's body vanished into the golden fire, swirled into the spinning ball. The fireball elongated into a thread, then shot out the window.

Stavark stood over the bloody body of the Maehka vik Kalik. He stared at her as Zilok's control drained from his body, freeing his thoughts once again.

A guttural cry of anguish ripped from him.

49

MERSHAYN

THE QUICKSILVER'S scream broke the spell that had been telling Mershayn to stand silently where he was. He shook his head, and like a fog burned away by the bright sun, he could suddenly see the horror all around. Sym's soldiers had been hacked and burned by Medophae's rampage. And Mirolah—

"Gods!" He leapt forward, but before he could take a step, something hard hit him in the back of the head. He crashed to his knees.

He looked up. Stavark sobbed, holding Mirolah's bloody hand.

A loud *twang* sounded from the gallery above, and a giant crossbow bolt slammed into Stavark's calf. He screamed as it drove through flesh and into the stone, pinning him to the floor. He transformed, but the silver flash just glimmered around the bolt, unable to remove it. Then Stavark reformed, his chest pumping like a bellows, face-first on the stones, teeth clenched in pain.

A soldier stepped forward and hit him in the side of the head with a war mallet. The quicksilver crumpled into a heap, and he didn't get up.

Mershayn roared and surged to his feet, but soldiers swarmed him, hitting him, kicking him. His sword clanged to the ground.

Boots rammed into him until he fell onto his back. He groaned, grasping for his sword, and someone stepped on his hand. The last thing he saw was a boot poised over his face. It descended, and Mershayn saw nothing else.

6§

HE OPENED HIS EYES, and the first thing he could feel was the throbbing in his face. His cheek, lips, and nose felt two times too large. Gradually, his vision came into focus. Grendis Sym crouched before him, smiling.

"Well, bastard," Sym said. "How do you feel?"

Mershayn looked for any sign of Mirolah or Stavark. The quicksilver was gone, but Mirolah's body still lay in a pool of her own blood in the center of the throne room. She wasn't moving. Her skin was pasty white. Her eyes stared at nothing.

"Gods, no..." he sobbed.

Sym followed his gaze, then looked back at him. "And here I thought she was Captain Medophae's woman." He gave Mershayn a smile. "But wait, I forgot. You don't pay attention to such distinctions, do you?"

Mershayn lunged at Sym, but the rope that bound his hands pulled him up short, sending spikes of pain up his arms.

Sym watched him struggle. "But I'm thankful for your base nature," he said. "If not for your indiscretions, Collus would still be on the throne." Sym grabbed Mershayn's chin, forced his gaze up.

"You'd best kill me," Mershayn growled. "Or I'll make you sorry you didn't."

"Oh, you're going to live. You're going to live a long life without your balls." He grinned, showing teeth. "I intend to parade you in front of the witty, breathy, vivacious Ari'cyiane once

I've castrated you. I'll show you to her, every missing part of you, and you'll see how much she favors you then."

Mershayn fought down his fear, the knowledge that he was helpless in the hands of this jackal of a man.

"I don't know how you escaped me before," Sym hissed in a low voice. "But this time, you're out of friends. This time, you'll stay where I put you."

Sym stood. "Get him up," he said to the guards. Sym's soldiers dragged Mershayn to his feet. The guards guided him to a door behind the throne.

"What should we do with her?" one of Sym's soldiers asked, nudging Mirolah's ruined body with his toe.

Sym did not even look back as he followed Mershayn. "Throw her out the window. Let the gulls and the surf dragons have her."

"No!" Mershayn pulled against his guards. They wrenched his arms, and he fell back in line. One of them punched him in the gut.

He doubled over. Through watery eyes, he looked up at Sym. "Please..." he said. "Bury her. She deserves that. Please..."

Sym smiled at his desperation. He looked thoughtful for a moment, then leaned down close to Mershayn's face.

"No."

As they hauled Mershayn to the door, the guards dragged Mirolah's body to the window. With a grunt, they shoved her through it.

"Mirolah!" He shouted. His shoulder screamed in agony as they yanked him back around and forced him through the door.

"And get someone to clean up this mess," Sym said, following closely behind.

50

BANDS

SNOW FELL SOFTLY, and Zynder huddled low, backed up against the edge of the cliff. He had dug a deep groove in the snow when he'd crashed to the ground, and his sinuous neck bent awkwardly where Bands had scored on him a moment ago. Blood coursed down his white scales to his chest, falling in a dripping sheet, staining the snow black in the moonlight. He'd managed to rip himself free of her and plummet this far, but his wings were ruined. Her last spell had seen to that. They curled into his body, pitiful melted gray nubs.

Bands folded her wings gingerly against her body. The left was injured, but not badly. What she truly worried about was the savage bite Zynder had given her foreleg. Avakketh's elites had poison on their teeth, a gift from their god, and that poison was not easily healed. The wound oozed, leaking between her scales down to her claws.

She crept forward, leaving bloody claw prints on the snow. Her vision blurred from his last spell, but she was still able to keep her focus. She'd identified it in time to counter most of the effects. She couldn't see perfectly, but it was better than being blind.

That attack had been Zynder's kill strike. Simple and powerful, he'd intended to blind her and bite her neck in two.

She had lured him in, making him believe she was blind, and then she had struck. He hadn't been expecting that.

Zynder, like so many of dragonkind, considered humans lesser beings. Zynder would compare the convoluted spells of Zilok Morth to the low cunning of a weasel. He would call Daylan Morth's achievements an aberration. He would call Difinius's intricate stylings a branch of human insanity. He thought human threadweaving was laughable compared to the power given by Avakketh. Therefore, Bands couldn't be a true threadweaver now that she was cut off from the dragon god.

Arrogance. Overconfidence. It had cost him.

He was wounded badly in several places, much worse than her, but he would fight hardest at the last. He did not fear death, only the shame of failure.

She crept forward, alert.

His breath came out in white plumes. They had been fighting for days in these snowcapped mountains. Zynder tried over and over to break free of her, to escape north to Irgakth. Each time, she had stopped him, corralled him back to these peaks. They were both exhausted, but Bands had the upper hand now. This battle was almost over.

Zynder mumbled quietly under his breath. Bands countered, speaking three words and twisting the threads.

The wind whipped Zynder in the face, scrambling his words and shaking his concentration. He sneered, bloody teeth clenched. "Traitor," he growled. "Human-lover!"

"I am." She tried to pretend his words didn't sting, but she wasn't just an outcast from dragon society now. She was an enemy. Zynder's words were the same words that would be spoken by any dragon she would encounter now, even her parents. She would live and die in Amarion, no matter what came next. Irgakth, the company of her own kind, these would be forever denied her. The human lands were her only home now.

"What you do to me does not matter," he breathed. "Avakketh will crush you. He will turn the lands upside down to find you. He will make you suffer. Your screams will last for an age."

"Maybe."

He snorted. More blood flecked the snow. "You are nothing without him!"

"What were you doing in Teni'sia, Zynder?" she asked calmly.

He sneered. "Ask the snow. Ask the sky. You will get more from them than you will from me. I will gladly die for Avakketh."

She crept closer.

His hind leg scraped off the edge of the cliff, and he pulled it back. He could not fly. He could not retreat. "If you kill me, your fate is sealed," he growled.

"My fate was sealed when I fell in love with Medophae," she said. "Avakketh is wrong. Humans are our equals."

He hissed, showing his teeth. He didn't understand. By the gods, she was not sure she understood.

She attacked. He pulled GodSpill from Avakketh, tried to harness the wind to blow her off the cliff. It was a desperate spell. She turned his hurricane blast into a breeze that circled around her, then looped her neck low. He raised a wounded claw, trying to block her, but he wasn't fast enough. She dodged underneath it, kicked his face away, and sank her teeth into his neck.

He did not have the strength to tear away this time. She crunched down with all her might, killing him.

She backed away from the body, blood running down her chin. Shaking her head with disgust, she scooped up a mouthful of snow, chewed, and spat out red. She repeated this until she cleaned his taste away.

There was no going back now. No dragon had ever killed another in the history of the world. Only the elites were given permission to kill, and that permission only came from Avakketh.

In Irgakth, she would be painted the most vile villain imaginable, the monster who had gone insane. Betrayer. Dragon-killer. Those would be her new names.

Her people were now humans. Zynder had been right about one thing—she wasn't actually a dragon anymore. She didn't think like them. She didn't share their values. She couldn't imagine returning to Avakketh's dominance and passionless endeavors, where all certainty rested upon his word, and to challenge his lies meant exile or death.

No. Everything she truly loved walked on the ground in the human lands.

Snow swirled around her, heavier than before. She looked up. It was worsening.

She turned her great, sinuous neck towards Teni'sia and stretched her wings, testing. Her left wing was weak, but if the winds did not gust too strongly, it would hold. Still, she needed to start back soon.

She launched herself straight up and beat against the air, sending snow swirling behind her. She hovered over Zynder and murmured the words that guided her threadweaving. She unraveled the protections on his scales, spells that were every dragon's birthright, and that protected them from the flame of another dragon. In life, no dragon could undo those spells. In death, it was tradition, ever since Dervon the Dead had twisted the corpses of dragons into the vicious neila. It took most of her reserves to remove them.

Once she was done, she gave him the Death Blast. Orange flame shot from her mouth and engulfed his body. The flame turned blue, then white as it grew hotter. She kept it on him as long as she could. Snow hissed, turning to steam. Rock bubbled beneath him. When she had finished, Zynder was no more. His scales, flesh, bones were all burned to ash.

The cliff above Zynder's body, weakened by the heat, rumbled, and an avalanche crashed down, erasing all evidence that there had ever been a dragon fight here.

She wheeled about and pumped her wings southward. Teni'sia was close. She lowered her head and raced to escape the growing storm.

EPILOGUE

THE EARLY AFTERNOON turned to night as the first storm of winter set in, unseasonably early and growing in strength with every hour that passed. Throughout the city and the surrounding countryside, Teni'sians gathered wood into their houses for fires and closed their shutters. A few had seen fiery lights above the Corialis Mountains, and the word had spread through the entire city and beyond.

By the time the sun set, even the brave took shelter from the whipping wind and snow. The blizzard howled into Teni'sia as though furious. Some said they heard the voices of dramaths on the wind, whispering maniacally as they scrabbled against shutters and doors.

A single creature did dare the storm, though, and those huddled warmly within their houses wondered what kind of evil beast it might be. The howling began at midnight and continued until just before the dawn. It chilled every listener, raising the hairs on their arms.

It would later be told that Ti'lishden the cobbler's son took a dare and went to capture the sad wolf. He ventured into the teeth of the storm and those teeth closed over him forever. In another part of the city, it was told that the bard Crystal Vander also sought immortality. She told the huddled group at the Hot Pot Inn that she would find the wolf, listen to its pain close up, and capture a song none had ever captured before. But the last note anyone ever heard from Crystal Vander was her musical goodbye as she stepped into the swirling white.

⅘

SNIFF SAT ALONE at the edge of the surf, crying over the broken body of his mistress. Early in the night, despite the storm, a few desperately hungry surf dragons came for the body. They each died in bloody conflict with Sniff, and he fed on them, tearing away large chunks of their scaly flesh with his jaws and swallowing them whole. He stood guard over his mistress, waiting for any others who would desecrate her. And he howled.

The pain of his loss drove him mad, and he howled until his throat was raw. Then he howled more. He did not stop. He would not stop, not until he died alongside her.

Sometime before dawn, limbs frozen and covered in frost, Sniff stopped howling. Something flickered over the body of his mistress.

The skin above his shoulders bunched, and ice cracked and fell from his body. He bared his teeth, ready to attack. Sniff smelled the GodSpill as only his kind could. He moved forward stiffly, standing over his mistress's body, looking for the thread-weaver who approached.

But it wasn't an approaching threadweaver. It was an actual spell, swirling around. He growled and spun, but then sniffed again, recognizing it.

With a whimper, he backed away. Slowly, his mistress's leg, severed from the sharp rocks when she fell, slid back to her body and butted up to the wound. Her back, spun and broken from the fall, twisted back around. Her shattered face reformed.

Flesh joined. Bones knitted. Blood ran afresh as life coursed through her, running in drips from healing wounds, and then running no more as the wounds closed.

When all of her pieces had joined together, his mistress shook her head and sat up. She glanced at Sniff, then at the swirling snow, then overhead at the tall walls of the castle. She stood up.

His mistress looked down at her torn clothing. Her shirt hung from her in rags, slashed into strips by the sword that had killed her. Her skirt twisted about her legs, covered in blood. Her breeches were in tatters. She gestured. The bloody garments came away from her body, and she stood naked in the snow.

With hollow eyes she looked down at Sniff again. He whined and crouched away from her.

Slowly, her feet left the ground, and she hovered over him. She floated northward away from him and disappeared into the storm.

Sniff barked and sprinted after her.

Dear Reader,

As I mentioned in my last author's note, *Wildmane* was written in college in Colorado Springs. The rough draft of *The GodSpill* was written many years later in New York City, ironically after a failed quest of my own.

After college, I moved to northern California, grabbed a temp job at a shampoo manufacturing company and got promoted a few times, eventually to Brand Coordinator, over the course of a year and a half. As soon as it looked like the job was turning into a real career, the pressure valve went off in my head, and I quit. I didn't want to be a Brand Coordinator. I wanted to be a writer.

Now unemployed, I flew to Denver for New Year's Eve, then went on a road trip through the frozen north (Minnesota, North Dakota and Utah) in January. This intrepid leap into winter included broken-down vans on snow-swept roads, fantasies of ax murderers in desolate garages, and inhuman yawns. I wrote it all down. Ask me about the Jack Journals someday.

After that misadventure, my intention was to settle down in Placerville, CA with my friends Brett and Kathryn, find a job as a dishwasher, and write books. Before taking that plunge, though, I hopped on my motorcycle to visit my friend Shona in San Francisco for one last weekend hurrah before looking for a job.

While I was there, my best friend Giles showed up. He had been writing screenplays in L.A., and to suddenly find him at Shona's doorstep in San Francisco was a shock. As it turned out, he had tracked me down to Placerville, then followed my trail to the city by the bay. He told me that we needed to go on a quest to find magic.

I said, "No way. I have a plan."

He said, "Wrong answer." Then he proceeded to explain to me why we needed to drop everything and begin a quest to the east coast. By the end of his story, I was inspired. I agreed to go.

So we jumped into his dilapidated Ford truck, nicknamed "The Drudge Skeleton" after a *Magic: The Gathering* card, and we went driving in search of proof that magic exists in a cynical world. (For those of you unfamiliar with *Magic: The Gathering*, the Drudge Skeleton is a weak little creature that can be resurrected time and again. A perfect moniker for a car that kept breaking down, but being resurrected.)

We didn't find what we were looking for, a definitive proof of the supernatural, but the trip defined our later lives. New York opened numerous doors. We settled in Queens, and I began writing in earnest. The quest had failed, but at least I could write about it. Probably in response to our failure, the adventures of Mirolah and Medophae took a dark turn in *The GodSpill*, and Mershayn, with his devil-may-care attitude, was born.

The GodSpill is an important volume in the *Threadweavers* trilogy, perhaps the most important. It is a book where the characters fail more than they succeed, and they have to face their own shortcomings. I hope you enjoy walking with them down their the dark tunnels. We all have our dark tunnels and, I know that for me, they have determined who I became more than my successes.

Thank you for reading *The GodSpill*. Please take a moment to leave a review. Also, if you would like to stay informed about upcoming book releases, giveaways, or to enter contests I hold for readers, be sure to subscribe to my mailing list, Todd Fahnestock's Readers Group: https://tinyurl.com/ToddNewsletter

Your email will never be shared and you can unsubscribe at any time.

Todd Fahnestock

ABOUT THE AUTHOR

TODD FAHNESTOCK won the New York Public Library's Books for the Teen Age Award for one of his short stories and is a writer of fantasy for all age ranges. He wrote the bestselling *The Wishing World*, a middle grade portal fantasy series that began as bedtime stories for his children. With Giles Carwyn, he wrote the bestselling "George R. R. Martin-esque" epic fantasy Heartstone Trilogy: *Heir of Autumn, Mistress of Winter,* and *Queen of Oblivion.* He just finished the *Threadweavers* series, which includes *Wildmane, The GodSpill,* and *Threads of Amarion,* and is now working on *The Whisper Prince* trilogy. Stories are his passion, but Todd's greatest accomplishment is his quirky, fun-loving family. When he's not writing, he goes on morning runs with his daughter, who helps him plot stories. In the afternoons, he practices Tae Kwon Do with his son. In between, he drives his beloved wife crazy with the emotional rollercoaster that is being a full-time author.

Connect with Todd at ToddFahnestock.com or on Facebook at Facebook.com/todd.fahnestock/

ALSO BY TODD FAHNESTOCK

Threadweavers Series

Wildmane

The GodSpill

Threads of Amarion (coming July 2018)

The Whisper Prince Trilogy

Fairmist

The Undying Man (coming September 2018)

The Slate Wizards (coming October 2018)

The Heartstone Trilogy

(with Giles Carwyn)

Heir of Autumn

Mistress of Winter

Queen of Oblivion

The Wishing World Series

The Wishing World

Loremaster

The Hate Man (coming 2019)

Made in the USA
Columbia, SC
15 July 2018